Diane Hammond is the author of two novels previously both set on the Oregon coast. A recipient of an Oregon Arts Commission literary grant, she has made Oregon her home since 1984, except for brief stints in Tacoma, Washington, and Los Angeles. She worked in public relations for twenty-five years, most recently acting as media liaison and spokesperson for Keiko, the killer whale star of the hit movie Free Willy. She currently builds Web sites for small businesses and nonprofit organizations and lives in Bend, Oregon, with her husband Nolan, daughter Kerry, six very large cats, and a Pembroke Welsh corgi named Petey.

For more information visit Diane online at www.diane hammond.com

Diane Hammond

Hannah's Dream

piatkus

PIATKUS

First published in the US in 2008 by Harper,
An imprint of HarperCollins Publishers, New York
First published in Great Britain as a paperback original in 2010 by Piatkus

A CIP catalogue record for this book
is available from the British Library

ISBN 978-0-7499-4278-6

Typeset in Bembo by Palimpsest Book Production Limited,
Grangemouth, Stirlingshire

Printed and bound in Great Britain by Clays Ltd, St Ives plc

Papers used by Piatkus are natural, renewable and recyclable
products sourced from well-managed forests and certified
in accordance with the rules of the Forest Stewardship Council.

Piatkus
An imprint of
Little, Brown Book Group
100 Victoria Embankment
London EC4Y 0DY

An Hachette UK Company
www.hachette.co.uk

www.piatkus.co.uk

Acknowledgments

From 1995 to 1998 I was lucky enough to work with an ailing killer whale named Keiko – the star of the movie *Free Willy* – and the staff that rehabilitated him. The Keiko project had all the makings of an epic story: there were heroes and villains, huge sums of money made and spent, complex issues and passionate declarations, organizational politics, and public and private struggles over control and recognition, often played out on the front pages and television sets of major media outlets around the world. At the center of the vortex was Keiko himself: a smart, wily, keen, silly, luminous soul that burned more brightly each month as his health was restored; and the handful of men and women who spent hours in an icy pool to swim with him, pet him, challenge him, play with him, teach him, and be taught by him. (They also joined him for the Fourth of July, Thanksgiving, and Christmas, and spent countless evenings watching television with him on a donated wide-screen TV.) From

Keiko's keepers I learned the extraordinary lengths to which good people will go – often without recognition – for the sake of the animals in their care. Keiko's was, in the end, a love story.

When the killer whale was moved to Iceland and my part in the project ended, I thought I would write about the experience, or at least about some of the issues and conflicts it raised, but the story was simply too close. So I let the idea go and wrote *Homesick Creek* instead.

Then, in 2001, I stumbled upon television footage of a man named Solomon James Jr., unshackling for the last time the Asian elephant he had taken care of for twenty-two years. Her name was Shirley, and he had just transported her from the Louisiana Purchase Gardens and Zoo to the Elephant Sanctuary in Hoehenwald, Tennessee. He was struggling to maintain his composure as millions of people watched their parting on television. It was clear that theirs had been a long and complex journey. Out of this remarkable moment, and informed by my experience with the Keiko project, Samson Brown and Hannah were born.

Thus, my thanks go first to Phyllis Bell and Beverlee Hughes, two extraordinary women who allowed me to be part of Keiko's story. I am also indebted to the men and women on Keiko's staff who so graciously shared with me their knowledge, patience, and friendship, especially Mike Glenn, Mark Trimm, Ken Lytwyn, Jeff Foster, Karen McRae, Brian O'Neill, Tracy Karmuza, Steven Claussen, Jen and Greg Schorr, Nicole Nicassio, and Cynthia Alia-Mitchell. My thanks, too, to Earth Island Institute's Dave Phillips, Eagle River's Craig McCaw and Bob Ratliffe, Joe Gaskins, veterinarian Dr Lanny Cornell, and trouble-shooter extraordinaire John Scully.

In the realm of elephants I would have been lost without the elephant keepers at the Point Defiance Zoo and Aquarium. Craig Wilcox, Shannon Smith, and Dr Holly Reed gave me not only their professional insights but also a further glimpse into the depth of commitment that became the centerpiece of Sam's character. Sally Joseph and Dr Brian Joseph were both generous teachers and invaluable fact-checkers when this book was very new, and they saved me from untold gaffs, goofs, and errors.

My heartfelt thanks also go to Beth Basham, Caryn Casey, Richard Liedle and Debbie Coplin for reading drafts of *Hannah's Dream* and giving me their thoughts and encouragement. My gratitude, too, to Kate Nintzel and her team at Harper Perennial, and to Jennifer Rudolph Walsh, Anna DeRoy, and Erin Malone at William Morris, for being Hannah's champions.

To Jeannie Reynolds Page goes my continuing amazement at finding such a friend and supporter in the lunatic world of writing. I land in your e-mail with doubts and fears and you just *know*: what to say, how it feels, why I worry.

To my daughter Kerry, who is beginning to discover the magic of fiction, go my thanks for sharing your insights and revelations. The world of books and writers is lucky to have you in its midst. I hope that for you, as for me, it's a passion that will last a lifetime.

And finally, no words can sufficiently express my love and gratitude to Nolan Harvey, my husband, teacher, supporter, guide and friend, for believing in Hannah and Sam even when I doubted them. Without you, this book would never have been.

Chapter 1

Samson Brown loved exactly two things in this world: his wife and his elephant. He *nearly* loved lots of others, of course, and had loved dearly some who were now dead and gone – his folks, his twin brother Jimmy, an old blue dog he'd had once – but real love, in the here-and-now, he reserved for Corinna and Hannah. He knew it, and he made sure they knew it, too. Loving that hard and exclusive didn't make up for the things he couldn't give them – and there were lots of things he couldn't give them – but it went a ways. To a man like Sam, a realistic man, that was something.

The hot-poker truth about the limitations of love was something they'd learned from the dead baby girl Corinna had delivered forty-three years ago, a perfect child with hands as small and tight as fiddleheads. The grief had nearly killed them, grief as solid and mean and unyielding as an anvil that they'd carried with them everywhere until they were shaking from the weight of it and had no choice but to put it down. The doctor had told them there was nothing they could have done to bring their baby out alive; things like that just happened, he said, and sometimes no one knew why. Whatever the reason, the loss of that baby had changed them forever, especially Corinna, a woman who'd wanted only three things out of life: Sam, a child to raise, and a reasonably good relationship with the Lord. She'd gotten Sam all these years. Her relationship with the Lord was another thing.

Still, at sixty-five Corinna was solid as an old tree, someone you could get a purchase on even in a high wind. Many a time she'd kept him going, this big, beautiful woman who always had time when people came to talk or asked her thoughts about something. And Lord God, but Corinna did have her thoughts. *I've got opinions I'll give away for free to anybody who wants them,* she was fond of saying. *Sam's already heard them all, and God stopped listening a long time ago.* And she'd laugh a laugh that was like warm syrup pouring from a jug.

Sam turned at the corner of Powers and Luke Street and then into the Dunkin' Donuts drive-through.

'Hey,' he greeted Rayette at the window.

'Hey, sugar,' she said. Rayette was a nice-looking young woman who wore her hair in a million tiny braids Corinna did for her once a month. One thing about Rayette, she always made sure she looked good, never mind anything that might be going on with her two kids and occasional husband – and it seemed like there was always something going on. 'You want Bavarian cream today? They just came out,' she asked him.

'Nah. She doesn't like them as much as she used to.

2

How about two custards and a jelly? You got any of those strawberry ones? She likes those best.'

'Sure thing, hon.' Rayette ducked inside.

She'd been selling him donuts for years. When she fetched up at the window again, holding his bag of donuts and some coffee, he asked her, 'How long have you been doing Dunkin' Donuts? Ten years, maybe?'

'More like fourteen, honey. Where've you been?' Rayette frowned. 'Be fifteen at the end of November.' It was September, now. 'We're getting old, hon.'

'Don't I know it,' Sam said, shaking his head. Rayette held onto the bag of donuts for him while he fussed up some change from under the driver's seat. 'Shoot. I'm sorry, I know I've got another couple quarters down here —' He found them and handed them over. Rayette passed him the donut bag and a cup of coffee hot enough to scald a rhino. One time Sam hadn't set his cup securely and it had tipped while he was driving, raising up a nice big blister on his leg. He knew why that woman had won her lawsuit against McDonald's, even if most people thought she was a gold digger.

'What happened to that new girl you had?' he asked, stowing the coffee in a cup holder clear on the other side of the car. 'She gone already?'

'Well, you know how they are. Kids got no staying power these days, think they should get rich overnight and when it doesn't happen they dump you like it was your fault.'

'Mmmm hmmm.' Sam breathed in the scent of donuts. He'd had to give them up a year ago, when he was diagnosed with the diabetes.

'Corinna said you were thinking about retirement

again,' Rayette said, leaning out the drive-through window on her elbows.

'Yeah, I've been thinking about it.'

'Well, you just go through with it this time, hon. I never heard of anybody putting off their retirement twice like you.'

'When the time's right for Hannah, I'll go.'

Rayette just shook her head. 'She'd get over it, honey. God makes His creatures strong. I swear, the things you've done for her all these years.'

'Yeah. Well, I got to go,' Sam said. He would brook no negative comments about Hannah, never had. 'I'll see you.'

'I guess you will,' Rayette said. 'You watch yourself around that coffee, now.'

Sam steered his old Dodge Dart back into morning traffic, making sure the coffee and the bag of donuts were secure. He was a careful man and it paid off. At sixty-eight, even by his own lights, he looked damned good. He stood upright and proud, no gut whatsoever, not even a little one people would have forgiven him for, at his age. A little snowfall on the top of his head, just a light dusting; no gray at the temples, either. Seeing him from the back, you might think he was twenty, but when he turned around his face gave him away. It was deeply lined, like a roadmap starting someplace far away – Cincinnati, maybe, where he was born, or Yakima, Washington, where his daddy had had a truck farm; then Korea, where Sam had served in the war; and ending right here in Bladenham, Washington.

He drove the last mile to the Max L. Biedelman Zoo fighting a powerful urge to take a bite of one of the donuts.

4

He wasn't a drinking man or a smoker, never had been, but he did miss his Dunkin' Donuts.

In the Pacific Northwest eccentrics are as thick as fleas, but even so, Max L. Biedelman had stood apart. For starters, Max was a woman – Maxine Leona Biedelman, born in 1873 in Seattle, Washington, the only living offspring of timber magnate Arthur Biedelman and his wife Ruby. Both Ruby and Arthur came from solid, respectable San Francisco families, a fact about which Arthur didn't care a fig but Ruby clung to like a life raft. By the time Max was born Arthur had already made his fortune harvesting the foothills of the Cascades, and he spent his time indulging his lust for travel. The child was just six when he took her and Ruby on the first of many extended safaris in Kenya. Ruby, a fainthearted woman at best, would later claim that her prized auburn hair turned white within a week of their arrival in Africa, fearful as she was of everything that moved and much that didn't – rhinos, mud wallows, camp cooking, bugs, Mount Kilimanjaro, pit toilets, Masai men, rainfall, thunder, and every fresh food either bought or gathered. It was undeniable that her nerves were in a terrible state by the end of the trip. She took to her bed the moment they returned home and claimed to have stayed there for the next nineteen years, although Max would always maintain that her mother sprang out of bed with a full social calendar the minute she and Arthur embarked on their next trip.

Max herself was made of sterner stuff, for which her father nicknamed her Brave Boy. She loved being on safari and showed no fear even in the immediate presence of

5

lions – which, strangely, were sighted more than once lying nearby and staring at the girl as though mesmerized. Arthur especially liked to tell the story of a cheetah that allowed Max to come within thirty feet of her and her cub, blinking at her serenely out of honey-colored eyes.

When she was fourteen, Max and Arthur traveled to Burma and made the acquaintance of elephant keepers – mahouts – who had earned their living for generations cutting hardwood in the Burmese teak forests. Max was so taken with what they'd seen that she made the elephant her personal totem and would return to Burma and Thailand many times in later years, always staying among the mahouts and their animals.

Arthur's untimely death of fever in 1898, and Ruby's subsequent return to her family in San Francisco, left Max, at twenty-five, in possession of a sizable inheritance which included Havenside, her parents' three-hundred-acre estate in the small agricultural town of Bladenham, Washington. Their land included rolling hills and woodlands that, in the summer, smelled like hay and apples. In the winter, when the wind turned, it carried in the saltwater smell of Puget Sound.

Arthur had designed the fifty-room Victorian mansion in the tradition of the great houses of Newport, Rhode Island. After his death, Max opened Havenside to the public once each year without fail. She stood at her wrought-iron gate and greeted each person individually, a strapping, long-legged, long-toothed, silver-haired woman, a committed cross-dresser who wore men's bush clothing and carried a shooting stick or riding crop wherever she went. The only exceptions were the flowing

Turkish robes she sometimes donned on cool winter evenings. She maintained a canvas campaign tent on the Havenside grounds year-round, and often slept there when she was in residence, regardless of the season or the weather. Her neighbors considered her quite dashing, if odd.

By the mid-1950s, she had turned nearly half of Havenside's grounds into yards and outbuildings for a growing collection of wild and exotic species. The accommodations weren't luxurious, but for their time they were adequate, and the animals were well fed and cared for. Conical thatched huts, small barns and whimsical pavilions provided shelter for those animals in need of it; the tapirs, in particular, suffered for lack of a decent fur coat in winter. But Max's most prized possessions were two female elephants from Burma, retired from their work in the teak forests and given to Max as gifts by her mahout friends. She talked about 'my girls' at length, and brought them baklava every afternoon at teatime. She took an active part in all the daily work performed by her staff of keepers and gardeners.

In 1953 the first of her beloved elephants succumbed to old age, and to replace her Max purchased Hannah, a small, two-year-old female that had been partially blinded in Burma when she followed her mother into a plantation. At eighty years old, Max had already begun negotiations with Bladenham's city council to turn her entire property and animal collection over to the city upon her death, with the understanding that her animals would never want for anything.

At the time, it had been a promise sincerely made.

★　★　★

In the fall of 1995, the elephant barn was a shabby place despite a fresh interior coat of yellow paint. A lack of insulation made the damp a perpetual intruder, and the high, uninsulated ceiling and soaring hayloft gave the place a hollow feel. It was also outfitted with a small kitchen; a tiny office; an open space furnished like a living room with a couple of inexpensive armchairs, end tables, stacked TV trays, and a big-screen television; and Hannah's confinement area at the back. 'Hey, baby girl,' Sam said softly when he reached the back of the barn. 'How's my sugar?'

Hannah lifted her trunk and rumbled a greeting, the same greeting she'd given him almost every day for the last forty-one years.

'How was your night? You hear that thunderstorm come through? God almighty, Mama nearly jumped out of bed it scared her so bad. Big woman like her scared of thunder, that's a sorry thing. Here, look what Papa brought you.'

Sam took the donuts from the Dunkin' Donuts bag and lined them up lovingly on the sill of the one tiny window in Hannah's barn. Hannah investigated each one, inhaling delicately, exhaling small puffs of powdered sugar. 'Go ahead, sugar. They're those custards you like. Plus a strawberry jelly. I swear, it was all I could do to keep my fingers out of that bag. I'd have done it, too, if I didn't think Mama would catch me.' Sam chuckled. 'But she always does catch me, I don't know how. When the Lord made that woman he must have given her supernatural powers.'

While Hannah ate her donuts, Sam eased down beside her left front foot and unhooked the heavy chain from its shackle. The anklet had worn away the skin underneath and sometimes there were open sores. Not today.

'Let Papa have a look at that foot, sugar.' Hannah lifted her foot. Max Biedelman had told him an elephant's toenails should be smooth and the cuticle soft and close-fitting, but two of Hannah's bulged, foul-smelling from sores underneath; another had a split that Sam had been watching for signs of trouble. His girl had started getting arthritic ten years ago or more, from never having anything soft to stand on, and the more arthritic she got, the more she walked funny, and the funnier she walked, the more unevenly she wore down her foot pads, which put uneven pressure on her toenails, which busted. Sam spent so much time caring for Hannah's feet that he told Corinna sometimes he might hire himself out as a pedicurist at the Beauty Spot, Corinna's beauty salon.

Now he dug in his pocket and pulled out a small plastic jar of salve. 'Let's try this, sugar. Mama made this one up specially for you last night.' Sam had a bad foot, too, with a diabetic ulcer the size of a chicken wing along one side of his heel, so Corinna was always whipping up some new healing concoction in the kitchen. If it yielded any improvement, no matter how slight, Sam would bring it in the next day and slather some on Hannah's poor feet. Nothing ever really worked, but it made him and Corinna feel better, having something to try. Sam fished out a tongue depressor from a box he'd bought with his own money from a medical supply store in Tacoma, and used it like a paddle to apply the ointment. Hannah flinched but stayed put, like she always did. It nearly broke his heart. He patted her on the shoulder.

'Okay, shug, that's done – you can put your foot down.

9

You ready to go outside on this fine sunny day?' It was early September, when Bladenham smelled of apple orchards and harvested fields. 'You bringing your tire with you?' Hannah picked up an old, bald car tire she liked to keep nearby, especially when she was alone. Corinna said it was no different than those shreds of baby blankets that some kids kept with them for comfort, and Sam guessed she was right. He watched Hannah amble outside, blinking in the sudden sunshine after the barn's dim interior, before he climbed up into the hayloft. He loved the smell of clean fresh hay in the fall, always had. It reminded him of Yakima when growing season was over and new crops were still a season away. Quiet time; healing time. Every year his father's hands had bled from early spring clear through November – working hands like Sam's now, only his didn't ever heal, especially now, what with the diabetes. He knew what his daddy would say about that. *Sick or well, you take care of what you got to take care of. Ain't no such thing as a day off when it comes to living things.* He'd meant crops, not elephants, but it was just the same. Eustace Brown had worked right up until the day he'd dropped; died in his bib overalls, the way he'd have liked it.

Sam pitchforked some fresh hay down into the yard. Hannah shambled over, propping her tire against the barn wall in the exact same spot she always did, and began to eat. He loved to watch the way she pinched up a switch of hay with her trunk, tucked it inside her mouth, and chewed as slow and deliberate as if her thoughts were a million miles away. In Burma maybe, in those teak forests Max Biedelman had used to tell him about; the place where shug was born.

★ ★ ★

10

Max Biedelman had hired him after he came home from Korea in 1955 with nothing to show for his service time except a wicked case of shingles and an aversion to mess hall food. Some of his buddies who'd worked with him in the Army kitchens had said they were going to go home and open cafés, but not Sam. He was sure that hell was a mess hall line, with him on the far side slopping out chipped beef for all eternity.

So he'd gone to Havenside, instead, to see about work. Everyone knew that Max liked to support veterans just coming home, and kept her job notices posted at the Bladenham VFW hall. His first job was as a groundskeeper, which he thought of as temporary, not being overly fond of mowing grass and raking dead leaves. He'd been hired by a foreman, and though he knew Max Biedelman by reputation, he didn't meet her until he'd been on the job for six days. He'd been in the orchard pruning apple trees when he heard her call to him. When he looked up he saw her striding toward him in a tweed hat, houndstooth jacket, and high leather boots.

'Mr Brown,' she said, approaching with her hand outstretched, 'I don't believe we've had the pleasure. I'm Max Biedelman.'

Dumbstruck, Sam grasped the old woman's hand and found it as dry and light as an old corn husk.

'I understand you've been working here at Havenside for several days already. Please accept my apology for not having greeted you sooner. I've been unwell.'

'Yes, ma'am.'

She frowned. 'Please don't call me ma'am, Mr Brown. I answer to Max or to Miss Biedelman.'

'Yes, ma'am,' Sam said before he'd thought it through,

but the old woman only chuckled and patted his arm. 'Never mind,' she said. 'I make you nervous. I seem to have that effect on people.' She started to walk away but then turned back, calling to him, 'If you feel very strongly about your manners, Mr Brown, you may call me sir.'

Max Biedelman's second old elephant, Reyna, died less than a year later. Sam heard that the animal hadn't been able to get to her feet once she'd lain down, not even with an improvised winch thrown over the barn rafters. Max Biedelman, who had not attended her own mother's funeral, stayed with the old elephant until she quietly slipped away with her trunk in the old woman's lap. Sam kept a lookout for her for two days, until he finally saw her walking in the farthest part of the property, where wildflowers grew.

He approached her with his heart beating hard. 'Me and my wife, we want to extend our condolences, sir,' he said.

Her face was ravaged, but she managed a smile. 'Thank you, Mr Brown. It has been difficult. Do you have a moment – yes? Then walk with me.'

Sam fell into step beside her. She matched him stride for stride. 'I understand that you and your wife lost a child.'

'Yes, sir.'

'Then you know how hard it is to part with a loved one.'

'Yes, sir, I do.'

She looked at him closely, as though she were trying to decide something. 'You were a farm boy, weren't you, Mr Brown?'

'Yes, sir. My daddy had a farm outside Yakima. He raised

vegetables for the family, grew hops, wheat, and alfalfa to sell. He did pretty good, too. Hard work, though.'

'And did he have animals?'

'A few – milk cows, goats, a couple of sheep. Not for selling, just for the table.'

'Yes, I thought so.'

Sam wiped his palms on his pants.

'Tell me what you think of my Hannah, Mr Brown.'

'Hannah?'

'Hannah is my elephant. My last elephant.'

'I don't know about elephants, sir.' He cast around for something to say. 'She's big.'

'Yes, Mr Brown, she is big,' the old woman chuckled. 'Unless I'm mistaken, you often watch her during your breaks and at lunchtime. I thought you might have some observations.'

Sam was sweating freely, trying to figure out where she was headed with this conversation so he could get out of the way. 'I've never seen anything like her before,' he ventured.

'Well, let me tell you about her, then. Hannah's actually quite small for her age, probably from malnutrition when she was still in Burma. Life in the wild is not always bountiful, Mr Brown. In 1952, she was found on a rubber plantation near her mother, who had been shot and killed for trespassing. Hannah was probably just two years old at the time, three at most, and she'd been wounded, but she was lucky. The plantation worker who found her had a brother who was a mahout – an elephant keeper – and he sent word that there was a young animal in need of care. All the plantation workers were under orders to destroy any elephant that trespassed onto the premises, but he managed to keep Hannah hidden for several days until his brother arrived, and in the meantime he dressed her wound and fed and watered her. When the brother arrived, he saw that Hannah would be useless for work in the teak forests because of her partial blindness and small size, but he also realized that simply releasing her would be a death sentence. The mahout was a good man, as most of them are, in my experience, so he agreed to take the elephant and care for her until a buyer could be found. I was well-known to the mahouts by then, and they contacted me and asked if I'd like her – as of course I did. It's quite a story, isn't it?'

'Yes, sir.'

'Hannah is resilient, Mr Brown; she's quite healthy now, and has a long future. She may be sixty years old before she dies. But there are no other elephants here, and in all likelihood there never will be again. Hannah has a future, you see, but not an especially bright one.' The old woman stopped walking and turned to face him. 'I'm going to ask you to do something, Mr Brown. It's very important to me, so I would like you to be honest with me when you answer.'

Sam waited with a keen dread.

'I'd like you to be Hannah's keeper, Mr Brown.'

'Keeper?'

'I'd like you to take care of her from now on.'

'Isn't there somebody already doing that, sir?'

'Not someone I trust, Mr Brown, and trust is very important to me. It's also very important to Hannah. Please understand that you'll be well paid for your work.'

Sam was struck dumb. This old woman was asking

14

him to take responsibility for an animal the likes of which he had never even seen, except in pictures, until he came to Havenside – an expensive animal, he was sure. And yet, when he watched Hannah he felt he was in the presence of a sharp mind and a gentle heart. Before he had a chance to change his mind he said, 'I believe I could do that, sir, but who's going to teach me how?'

Max Biedelman clapped him on the back and crowed, 'Hannah, Mr Brown! Hannah will teach you.'

And so she had.

Sam found it ironic that although he'd sworn never to work with food after Korea all those years ago, here he was, the same as every day, in the little kitchen in the barn, prepping groceries. He quartered apples, sundered yams, halved bananas and carrots and melons to make them all last longer. Corinna used to tease him about being Hannah's personal chef, and damned if it wasn't true. He didn't mind, though. Hannah's food meant a lot to her.

Now, he strapped around his waist a canvas pouch filled with fruit, and went out into the elephant yard.

'You want to go for a walk, baby girl?' he asked her as she reached for the pouch with her trunk.

Sam imagined the Lord must have been in an odd frame of mind the day He created the Asian elephant. When he first met her, Hannah had reminded him of nothing so much as a worn-out, hip-shot, low-slung, dog-ugly, poorly dressed old floozy in bad shoes. And what about that tail, scrawny thing with a little hairy flywhisk on the end; looked like something picked up late on the last day of a church sale. And yet there was a soul, a thing of pure beauty, behind those eyes. Max Biedelman had seen it clearly all those years ago and, walking in her footsteps, Samson Brown saw it shining there every day.

'Come on, sugar,' he said, handing Hannah half a banana as she went through the gate leading out of the elephant yard and into the visitor area. She wore no harness or restraint of any kind, and she never had. Sam carried an elephant hook, a short stick with a blunt metal hook on the end, that had once belonged to Max Biedelman. He brought it along more out of habit than anything else. Hannah was like a big, placid dog padding along beside him on her poor feet. They walked at least once a day when the weather was fine and often when it wasn't, because Sam thought it did her good to walk on grass or even the asphalt paths when she could – anything softer than concrete. And it gave her a change of scene.

Surprised zoo visitors cut wide paths around them, or followed alongside whispering to each other, as they walked all the way up the hill past the rhino, around the tapirs and past the monkeys and the marmosets, shooing a couple of wandering peacocks out of the way, before they headed back down to the elephant barn, which was nestled in a small depression at the bottom of the hill. Sam stayed on Hannah's right side – her seeing side – so she'd know that he was there, watching out for her. She might be big, but she was timid even after all these years.

He heard someone call, 'How come you're walking that elephant, mister?' A boy appeared at his elbow, a small but good-looking kid about eleven years old.

'How come you're walking around the zoo?' Sam asked.

The boy shrugged, falling into step beside Sam. 'To see stuff.'

'Guess you answered your own question, then,' Sam said.

'Can she see me? She's awful damned big.'

'She can see you just fine. Say hello to her. Her name's Hannah.'

The boy lifted a hand self-consciously. 'Hey.'

'Hey, *Hannah*. Elephant's got the right to expect good manners.'

'Hey, Hannah.'

Sam handed Hannah a yam. 'What's your name?' he asked the boy.

'Reginald.'

'Reginald. That's a pretty big name for a small fry.'

'I'm not small,' the boy said, puffing up a little.

'Your daddy a big man?' Sam asked him.

'He's big.' The boy's eyes got shifty: no daddy.

'You got any questions about Hannah you want to ask me?'

The boy looked around Sam at Hannah chewing placidly on a cantaloupe half. 'She got teeth? She don't look like it.'

'She's got teeth the same as you, just not as many,' Sam said. 'She's got four; two on top, two on bottom. Big molars, look like your sneakers, maybe; about that size. She loses one, she gets another in. Let me see your teeth, Reginald.'

The boy bared beautiful, white, even teeth in healthy pink gums. Someone was taking good care of him.

'So how come her chin's all wobbly?' the boy asked.

'That's not her chin, it's her lip,' Sam said, slipping

17

Hannah a couple of apple quarters. Hannah chewed with great solemnity. 'She can make that lip work just like a funnel. You ever seen someone pour oil into a car engine using a funnel? Same thing – she doesn't lose any food or drink that way, it all goes in just where it's supposed to. You grow up in a hot jungle, you don't want to miss even a drop of that cool stream.'

'Give her one of those cantaloupes,' Reginald said.

'You want to give it to her?'

'Yeah, I'll give it to her,' the boy said, voice shaking a little.

Sam put a cantaloupe half in Reginald's hand. 'Come around me, now, so you can get closer to her. Move slow, so you don't startle her. Girl doesn't like being startled.'

The boy went to stand behind Sam.

'Go on, now,' he said, pulling the boy around him by the arm. 'You've got to hold it out to her, or she won't know to take it. Shug's real polite that way.'

Reginald held the melon out to her, and Hannah picked it off the boy's palm with great delicacy.

'You see that?' he crowed. 'You see her take that right out of my hand? She likes me, I bet.' Still, he hurried back to his place on Sam's far side. 'Where are you going now?'

'Just around. No place in particular. Does her good to just meander.'

'Reginald!' A shrill female voice called out from behind them on the path. 'Lord, boy, you scared me half to death wandering off like that.'

'That your mama?' Sam asked.

'Nah, she's my aunt. I live with her.'

'Where's your mama, son?'

18

The boy shrugged.

'All right, go on. Don't make her chase you, now.'

Reginald started off, turned back. 'I'll see you, mister.'

'Yeah, I expect you will. Next time you come here, you ask for Sam Brown. Just tell them you're a friend of mine and they'll let you in to see me.'

As he and Hannah moved on, Sam could hear the boy calling excitedly to his aunt, 'Hey, I fed that elephant. I fed her right off my hand!'

Sam reached up and patted Hannah's shoulder. 'You were real good with that boy, sugar. That was a nice thing you did for him.'

When they got back to the barn, he found a voice-mail message waiting in the tiny office where he kept food and medical records. It was from Harriet Saul, the zoo's director. Her message said, 'Sam, please remember Neva Wilson will be here tomorrow morning. Do you have her uniforms and key? If not, I'll have Truman bring them down.'

Sam sighed. He'd had so many keepers teamed up with him over the years, he didn't even bother keeping track of them anymore. They were either earnest know-nothings or gone to seed. This Neva Wilson would be the first woman, though, and he wondered how that was going to work out. He didn't know if Hannah would like a girl much. Truman Levy, the zoo's business manager and Harriet's right-hand man, had told Sam she'd been impressive at her interview, but Sam wasn't setting any store by it. He and Hannah would just have to see.

Chapter 2

In her negotiations with the City of Bladenham, Max Biedelman had arranged for an exemption to the normal burial regulations that required all human remains to be interred in one of two small cemeteries on the outskirts of town. Instead, she was given a variance to be buried on her own property, beside Hannah's little elephant barn. The site was identified only by a discreet brass plaque on the barn's north wall: MAX L. BIEDELMAN, 1873–1958. FOREVER WITH THE ANIMALS SHE LOVED.

There were many days when, if Max Biedelman was watching over her zoo from the hereafter, she'd be appalled. Most of the exquisite landscaping had been replaced by asphalt and concrete. Nocturnal animals like the slow loruses, difficult to see by daytime visitors, were no longer replaced when they died. One by one their areas were converted into snack or trinket kiosks. When the last zebra succumbed to hoof-and-mouth disease, the zebra yard had been turned into a petting zoo of common

goats, sheep, and a large, bad-tempered sow named Hilda. By 1995, what had once been one of the country's foremost private exotic animal collections had become a seedy third-rate zoo.

Harriet Saul had been hired five months earlier to change all that. In middle age she was stocky, shrewd, and focused: fifty-two years of plainness had tempered her like hand-forged steel. She knew by then that it was her lot to fall in love with institutions instead of men. Her previous love affairs had been with a regional science museum, a library system, and a dairy cooperative. Now, when she closed her eyes at night, she dreamt about the barns and huts and pavilions of the Max L. Biedelman Zoo.

The zoo's offices were on the ground floor of Havenside, the old Biedelman mansion, long past its glory days. Bladenham was not a city with money to spare for beautification unless it was backed by local business interests. The zoo, though a venerable institution in the minds of the town council, returned relatively little in the way of taxes, prestige or tourism revenues. When it came time to allocate the city's public works budget each year, installing handicapped-accessible curbs, repairing roads, upgrading the wastewater treatment plant and buying new play equipment for the parks all came before the massive investment that would be needed to properly renovate the old Biedelman home. It was enough that the city council allowed the place to run in the red year after year.

In its halcyon days, Maxine Biedelman's home had been as exquisite as it had been out of place. She'd kept an office on the second floor, overlooking the grounds.

After her death, however, as the house continued to age and maintenance fell woefully behind, the second floor had been closed off and the offices moved into what had once been a large library on the first floor, now divided into Harriet's office and a half-dozen cubicles.

This Monday morning, she yelled through her office doorway, 'Has Geneva Wilson showed up yet?'

Truman Levy, her director of operations, sat in a cubicle no more than ten feet from her office door. He glanced up from his paperwork. 'It's only five past eight,' he said.

'Well, *I'm* here,' she said. 'You're here. Even Brenda's here. Neva Wilson is late. Has she called in? Brenda, has she called in?' The receptionist maintained a stony silence. She and Harriet detested each other, and their latest battle was over Harriet's insistence that Brenda wore too much makeup. *People can see right through it, you know,* Harriet had recently told her. *You're not fooling anyone.*

Truman stood and walked six steps to the reception desk. In a modulated voice and with exquisite politeness he asked Brenda if Neva Wilson had called in yet.

'Nope,' Brenda said, smiling at him nicely.

Truman took four steps to the doorway of Harriet's office and said, 'Apparently she hasn't called in.'

'I am not pleased,' Harriet intoned.

'She'll be here,' Truman said. 'It's her first day, and she doesn't know the area yet. She might have gotten caught in traffic, or forgotten the way.'

'I don't care.'

Truman withdrew to the relative asylum of his cubicle, where he chewed his first antacid of the day, reflecting gloomily that it was the earliest he'd taken one yet, beating by ten minutes his previous record. Ever since he'd gone to work for Harriet Saul he'd been buying Tums in bulk from Costco. There had been a time when he would have earnestly, even passionately, argued that appearances – especially appearances as unprepossessing as hers – shouldn't matter. Several years ago Truman's ex-wife Rhonda, a sculptor, had challenged that opinion. She'd said, *Let me tell you something, Truman. You know the only people who really believe appearances shouldn't matter? Ugly people.*

She'd been right, of course, about this and many other things. Last year, when she left him and their eleven-year-old son Winslow, she'd accused him of being the least memorable person she had ever known. *And it's not just me*, she'd said. *You're the least memorable person anybody's ever known. You know I'm right about this, Truman.*

It was true. People sitting directly across a dinner table from him for an entire meal consistently failed to recognize him the next time they met. This had happened not just once, but time after time. He seemed simply to disappear from people's memories. Rhonda had taken to calling him Truman the Bland. *You're rice pudding, cream of wheat. I want jambalaya, paella. Is that too much to ask?*

Truman had thought that, as a matter of fact, it *was* too much to ask. He didn't say so, of course. One didn't, with Rhonda. She'd asked him once if he thought she was destined to accomplish great things, and he'd said probably not. He'd only meant that the statistical probabilities were against her, but she'd thrown an expensive dried flower arrangement at him and stalked out of the house; a prelude, as it turned out, to leaving them for good. Truman had appealed to her to stay,

24

if only for Winslow's sake. The boy was then ten years old; he needed his mother. Rhonda had sighed, *He's your son, Truman. He takes after you. You'll know what to do with him. I'd just lose my temper.*

After she'd brained him with the dried floral wreath and left, he'd been sitting glumly in the living room when Winslow approached to ask why he had bits of dried bachelor buttons in his hair. Truman said a wildflower fairy had swooped in unexpectedly and anointed his brow with blossoms, but Winslow hadn't bought it. He was, indeed, Truman's son, the sort of analytical boy who weighed the possibility of being struck by lightning while riding his bike; who wondered if you could create a robot that would dress you from head to toe while you were still in bed. He could sit perfectly still for an hour or more, roaming the galaxy inside his own mind. He kept his room spotless, his socks neatly paired in his designated sock drawer and his closet organized by color. He'd driven Rhonda to frenzy. She used to scream at him, *You're a child! You're supposed to be messy!* To Truman she said, *My god, he's like an accounting savant.*

Rhonda had left them just over a year ago, several weeks after the debacle of the flower arrangement. At no time since then had Winslow commented on her absence except factually and in passing. He did not require heart-to-heart, father–son conversations, nor had Truman heard him weeping when the boy thought he was alone. He didn't have nightmares or act out either at home or at school. He seemed perfectly satisfied with the way things were, and for that, as much as for anything else, Truman loved him fiercely.

Neva Wilson arrived at last, forty-two minutes late.

She was slight and tensile, red-haired and freckled, with the thin, smart face of a fox. Truman winced as she stepped into the minefield that was Harriet's office. Neva Wilson was, beyond the shadow of a doubt, screwed.

'Am I late?' he heard Neva say.

Dead silence. Harriet would be looking pointedly at her watch.

'I'm sorry,' he heard Neva say, clearing her throat. 'I made a wrong turn, and by the time I figured it out, I was ten miles out of town.'

'Well,' Harriet said; and then, no doubt having made her point, her voice lightened beneficently. 'When did you get to town? Are you all settled in?'

'Yesterday. And settling in is never a problem. Everything I own fits in my car.'

Truman quietly approached with a stack of Max L. Biedelman Zoo uniform shirts and paperwork, announcing himself by knocking on the wall outside Harriet's doorway.

'Excuse me,' he said. Harriet, sitting at her desk with her hands clasped, nodded that he might approach. He handed the clothes and papers to Neva, whose coloring was livid, and said, 'You can fill these out anytime today. Just leave them with me before five. You'll have a locker at the elephant barn where you can put your uniforms for now. Shall I take you down there? I'm sure you're anxious to start.'

'I can find my way.'

'I don't mind.' Ignoring a disapproving look from Harriet, he quickly stowed his work as they passed his cubicle. It was nothing more sensitive than employee timesheets – he'd been working up the payroll – but

Harriet made a point of sitting at his desk when he was away from it, gathering intelligence. She was not beyond docking an employee fifteen minutes of pay, claiming she saw him or her malingering someplace on the grounds or in one of the outlying zookeeper workrooms.

'I'm sorry, but I don't think we've met,' Neva said, holding out her hand once they'd emerged into the watery fall sunlight. Truman took it.

'I was on your interview panel,' he said. 'It's a pleasure to see you again.'

'God, I'm sorry.' Neva clapped her hand to her forehead.

'Please don't be. It happens all the time.' Truman smiled sadly.

'No, it's me. I do this. And here's the weird thing: I can remember the face of every animal I've ever worked with. I don't mean just general features, either – I remember the exact markings and the way their ears feel when you rub them between your fingers and what their favorite foods are and whether or not they like to be sung to. But I never remember people. Introduce me to a new person and within ten minutes it's like I was never there. I think it's some kind of learning disability.'

Truman smiled as Neva gabbled a little at a passing peacock, a moth-eaten specimen fanning his ratty tail beside the path.

'So tell me about Harriet Saul,' she said.

'Ah,' Truman said. 'She can be a bully, but her heart's in the right place. She was brought in by the city to turn the zoo around. We have some financial challenges.'

'You've got a charismatic mega-vertebrate, though. That always helps.'

27

'I beg your pardon?'

'Charismatic mega-vertebrates,' Neva repeated. 'Whales, dolphins, elephants. They're the money animals. They're what people come to see. Of course, you've only got one, and she has some problems.'

'Her feet, you mean.'

'For starters.'

'Something about her toenails, I gather.'

Neva looked at him and smiled. 'I know, you're probably thinking it's no big deal, like a hangnail. But foot problems are one of the primary causes of death for a lot of elephants at older zoos like this one.'

'*Death?*'

Neva nodded. 'Mother Nature didn't take concrete into account when she designed the elephant. A three- or four-ton animal is going to break its feet down if there's nothing soft to stand on.'

'What does that mean?'

'Say you have a sore foot, right? What are you going to do?'

'I suppose I'd try to stay off it.'

'Exactly. But if an animal this heavy lies down for more than a few hours, it crushes its internal organs. So they have to stand up, bad feet or no. And if you're kept indoors all night, which Hannah is, you're standing in a toilet, which leads to intractable infections and blood poisoning. Which leads to death.'

'Good Christ.'

They completed the walk in silence. Truman thought that walking beside Neva Wilson was like walking beside a high-voltage electrical transformer. He could almost hear the hum, feel the heat.

Just as he pulled open the door to the elephant barn, the wall phone rang. He saw Harriet's extension flashing on the console, and picked up the receiver.

'You need to come back,' she said.

'Yes, I was just ready to.'

'She could have found her own way, Truman.'

Truman sighed. It was only two minutes after nine, and it was Monday.

Sam was in the elephant yard, looking at Hannah's bad foot in the sunlight. Even through the ointment he'd slathered on, he could see that the foot was worse. 'Okay, baby girl,' he murmured, patting her foot down gently. 'Guess Papa's going to have to find something different to try.' He stood beside her, reaching up to stroke the back of her ear. She touched his face with her trunk, blowing lightly and smelling of guavas. Someone had sent a tropical care package, guavas and papayas. The zoo got gifts like that all the time. His girl had thousands of friends and well-wishers.

'Good morning.' Neva Wilson came out of the barn and into the yard, wearing a zoo sweatshirt so new it still had fold marks.

'Morning, miss. I didn't hear you come in. Me and Hannah were catching up on the day.'

She nodded at the foot. 'That's a pretty nasty abscess.'

Sam remembered thinking the woman was a tad high-strung when he met her after her interview three weeks ago. Then again, that Harriet Saul had only let her stay in the barn a few minutes – big, bossy thing.

'Hey, baby girl,' he said softly to Hannah. 'Look who's here. Hannah, this is Neva Wilson. Miss, meet Hannah.'

'Please don't call me miss,' Neva said, flushing. 'I hate formality.'

'All right, miss.'

Neva sighed. 'Is that getting worse?' She nodded at Hannah's foot.

'Yeah, a little bit. Nothing new about it, though. Seems like she always has some foot problem. Shug's worse than an old woman with bunions.'

'May I see?'

'Foot, sugar.' Hannah lifted her bad foot again, looking nervously at Neva. 'It's okay, sugar, she's just going to take a look.'

Neva looked at the shattered nails and underlying abscesses. 'What medication's she on for this?'

To Hannah Sam said, 'It's okay, baby, you can put your foot down now.'

Hannah put her foot down.

'Right now, nothing. We tried everything the zoo doc recommended, but it seemed like none of it made any difference, plus it put the girl off her hay. So me and Mama – that's my wife, Corinna – we've tried some homeopathic cures, you know? Looks like they haven't helped much this time, though.'

'Homeopathic cures? Like what?'

'Well, Mama could tell you more about that than me, but let's see.' Sam leaned against Hannah, thinking. The elephant wrapped her trunk around his head affectionately. 'Ointments and creams, mostly. Baby doesn't like to stand still for poultices. Right off the top of my head, there was witch hazel and ribwort, calendula, comfrey, and that's about all I can remember. We'll have to ask Mama. We were thinking about trying echinacea tincture, but I don't think shug would take to that. Her stomach gets upset real easy.'

'Did any of them help?'

'The comfrey helped some. The witch hazel seemed like it was soothing, but I don't know if it had any healing powers.'

'Have you tried applying Copper-Tox over the top of them?' Neva said.

'Don't know that one, miss,' Sam frowned.

'It acts as a sort of liquid Band-Aid, sticky so it stays on for a long time. Stuff smells to high heaven and it'll give you one hell of a headache if you're around it too long, but I've seen it make a difference at least in keeping medication in place so the abscess has a chance to heal.' Neva put her hands in her pockets.

'I'll ask Doc. Maybe he doesn't know about that one.'

'Who's the vet here, again?'

'Doc Richards.'

Neva frowned. 'I guess I don't know him.'

''Bout my age, ready to retire soon. He worked for Miss Biedelman when she was still alive. He's been around here longer than anyone but me and Hannah.'

'Is he a good vet?'

'He never killed anything, at least as far as I know. He usually comes to see Hannah every week or two.'

'Has he ever had you give her footbaths of peroxide, betadyne, and chlorhexidine?'

Sam frowned again, raking his fingernails up and down Hannah's side. She made a low, contented rumble and put her trunk into the canvas treat bag Sam wore strapped around his waist, fetching up two chunks of apple and popping them in her mouth like candy. 'Not those, miss, but we've tried Epsom salts,' Sam said as he pushed her trunk away. 'Warm water and salts a couple times a day. She took it all right, but it didn't seem to do anything besides make her sleepy. By the time the ten minutes was done, why she'd be sawing logs.' Sam chuckled gently. 'Breaks my heart, seeing the girl in pain.'

'Does she limp?'

'Not much. I believe she has a touch of rheumatism in the joints, though – she takes after me that way. Seems like she stands still more than she used to. Except for our walks, of course.'

'You walk her?'

'Sure,' Sam said. 'It does her good, gives her a chance to see some things, stretch out a little, let her poor feet touch some grass. Plus you meet people. Yesterday we met a real nice boy, lives with an aunt. Too many kids out there are bringing themselves up these days. My folks never did have a lot, but there was plenty of love to go around. My mama used to say to all us kids, *You help yourself to a hug whenever you want one, sugar. They're warm, and they're free.*'

Neva smiled. 'Do you ever put sand in her yard?'

'Never have. Just hay.'

'So how does she show pain?'

Sam smiled. 'She doesn't show it, she just comes right out and says it. She's a talky thing, talks all day long.' His smile faded. 'I love my girl, miss. Me and Hannah, we've been together forty-one years. Miss Biedelman trusted me to take good care of her, and I've done the best job I could. It's about time for me to be retiring, been time for a couple of years already, but I can't do it unless I know my baby's in good hands. You show me you've got those hands and I'll do anything I can to make the rest easy on you. I will, and Mama will, too.'

Neva folded her arms and regarded him for a minute. 'If you could give Hannah anything in the world, what would it be?'

Sam rubbed his cheek along Hannah's leg absently. 'That's easy. I'd give her a good place to live and someone who'd never leave her.'

'But she could easily live for another twenty years. No keeper's going to commit to being in one place that long.'

'Didn't say anything about keepers, miss,' Sam said quietly.

'I'm sorry?'

'I meant other elephants.'

Neva sighed. 'Well, given what I know about this zoo, that would take a miracle.'

'I dream about it sometimes,' Sam said before he could think better of it.

'Sure. We all dream about having more money and better living conditions for our animals.'

Sam nodded, but it wasn't what he'd meant.

Chapter 3

Neva Wilson prided herself on both her nerve and durability. In fifteen years as a zookeeper she had worked with large, intractable animals from killer whales to polar bears. She seldom cried, never balked, and rarely wavered in her opinions. She had been married once, but that was a long time ago. She was a zookeeper's zookeeper, fierce, tough, single-minded, and dedicated to the animals in her care.

Unlike any of the dozens of backup keepers Sam Brown had been given over the years, Neva had not washed up on the unpromising shores of the Max L. Biedelman Zoo because of diminished circumstances. She had worked at some of the best zoos in the country, and trained under some of the finest senior elephant keepers in the world. But lately she'd begun to believe that she needed something more; some sort of purpose. She'd decided that she would become an elephant-care ambassador, bringing what she knew to one of the country's many mediocre, backwater, needy facilities. The Max L. Biedelman Zoo had advertised for an elephant keeper less than three weeks later. It wasn't accredited by the American Zoo Association, and neither Neva nor any of her colleagues had ever heard of the place before. A week later her interview with Harriet Saul and the zoo's top management convinced her that the zoo's leadership was clueless, arrogant, misguided, and blind. It sounded perfect. No missionary to the darkest heart of Africa brought along more zeal than Neva Wilson did. When she was offered the job at a salary that was not quite half what she had been earning, she accepted on the spot.

At the end of her first day, she pulled into her driveway and climbed out of the beat-to-shit tin can that was her current car – the latest in a long line of beater vehicles reaching all the way back to her sixteenth birthday. She took perverse pride in the fact that not one of her cars had ever rated a Blue Book value of more than fifteen hundred dollars, and many had been worth significantly less. She was, by necessity, a fair mechanic.

Instead of an apartment, she'd rented a detached, converted garage in Bladenham's historic neighborhood. It was just her kind of place: carpeting laid directly over the concrete slab, tiny kitchenette, tinier bathroom, dirt-cheap rent. She wouldn't be there much, anyway – she was used to spending up to twenty hours a day at work, coming home only to shower, sleep, and change clothes.

She pulled into the driveway just as her landlord, Johnson Johnson, came out the back door of his house and approached her across the narrow lawn that separated her apartment from his house, a 1920s craftsman bungalow with a deep front porch and leaded windows.

36

She guessed he was in his late thirties, tall, balding, and impossibly thin, with a sweet, vague air about him. Neva couldn't decide whether he was afflicted or simply shy. He lifted his hand uncertainly and said, 'Hi.'

Neva pulled a stack of Biedelman Zoo uniform shirts out of her car. 'Would you mind?' she said, handing them to him so she could reach in and extract a second pile of sweatshirts. 'Okay, you can just set those on top of these,' she told him. He did. 'Thanks.' And then, because he was still just standing there with his mouth slightly open, she added, 'That should do it.'

'Okay,' he said, nevertheless failing to walk away. 'You work at the zoo?'

'My first day.'

'I like the zoo.'

'Really? What's the best thing about it?'

'They have animals.'

She waited for more, but evidently he was done. 'Well, it is a zoo,' she said. 'What is it that you do?'

Johnson Johnson looked at his feet. 'I make things.'

'What kinds of things?'

He shrugged. Neva thought it was as though he had learned social discourse from a book.

'Look,' she said, beginning to run out of patience, which had never been a strong quality of hers. 'Is your real name Johnson Johnson?'

'Yes.'

'I can't imagine anybody actually naming a baby Johnson Johnson.' She kicked her car door shut with her foot.

Johnson Johnson flushed with pride.

'Okay,' Neva explained. 'I have to go in now.'

'Okay,' he said, but it was as if she'd never spoken. 'Have you seen my cat?'

'You have a cat?'

'Yes. He's an orange tabby. He has six toes on each foot.'

'A polydactyl,' Neva said, brightening.

Johnson Johnson looked at her uncertainly. 'Well, a cat.'

'Yes – polydactyl is the term for six-toed cats.'

'His name is Kitty.'

'Of course it is.' It had been a long day; Neva felt hysterical giggles rising. Trying to outrun them, she said, 'Look, I'm sorry, but I really have to go in now.'

'Oh.'

And so she did. As she took the key from the lock and closed her door, she could still see Johnson Johnson standing in place, his hand finally lifted in farewell.

The interior of her tiny house was cheerful, even incandescent, with bright yellow doors, orange walls and fiery red baseboards. Somebody in its past had had color-courage. She put her things away and dumped canned chicken noodle soup into a pot, encouraging the front burner of her little Pullman stove to choose life. Chances were excellent that she would stand right there and eat her soup directly from the pot once it was heated. For years she had resisted her mother's efforts to teach her to cook. *You can only eat tuna casserole so many times, Neva,* she had told her a hundred times. *Sooner or later the body will rebel.*

In the end it hadn't been the body but Neva's ex-husband Howard who had rebelled, not against her tuna casserole but Neva's refusal to choose a different career path. He'd wanted to know how she could be passionate

38

about jobs that listed shoveling shit as one of their major duties. When Neva was promoted out of the San Diego Zoo's African savanna exhibit to become a full-time elephant keeper, he'd said, *So, what – you go from small shit to bigger and more dangerous shit, and that's the dream of a lifetime?*

As she ate her soup, Neva thought about Samson Brown. She'd never met a keeper with so little training. He knew nothing about protected contact, operant conditioning, environmental enrichment, or any of the other cornerstones of modern animal husbandry and training. Still, it was clear that he had enormous natural gifts. His work with Hannah showed flawless instincts as well as obvious devotion. By taking Hannah for walks around the zoo each day, he gave her feet some relief from the unyielding concrete in her barn and small yard. It also gave her a change of scene, a relief from the sameness of her exhibit. Her diet was good, her appetite excellent, and her attitude seemed positive, even in light of the poverty of her surroundings and her complete and nearly lifelong isolation from other elephants.

And though Hannah's feet were ugly and she already had arthritic knees and hips, they weren't nearly as bad as some she'd seen. Maybe there was something to Sam's wife's homeopathic remedies. They had certainly done the animal no harm, which was probably more than could be said of the zoo veterinarian, a local DVM who, she'd learned, spent most of his time working with cows.

'Truman, come here for a minute,' Harriet called from her office as Truman tried to slip past her door to go home. He stopped with a sigh: she seemed to take a

39

perverse pleasure in preventing him from leaving on time. Nevertheless, he stepped into her office and shut the door part way, raising his eyebrows at Harriet: *Close it?* She nodded, and he pulled it to. Outside the door, Brenda would be all ears. Truman had known her to turn the entire switchboard over to auto-answer if she thought she might overhear something juicy.

He stood in front of Harriet's desk, or in front of what he assumed was Harriet's desk if only he could see it beneath the mounds of paper. The office was squalid with half-filled coffee mugs and partially eaten nachos teetering dangerously atop shifting dunes of paper. Mess notwith-standing, she seemed to know the exact location and content of every single memo, report, spreadsheet, and phone message, right down to the bare wood.

Harriet nodded toward a visitor's chair that was rela-tively clear of debris. A single pink message slip had floated down from above to rest there, but it was an old message so Truman just sat on it. He needed to be out the door in no more than ten minutes if he was going to pick up Winslow from his piano lesson on time.

'I've been looking at this,' Harriet said, holding out a financial statement he had prepared for her earlier in the day. 'Are you sure about the numbers?'

'Very sure,' he said. 'A number of school groups cancelled last month.'

'Do we know why?'

'Evidently the Pumpkin Patch had a corn maze.'

'We're losing business to a *farm stand*?'

'Apparently so.'

In disgust, Harriet tossed the sheet of paper on top of a half-eaten grilled cheese sandwich.

'Look,' Truman said. 'I'd like to ask my father to review the old City files pertaining to the zoo.' Matthew Levy was a retired federal court judge and lifelong Bladenham resident. 'Maybe there's money we're entitled to that no one remembers anymore. Special funds of some kind, or maybe a small endowment. With the kind of administrative turnover the zoo has had in the last decade or so it's a long-shot, but I think it's worth looking into.'

'Well, I can't pay him,' Harriet said. 'That's the first thing.'

'No, that's just fine.'

'Tell him to go ahead, then.'

Truman smiled. You didn't *tell* Matthew anything. You laid out a case as carefully as you could and then you stood back to see if it stuck. He stood up. 'I'm sorry, Harriet, but I've got to go pick up Winslow. You're leaving soon, too, I hope?'

'Eventually.'

'It would probably do you good to take the evening off.'

'Maybe when things slow down,' she said vaguely, already mining her desk for a buried document. She didn't seem to have much of a home life. He gathered that she lived alone, and kept birds – finches, as he remembered.

As he closed Harriet's office door behind him, he saw the hem of a coat whip out the main door. Brenda, with her sly sense of timing, was done for the day.

Winslow was in the front window of his piano teacher's house, watching for him. Truman could see the boy's pale moon face, framed by curtains, sweeten with relief as he saw Truman's car pull into the driveway.

41

'Hey,' Truman greeted the boy as Winslow climbed into the car. 'How was Mrs Leahey? How was the lesson?'

'It was okay. She gave me a new piece.'

'Still Mozart?'

'Yeah.' Winslow nodded. 'It's hard.'

'Well, she's always going to give you something hard,' Truman said. 'She warned us.'

'I know. It's okay.'

'Homework?'

'Math.'

'Ah.' The day's inventory behind them, Truman fell into a reverie for the rest of the drive home. The boy might have the demeanor of an accountant, but he had an artist's soul. Shortly after Rhonda left them, Mrs Leahey had called him at work and said, *He's very musical, Mr Levy. With your permission, I'd like to push him, see what he's capable of.* Truman had agreed, of course, and on the wings of Mozart, Winslow had risen and soared. Truman often sat just outside the den while he practiced, listening. In Winslow's playing the boy was all brilliant hues and soft, rich shadows. Truman wondered sometimes whether, if the two of them had been outwardly vivid people, Rhonda would have stayed with them. But he was not a colorful man. Winslow was not a colorful boy. Their riches were subterranean.

Once home, Truman sent Winslow upstairs to begin his homework while he thawed a Tupperware container full of spaghetti sauce he'd prepared over the weekend. His freezer was neatly stocked with chili, stew, chicken tetrazzini, beef stroganoff, all meticulously labeled and dated. He liked to cook and got a quiet satisfaction from maintaining order and readiness in the household. If he had been a caveman, he would have been the one awake late into the night, taking inventory of the spear-points and stone axes.

Rhonda had been a disorganized, impulsive woman as likely to leave discarded pantyhose on the living room floor as in the dirty clothes hamper. She prided herself on being a strewer. *Order is for mediocre minds, Truman,* she had often told him. She mocked the absence of clutter in the house now, mocked the way Truman and Winslow arranged the books alphabetically, stored CDs by musical genre and composer. *My god,* she'd told him after she'd moved out, *it's as though dead people live here.*

It was true that Rhonda was not an easy woman to survive.

When the pasta was ready, Truman called Winslow and while they ate in companionable silence, Winslow patted his foot on an imaginary piano pedal, keeping time to some piece of music shining in his head.

The Beauty Spot hair salon was in the half-basement of Sam and Corinna Brown's small white clapboard house. Corinna had fixed it up with gingham curtains and a pink salon chair and big mirrors on the walls that had little etched doodads in their corners. Her sink was pink, too, and her customers' protective smocks were black with pink musical notes spilled all over them like someone had had an accident with a tune. No one she knew could read music, so she'd never figured out if the notes went to a real song. Not knowing was fine with her, though; in her opinion, it didn't always do to know the exact nature of things. The best moment for a box of chocolates was before you bit into one. Once you knew it was coconut, the magic was over.

'How are you doing under there?' Corinna hollered, thrusting her hand under the hairdryer hood and poking at Bettina Jones's curlers. Bettina was half deaf anyway. Put her under a hair dryer and she became a gently smiling imbecile.

'Honey, you're just about done!' Corinna shouted.

Bettina smiled expansively and without a shred of comprehension. She'd been one of Corinna's customers for nearly forty years. When Corinna had first started doing her hair, neither one of them showed a single sign of wear, and now look at them – Corinna with her stout bosom and Bettina with all that gray, which Corinna could never talk her into coloring. *I'm exactly the age I am, girl, and I've got nothing to apologize for,* Bettina was always saying. As a beautician, Corinna thought Bettina had plenty to apologize for, Bettina being a naturally homely woman who failed to even attempt improvements, but she'd learned to keep her thoughts to herself.

'Let's comb you out, honey,' Corinna said now, flipping up the hairdryer hood and clicking it to off.

'Whew,' Bettina said. 'You could drop an atom bomb and I wouldn't hear it under there. It's kind of peaceful. You ever sit under there, Corinna? It might be a good idea from time to time. You never know – you might just find God under there, honey.'

'I may not know a lot,' Corinna said, 'but I do know God doesn't live inside a hairdryer. If He's worth His salt, He's living right out in the open where anyone can find him.' Corinna unwound Bettina's curlers and tossed them into her disinfectant soak.

'He works in mysterious ways His miracles to perform,'

Bettina said primly. 'You just haven't been of a mind to see them.'

'You're right about that, honey.' Corinna fluffed Bettina's hair to cover up her receding hairline with a puff of bangs. Bettina might have laid down a good foundation with the Lord, but she sure was losing the war with her hair. Sometime soon, Corinna was going to have to talk to her about Rogaine.

'How's Sam doing?' Bettina asked. 'He keeping that diabetes under control?'

'He's doing the best he can, but it's hard on him. He always was one for an apple brown betty or a fudge cake.'

'He set another date to retire?'

'Naw. Not yet.'

'I'm telling you, if that man isn't careful he's going to kill himself.'

'He's not ready to retire yet. When he's ready, he'll go.' Corinna looked at the clock. Sam should be getting home in fifteen minutes, and she didn't like him waiting too long for his supper. 'Looks like you're all done, honey.' She whisked the nylon smock off Bettina and brushed the little hairs off her neck with a badger brush.

'Let me just get you a check.' Bettina grabbed her purse and wrote a check in record time, including a two-dollar tip. Bettina was always good that way, even though she lived on Social Security. One day Corinna and Sam would be living like that, too, but it didn't look like it would be any time soon.

Corinna set a plate of meat loaf, peas, and mashed potatoes on the table for Sam – good food, country cooking like they'd both grown up on.

45

'Thank you, Mama.' Sam lifted his fork as though it was a heavy weight. He must be having another bad day. He worried himself sick; worried even when he said he wasn't worried. When he *said* he was worried, Corinna knew he'd be sitting up in his chair all night. Her heart ached for him.

'How'd it go with that new girl?' Corinna asked.

Sam chewed thoughtfully. 'Went okay, I guess.'

'You guess?'

'I don't know – she knows a lot of things I never heard about before. At least she's not like that Harriet Saul, always bossing everybody around like they're some fool.'

'Sugar, you know everything there is to know about Hannah.'

Sam set his fork down, his face full of heartbreak. 'What if there was something the baby's needed all these years, and I didn't know it?'

Corinna pressed his hand hard. 'You've done the best you could for that girl, sugar. No one would say any different.'

Sam nodded and lifted his fork again. 'Sure is a good meal, Mama.'

They ate in silence.

'What did Hannah think of her?' Corinna said after a while.

'I think she'll take to the woman. Ate a yam right out of her hand already.'

'You think it helps that she's a woman?' Corinna asked.

'Don't know.' Sam started clearing the table. 'Could be.' He brightened a bit. 'She says she's got some ideas for us to try, things that'll be fun for the girl.'

'You tell her about TV?'

'Nah. She already looks at me like I'm crazy because I talk to shug like I do.'

'Don't you stop talking to her, now,' Corinna warned.

'Nah. There's nothing out there that can shut me up, you know that. Hannah knows it, too. It would probably scare her half to death if I came in quiet.'

'What kind of donuts did you bring her?'

'Custards, plus the strawberry jelly.'

'Uh huh.' Corinna spooned out some sugar-free ice cream for them both. It tasted like hell, but they pretended to like it. 'You didn't cheat, did you? Take a little bite?'

'Nah.'

They finished their ice cream in silence. When they were done, Corinna went into the kitchen and came back with a tongue depressor, some bandages, and a little plastic jar. Sam took off his left shoe and sock and untaped a square of gauze on his foot and lower leg, exposing a wet, livid, diabetic ulcer.

'Looks a little better,' he said.

Corinna just looked at him and he looked away. 'You can't keep going like this, honey,' she said softly. 'You think maybe this girl's the one?'

'I don't know, Mama. It's awful soon.'

Corinna scooped some ointment from the jar and put it on the wound gently. Not that she had to. He hadn't been able to feel that foot right in almost a year. It might be ugly, but there wasn't any pain.

'Comfrey root,' Corinna said, deftly screwing the lid back on the little jar.

'Thank you, Mama.'

Corinna taped new gauze over the wound and said,

47

'You talk to her at all about maybe getting another elephant?'

Sam put his sock and shoe back on. 'It came up.'

'What'd she say?'

'Said it would take a miracle.'

'That's one thing that's in short supply, honey,' Corinna said dryly. 'Guess we'll have to figure out something else.'

That night, for Sam, was a dream night. As always, he found himself in a meadow full of high grass and rolling hills, with a pond deep enough for an elephant to belly down in. It smelled like summer, like a tonic made of growing things and sunshine and bugs and good rich dirt, though he'd also dreamt that meadow in every season and all kinds of weather. No matter when it was, he always found himself there with a joyful heart. Not that he was himself. No, he moved in a herky-jerky sort of way, so that even when he was going forward, he was also swaying from side to side. It was like being on a hayride, way up high, but there was no hay, no wagon. When he looked down he saw perfect feet, healthy feet. Elephant feet.

And as always, he ambled around the dream-meadow smelling everything, feeling the warm sun on his head and the cool earth underfoot as he browsed. When he was done he wallowed in the pond, pinching up gobs of good thick mud that he flung over every part of himself. And then he heard a trumpeting, a rumbling, the low thrumming of elephants; first one, then a second and a third. As they ran towards him he could feel the very ground shake. His heart filled to nearly overflowing, every beat sending out a prayer of thanks: *O Lord, for giving me this place, these elephants, I will worship at Your feet forever.*

48

Next morning, like all the mornings after the dreams, he felt the way he always did after a sickness, heavy and slow and filled with the unyielding knowledge of all the things he couldn't do, couldn't give; knowing, too, that he would go back to the zoo to find his sugar chained to the wall in her little barn at the zoo, waiting patiently for him to come back to her one more day. It was on those mornings, not being able to bear showing up empty-handed, that he brought his baby donuts.

Chapter 4

When Sam arrived at work the next day he saw that Neva Wilson had gotten there before him. She waved gaily from the elephant yard as he pulled in. He didn't see his baby, though. Hurrying into the barn, he found her still standing in her overnight mess and shackled to the wall, rocking back and forth in great agitation. And her tire was gone. How could he have forgotten to bring her the tire last night? It was usually the very last thing he did, and in all these years he'd never forgotten it.

He laid hands on, murmured quietly, 'Hey, sugar; c'mon now, baby girl. How's my sugar this fine morning? How's Papa's girl? Come on, sugar, come on now. Let's get that chain off.' He leaned down and unclipped the heavy chain from her shackle as she continued to rock beside him, swaying back and forth rhythmically like some kind of broken thing. The skin under the metal anklet was rubbed raw again after a month of healing, and every

51

time she swayed it got just a little bit worse. God*damn*. Sam kept his voice soft, though, as he murmured and worked around her, crooning and petting and clucking and soothing; bringing her down. Later he'd have to do the same for himself. Right now, he was steaming.

'That woman talk to you at all? What in hell was she thinking, leaving you chained up in here when she's out there all sunny and smiling like some damn Florida orange juice commercial?' Sam muttered, moving around Hannah with his hand on her the whole time so she knew where he was; talking and talking, until he finally got her still and calm. He made sure to save out a word or two for the young lady, and not a kind word, either.

'Good morning!' she sang from the door leading out to the yard.

'No, it's not,' Sam snapped. 'What in the name of God were you thinking, miss, leaving Hannah in here in her own filth while you were out there doing whatever it was you were doing? The girl's been in here all by herself since six o'clock last night.'

Neva winked at him. *Winked*. 'Can you keep her busy for about five more minutes? I'm just about ready.'

'Girl, you and me are going to have some *words*, and they ain't gonna be pretty, neither.'

'Okay, but first give me five more minutes.' And damned if she didn't sail out to the yard again, leaving Sam muttering things it was good that no one but Hannah could hear. He forked down a flake of hay from the loft, and was about to start getting the day's fruit and vegetables ready in the kitchen when he found two big pans already filled with cut-up produce.

'Okay,' Neva called from out in the yard. 'Let's have some fun. Go ahead and bring her out!'

'C'mon, sugar. Let's get you out of this mess and into some fresh air,' Sam said to Hannah, clucking a little to encourage her. They both blinked as they stepped into sunshine as powerful as a searchlight after the fetid gloom of the barn.

Neva was solidly planted next to the door with her arms folded across her chest, grinning like a fool. She put a finger to her lips to shush him. He was about to let his words fly when she motioned for him to turn around quick. When he did, he stopped dead in his tracks.

Hannah was rushing around the yard. Bewildered, he looked at Neva, who just smiled and said in a low voice, 'Watch. Just watch! She's already figured it out. She's a smart girl, your elephant.'

So Sam watched as Hannah lumbered over to one of the trees and found her tire in the highest notch in the branches. She ran her trunk around the outside of it, and then around the inside – withdrawing a banana, which she neatly ate. Then she went back to the outside of the tire again, working on something Sam couldn't see.

'Peanut butter,' Neva said. 'She's found the peanut butter.'

Sam just stood there.

'Just wait,' Neva said, clapping her hands. 'Wait until she starts finding the pumpkins. There are eleven of them, and I filled them all with raisins and jelly beans.'

'A scavenger hunt,' Sam said in wonder. 'You've given shug a scavenger hunt.'

Neva grinned. 'It's one of my all-time favorite things. The animals light up just like it's Christmas.'

53

Sam shook his head. Hannah was hustling around pulling bananas from branches, a pumpkin from inside a hollow log, squashes from the little wallow Sam kept for her. 'Looks like Christmas came early this year. What time did you get here to do all of this?'

Neva shrugged. 'Six, six-thirty.'

'Lord.'

Neva shrugged again. Sam watched as Hannah polished off a cache of bananas.

'Guess I owe you an apology, miss.'

'No you don't,' Neva said. 'How could you have known?'

In the beginning, Max Biedelman had checked on Sam often. He would be hosing Hannah down or cleaning her with a scrub brush when he'd see the old woman out of the corner of his eye, resting on the little folding stool she carried wherever she went. Sam thought the eyes of God must be something like Miss Biedelman's, bright and all-seeing, snatching things up as quick and strong as a rat-trap. It had occurred to him more than once to wonder whether Max Biedelman was an emissary of the Lord, sent down to protect His earthly creatures.

Sometimes she brought Miss Effie with her, and those were good days when Sam could count on the old woman smiling, showing the yellowed ivory of her excellent teeth. She introduced Miss Effie to Sam as her personal secretary. Effie was nearly as old as Miss Biedelman, but still a beautiful flower, small in her bones and figure, skin like fine silk crepe: a lady. She always carried a perfumed white lace handkerchief as insubstantial as a spider web, which she kept tucked inside her cuff. When they visited an animal that was especially strong-smelling, Miss Effie held the scented lace to her nose.

'Effie was brought up in genteel surroundings,' Max Biedelman told Sam on a day when she came to visit alone, her eyes full of hell and wickedness. 'She would have done very badly in Africa, don't you think, Mr Brown?'

'Don't know, sir. I've never been there.'

'If I were a younger woman I'd take you. I think you'd find it quite splendid. The world is simpler in Africa, Mr Brown. Not in all ways, of course, but in the important ones. You eat when you're hungry and sleep when you're tired and you know you're nothing more than a gnat, a visitor, forgotten even before you're gone. Africa belongs to the land and the animals. It's no place for the high-strung. Effie did not find it to her taste.' The old woman smiled fondly. 'But I would have enjoyed showing it to you, Mr Brown.'

'Thank you, sir. I see it in my mind as plain as day from your stories.'

'You're just humoring an old woman.'

'*No* sir.'

'Well, I thank you just the same. Talking makes it seem real again.' She sighed. 'I do miss it, but Effie is happier keeping me at home, now that we're in our dotage.'

'I've never been anyplace but Korea and here, and I sure didn't think much of Korea,' Sam said. 'Course the circumstances weren't what you'd call inviting. I came home alive, though. Me and Corinna never took that for granted. A lot of men came home the other way.'

'War is dreadful, Mr Brown – a male vice, if you'll

55

forgive me for saying so. Tell me, do you believe in reincarnation?'

'I might, if I knew what it was.'

'Ah. Hindus believe that after we die, we are reborn – reincarnated – as another being.'

Sam frowned. 'The Bible doesn't say anything about that.'

'And you believe in the Bible, do you, Mr Brown?' Max said. Her sharp old eyes twinkled.

'Mainly.'

'But it's very limiting, isn't it?'

'Corinna would probably agree there. Ever since the baby died Corinna hasn't had much use for God or the Bible. She says when God lets you down like He did to us, He doesn't deserve our respectfulness. Corinna's got high standards. High standards and an unyielding nature.'

'I'd like to meet her.'

What a picture – his Corinna and Max Biedelman together, two towering priestesses toe to toe, and no telling what wonders they could perform. Sam shook his head admiringly. 'If you'll pardon me for saying so, we've never met anyone like you before. Probably never will again.'

'Thank heaven for that, Mr Brown.' The old woman had chuckled, clapping him on the back with a dry, hard hand. 'Thank heaven for that.'

By noon Hannah was dozing peacefully in the sun, sated with treats and happiness and hay. Neva hoisted herself onto a counter in the tiny office inside the elephant barn. It was a small room to begin with, more like a glorified closet, and it was furnished with a rickety old desk and

56

a rolling wooden chair that tilted dangerously to the right. She'd had furniture just like it for years – had it and abandoned it in four cities and three states. Howard had laid claim to most of their good things when they split – the rope bed they'd found and refinished, the washstand with the Delft tile backsplash, a rocking chair with beautiful acanthus-leaf arms. Neva's mother had been appalled, but as far as Neva was concerned Howard had been welcome to it all. She'd never been any good at decorating or at organizing belongings. Better to just give things away or throw them out and start over again later. There was something cleansing about abandonment.

She unwrapped a Milky Way bar. 'Want some?' She held out the candy to Sam. 'I can split it.'

'Can't, miss – diabetes. Found out last year. It's a damned shame, too. I sure do miss my sweets. Me and Hannah, we could go through a bag of Hershey's Kisses in a day. Baby Ruths, too. And Paydays.' Sam's eyes took on a dreamy, faraway look.

Neva knew other old zookeepers who, like Samson Brown, had been hired right out of the military by municipal zoos and animal parks in the 1940s and 1950s, but most of them were so unsuited to their work that they had been transferred to park maintenance or food preparation on graveyard shifts – anything to get at least a minimal return out of them while keeping them away from the animals. Neva remembered one man who was so terrified of the bears he took care of – sun bears, strict vegetarians; sad, sleepy, fly-blown old animals – that he insisted on carrying a switchblade with him at all times. You would have to shoot flaming darts into those bears at point-blank range to get a rise out of them, but the keeper only shook his head and whispered to Neva, *I see them watching me – I see them watching me all the time. You look in those eyes and you can see murder, plain as day.* Mercifully the man had been transferred, eventually finishing out his working life taking care of butterflies.

Neva chewed in companionable silence while Sam finished entering food records for the morning – how much fruit Hannah got, how many vegetables, how much hay. 'So how do you think this morning could have gone better?' she asked when he was finished.

'I haven't seen her playful like that in an awful long time, kittenish that way.'

Neva smiled.

'But she gets real upset if somebody gets here in the morning and they don't unchain her. It makes her feel bad, and then she starts rocking, and once she's rocking it's hard to get her to stop. She can keep it up for days, I've seen her do it. When she does, that metal anklet of hers just digs up her leg something awful. Took three months to heal, last time.'

'Has she always done that?'

'Long as I've known her. When she first came over from Burma, I guess the only thing that calmed her down was old Reyna, the elephant Hannah was supposed to keep company. Course, Hannah was nothing but a little tiny thing then, especially compared to Reyna. Reyna was a big old cow, and she'd stand right next to shug in the barn for hours, right up against her, not enough room between them for a flea to pass. Guess it made Hannah feel secure, having old Reyna plastered on her like that. She quit rocking after a while.'

'How old was she then?'

58

'Shug? Course nobody knows for sure, but Miss Biedelman figured two, three maybe. And you should have seen her run in those days. We used to use golf carts to take care of the grounds, take weeds to the back lot, bring new bushes, animal chow, like that. Well, Hannah, she liked to charge at that golf cart when it came by outside her fence. Her stumpy little trunk would be up and she'd just be trumpeting away.' Sam laughed. 'The girl was afraid of her own shadow, but she wasn't going to take no guff off that golf cart, *no* sir. Sometimes me and Miss Biedelman got Little Jim to bring that cart around just to give the girl some exercise.'

Neva laughed. Sam subsided, saying quietly, 'My Hannah's a good girl, miss. She's never done anything bad, never hurt anybody even when she was scared.'

'I can see that.'

'It was awful bad for her when old Reyna died. Shug didn't stop rocking for two weeks; girl even rocked in her sleep. Miss Biedelman was almost as bad off, slept with Reyna for three days and nights before she passed, then stayed with the body another whole day before she'd let them take it away. That was a long time ago and I wasn't working with shug then, but I remember it as plain as yesterday. The baby rocked and Miss Biedelman wouldn't come out of the house – wouldn't talk, either, not even to Miss Effie, and that was saying something. A couple of weeks later was when she asked me to take care of Hannah. Been doing it ever since.'

'She has some bad scars on the sides of her head and on her shoulders. Do you know why?' Neva asked.

'Miss Biedelman thought someone beat her on the boat that brought her over here from Burma. Miss Biedelman said the mahouts would never have done it, but no mahouts came with her, just somebody hired to stay with her on the boat so she didn't make trouble.'

Neva sighed. 'Even keepers beat elephants sometimes. It used to be an accepted way to establish dominance over them.'

'Nobody's got the right to beat an animal,' Sam said quietly. 'No more than they've got the right to beat a child.'

Neva agreed. 'How does Hannah do when you go away for a few days? Is there anyone else she trusts?'

'Hasn't been anyone who stuck around long enough for her to get to know. Anyway, I don't take much time off. Longest time was when I was in the hospital last year. That's when we found out about the diabetes. It took me nearly a month to get back on my feet. Sometime in through there, somebody left shug chained up in the barn for three days straight. Like I was saying, she gets real spooked now being in that barn too long, especially when someone besides me comes around and doesn't unchain her.'

'And that's why she was rocking this morning?' Neva said.

'Uh huh.'

'*Damn* it.'

'Next time you want to do some game, just let me know ahead of time and I'll come in early and keep Hannah company, let her know things are okay while you set up.'

'You're very good to her,' Neva said.

'Well,' said Sam, 'I had a good teacher.'

'Miss Biedelman? So who was *Mr* Biedelman?'

Sam grinned. 'Wasn't one. Maxine Leona Biedelman's the whole name, except she never used the Leona part except as an initial. It sure made her mad when someone called her Maxine. *Real* mad. She was a fine old lady.'

'Haven't you ever wanted to work with other elephants besides Hannah?'

'Nah. Miss Biedelman asked me to take care of Hannah for her, and that's what I've done. Can't imagine caring for any other elephant, though.'

'But don't you want variety?'

'Nah. If me and sugar want variety, all we have to do is go for a walk. There's plenty of variety out there. She sure does like her look-around.'

'And that's enough? Doesn't it make you want to see what's out there beyond the zoo?'

'I did that, miss. Before you were born I was in Korea. I saw that. Don't need to see any more.'

Neva touched him on the shoulder lightly. 'You're a very good man,' she said, and then flushed. She hadn't intended to say it; she hadn't even been aware of thinking it until it slipped out. But she'd meant it. This morning she had been arrogant enough to plan on teaching him all she knew about elephant care and zookeeping in general. Now she understood that it wasn't going to be like that at all.

Chapter 5

For Winslow's eleventh birthday Truman Levy had agreed to get him a pig. Possibly to counter Rhonda's knee-jerk negativity, he hadn't been able to come up with a credible reason to say no, except that he didn't want a pig in the house, which didn't seem good enough even to him. So he'd said yes, despite the fact that he knew nothing about pigs in general or potbellied minia-ture pigs in particular; and despite the certainty that he would come to regret this decision in ways he couldn't even begin to imagine.

So Sunday afternoon, in a light drizzle, he and Winslow had driven to a pig breeder at a rundown farm, squished through the muck, and surveyed the squealing piglets. The farmer pushed a few piglets aside to reveal one sitting calmly amid the chaos.

'That little male's a good one,' the farmer had said.

'How do you know?'

'He ain't runnin', is he?'

63

Though far from reassured, Truman paid $125 in crisp new bills and they became the owners of a twelve-pound pot-bellied piglet named Miles. Miles was black and white, had tiny, wicked black eyes and a nose like a tin can hit head-on by a truck. His coat felt like something between human whiskers and toothbrush bristles, and he rode home beside Winslow in a cat carrier.

On the boy's other side was nearly a hundred and fifty dollars' worth of essential pig-nursery items he and Truman had purchased that morning. These included a sack of feed, a hoof trimmer, an untippable food dish and water bowl, a dog bed with fleecy liner, a collar and harness, a litter box with wood shavings to fill it, rubber balls in an assortment of sizes, rawhide chew treats, a selection of stuffed toys, and a book called *Miniature Pigs and You: A New Owner's Guide to Love and Happiness*. Truman had also signed up for the store's preferred customer program, written down the Internet address of several informational Web sites about miniature pigs, and bought Miles a small engraved ID tag shaped like a heart.

Distantly but with perfect clarity he heard Rhonda's voice say, *Oh, for god's sake, Truman. Really. You could have simply said no.*

Yesterday they had created a pen with wire fencing that would be Miles's outdoor domain, reached from the den through a dog door. Now, while Winslow kept the piglet busy out back, Truman closely consulted the *Guide to Love and Happiness* and arranged a cozy living space for Miles in the den. Per the instructions, he artfully strewed old towels around for Miles to root through, this evidently being a pig behavior as elemental as eating, only far more destructive when mishandled. With growing horror Truman read that if the pig was allowed to become bored he could be expected to tear up carpeting, eat drywall and baseboards, tip over and root through potted plants, and generally destroy at will any luckless object or architectural feature upon which he chose to lavish his attention. And, the book made clear, it would be the owner's fault for his lack of foresight and imagination in meeting the pig's basic needs, never mind keeping its superior intellect more productively engaged.

Filled with dread, Truman opened the sliding glass door into the backyard and summoned Winslow and Miles. The boy came in first, followed closely by the pig, which emitted a steady stream of old-mannish grunts, snorts, and general muttering.

'I think he likes me,' Winslow said.

'Thank god.'

The pig approached a pile of towels, buried his nose, and began sorting through and rearranging them. Truman had had an Aunt Tilda who did the same thing when presented with a pile of partygoers' coats in a back bedroom.

'What's he doing?' Winslow said.

'Rooting. Either rooting or wallowing.' Truman thumbed through the guide. 'Yes. This would be rooting.'

'Why?'

Truman sighed deeply. 'Because he's a pig. We can't always expect to understand these things, Winslow.'

'So what's wallowing?'

'Technically, rolling in mud and filth. According to this, though, a mainly indoor pig will be satisfied wallowing in blankets and towels.'

And then, purely by chance, Truman's eye fell on a

page of the book subtitled *Screaming*. 'Good Christ. It says here that if we pick him up he may scream. Evidently pigs don't like to be picked up – it makes them think they're prey. It says here that the scream of a pig has actually been recorded at higher decibels than a jet engine at takeoff. Oh, but here's the good news: if he's properly socialized, he'll only scream for ten to thirty seconds.'

'What if he isn't socialized?'

'The neighbors will turn us in.' Truman regarded the small pig, appalled.

'Maybe we should have gotten a dog,' Winslow said.

Oh, for god's sake, said Rhonda.

'Let's give him some time, Winnie. Let's just give him some time.'

Harriet Saul had recently commissioned a marketing study that would help her revitalize the zoo. She wanted to know who came to visit and why; when they came, what they saw while they were there; how long they stayed; and how much money they spent per capita in the gift shop and food concessions. She intended to double the zoo's attendance and triple its income within the next two years. It was ambitious, but Harriet had turned far less promising organizations around. At least the zoo had animals, and animals brought people – people with money to give away.

Finches were her own – and only – true love in the animal kingdom, though they weren't pets in the sense that you could hug them or take them for a drive in the car. No, they were miraculous little fairy-creatures, all air-filled bones and fluff and down and feathers that resolved, however improbably, into a creature that could take flight.

They were, in every way, not human. She loved that about them. Harriet didn't share the prevailing worship of wolves and whales and dogs of all descriptions. They looked out of eyes just like hers.

Now, sitting at her desk on Sunday morning, she reviewed the marketing firm's preliminary report. It told her what she had already assumed: Hannah was by far the zoo's biggest draw. Parents brought their children to the zoo, but children brought their parents to see Hannah. An incredible one out of every three children under the age of twelve in the greater Bladenham area had visited Hannah, either with a school group, a family member, or both. Twenty-eight percent of all monetary donations to the Biedelman Zoo were made directly or indirectly to Hannah. Hers was the only animal's name the majority of those interviewed could remember. The elephant *was* the Max L. Biedelman Zoo.

Thus armed, Harriet intended to put Hannah's picture on billboards, print ads, mugs, hats, T-shirts, sweatshirts, posters, postcards, trinkets, balloons – the works. She intended to make Hannah the most famous elephant on the West Coast. She'd already selected a Seattle ad agency that she would ask to execute an ad campaign pro bono. For the agency, the campaign would be the perfect plat-form for innovation, and innovation won national awards, which in turn lured new clients that would more than pay the agency back for the time they donated to the zoo.

Closing the report summary and locking duplicate copies in a desk drawer, she pulled on a baggy Biedelman Zoo cardigan and left the office – a walk would do her good. It was a glorious October day. The smell of burn piles, apples and dying annuals made a perfume more intoxicating than springtime. Harriet had always seen the waning days of autumn as times of hope and renewal. School was back in session, and winter clothes hid her hefty figure. Her Aunt Maude, with whom Harriet had lived from her ninth birthday until she was eighteen, used to tell her to cover up, for God's sake, as though the big bones and dumpy figure she'd inherited from her father's side of the family were her fault. Harriet would often hear Maude looking through wastebaskets for wrappers that would prove Harriet was sneaking candy bars – which she was, although Maude never caught her because Harriet put the wrappers between the pages of her textbooks and threw them out at school.

Maude had also looked to see if Harriet was discarding the tubes of her acne medicine before they were completely exhausted. *We do not waste in this house,* she'd sniff if she found something that offended her. *Despite what you may think, I am not made of money.* Maude had made no secret of her displeasure at being stuck with Harriet after her mother, Maude's sister, died of a brain aneurysm. *She always was one for passing off her work to others,* Harriet once overheard Maude say about her mother. Maude disliked children, especially large, messy girls like Harriet. As a senior in high school, Harriet had saved her money for months to have a beauty makeover at Nordstrom's. The beauty consultant had cracked a tiny piece of gum as she'd circled Harriet's high barstool with her brushes poised, sighed, then circled again. At the end of the hour Harriet had spent one hundred and thirty-two dollars on a pore minimizer, skin tightener, ultraviolet blocker, under-eye concealer, eyebrow lightener, six complementary shades of eye shadow and two complementary lipsticks. When she got home Maude's single comment was, *Dear god. I assume you intend to demand your money back.*

Now, as Harriet walked down the path past the elephant barn, en route to the employee parking lot, she saw the new girl, Neva Wilson, out shoveling a thick layer of sand onto the concrete pad of the elephant yard. When she looked up Harriet lifted her hand in greeting and called, 'How's our elephant this morning?'

'Actually, the abscess is a little better,' Neva called back. 'Plus this sand should give her a softer substrate.'

'Excellent! Anything to keep our star happy!'

'How about another elephant?'

Harriet pretended Neva had said something amusing and walked on. The girl was far too intense for Harriet's taste, too ready to point out a shortcoming or an unfilled need. On her third day at the zoo she'd sent Harriet a handwritten note, requesting petty cash for jumbo bags of jelly beans and raisins – snack food. Harriet had declined the request with a written note advising her that vending machines were located both in the employee lounge behind the zoo cafeteria and near the food and gift concessions; and that an institution belonging to a municipality had to be especially careful about impropriety, or even perceived impropriety, including making purchases that benefited employees who were already fairly compensated. It surprised Harriet that the woman had made the request in the first place. Neva had come with an excellent background and the most glowing references, but Harriet was still reserving final judgment. Either she had pulled off a coup by hiring someone with

Neva's experience for the low salary she could offer, or the woman was on her way down for a reason Harriet hadn't managed to determine during the selection process. If she turned out to be a drinker or drug abuser, Harriet wouldn't hesitate to let her go. She'd already explained this to Truman, who seemed unnecessarily attentive to her – and on zoo time, one of Harriet's pet peeves. She was paying her people a fair living wage, and expected them to earn it. They could socialize on their own time.

Harriet walked the entire loop through the zoo, picking up trash here and there, fluffing up some new landscaping she'd had installed and greeting the few visitors in attendance – most people were still in church. According to the marketing summary, which confirmed Harriet's own observations, the numbers would spike between twelve and one o'clock, especially on such a beautiful day. Harriet had never been a churchgoer, herself. She found the praying and hymn-singing bizarre, like a collective, delusional belief in Santa Claus.

Back in her office, she stood at her window, pink-cheeked and too full of energy to settle down. On a sudden impulse she grabbed her bundle of keys, including the heavy old skeleton key that supposedly unlocked any door in the house, and headed up the grand staircase to the second floor. She'd been saving this exploration for just the right day. She had very little family memorabilia of her own – Maude considered scrapbooks and old yellowing photo albums maudlin and irrelevant.

The first three rooms seemed to be bedrooms, with handsome mahogany beds and dressers, huge armoires and little else. But a fourth door led into a room furnished with huge old oak file cabinets and a map case that held sixty or seventy old maps. Harriet glanced at maps of southern Africa, India, Thailand, Burma, Indonesia. Someone had clipped slips of paper to them, with code numbers printed in a firm, dark hand. A methodical thinker herself, Harriet turned to the oak filing cabinets and found each drawer labeled with corresponding code numbers. In those cabinets she found hundreds and hundreds of photographs, old sepia prints, gorgeous black and white studio shots, and more modern color snap-shots.

She dragged over a heavy oak desk chair and, one drawer at a time, brought the photographs out into the light. Early pictures showed a sturdy little girl, handsome rather than pretty, standing outside a canvas tent or near a camp table. In some she wore the clothing of a Victorian schoolgirl, but in others – the most striking ones, Harriet thought – the girl wore a pith helmet and boy's safari costume: baggy shorts, low sturdy boots, a khaki shirt, and incongruous hair ribbons, indifferently tied.

The girl was in the habit of looking straight and intensely into the camera lens, her light eyes as clear as rainwater. Many of the pictures also included a man whom Harriet assumed was the girl's father – an exceedingly handsome man, hard and fit-looking and very much at his ease, with the same light eyes as the child's. In most of the pictures he appeared to have glanced at the camera only coincidentally, as though caught in a momentary interlude.

Curiously, neither the man nor the girl carried guns, though guns could be seen in some of the pictures leaning against tents or tables, or in the hands of the guides who accompanied them. Instead, the man – her father, Harriet guessed – held a large pair of binoculars and the girl, who must be Maxine, sometimes wore a pair of smaller opera glasses on a ribbon around her neck. According to the maps, these photographs had been taken in the Ngong Valley in Kenya in the late 1870s and throughout the 1880s.

Harriet looked through all these photos once and then started over, lingering on those that showed Maxine's father. People thought that homeliness sought its own level, but it wasn't true; sometimes her heart ached for a man like this one. Maybe she could be this girl, so she could stand beside this man. Even as the daughter and not the lover, she would be blessed. Her own father hadn't been able to stand the sight of her or her mother. When he had been killed in a car wreck two days before her seventh birthday – and before she knew what lay in store for her at Aunt Maude's one day – she had considered his death a confirmation of God's goodness.

Harriet put away the first set of pictures, reached into the next drawer, and found herself at the turn of the century. There were no more photographs of Maxine's father; the cameras found Maxine herself grown into a tall, vigorous young woman with the same pale eyes, still amused, still youthful. These pictures were taken in jungles, in bazaars, and on plantations in Burma, India, Indonesia, and Thailand. Maxine was often riding or standing beside Asian elephants, or towering over dark-skinned men carrying short sticks with metal hooks on one end.

In several pictures Maxine led rather than rode an elephant, as though she had been allowed to work. In these she looked particularly strapping and contented.

Though Harriet knew she had died more than thirty years ago, it wasn't hard to imagine Maxine in the present day, haying a field or chopping wood, using her formidable energies in some hard physical labor. Harriet knew that restlessness, knew that so much energy was no gift unless it was matched with opportunity and circumstance. She had never been happier, more completely engaged, than on a grueling corporate five-day Outward Bound survival exercise in Montana, where she had welcomed the physical demands, greeted each day with vigor and keen attention. If she could have chosen an historical period in which to live, she would have homesteaded on the American frontier.

The next drawer of photographs had been taken during the first fifteen years of the new century, and for the first time they included cities – New York, London, Paris, Rome, Bombay. Even in these, a middle-aged Maxine wore men's tweeds. The camera often caught her scowling, as though she was in the cities by necessity rather than choice. In many there was a young woman, unidentified but exquisite, dressed in graceful Edwardian linen, high-collared lace blouses, and narrow pointed boots.

In the next several decades, the pictures often showed the zoo – still called Havenside – and the growing animal population, including the two old elephants to which Maxine had apparently been so devoted. In these photographs she was often pitching hay or hauling piles of dirt or building materials, as the property grew every which way into sheds and animal yards. Harriet recognized much of it, even in its current, rundown condition. For the first time, she understood the full extent of Maxine Biedelman's accomplishment.

Harriet flipped through the pictures with growing excitement. Here was a life she could use.

In the very early hours of Monday morning Truman dozed uncomfortably in an armchair in the den as Miles snuffled at his feet, ceaselessly rearranging his towels and an old sleeping bag of Winslow's. Truman's motivation for being there was somewhere between protecting his property and helping a child through its first night away from home. He recognized the absurdity of his situation, but he hadn't been able to relax in bed, listening for sounds of crashing furniture or piggy bereavement. In the end it seemed more bearable to doze upright in a chair than to lie wide-awake in bed, contemplating lone-liness beneath his roof. The *Guide to Love and Happiness* had been quite stern about not giving your pig more attention at the start than it would get later on: the pig would never understand what had gone wrong. Truman had been a pig owner for less than twenty-four hours and he was already making bad choices. The only pet he'd had in his parents' orderly home had been a turtle, which disappeared within twenty-four hours and who could blame it? Even Truman had found the little plastic desert island and single plastic palm tree depressing, and God only knew what kind of hell it looked like from the turtle's point of view.

Truman's mother Lavinia – ever regal in her signature pearls and twin sets, her elegant French twist – had been firm in enforcing the household rules that applied to him: no messes, no disorder, no tussling with other boys on the living room furniture. Not that Truman had been the sort of boy to tussle with friends or anyone else on the living room furniture; he had been a pale, bookish child whose boyhood energies went mostly into imagining himself as a pirate, an astronaut, a mountain climber, a spy. As an adult he was still leaving no messes or disorder, and abstaining from tussles on the living room furniture, but he was keenly aware that he had failed to mature into a dashing figure.

Truman sighed and switched on the nearest lamp. Its vibrant glass base had been made by a prominent glass artist, who'd given it to Rhonda in exchange for a bust of his young son. The lamp was a robust piece, the deep golden color of hope and joy, and he hoped she wouldn't remember to ask for it back. He needed it more than she did. Rhonda had a sinewy character and edgy resilience, heavy-lidded eyes and long hard bones. Had he ever found her beautiful? It was hard to remember. He supposed he had, in the beginning, when they were in college and under the influence of the twin stimulants of sex and sleeplessness. She had been so decisive, so sure of what she wanted, when she wanted it, and with whom. If he met her again now, for the first time, he would probably be just as vulnerable to her certainty, her supreme self-confidence. The road to Truman's beliefs was more circuitous, traveling as it did through the dense woods and bogs of indecision and doubt.

Indefatigable, the pig was still working on the towels beneath his chair. Miles. Truman could see Rhonda rolling her eyes at the name he and Winslow had deliberated over for so long. *It's a pig, not a banker. Why not name it Sir Francis Bacon, something clever?* But Truman and Winslow weren't clever, not in the ways Rhonda had expected.

Truman reached down and touched the animal's side.

The pig instantly dropped to the floor in bliss. Absently, Truman scratched the sparsely haired belly while Miles subsided into soft piggy grunts and then snores. Outside it was still pitch dark, the domain of the abandoned and the loveless.

Chapter 6

On Monday morning, Sam found a note taped to his desk in the elephant barn:

Come see me right away.

Harriet Saul

As far as he was concerned, the woman could hold on until he got Hannah comfortable. That meant cutting produce, pulling down hay, sweeping the barn, attending to his sugar's feet, and petting her a little bit before letting her out into the yard. The phone on the barn wall seemed like it rang every other minute, but Sam just let it go. Mama knew better than to call so early, especially on one of Neva's days off, and Harriet Saul could just wait; big noisy woman with a gift for making people feel small. In the end, it was ten-thirty by the time he made it up to the house. Poor place needed a new coat of paint for its trim in the worst way; that, and to have its drive re-graveled. Max Biedelman would have died, seeing it this way. She'd been proud of her house, showed him paintings and statues and furniture she'd brought home from all over the world. The place had looked just like a museum.

He and Corinna had been invited there to supper now and then. The first time wasn't more than a few months after Hannah had been given to Sam to take care of. Miss Biedelman and Miss Effie had set that huge dark table with a fine white tablecloth, china and crystal and silver, looked just like some movie. They'd sat way up at one end, but you could have fed a baseball team at that table and still had room to spare.

Sam had been self-conscious of his manners but Corinna settled in like visiting royalty, and that was just how they'd treated her, too. Asked her all sorts of questions about her grandmother and grandfather coming out from Chicago and settling a claim out near Bladenham, so poor they'd had to make their clothes from hides one year just like the Indians. They'd been too embarrassed to be seen like that, so they lived off the land until Corinna's grandmother had spun and woven enough cloth to make Corinna's granddaddy a proper suit of clothes.

Corinna had talked on and on, sitting up so straight and fine, her face glowing just like a polished chestnut. She had a smooth, rich voice, and she could spin a story as well as anyone he'd ever heard. Sam had been so proud of her he'd hardly said a word the whole meal, just watched her sparkle. When Corinna teased him about it on the way home, he told her he could talk to Miss Biedelman any time he wanted, but it wasn't every day he could see his wife doing herself so proud. Even now, so many years later, it was a memory that sustained him sometimes when he was feeling low.

When he came up the walk to the house, he saw Harriet Saul standing at her window, watching for him; by the time he walked in the office door she was fumbling with a slew of keys on a plastic spiral bracelet which she pushed up an arm as meaty as a ham. She pulled her office door shut behind her and led him upstairs and down the hall. He'd never been in this part of the house before, felt embarrassed to be here now, even with Miss Biedelman long dead. It felt like trespassing. But Harriet was already halfway down the hall. She moved real quick for such a stumpy woman; reminded him of the way Hannah moved out sometimes when she caught the smell of a treat in the wind.

Harriet unlocked a door and went inside, beckoning for him to follow. 'I want you to look at these and tell me anything you know about these people,' she said. She opened a big wooden drawer and pulled out a fistful of photographs which she handed to Sam. 'Start with these.'

'I'll be damned,' he said softly, because he was looking at pictures of Africa. 'That's Miss Biedelman. Wasn't she a fine-looking girl, though! I never saw her except as an old lady. Wouldn't have pictured her like this, but she sure does look like herself.'

'Maxine Biedelman,' Harriet said.

'No one else it could be, not with those eyes. She hated being called Maxine, though. Always had people call her Max, and she got real mad when they forgot.'

'I thought Max was her father.'

79

'No ma'am, his name was Arthur. Died of the fever when she was twenty-five. I guess it nearly broke her heart.'

Harriet took the pictures out of Sam's hand and thrust another one at him. 'Who's this with her? Is she a sister, maybe, or a cousin?'

Sam broke into a wide smile, saying softly, 'Well, I'll be. Naw, there never was a sister. That's little Miss Effie standing next to her. Doesn't she look just like a picture in all those pearls. And so young and pretty, too.'

'Who was Effie?'

'Miss Biedelman always introduced her as her personal secretary, though I never saw her working. Of course, that was when they were old, too. Didn't know Miss Effie knew Miss Biedelman when they were so young, though. Fine-looking women, both of them. Don't they just beat all in their fancy clothes.'

Sam handed the pictures back to Harriet, frowning. 'It doesn't feel right going through their personal effects like this. Miss Biedelman was a real private woman. She wouldn't like us pawing through her things.'

Harriet waved away his concern. 'She left them to the City of Bladenham, just like she left the house. I'll get hold of the historical society, so they can catalog everything.'

'Well, I thank you for letting me see them again. I still miss them sometimes, even after all these years.'

Halfway back to the elephant yard Sam felt a tug on the back of his shirt. 'Mister? Hey, mister.'

He turned around and saw Reginald Poole, the boy who'd come along for a walk with him and Hannah. 'Well, hey, boy. You come back to see my elephant?'

'Yeah, I came back like you asked me to. You remember me?'

'Of course I do. You treating your aunt right?'

'Yeah, I'm treating her good.'

'Glad to hear it, son. Treating women right's one of the most important jobs a man's got, seeing as how they give birth to us and all. It's the least we can do in return.'

'Yeah. So are you going to walk that elephant again sometime?' Reginald walked with a big-man, basketball walk, bouncing up on the balls of his feet.

'Guess we could. You got any fruit in your pockets, a banana or two, maybe, or a couple of apples? Apples are good right now – I've been picking them out of Miss Biedelman's orchard.'

'Nah.'

'Then you'll have to just come back to the elephant barn with me and cut some for us. Your aunt know you're here?'

'Yeah, she knows. She's going to come back for me later, maybe in a couple of hours.'

'Well, we've got some time, then. Tell you what. I've got some chores to do before we can go off with Hannah, but you can come along and give me a hand, as long as you don't get in the way and don't rile Hannah. Say that back to me.'

'Say what you said?'

'Yeah, what I just said.'

'I can come along if I don't get in the way and don't rile Hannah. That means don't piss her off, right, mister?'

'Yeah, just a prettier way of saying it. Your aunt, does she know what you were going to do, coming to see me

81

and all? I don't want to do anything that might upset her.'

'Yeah, she knows.'

'Okay.' Sam opened the gate leading to the barn and ushered Reginald in ahead of him. It wouldn't hurt to show him the ropes a little bit. It would be best not to tell Harriet Saul about it, though.

'How come it's so cold in here?' the boy asked as they went into the food prep room. 'Feels like the damn North Pole.'

Sam shot him a look that said, *Your language, son,* and Reginald looked away. 'It's not that cold,' Sam said. 'Course, I shouldn't say that, seeing as how I've never been to the North Pole myself. You been there, a great traveler like you?'

'Naw. I just imagine it.'

'Imagining is good. You know some grownups go through their entire lives without using their imagination a single time? Now, I call that a waste.' Sam set apples and bananas and carrots on the counter. 'All right, son, here's what I want you to do. You take these apples and bananas, and you cut the apples in quarters, the bananas in halves, and the carrots you can leave alone because they're just little ones anyway. Think you can do that? That knife's real sharp, so you've got to be careful, got to keep your mind on your work.'

'Yeah, I can do that. That's not hard.'

'Well you must be experienced, then. Me, I found it real hard at first – kept having to fetch my mind back every two minutes because it kept wanting to fly away like some big lazy bird. I nearly cut my finger off one time. See that scar?'

'Uh huh.'

'Happened when I was cutting a melon for my girl and forgot what I was doing for a minute. Next thing I know, I've got blood all over the place – took six stitches to get it to stop. Hannah wouldn't eat that melon, either. It must have made her mad, me getting so careless like that and ruining a perfectly fine piece of fruit, especially because melons are her favorite thing besides Dunkin' Donuts.'

'I got stitches once, in my head.'

'Is that right? You have a scar from it?'

'Right here.'

'Uh huh. I see that. You're lucky your brains didn't escape right out of there before you got it patched up. Brains like to go their own way sometimes. I had an uncle who got a cut no bigger than yours and next thing we knew, he couldn't even talk right.'

'Aw, that's just a story.'

'Nope. The poor man never did have a complete thought after that. He'd come out with a half-a-one sometimes, but he never could finish what he started. It was about the saddest thing I ever saw. Only thing he could do right after that was shuck corn. He was a champion corn-shucker, but where's that going to get you?'

Reginald shrugged.

'See there?' Sam waggled the knife at him. 'That's why you've got to start out your life with all your wits protected. You never know when you might lose a few, and you want to always have extra if you can, especially since the good Lord doesn't always start us out with an equal number. Now Hannah, she got extra wits right from the get-go, and not only because she's bigger. She's just plain smart and she always has been, as long as I've known her. You, now, I bet you're pretty smart, too. But I've only just barely got enough, so I've got to protect what I've got extra carefully. My wife Corinna's real smart. I bet your aunt is, too.'

'Naw. She's good at yelling, though. She can yell real loud when she wants to get on you about something.'

'Well, yelling real loud, that's an important skill to have, too. You never know when you might walk right in front of a train and her yelling's all that stands between you and eternity. But for that yell, you'd be flat, and there's nothing worse than a flat boy, just kind of ruins the day for everyone.'

Reginald started giggling. 'You tell a pretty good story, mister.'

'Me? Naw. I'm just an old man who's seen a lot of things in my time. One day you're going to be just like me, except better looking.'

Corinna didn't use to open the Beauty Spot on Mondays, but she'd started doing a half day to put a little extra money by for when Sam retired. She hadn't told him yet, even though she'd been doing it for a couple of months now. If he knew, he'd fuss, so she just happened not to mention it, though she wasn't used to keeping secrets.

The fact was, Corinna was worried almost to distraction. Sam was having those Hannah dreams three, four times a week now, and sometimes more. Before long Hannah was going to be getting donuts every single morning, and if they couldn't figure out what to do, Sam would die a working man.

Corinna sighed and turned the coffee maker on, then opened the door for her first customer of the day. Debby Mitchell was a pretty thing, tall and slender like a model, except she taught high school, not even thirty yet. 'Hey, sugar!' Corinna said. 'How're you this morning?'

'I'm okay now that I'm here. There was so much traffic I thought you might not see me until tomorrow.'

'Well, you're here now, baby. Just relax and settle back.' Corinna put a smock over Debby and rubbed her shoulders and neck, something she did for her favorite customers. Debby had been coming to the shop for nearly fifteen years now, since she was in high school herself. 'So what are we doing today? You want to relax it again?'

'No, I won't be doing that for a while.' Debby's eyes were full of sparkle.

'Girl, you got a secret?'

'I do, but if you promise not to tell, I'll tell you.'

'Honey, one thing I know how to do is keep my mouth shut. You should know that by now.'

Debby pressed her hands together, palm to palm. 'Louis and I are going to have a baby.'

Corinna took the girl's pretty head in both hands and gave her a kiss on the forehead. 'Aw, congratulations, sugar. When are you due?'

'Not until late May. I don't see how I'm going to last that long, though, I'm so excited to see her.'

'You pretty sure it's a girl?'

'Pretty sure.'

'I thought so, too, and you know, I was right. Course, that was a long time ago.'

Debby turned in her chair to look at Corinna straight

on, instead of through the mirror. 'I didn't know you and Sam had kids.'

'Just one. Things didn't work out, though.' Corinna got her scissors and a fresh comb out of the cupboard. 'So what are we doing, shug? Taking it down real close?'

'Yeah, I guess so.'

'That or we're going to be braiding 'til the cows come home, honey, with all the hair you've got.'

Debby twisted around in her chair again. 'Were you preoccupied when you were pregnant? I can't concentrate for beans.'

'I don't remember, hon,' Corinna lied. 'It was an awful long time ago.'

'I'm all over the place like a bead of water on a hot skillet, and Louis is almost as bad as I am. We've been trying for a while.'

'I'm real happy for you both,' Corinna said. 'If she looks even halfway like you, honey, she's going to be beautiful.'

'What a nice thing to say!'

Corinna patted the girl's cheek. 'You ready for me to start?'

'Go ahead and work your magic.'

'I don't know magic, sugar. I sure wish I did,' said Corinna, raising her scissors to begin. She had known the instant she became pregnant, had been so sure she'd never even had herself tested. She didn't know how she knew; she just had. She and Sam were wild in love, and then a baby coming. Their cup had been full.

Corinna had loved being pregnant. She'd been thinner in those days and she'd started showing early. She never had a day's sickness, never felt tired until the very end.

Sam had been proud enough to pop; sometimes when she'd looked up in the evening he would be watching her with tears in his eyes. He never would say anything, just those looks and a little extra blinking when he knew he'd been caught. How many nights she'd lain in the dark, her hands on her belly, and marveled at how much the Lord must love her, to bring such good fortune her way. There were no special vitamins in those days, no ultrasound or amniocentesis. Mostly Corinna had just let nature take her where she wanted, whether it was to a big plate of meat loaf or to fried chicken every night. The body took care of its own.

And the baby had been a dancer all through Corinna's waking hours, or at least it had seemed that way. Sam could feel the baby just about any time he wanted to, just put his hand on Corinna's big belly and wait a minute or two for her to swim over. Corinna saw a doctor two or three times, and every visit, the baby was just fine – good heartbeat, good weight gain.

Corinna's mother had come to be with her at the end; showed up with a suitcase full of crochet hooks and a rainbow of yarn, never having been one for idle hands. The night Corinna went into labor, Corinna, Sam, and her mama were laughing at some fool radio program when her water broke, making a spot on their brand-new sofa. You could still see its outlines like a ghost if you knew where to look.

Sam had called a taxi – they were still too poor to own a car – and helped her in. She had never known a short ride could take so long. Her contractions started hard and stayed that way. At the hospital Sam held her hand and told her that he loved her and then they made him go sit in the waiting room like hired help. Of course, that's the way they did it in those days. It didn't seem fair, though, not even back then.

Corinna had labored in silence so she could feel her body working, feel the baby working, too. And it was all fine for a long time, until all of a sudden, out of nowhere, she heard a soft beating of wings and a small, sweet whisper like a soul might make when it passed. She cried out, but the attending nurse said no, everything was fine. Then the baby came, and she was perfect in every way, except, of course, she was dead.

Corinna had spit on God that day; told Him she was turning her face away forever. She wanted nothing to do with a God who'd trick her like that, get her and Sam all saturated with love and then change His mind without so much as an explanation why. From then on, for Corinna, her life was just her and Sam and a little bit of luck thrown in from time to time.

Neva Wilson spent nearly her entire day off chasing down necessities: paper towels, Kleenex, and toilet paper; dish-washing detergent, sponges, canned goods, and soda; a new shower caddy, shampoo, conditioner, and soap. This was the part she hated most about moving. You went to make a sandwich and, damn it, you'd left your mustard in New York. Or you knew exactly which cupboard had the honey, but that was in San Diego. She'd be the first to admit she wasn't a homemaker. By six o'clock in the evening she was in a foul mood. Grabbing a baseball cap off the top of her TV set she stuffed her not-quite-clean hair underneath, got back in the car, and headed for the zoo.

To her surprise, she saw flickering lights in the elephant

barn when she pulled up. She looked in the window as she approached and, of all things, she saw Hannah watching *Star Wars* on the barn's wide-screen TV with Sam and Corinna. Sam was sitting in one of the armchairs with his foot up on an overturned steel bucket, while a big, beautiful woman removed a gauze dressing. As she pulled the barn door open, Neva overheard Sam saying, 'I know, Mama.' Both of them jumped when she appeared in the doorway, which made her jump.

'I'm sorry – am I interrupting?' she said.

The wound on Sam's foot looked old and serious. The woman moved to block Neva's view, quickly finished applying ointment and a fresh dressing. 'Mama was just fixing up a cut I got the other day,' Sam said, pulling his sock up over the bandage. 'Just me being clumsy, miss. How come you're here so late?'

'I didn't want to be at my apartment anymore, and I'm sick of running errands, so I thought I'd come down here and keep Hannah company for a little while.'

'Well, pull up a chair,' Sam said. 'This is my wife Corinna. Sugar, this is Miss Wilson.' To Neva he said, 'Course, she knows all about you.'

'Uh oh.' Neva smiled as Corinna held out a warm, soft hand.

'Sam's told me all the good things you've done for the baby.'

'We're just getting started,' Neva said.

Hannah wandered over, stood behind Corinna's chair and put her trunk over Corinna's shoulder, sniffed beneath Corinna's ear. When Corinna held up her hand, Hannah blew a soft breath or two into her palm. 'Aren't you the sweetest thing,' Corinna crooned.

Neva smiled. It was unusual to find a zookeeper's spouse who wanted to be included in an animal's care, never mind develop a relationship. More often, they became resentful. 'Do you do this often?' She indicated the television.

'Two, three times a week, maybe,' Sam said. 'We've been doing it for years now. Down at the video store they've got a little display, "Hannah's Pick". She gets new releases, whatever she wants, for free. She likes action pictures. *Independence Day*'s one of her all-time favorites. She likes all the *Star Wars* pictures, too.'

'She has an eye for men, too,' Corinna said. 'Danny Glover and Mel Gibson – she's seen all the *Lethal Weapon* movies four, five times now.'

Hannah shuffled and made low rumbles in her throat. Sam said to Neva, 'You're sure welcome to join us, if you want to.'

So Neva rolled out the office desk chair and settled in. Corinna took Sam's hand while Hannah watched the screen with her good eye, her trunk draped gently over Corinna's shoulder, chuffing now and then. Neva thought there was something surreal about the scene, if soothing.

'My father was diabetic, too,' Neva said when the movie was over. 'He lost a foot from an ulcer like yours.'

Sam and Corinna exchanged a look. 'Anyways, it doesn't hurt,' Sam said.

'Doesn't mean it can't kill him, just the same,' Corinna said to Neva. 'He can't even feel that foot anymore. That's why it doesn't hurt.'

'Neuropathy,' Neva said.

'Uh huh,' Corinna said.

'Me and shug,' Sam said. 'We've got our bad feet in common.'

'Doctor's told him he could lose that foot if it doesn't start getting better,' Corinna told Neva. 'And it's not going to get better as long as he's got it rubbing around inside a shoe. Man's a mule, though.'

'You find me someone for Hannah and I'll be done tomorrow,' Sam said to Neva, then jerked his head toward Corinna. 'She knows that.'

'When's the last time Hannah saw another elephant?' Neva asked.

'Forty-one years ago this November. November 24,' Sam said. 'That's the day Reyna died – Miss Biedelman's other elephant. Reyna and shug were real close. Shug started rocking right after she passed, and she's been doing it ever since. Truth is, I believe she's afraid of the dark – that, and being alone.'

After that, there was nothing left to say. Neva helped Corinna shut off the TV and roll it back to its place along the wall, while Sam led Hannah to the back of the barn and the windowless stall where she spent the night. She could hear the clanking of the chain and shackle as Sam secured her, turned on a nightlight, gave her one last yam, and tuned a radio to an easy-listening station.

'You be good now, sugar,' he said in the gloom. 'Morning'll come soon.'

It was the one thing she'd ever heard him say that wasn't true.

Chapter 7

By Tuesday morning Harriet had almost finished assembling her kit. She'd ordered a safari hat, safari boots, four pairs of khaki pants, four big-game-hunter shirts, a whistle, and a lanyard from a safari outfitter. She'd even found Max's riding crop and shooting stick in a huge armoire in one of the bedrooms. She was so excited she was trembling. Every couple of minutes she paused, thinking she heard Truman's feet outside her office door. When he did finally arrive she leapt out of her chair and pulled him into her office by the arm.

'Truman, I've had the most brilliant idea!' she cried, solicitously pushing a pile of papers from the visitor's chair onto the floor to make room for him. 'I want to show you something.'

Truman nodded in bleary agreement. It had been another long night with Miles, and Winslow had woken up with an ominous cough.

Harriet took in the wreckage and asked, 'Coffee – do you need coffee?'

'That would be merciful.'

Harriet trotted to the little coffee station near Brenda's desk, poured Truman a cup, and set it before him on her desk. She was trembling with excitement as she circled around to her side of the desk and handed him a stack of Max Biedelman's photographs, which he looked through with faint enthusiasm. 'They're very striking. Thank you for showing them to me.' Truman rose, clutching his coffee cup.

'No, no!' she said. 'I haven't even started yet. Sit!'

Truman sat.

'I got the preliminary marketing report on Saturday, and of course Hannah's the big draw, no surprise there. I'd already decided to have an agency do a big ad campaign featuring her. But – *but!* – I came up with something else.' She paused for dramatic effect. 'I will *be* Maxine Biedelman.'

'What?'

Harriet unveiled her plan: she would incorporate living history into the zoo by impersonating Max Biedelman and re-enacting her experience with elephants – Hannah, in particular. She would give lectures, make informal appearances around the facility, the works. And the program would be supported by an exhibit of the pictures and maps she'd found upstairs. 'You can just imagine the merchandising opportunities!' she said. 'Those pictures can go on coffee cups, refrigerator magnets, notebooks, a line of greeting cards, T-shirts, sweatshirts, postcards, you name it! Don't you think it's brilliant?'

'You don't think it'll look like we're exploiting her?' Truman asked.

'Who?'

'Hannah.'

'No.'

'Oh.'

'You don't like it?'

'No, no, I didn't say that,' Truman said. 'It certainly has merit. The educational possibilities—'

'You don't like it,' Harriet said flatly.

'Yes, I do, Harriet. I do.'

Brenda knocked on the door jamb and said, 'Truman, Winslow just called from school. He says he doesn't feel well, and can you pick him up. He says he'll be waiting for you in the nurse's office.'

'Did he say exactly how he didn't feel well?'

'No, but he was coughing.'

'Go,' Harriet said coolly, dismissing him.

As Truman drove to Winslow's school, he found himself wondering if there were such a thing as anti-luck, because if there was, he was suffering a string of it. Not only was Harriet preparing to launch a megalomaniacal marketing campaign balanced on the back of an ailing elephant, but last night had been Truman's third night in a row of pig-sitting, fueled by dire warnings in the *Guide to Love and Happiness*. From what Truman could gather, he and Winslow had only a matter of weeks to cement the life-long bond that was their only insurance against ruined upholstery, splintered woodwork, shattered dreams, and porcine misery. *Pigs that are poorly bonded with their owners are too often turned into pork,* the *Guide* intoned, *and who is at fault? Surely not Piggy.* He took the most limited comfort from the fact that the pig appeared to be in fine fettle, perky and bright-eyed and hellishly busy. Miles loved his pen in the yard and during his first two days in residence had rooted up a whole section of lawn to form a shallow, pig-shaped pit in which to snooze. Teenage boys ate less. Worse, whenever he caught sight of Truman, the animal trotted toward him with piggish declarations of love. And then there was the grim prospect of Porcine Stress Syndrome, a potentially fatal condition brought on by restraint, predation, medical attention, or pique. Truman had found this in the *Guide* as a follow-up to the section on *Screaming*. As a result, neither Truman nor Winslow had had the courage to pick up the animal even once. He slept at Truman's feet – *when* he slept – pressed up hard against his calves and snoring like a wino.

Truman found Winslow sitting forlornly on a cot in the school nurse's office, coughing dryly and staring at his shoes.

'Hey, buddy,' Truman said. 'Feeling crummy, huh?'

'Kind of.'

Truman signed him out and walked him to the car with a sorrowful hand on his back. Winslow rarely got sick. He put his hand on the boy's forehead. Winslow felt hot, but Truman's hand was cold with fatigue and cold weather, so who knew?

'So how bad do you feel, exactly?'

Winslow shrugged.

'On a scale of one to ten, ten being the worst?' He often asked about things on a scale of one to ten. He'd found it clarified things, but it had driven Rhonda crazy.

'I don't know. Six.'

If the boy had a severed arm, he'd probably give it a seven. Kids were supposed to complain, but Winslow rarely did, even when he would have been justified. Truman brought him back to the zoo and kept him in his cubicle for an hour, but when Winslow got restless and asked if he could take a walk, Truman said yes. A little fresh air wouldn't do the boy any harm; in fact might do him good, and he wasn't coughing all that much. Truman was working on letting go. *You smother him,* Rhonda had said the last time he saw her. *He's not disabled, you know.*

'All right,' he told Winslow. 'But wear my sweatshirt, and keep the hood up. And be back in an hour, please.'

Winslow wandered down the path to the elephant barn. A lot of the kids said he was lucky having a dad who worked at the zoo because he probably got to do neat stuff no one else did, like feed bugs to the aardvark. They also thought it was cool that he had a pig, but the only cool thing Miles had done so far was suck a piece of Kleenex up his nose, and Winslow was pretty sure that hadn't been on purpose.

When he reached the elephant yard he stood outside the fence, watching Hannah fling mud over her back. A woman he didn't recognize was with her, hosing the wallow to keep the mud gloppy. Winslow admired the elephant's ability to shape and then pinch up a precise gob of mud in a bend in her trunk. It was like watching someone knit using only their elbows – it didn't look like it should work.

The woman noticed him. 'Hi. Can I help you?'

'No, thank you,' Winslow said. 'I just like to watch her sometimes.'

'Really? Do you come here a lot?'

Winslow nodded solemnly. 'I like her trunk.'

'One hundred thousand muscles, all perfectly coordinated. She can shell a peanut. A single peanut.'

'Yeah,' Winslow said appreciatively.

She looked him over. 'Do you work here?' She indicated the zoo sweatshirt he was wearing.

'No, just my dad. His name's Truman Levy.'

'So that's why you looked familiar.' The woman turned off the water, came to the fence and stuck part of her hand through the chain links. 'I'm Neva,' she said.

Winslow shook the fingers solemnly. 'My name's Winslow. My mom named me after Winslow Homer, the painter.'

'Are you an artist?'

'No,' Winslow said. 'She wanted me to be, though.'

'Well, we can't always be what other people want.' Neva turned the water back on, brought the hose around Hannah and blasted a jet of water straight into her open mouth.

'Does she like that?' Winslow asked. 'It looks like it'd hurt.'

'I know, but it's one of her favorite things. So how come you're here on a school day?'

'I didn't feel well, so I left early.'

'Well, that's okay, right?' Neva said, training the hose at Hannah's flanks. Hannah blinked with bliss. 'Kind of like getting a snow day.'

'Yeah, but I was supposed to have a piano lesson this afternoon, and now I won't.'

'And that's a bad thing?'

Winslow shrugged. 'I wanted to play something for my teacher.'

98

'I took piano for years. Back before the flood. What were you going to play for her?'

'Mozart's *Fantasia in D Minor*.'

'Whoa,' Neva said. 'How long have you been playing?'

'I started when I was six. So' – he counted quickly on his fingers – 'five years.'

'You must be good. Not so much with the math, though, huh?'

'Yeah. Music is easier. I hear it in my head.'

Hannah approached the fence carrying her tire. 'How come she carries that around all the time?' Winslow asked.

'Do you know a little kid who sucks their thumb, maybe, or carries an old blanket around all the time? Same reason. It makes her feel safe.'

'She's pretty big to be scared of anything.'

'You know that, and I know that, but Hannah doesn't seem to, at least not in her heart.'

When Hannah got close enough, she set down her tire, extended her trunk straight at Winslow through the chain link fence, and blew a breath of air at him. He took a cautious step back.

Neva patted Hannah's leg. 'She's just trying to get your attention. Here.' Neva fished around for something in her pants pocket. 'Hold out your hand.'

Obediently Winslow held out his hand. Neva dropped in a red jellybean, a green jellybean, a white jellybean, and four raisins. 'Get ready,' she said. Hannah's trunk was already snaking through the fence. Winslow trembled slightly but held his ground as Hannah daintily picked off the jellybeans and then the raisins, popping them into her mouth one by one. When she was done she reclaimed her tire and moved off, blowing bits of hay around the yard.

'Good job,' Neva told Winslow. She began coiling the hose. 'Well, at least you have the chance to goof off. By getting out of school early, I mean.'

'I don't like to goof off that much,' Winslow said.

'No?'

Winslow shrugged. 'I don't really like kids my own age. There's this one named Simon who's okay. He used to come here with me sometimes after school, but not so much anymore. He says he has a girlfriend. My dad says it's just a phase.'

Neva manhandled the coiled hose over to the barn and hung it on a hook. 'Your dad seems like a pretty nice guy.'

'Yeah,' Winslow said. 'He worries a lot.'

'About you?' She wiped her hands on her pants and came back to the fence opposite Winslow.

'Uh huh. He wants me to have other interests besides music. He gave me a pig for my birthday.'

'A pig?'

Winslow nodded. 'Miles.'

Neva grinned. *'Miles?'*

'My dad named him. He's a Vietnamese potbelly. He doesn't sleep.'

'Ever?'

Winslow shrugged. 'Not so far. We've had him for three days.'

'Is he a house pig?'

'Sort of. He stays inside with us until we go to school and work. Then he has to go outside so he doesn't wreck the house.'

'Do you like him?'

Winslow shrugged. 'He's okay. He likes to listen when

I practice piano. Kids just say they're bored or cover their ears and stuff.'

'Well, they'll regret it when you play Carnegie Hall.'

'Yeah.'

'Your mom must be proud of you.'

Winslow shrugged. 'She used to get mad at me because I didn't have play dates. She used to say if there was no one left in the whole world but me and one other kid, I still wouldn't invite him over.'

Neva laughed. 'Well, blessed are the self-reliant. Doesn't she say it anymore?'

'Who?'

'Your mom.'

'No. She lives in Colorado now. There's an artist colony there. She makes sculpture out of nails and rusty cans and barbed wire and stuff.'

'Sounds dangerous.'

Winslow watched Hannah across the yard, where she was methodically breaking up a pumpkin shell by hitting it on a rock. 'Do you think she's pretty?' he asked Neva doubtfully.

Neva smiled. 'If I were another elephant, I'd think she was beautiful.'

'Because she's kind of funny-looking. Her skin's baggy.'

'Well, beauty's in the eye of the beholder,' Neva said. 'Look, can you keep a secret?'

'Usually.'

'Do you ever come here after school? If you're not home sick, I mean?'

'Sometimes.'

'Well, see if your dad can bring you here tomorrow

at three-thirty. We're going to try something with Hannah, but it's a big secret.'

'Try what?'

Neva lowered her voice to just above a whisper. 'We're going to teach her to paint.'

'You mean like buildings and stuff?'

'No, like pictures.'

'Why?'

'Because it's something new. We're trying to find things to keep her from getting bored.'

'How are you going to teach her?'

'Come back tomorrow at three-thirty and see. You can tell your dad, but you can't tell anybody else. And your dad can't, either. Swear?'

'Swear,' Winslow said. 'I probably better go.' He turned to leave, and then turned back. 'It was nice to meet you and everything.'

'It was nice to meet you, too, Winslow. Come back tomorrow, but remember – *don't tell anyone* besides your dad. Oh, and listen. Pigs are very smart, so don't let yours boss you around.'

'I won't,' Winslow said, and then he trotted up the path in the direction of the Biedelman house.

The next afternoon, in thin, brilliant sunshine, Neva set up a sturdy wooden easel outside the barn and clamped a pre-stretched canvas to it, then squeezed blobs of acrylic paint in primary colors onto an oversized artist's palette and took a big new brush out of its cellophane wrapper. Winslow and Truman stood outside the fence, watching as Neva gave Sam the go-ahead to bring Hannah over. The elephant brought her tire along, carefully setting it at her feet as Neva dipped the brush into red paint, made a bold swipe at the canvas, and then held out the brush.

Truman nudged Winslow and whispered something to him.

Hannah grasped the brush handle in her trunk and waved it around.

'Put it on the canvas, shug!' Sam encouraged. 'Make us a picture!'

Hannah swiped at the canvas with the brush, crossing the mark Neva had made.

'Good girl!' Neva and Sam cried in unison. Neva took the brush back so Sam could reward her with a yam. 'Who'd have thought shug was an artist?' Sam marveled as Neva loaded the brush with yellow paint this time. Hannah brought it from the upper left corner of the canvas to the lower right, and then made a series of jabs and swipes.

'I'll be damned,' Truman said softly to Winslow.

'She's pretty smart, huh?' Winslow said.

'She's certainly got the idea,' said Neva, loading the brush with blue paint while Hannah waved her trunk impatiently.

'Just look at her,' Sam said.

'What made you think of doing this?' Truman asked Neva.

'It's not my idea. It's been done before at other zoos. It gives the elephants something fun to do, and the zoos can sell the paintings to raise money to improve the elephant yards. They seem to like the challenge.'

'I'll be *damned*,' Truman said. 'I never would have guessed she'd be so dexterous.'

'They have one hundred thousand muscles in their trunk,' Winslow said. 'They can take the shell off a peanut.'

Neva smiled. The canvas was filling up with strokes and splashes of color. It could have been art, or it could have been accident. Either was okay with her.

'I'd better go,' Truman said regretfully. 'Harriet had an appointment in town, but I'm sure she'll be back soon.'

'She keeps you on a pretty short leash, huh,' Neva said.

'She does have a hands-on style,' Truman said.

'You mean she's a control freak.'

Truman smiled sadly. 'Yes, well. Are you ready to go, Winnie?'

Winslow sneezed. 'Fifty-nine.'

'Fifty-nine?' Neva said.

'That's how many times he's sneezed today,' Truman said.

'My dad bought me some of that Kleenex that has lotion or something in it. It's supposed to keep your nose from getting chapped, but it's not working. Plus I have a cold sore.' Winslow opened his mouth and turned his cheek inside out for Neva's inspection. 'See?'

Neva peered out through the fence. 'Ow. So I'm guessing no school again today, huh?'

'Nope. I'm missing a social studies quiz.'

'He'll probably be well enough to go back tomorrow,' Truman said. 'Anyway, here's hoping. Come on, Winnie. Time to go.'

'Well, you two take care.' To Winslow Neva said, 'I bet you get to eighty-six. No. Eighty-two. I bet you get to eighty-two sneezes by the end of the day.'

'A hundred and seven,' Winslow called over his shoulder as he and Truman started up the hill. 'Bet you a buck!'

'You're on!'

As the two turned to leave, Neva heard Truman say, 'Well, you're as thick as thieves.'

'Yeah,' Winslow said. 'She's nice.'

Neva rinsed out the paint brushes with the elephant yard hose. Sam had gathered up the easel and canvas. 'Why don't you take the painting home?' she told him. 'You can have it framed and then hang it in the living room or someplace. It's colorful. And it's her first.'

'Nah. It's zoo property and all.'

'If you don't take it, you can bet Harriet will. You know I'm right.'

'Well, it would look real pretty in the kitchen. Imagine, me having a shug original on my wall. It's too bad Mama had a customer. She'd have loved seeing the girl rushing around all important like that.'

'Next time we'll plan ahead, so she can be here.'

Neva took the brushes, palette, and paint cans into the elephant barn while Sam took the canvas to his car. She was glad their experiment had gone so well, and not just for Hannah's sake. She'd gotten up this morning in a melancholy mood and hadn't been able to shake it. At first she hadn't known why, but then she'd seen the wall calendar in the elephant barn. The boy turned twelve today. His hair, Neva was sure, was dark red like hers, thick like hers; it had been when he was born. Would his build be hers, too? She had small bones, but so dense that even when she was a child they'd weighed her down. Her father, when he'd taught her to swim, would say in exasperation, *You're sinking on purpose! You're just not trying.* But she had been trying. The only time she'd been buoyant was when she had been pregnant. She'd been twenty-four.

105

It had been an awful time. She and Howard had fought about everything – her choice of career, his misery at a dead-end job selling athletic shoes, their crappy little apartment above a crappy little bar.

We don't have the money, he'd said to her over and over. *And if you have this kid, we never will.* Neva hadn't wanted to raise a child any more than Howard did, but she couldn't bring herself to abort it, either. In the end, the free health clinic had referred her to a private adoption attorney who represented an infertile couple willing to pay all Neva's prenatal and delivery expenses in return for a closed adoption – no contact between biological mother and son, ever. The baby had been whisked away within minutes of his birth, and Neva was left with an aching perineum, leaky breasts, and a fatally compromised marriage. She and Howard hadn't officially divorced for another two years, but the outcome hadn't been in doubt, only the timing. Ironically, it was Neva's first-ever bonus check that had set them free, though they'd been living apart for over a year by then – Neva in New York, Howard in Seattle. By now memories of that time had faded into neutrality except for this one day a year.

Fifty-nine sneezes. She picked up the phone in the tiny office, dialed Truman's extension, and asked for Winslow.

'Sixty-eight,' she said when he came on the line.

'Seventy-one. But my dad made me take a decongestant, so I'm never going to win now,' the boy said disconsolately. 'I haven't sneezed in half an hour.'

'Bummer,' Neva said. 'You're probably a lot more comfortable, though.'

'Yeah.'

106

'Look, let's do this. After you're better, we'll just bet on something else.'

'Like what?'

'I don't know. Number of farts?'

'No way!' he said in the tone of someone who considers himself to be in the presence of greatness. 'In a day?'

'In a day. Pig-farts, not boy-farts.'

'Awesome!'

She could hear him telling Truman all about it as he hung up the phone.

Corinna's new customer had given her name over the phone as Maxine. Corinna hadn't thought much about it until she saw Harriet Saul stumping through her beauty shop door.

'Ms Saul,' Corinna said. 'I never would've expected to see you here. I thought you said Maxine over the phone.'

'I did.' Harriet rummaged around in a bulging leather briefcase and took out a stack of photos of Max Biedelman which she handed over to Corinna. 'I want you to make me look like her,' she said.

'She sure was a fine-looking lady.' Corinna studied a studio portrait taken in the mid-1930s. 'I wish we'd have known her when she was as young as this, instead of already old. Course, she was still a fine-looking woman even then – always looked like she was going to fix things once and for all, like there wasn't a problem in the world she couldn't make right.'

'Can you do it?'

Corinna frowned. 'Well, first we're going to need to turn your hair white, and that's going to take a bunch of chemicals. That all right with you? Because it's going to play hell with the cuticle.'

'Do whatever you have to,' Harriet said.

Corinna shook out a smock. The musical notes looked small all bunched up in Harriet's lap that way.

'Won't I make a good Maxine Biedelman?'

'Well, she was one of a kind,' Corinna said doubtfully. 'But we can sure give it a try.'

Corinna laid out scissors, combs, and chemicals as precisely as a surgeon and settled down to work. 'Last time I saw Miss Biedelman she probably only weighed a hundred and twenty, hundred and twenty-five pounds, and that was nowhere near enough. She was a big woman. Tall, too, almost as tall as Sam. She just lost her spirit after Miss Effie passed.'

'She was the personal secretary, right? She was in some of the pictures. Sam said you didn't know much about her.'

'We knew enough. You never saw two people more devoted to each other than those two. Miss Effie, she didn't weigh more than ninety-five pounds dripping wet, just like a little bird, like a sparrow. Her people were all from the South – Virginia, maybe, or North Carolina. She was always saying, *Oh, my land,* and things like that, that would have sounded foolish coming from anyone else, but Miss Effie was a lady, so it sounded right. It broke Miss Biedelman's heart when she passed away. She never would let herself see it coming, even with Effie getting so frail and all. By the end you could have snapped her arm like a twig. You going to have someone play her?'

'No.'

'Why's that?'

'She wasn't important.'

108

'Is that right?' Corinna said. 'Well, it's nobody's business, anyway.'

An hour and a half later, Harriet Saul took one last look at herself in the beauty salon mirror. Her new hairstyle was as near to Max Biedelman's as she could have asked for. And she looked good with white hair — it gave her a dignity she otherwise lacked.

Thus armed, she called Howard Bolton, mayor of Bladenham, and made an appointment to talk. It was time to get things started.

Chapter 8

Next morning, Harriet set aside two hours to get ready for her debut as Maxine Biedelman. Normally she dressed in her outfit for the day in five minutes flat: a Land's End T-shirt in one of six colors; a pair of polyester, elastic-waisted slacks in black, brown, or navy blue; black, white, or tan-colored Reeboks, and a baggy Max L. Biedelman Zoo cardigan or sweatshirt. If she had a meeting, she simply exchanged her T-shirt for a polyester crepe blouse. No one had seen her in a dress in years. She didn't even own a full-length mirror – the last one had broken several months ago, when she slammed the door on her reflection. She didn't need a mirror to know what she looked like. What she looked like was fat. She'd been fat, and was getting fatter at the rate of almost twenty pounds a year – more, since coming to the zoo. If she still had a mirror, she knew exactly what she'd see – the jutting bosom, Tweedle-dee belly, heavy arms, thick waist, legs that fit better in a pair of men's suit trousers than the detested panty hose that were always too short and too narrow. She even shunned the impeccable fingernails that were so often dear to big women. *Oh, please,* Maude had told her after she'd gone to the cosmetology school to get a free manicure. *You have the hands of a plumber.* People blamed unattractive people for their ugliness, but Harriet Saul knew better.

Now, standing in front of the medicine cabinet mirror on a cold and gloomy morning, she dressed in her new safari things and arranged her hair to look as much as possible like the pictures of Maxine that she had stood on the shelf by the sink. To her surprise, her new look suited her – the white hair flattered her dark eyes and energetic smile, and the loose-cut men's safari shirts minimized her breasts. She carried a pith helmet in one hand and Max Biedelman's riding crop in the other. From what she could see – and, granted, it was only from the waist up – she cut a surprisingly dashing figure. Here was a woman who was confident, leaderly, and strong.

Maybe there was an Almighty God after all.

She stayed at the zoo offices only long enough to collect Truman and a briefcase she'd filled to the gills the night before. He did a double-take when he saw her, and she instinctively crossed her arms over her breasts, tried to pull in her stomach and tuck in her sizable back end. *You don't* have *to look this big,* Maude used to tell her. *You're* choosing *to. Stand up straight, for God's sake.*

'Wow,' Truman said. 'You look – '

She prepared herself.

' – like Max Biedelman.' And he said it like he meant it.

112

There could have been no higher compliment.

Outside, the moisture-saturated air tasted metallic. Truman drove them to City Hall and hoisted Harriet's things from the back seat. Mayor Howard Bolton was already in the conference room waiting for them. He was a big, florid man with the over-hearty manner of a small-town politician. Shaking Harriet's hand, he said, 'Good to see you, Harriet. And you are . . . ?'

Truman held out his hand. 'Truman Levy.'

'For heaven's sake, Howard!' Harriet said. 'You've met him half a dozen times. He's my business manager.'

Truman gave a small, embarrassed smile and put Harriet's briefcase on the table.

The mayor gave Harriet a once-over and said, 'So what's with the getup, there, Harriet?'

'I'm going to save the zoo.'

'You moving it to Africa?' Howard cracked himself up, punching Truman lightly in the arm to share the joke.

Harriet gave him a withering look. 'What's our ad budget, Howard?'

'I don't know – off the top of my head? Ten thousand. Maybe.'

'For the quarter?'

'Yeah, right. For the year.'

Harriet and Truman exchanged glances. 'Find more,' Harriet said.

'Beg your pardon?'

'Find more. Ten thousand, at least. Or find me a travel magazine or two that'll run our ads for free.'

'Is she kidding?' the mayor said to Truman.

'I'm not kidding,' Harriet said. 'If you want me to save this zoo, you'd better give me the tools to do it.' She

113

hauled a stack of photographs and a neatly bound proposal out of her briefcase. 'Now, listen. It's all going to be about the elephant.'

Two days before Thanksgiving, 1956, Sam had sought out Miss Biedelman about something that had been on his and Corinna's minds. It was late morning, and cold; in the fields, wisps of ground fog were still caught in the corn stubble, and the air smelled like animals and loam. Sam found the old woman moving painfully across the front lawn. Her arthritis had been worse lately – he could see it in her face as well as her walk. He'd taken a strengthening breath and approached her. 'Excuse me, sir.'

'Good morning, Mr Brown,' she said.

'I wonder if I could ask you a question.'

'Of course. You may walk with me. Let me take your arm.' Sam held out his elbow and she slipped her arm through his; and though she gave him most of her weight, it was surprisingly little – she was as light and dry as cured tobacco. 'Now, what is this question of yours?'

'Well, sir, you remember that reincarnation you were telling me about?'

Max Biedelman nodded. 'I remember.'

'Me and Corinna have been talking about it, and we wanted to know, can a person come back as an animal?'

'According to the Hindu faith it happens all the time. Why?'

Sam was perspiring lightly despite the chill. He breathed in, breathed out for nerve. 'We think Hannah's our baby girl.'

Max Biedelman pressed Sam's arm; they'd stopped

114

walking without his noticing. Then they started again. 'Yes?' she said. 'And why is that?'

'Well, sir, from the very first time I set eyes on shug I thought there was something familiar about her. That's why you used to see me watching her at lunch and all. And Corinna, she took one look into shug's eye and started crying, and Hannah, she wrapped her trunk around Mama's head and started making this low sound, this humming, you know how she does. And Corinna says to me, *She's talking to us, honey.* She meant *her* – that she'd lived after all, only she was doing it as Hannah. We figure her soul must have passed from one of them to the other, like you can pass along a flame from candle to candle. Call us damn fools, but we both saw it as clear as if God Himself came down and shined His heavenly light.'

'Well, Mr Brown,' Max Biedelman said, 'I can't speak for God, of course, but I believe you've already answered your question.'

'Yes, sir. I guess I did.'

'Please tell Corinna she's welcome to visit Hannah whenever she'd like.'

'Thank you, sir. She doesn't like to presume.'

They had reached the house. Max Biedelman had withdrawn her arm from his and pressed his hand warmly.

'Thank you, sir.'

'Of course, Mr Brown. If the truth be told, I'm envious. I've been all around the world, but I have had precious few revelations. And to think one was right here all the time.'

Corinna set a plate of beef stew and biscuits down on the table in front of Sam. She prided herself on her stew,

115

using herbs that she'd grown in a little greenhouse she kept behind the Beauty Spot. 'Have you seen that Harriet Saul in her Miss Biedelman outfit yet?'

Sam nodded glumly. 'Yeah, I've seen her.'

'She wearing those clothes and all?'

'Yeah. She's carrying one of Miss Biedelman's riding crops, too. She even got herself a nametag, says MAXINE L. BIEDELMAN, OWNER, like Miss Biedelman's some suit of clothes she can just put on.' Sam shook his head, chewing. 'She doesn't like Neva, either – gave her a hard time for buying Hannah a new ball that cost twenty-five dollars because a gorilla could slam it around and the thing won't even crack. It has a couple holes, and Neva put raisins and grapes inside. You should have seen shug shaking it – just like watching a little kid emptying their piggy bank. Girl's still got plenty of spunk left in her. Neva thinks we should spread some smells around, too – tiger pee, maybe, or antelope dung. It'd sure give shug something new to think about. Bet Miss Biedelman's real impressed with her, if she's up there watching.' Sam wiped his bowl clean with a biscuit. 'This was a real good meal, Mama.'

'Have you told her about your dream yet, hon?'

'Nah. She'd probably think I was crazy, dreaming someone else's dream like that.'

'You're already crazy. What kind of harm could it do? Besides, we're out of ideas. And you're coming home tired all the time now. *All* the time.'

'I'm fine, Mama.'

'Yeah, and that's what you're going to tell me right up to the day you drop.'

'Maybe so, but I don't know what else to do. We're

just going to have to wait for something to come to us.'
Sam began clearing dishes off the table. Corinna tried to
stop him, but he said, 'Let me do this. You've been on
your feet all day long. Go on now, you just sit there. *Sit*.'

'If you start spoiling me, there's no telling where it
could end,' Corinna said. 'You'll be doing all the chores
and I'll be sitting in a big comfortable chair by the
window fanning myself and eating chocolates.'

'Nothing wrong with that.'

Once the dishes were done Sam rounded up the paper
and sat in his easy chair, the same one they'd bought so
many years ago on credit at Sears. It had taken two years
to pay it off, and they'd had it reupholstered twice since
then. Both times, Corinna had been after him to buy a new
one, but Sam was partial to things being the same. He'd
broken in that chair just right, and he wasn't about to start
over. When they were young they used to talk about moving
to a fancier house, but they didn't have the heart, once they
found out Corinna couldn't bear any more children. There'd
been bleeding, complications, surgery, and scar tissue, and
after that Corinna didn't want to live on some other street
that might have mothers and kids on it, said it would break
her heart every morning just to get up. So they'd stayed,
fixing up this house little by little – new roof, new shut-
ters, a new window or two, and of course Corinna had
opened up the Beauty Spot in the basement. She had her
customers and he had his work and they both had Hannah
and each other, and if it wasn't anything like what they used
to dream about, it was mighty close to being enough.

When the dishes were done, Corinna came into the
living room with her crochet hook and a pile of bright
pink yarn, and settled into her chair with a soft grunt.

Sam looked at her over the tops of his reading glasses. 'Go ahead and turn on the TV if you want to.'

'Nah. You read your paper,' Corinna said. 'I'll just listen to myself think for a while, then maybe we'll see.'

Sam pretended to go back to his paper, but what he was really doing was watching her. She was making a blanket for some customer who was having a baby, like she'd always done, all these years. Not one of them knew what it cost her.

The next morning, Harriet cleared a space on the desk between herself and Truman, and laid out a half-dozen receipts. 'She's spending money like water,' she said. 'Look at these! Art supplies. *Art* supplies for forty-seven dollars and thirteen cents.'

'I authorized it. She wanted to surprise you.'

'Well, she did,' Harriet said. 'And frankly, you've surprised me, too.'

'If I may finish,' Truman said quietly, 'she wanted to surprise you once she and Hannah were ready.'

'Ready for what, unveiling some kind of mural?'

'She's taught Hannah to paint.'

'What do you mean?'

Truman smiled faintly. 'Hannah paints pictures.'

'That's ridiculous. Get her on the phone.'

'I can try, but they usually work outside until late morning.'

'Truman.'

Truman sighed, lifted the phone receiver, and entered the extension for the elephant barn. The phone rang into an empty building, as he had known it would; Neva and Sam were always busy outdoors until late in the morning.

118

He switched to the phone's speaker so Harriet could hear it for herself. Three times. Four times. Five times, and then to voice mail. He watched Harriet mildly. She picked up the receiver and dropped it down again to disconnect the call, leaving no message. Then she folded her hands in front of her.

'Truman, I've been in the workforce much longer than you,' she said. 'And one thing I've learned is that work-place relationships rarely work out.'

'Relationships?'

'You seem to know a lot about her,' Harriet said.

'I know nothing about her. She's had some entirely appropriate questions, and I've tried to give her answers. Period.'

'I'm just saying,' said Harriet.

'Look, would you like me to set something up so you can see Hannah paint?'

'I think that would be appropriate,' Harriet said, straightening in her chair. 'Don't you?'

Several hours later, Neva set up Hannah's easel in the sunny part of the elephant yard. Hannah was all over her, watching and reaching for paint tubes and brushes with her trunk. Curious zoo visitors were gathering along the fence.

'Sam,' she called, 'can you come do something with this girl? She's all wound up and we've still got five minutes until Harriet and Truman get here. Did you get hold of Corinna?'

'Mama's on her way.' Sam laid down his pitchfork and came over. 'Shug sure does like all these new projects.' Hannah shifted from foot to foot in excitement as Sam

119

pulled several peppermints from his trouser pocket and unwrapped the cellophane. It had already been a Dunkin' Donuts morning; his girl was sure getting to indulge her sweet tooth today. She let Sam lure her with candy to the other side of the yard. Sam made sure he kept her back to Neva so she couldn't see the preparations, and once she'd eaten her peppermints he rubbed her tongue, which made her go piggy-eyed with bliss. Finally he heard Truman and Harriet coming into the yard.

'Looks like it's show time, baby girl,' he said to Hannah.

Neva was telling Truman and Harriet, 'I'd prefer that you stay over by the barn wall. Hannah's very excited, and we don't want to give her too many distractions.'

'But you can't see from over there,' Harriet said.

'You can see well enough,' Neva said. 'Please.'

Sam saw the muscles flex in Harriet's jaw – two strong women in a struggle to dominate. As he brought Hannah over he saw Corinna hurrying up from the parking lot. ''Scuse me,' he said to Neva, leaving Hannah with her so he could go around to let Corinna in the barn gate without Harriet's seeing her. 'Hi, hon,' he whispered. 'Harriet Saul's here, and she's in a mean mood. Best to stay out of the way.'

Corinna looked to the heavens and slipped inside the barn. She'd watch from the office window.

When Sam got outside again, Neva was talking to Hannah. 'Do you remember this?' She held up a brush loaded with blue paint. Hannah took it in her trunk and without hesitation laid down a track of blue from the upper left to the lower right-hand corner of the canvas. Truman shifted a few feet along the barn wall to get a better view. Harriet strode directly across the yard until

120

she was standing right beside Neva. Hannah's eye rolled nervously.

'It's much safer if you don't stand right here,' Neva said in a low, quiet voice. 'She's very excited.'

Harriet folded her arms in defiance.

Sam saw Truman catch Neva's eye and make the slightest gesture: *Unless she's about to be killed, let her be.* Neva collected herself and turned back to the elephant, saying, 'All right, Hannah. You're doing a great job. Do you want more paint?' She offered the palette and Hannah dabbed her brush and made a tornado of red at the bottom of her canvas. Zoo visitors were piling up along the fence, including a young man who was frantically scribbling notes in a small reporter's spiral notebook.

Hannah switched to orange paint and then black. The canvas was filling with strokes and color, swoops and dots and vortexes. Inside the office Corinna, seen only by Sam, laughed in amazement and lifted her hands to her mouth.

The young man with the notepad took several pictures of Hannah painting, and of Harriet and Neva watching. Then it was over. Hannah returned the paintbrush to Neva and walked off to her mud wallow without a backward glance.

The visitors applauded.

Neva unclamped the canvas, handed it to Harriet without a word, and began to clean up.

Sam gave Hannah six apple quarters and a banana. Unseen except by Sam, to whom she blew a kiss, Corinna hurried back to her car: she'd left a customer under the hair dryer back at the Beauty Spot.

★ ★ ★

Harriet walked out of the elephant yard without a word. Truman closed the gate carefully behind them and said, 'She was just doing her job. Hannah was agitated, and I'm sure that can be dangerous.'

'My ass,' Harriet said bitterly. 'And I want you to talk to Sam. I won't have family members in the exhibits during work hours.'

She was furious. These two employees were completely out of hand. Harriet had been so involved with her own projects that she'd allowed Sam and Neva too much freedom, and this was what it had led to: insubordination. Harriet wouldn't stand for that. She expected – no, she demanded – respect for her office if not for herself. Without that, Harriet could never move the zoo into the future she envisioned, a brilliant gem in Washington's tourism crown.

When they arrived at the office, they found the young man from outside the elephant exhibit talking to Brenda at the reception desk. He was trying to take notes while juggling a great deal of camera gear.

'Hello,' Harriet said coolly, cutting Brenda off in mid-sentence. 'Brenda, please don't speak.' To the young man she said, 'I am the zoo's director. May I help you with something?'

Brenda flushed to the roots of her hair.

The young man looked up. 'Oh! Sorry. My name is Martin Choi.' He held out his hand. 'I'm a reporter with the *Bladenham News-Gazette*.'

Harriet grasped his hand and smiled. 'It's a pleasure.'

'Sure. I was just getting some information from, ah . . . '

'Brenda doesn't speak for the zoo.'

'Yeah? Well, okay, then maybe I can talk with you.'

The reporter looked with confusion at Harriet's badge. 'Maxine Biedelman?'

'My real name is Harriet Saul.'

'Oh. That's kind of confusing, isn't it?'

'No,' Harriet said.

'So who's Maxine Biedelman? She his daughter or something?'

'Whose daughter?'

'Max Biedelman's.'

'Max *was* Maxine,' Harriet said. 'It's what she called herself.'

'No shit? I thought it was a guy.' Martin scribbled a note.

'No.' Harriet took a strengthening breath.

'Wow. So when did you meet her?'

'Who?'

'Maxine Biedelman. You knew her, right?'

Harriet gritted her teeth. 'She died in 1958.'

'So that would make it a while ago. You grow up around here?'

'No,' Harriet said. 'I wasn't born until 1956.'

Martin furrowed his brow. 'So how does that work?'

'It doesn't!' Harriet cried. 'I never met Maxine Biedelman!'

'Yeah? Huh.'

'Look.' Harriet pulled several photographs out of her pocket. 'Meet Maxine Biedelman.'

Martin looked through the pictures. 'Not a very good-looking old broad, was she? No wonder she called herself Max.' He cracked himself up.

Harriet reached for the photos, snatching them out of his hand. 'Let's start again. I'm Harriet Saul, the director of this zoo. I'm re-enacting the role of Maxine Biedelman as part of a brand-new living history program. This is the first day, in fact. I'll be giving daily lectures so our visitors can get a better feel for the zoo's roots. We have colorful beginnings.'

'Yeah?'

'Why don't we go into my office?'

Harriet led the way. Inside her office door Martin stopped, surveying the wreckage. 'Whoa! This looks like my apartment. No kidding. Looks like you should fire your janitor, huh?'

Harriet swept the visitor's chair clear. 'We're a nonprofit organization. We don't have a janitor.'

'No kidding.'

A small vein pulsed in Harriet's temple. She sat down behind her desk, took a fortifying breath, and outlined the history of the Max L. Biedelman Zoo in extreme, even numbing, detail, as her little act of revenge. When she finally stopped at somewhere between forty-five minutes and eternity, Martin Choi squinted at her and said, 'Okay, but so wait. There was never a guy named Max? It's kind of funny to have a zoo named after a nickname, huh?'

Harriet shrugged. 'It was a personal quirk of hers, I gather.'

'Well, hey, you've given me lots of great information. I have to talk to my editor, but maybe we'll be able to run a feature story. I'd love to get some pictures, maybe some of you with the elephant. That painting, that was some cool stuff. Would you have a few minutes to go back down there with me now?'

'Of course,' said Harriet.

She continued to brief him as they walked. Her

124

twice-daily interpretive performance as Maxine Biedelman was to be called *My Walks on the Wild Side*, which she believed was sexy enough to draw at least a small crowd to her impromptu stage on Havenside's marble steps at ten every morning and three every afternoon. She would give a dramatic recitation of Max Biedelman's travels in Burma, using as props Max Biedelman's own elephant hook, shooting stick, and old Haaselblad camera. Except for her photographs, Max Biedelman had left behind very little anecdotal information about her life, so Harriet would have to take a certain amount of dramatic license with the contents of her monologue. She had been preparing and practicing for a week; last night she had set up a video camera and taped herself. Though she was by no means a professional performer, she thought zoo guests would find the result moving.

The elephant yard was quiet when they arrived. Hannah appeared to be dozing against the fence, her eyes closed and trunk moving only now and then to check on the tire leaning against her ankle. Rather than enter the elephant yard, Harriet suggested that Martin shoot his photographs from outside the exhibit, but from an angle that would make it look like she and Hannah were only inches apart. They never even saw Sam or Neva, which was exactly what Harriet had intended.

When her work with Martin Choi was finished, she sat at her computer and composed a memo for all employees to receive in their paycheck envelopes first thing Monday morning. It read:

Today, as part of our recent focus on revitalizing the Max L. Biedelman Zoo, we will begin offering a

125

living history program that will feature two daily presentations of the life and accomplishments of our founder, Maxine L. Biedelman. Please be advised that in support of this new effort, I, Harriet Saul, will be costumed as Maxine Biedelman, and during zoo hours am to be addressed exclusively by her name. You may also be called upon to improvise in a supporting role from time to time as Maxine moves through the zoo in character, costumed as Ms Biedelman would have appeared in the late 1930s. Presentation times will be at 10 a.m. and 3 p.m. daily. Your cooperation is appreciated.

Signed, Maxine Biedelman, née Harriet Saul

That done, Harriet nipped into the administrative bathroom to take one last look at herself. She put on the pith helmet, tipped it to a jaunty angle, and walked outside. A family of four was coming toward her along the path. Harriet grinned broadly and extended her hand.

'Good afternoon!' she cried. 'I am Maxine Biedelman. Welcome to my zoo.'

Chapter 9

When Neva got out of her car at home that evening she smelled something miraculous in the air. Cookies. Sweet, sweet chocolate chip cookies. The aroma was wafting from the kitchen of the Big House – her landlord Johnson Johnson was baking. To her annoyance, she felt weepy. Her missionary zeal was leaching out of her like heavy metals, contaminating everything she'd touched since she'd arrived at this godforsaken place and its third-rate zoo.

A foil-covered plate sat on the stoop of her garage-cum-apartment. It was the third time she'd received cookies since moving in. With trepidation she walked up to Johnson Johnson's door. He answered her knock at the exact moment that she had decided to turn and run. Spectrally thin in battered jeans and a T-shirt that said JESUS IS COMING: LOOK BUSY, he appeared at the door holding a spatula.

'Hey!' he said. 'Did you get the cookies? Did you taste one?'

'No, I just got home, but I wanted to thank you.'

'Sure.' A timer went off inside the kitchen, and Johnson Johnson began windmilling with his arm. 'Come in, because I better get this batch out before they burn.'

'No, no – '

But he was already across the kitchen. She followed – and found, to her astonishment, that the kitchen was painted, even saturated, in the colors of a Mexican fiesta: brilliant yellows, reds, oranges, and greens. In place of baseboards, a seven-inch band of black-and-white checkerboard wrapped all the way around the room, and above that ran what appeared to be a poem. No – Neva recognized it as the opening lines of Lewis Carroll's *Jabberwocky*: T'WAS BRILLIG, AND THE SLITHY TOVES DID GYRE AND GIMBLE IN THE WABE . . . Along the tops of the walls, at the ceiling-line, Johnson Johnson had painted fragments of a dinner conversation: MY, WHAT A LOVELY HAM! and HAVE THE BROCCOLI – IT'S DELICIOUS. Even the wood floor had been painted brick red, with a compass dial beneath the kitchen table.

'It's so I know where North is,' Johnson Johnson said, sliding hot cookies onto a cooling rack, his mouth slightly open. 'In case, you know, I forget.'

'Why do you need to know?'

He looked up at her. 'Well, you're supposed to.'

'You are?'

'Course.'

Neva was reminded anew that it was best not to expect clarity from the funhouse that was Johnson Johnson's mind. 'So did you do all this yourself?'

'Yeah,' he said modestly. 'I don't like white, so, you know.' He spaded gobs of cookie dough out of a mixing bowl and onto the cookie sheet. 'Did you see Kitty anywhere?'

'No. Is he supposed to be in the house?'

'Yeah, he doesn't go out much anymore. Check the living room, okay? He gets nervous when I use the oven.'

Neva didn't have the strength to ask why. She opened the door leading into the living room and found herself trying to take in a series of wall-mounted ramps, runways, platforms, small hammocks, and tunnels that encircled the room, rising from the floor to the ceiling – a gloriously outfitted feline jungle gym. In a far corner, a narrow carpeted ladder rose through a cat-sized hole in the ceiling. Halfway up one wall, draped across a sleeping perch, she spotted a battered orange tabby with a significant gut. He didn't so much as glance in her direction. 'I think he's in here,' she called. 'He's out like a light.'

She returned to the kitchen. Johnson Johnson was deep inside his refrigerator. 'So, you want a glass of milk with your cookies?' he said. 'I even have' – he waited a reverential beat – 'strawberry milk.'

'No, no. I just wanted to say thank you. Your cookies were the best things that happened all day.'

'Uh oh,' he said.

'Yeah.'

'Hey! If you're hungry we could get a pizza, maybe.'

Neva immediately put her hand on the doorknob. 'Look, I'm sorry. All I can think of is a shower and then bed. I'm beat.'

'You do, like, smell of something.'

'Elephant.' The subject was getting a little too personal. Neva backed out the door. 'Okay. So thanks again, okay?'

'Okay,' said Johnson Johnson. As she was pulling the

door to, Neva saw him bite into a cookie and close his eyes.

Neva had just finished drying off after her shower when the telephone rang. She considered not answering it, but she was trying to freshen up her social skills, and as her mother often admonished her, socially successful people answered their phones when they rang. Truman Levy was on the other end of the line.

'Look, how are you?' he asked.

Neva let out a long breath. 'Okay. My landlord gave me a plate of home-baked chocolate chip cookies, so that's one good thing.'

'Tough day?'

'Yeah.'

'Please tell me you're not going to quit,' Truman said.

'What a strange thing to say. I'm not going to quit. I may start taking tranquilizers, I might even consider something stronger, but I have no intention of quitting. I wouldn't mind a few suggestions about how to go below her radar, though.'

'It helps to be male.'

'So that's out. Am I the only one she doesn't like?'

'No, you're just the most recent. Here's my suggestion: steer clear of her whenever you can, and avoid disagreeing with her when you can't.'

'Like that's going to help,' Neva said. 'Thanks for the concern, though.'

'All right,' said Truman. 'Good night, then.'

'Good night.'

Just as Neva hung up the phone, she heard a faint porcine

130

grunting coming through the receiver, and smiled the first real smile of the evening.

Truman hung up the phone with a mighty sigh. At his feet, Miles was pushing around a child's plastic ring-toss ring, bright pink and filthy after days of pig slobber, backyard mud, and carpet fibers. Truman reached down absently and scratched him behind one ear.

Harriet had shown him storyboards of the zoo's new ad campaign. There was a three-quarter profile of Hannah and, ghosted behind her, a picture of Harriet as Maxine Biedelman, squinting heroically into the jungle interior as suggested by a few ghosted palm fronds. Truman hadn't given her much of a reaction, buying time by saying he would prefer to give the matter a night's thought before offering his opinion. Of course, this amounted to feet of clay, since he knew that tomorrow he'd advise her to use a picture of the real Max Biedelman instead. God knew how she would take it. He wondered how much unemployment he might be able to collect if he found himself suddenly out of work. Not enough, probably, to cover Winslow's art and music lessons, plus Miles and his expenses, including food, ring-toss games, other miscellaneous toys, and new blankets and towels.

Miles and Truman had bonded.

It was not what Truman had had in mind.

The little pig followed him everywhere, and when Truman went beyond the baby gate that limited Miles to the kitchen and den, the pig cried, making little snuffling sounds. It was heartbreaking. He showed no such devotion to Winslow. Happily, the boy didn't seem to mind, taking only the faintest interest in the animal he'd once so desperately wanted.

Truman heaved himself up from the depths of the sofa Rhonda had insisted he keep because she knew he hated it. Why weren't more women like Neva Wilson? Though he would be the first one to concede that he didn't know her, really, she seemed balanced, reasonable, and completely professional. She even seemed to have a sense of humor. He wondered what she would think of Harriet's ad campaign.

As he began dinner preparations, Winslow shuffled into the kitchen in his socks. Truman wondered for the zillionth time why no matter what brand or style of socks he bought for the boy, they all ended up flapping off the ends of his son's feet like clown shoes. He had always held to the highest standards of personal grooming – one thing he had very much in common with his orderly mother, Lavinia. While Truman was growing up she had brooked no compromise, insisting that his shirt be tucked in, its elbows intact, and all buttons accounted for. He had never been allowed to wear badly fitting slacks or messy shoes.

'Pull up your socks, Winnie.'

'What?'

'Your socks. They're bagging.'

Winslow shrugged and halfheartedly pulled up his socks. Miles came over to investigate.

'He's got such little tiny eyes,' Winslow said, peering at them. 'They look like polished onyx.'

'Where have you seen onyx?'

'Morris brought some into school once. He has a rock tumbler.' Morris was a brainy kid with whom Winslow was often paired for science projects. Last year, they'd

132

performed elaborate experiments with bread mold that Truman had never quite understood, but which had won first place at the school's science fair.

Truman assembled chopped meat, an egg, fresh breadcrumbs, and ketchup in a mixing bowl and, shuddering, plunged his hands in. The combined feel of cold animal fat and raw egg was almost more than he could bear. He squished the stuff through his fingers. 'Hand me that pan, would you, Winnie?'

Winslow handed him a glass baking dish, and Truman dumped the meat loaf out of the bowl. 'You want to shape it, or no?'

'You can.'

Truman slapped the clammy stuff into a tidy loaf, iced it with ketchup, and, with infinite relief, slid it into the oven. He set down the bowl for Miles to lick. The pig pushed it around the floor, running it into the baseboards, cupboard doors, Truman's feet and ankles, and Winslow's terrible socks.

'Do you think he's smart?' Winslow said.

Truman regarded the pig doubtfully. 'They're supposed to be.'

'But is *he*?'

'It's hard to imagine.'

'Yeah,' said Winslow.

'So tell me about your day.'

The boy shrugged. 'It was okay.'

'Okay, like you couldn't wait for it to end, or okay, like there were some bright spots?'

'I don't know. We got to draw in art class. Mr Warner put some crushed cans, a fern, and two marbles on a table, and we were supposed to draw it.'

133

'Yes, it's called a still life. And did you?'

'Yeah, but I was the only one. Jeremy Ireland called me a kiss-ass.'

'I'm sure that Vincent van Gogh's classmates called him names, too.'

'I don't care, anyway.'

'Really?' Truman drizzled halved baby red potatoes with olive oil and rosemary. 'I always cared.'

'What exactly *is* a kiss-ass?' Winslow asked after a minute.

'Well, that depends. If you want to be literal, it's a person who kisses a donkey. I, for instance, might be called a kiss-pig, though I don't think I'll ever do it again because he didn't smell very good close up.'

Winslow snorted.

'Or it can mean a suck-up, a person who wants to win favor by helping or cooperating with a person in a position of greater power,' Truman continued. 'Personally I prefer the first meaning, but you can choose for yourself.'

He slid the potatoes into the oven with the meat loaf, and fished lettuce, carrots, cauliflower, and radishes out of the vegetable bin. He didn't feel that Winslow got enough vegetables, so he insisted on making a salad for them every night, a chore he detested. As additional penance, he refused to use pre-washed and bagged lettuces, struggling with messy heads of red leaf and romaine, vigilant for the omnipresent aphids.

'Have you talked to your mother lately?'

'Nah.'

'Why don't you give her a call while dinner's cooking?'

'That's okay.'

Truman decided to let it go. In his heart he was relieved

134

that the boy wasn't pining, though he worried about unforeseen emotional fallout in Winslow's later life. On the other hand, his reluctance might be simple dislike of talking to Rhonda on the phone, an experience Truman himself likened to a jousting match where only one person had a lance and that person wasn't you.

'Then go do piano until dinner's ready.' Truman tripped over Miles snuffling around under the open dishwasher door. 'And Winnie? Take Miles with you.'

'He doesn't want to come.'

'Yes he does, he just doesn't know it.'

One morning in early fall, 1956, Sam had found a note taped to the door of the elephant barn, asking him to come up to the house. He'd gotten Hannah squared away in a hurry and headed up the hill. Miss Biedelman and Miss Effie weren't strong, either one of them – Miss Biedelman's rheumatism was bothering her more and more, and Miss Effie had a nasty little cough. He was relieved when the old woman herself answered the door, her quick old eyes dancing with excitement.

'Mr Brown! It's a pleasure to see you. Come in for just a moment while I get my coat and see if Effie would like to join us. Sit, sit!' She bullied him into a chair in the front room and then hurried out. He could hear a faint conversation in the hall and then she came back alone, wearing a man's heavy canvas barn coat and brandishing one of her walking sticks. 'I'm afraid Effie won't be walking with us today – her cough is worse. I've insisted that she call the doctor. Come, Mr Brown.' She urged him out the door with a hand on his back. 'I'll explain as we go.' She led the way back to the barn, hobbling along at a remarkably fast clip.

'Looks like you're feeling better today,' Sam said.

'Yes, yes, I feel quite myself, Mr Brown. Slow as the dickens, of course, but never mind. At my age it's best to lower one's standards.' She chuckled to herself as they got near the elephant barn. 'Now here's my plan. We're going to take Hannah for a walk.'

Sam frowned. 'We don't have a lead or a halter.'

'We don't need one, Mr Brown! Could you restrain her even if we had? No, the mahouts work their elephants without restraints of any kind, and so shall we. Do you have an elephant hook? I know we did at one time. Go and see, Mr Brown.'

Sam went inside and rummaged around in a closet. The last keeper had had the habits of a hog, leaving nasty messes where you'd find them days later, stinking and caked onto something – the man hadn't grown up around clean folks, that was obvious. Sam finally found the tool beneath a pile of old feed sacks. The stick was about a foot and a half long, not quite as stout as an axe handle, and with a blunt metal hook coming out of one end.

'Yes, that's it!' Max cried when Sam reappeared with it. 'Yes, yes! Come on, then.' She took the stick from him, tucking it beneath one arm.

Sam regarded it doubtfully. 'Looks like a mean thing, sir, with that hook and all.'

'No, no. It's used to suggest, Mr Brown, not to punish. I'll show you. Why don't you bring her to the gate?'

Hannah was chewing her hay contemplatively when Sam approached her and said, 'Guess what, sugar? Me

136

and Miss Biedelman are going to take you out, give you a look at some things.'

Hannah sucked on her trunk apprehensively. Sam looked at Max Biedelman.

'It's all right, Mr Brown. We have to expect some nervousness. After all, the last time she was taken from her normal surroundings she was put in a cage for three weeks and brought here.'

'It about breaks my heart seeing her fearful, a big girl like her.'

Max patted Hannah's shoulder. 'She'll be fine, Mr Brown. You'll see. Go and load your pockets with fruit. Fill this, too, please.' She dug a string bag out of a trouser pocket and handed it to Sam.

'All right, sir, only take me a minute – I've got food cut up already from before I went home last night.' Sam hurried into the barn and filled his canvas pouch, then Max Biedelman's string bag, with yams, gourds, squashes, and apples. When he was done he found Max Biedelman patting Hannah and talking to her quietly. The elephant browsed around the old woman's feet, occasionally lifting her trunk to sniff her pockets.

'We're all set now, sir.'

'Good, good.' The old woman attached her bulging string bag to her sturdy leather belt, and Sam slung a leather pouch over his shoulder.

'Come along, Hannah,' she said. With the twin lures of apples and yams, Hannah took small steps forward until she was out of the yard, but there she stopped, lifting her head nervously.

'We're going to have an adventure,' Sam soothed. 'We're taking you places you've never been before, maybe let you root around in the woods. You might even find a sweet leaf or two.' He handed her another yam and, evidently resigned, she started walking again, following Max Biedelman.

'Why, what a very good elephant you are, Hannah!' the old woman cried, hobbling backwards, offering a trail of treats. 'Worlds will open up to her, Mr Brown, once she's regained her confidence. Small worlds, I'll grant you, but new ones just the same.'

'Think she remembers walking free?' Sam asked. The thought disturbed him, her remembering freedom and now this.

'Only Hannah knows that, Mr Brown, but I believe it's possible – even quite likely.'

'Makes me sad, thinking about that.'

'Yes, I can see why you might say so, but you must remember that in the wild she was starving. No one was cutting up cantaloupes for her, were they, Mr Brown? Nature is never so simple as we like to think, a veritable Garden of Eden. I have never seen the Garden of Eden, not in all my travels.'

'Yes, sir,' Sam said, but he still felt the way he felt.

They had reached the edge of Havenside's lawns, where a sketchy trail led into the woods. Sam had seen Max and Miss Effie go that way sometimes on their nature walks. Hannah drew up short.

'It's okay, shug,' Sam said, patting her. 'This right here is where the fun starts. You've been in forests before. There's nothing here to be afraid of. Miss Biedelman and me are going to be right here with you, sugar.'

Hannah rolled her eye nervously, first looking to Sam, then Max Biedelman. The old woman reached out and gently touched Hannah's right knee with the hook. 'Come along, Hannah. There's a good girl.' Slowly, Hannah walked into the woods. Max Biedelman continued to coax with the elephant hook and Sam kept a firm hand on her for reassurance. She trumpeted once and tossed her head a time or two, but out of a growing excitement rather than nervousness. Finally she began browsing among the leaves and ferns on the forest floor. Max folded her arms across her chest and watched with keen satisfaction.

'Hannah has done very well, indeed,' she said. 'I think this is as far as we'll take her today, Mr Brown. It would be best if we just let her root and get comfortable.' The old woman opened her shooting stick, turning it into a little seat and settling herself with a small grunt of discomfort.

'Now, isn't that handy!' Sam said. 'I've never seen anything like it before.'

'Yes, the British have always been good at coming up with this sort of thing.'

Sam crossed his arms over his chest and watched Hannah bend several small alder trees with her trunk to strip off and sample the leaves. When he took a step or two away from her and sat on a tree stump, she lifted her head, but Sam said, 'I'm right here, sugar.'

'May I ask you a question, Mr Brown?' Max Biedelman said.

'You go right ahead.'

'When you were a small boy, what did you dream of?'

'Well, now, that's a hard question. I don't know that I had any dreams. I always figured I'd have to help my daddy on the farm. Took him dying for me to figure out I could go my own way.'

'I don't mean practical considerations, Mr Brown. I mean

139

if you could have been anything, what would you have chosen?'

Sam shifted, patting Hannah. 'You've got to understand that my kind of people, sir, we don't always have dreams, at least not in the way you're thinking. It's better not to, sometimes.'

Max Biedelman looked at him keenly. 'Why is it better? One should always dream, Mr Brown, even if we know the dream can only come true in our imaginations.'

'Well, maybe that's so, sir, but I'd rather appreciate what I've got than die of wanting what I can't have.'

'And what is it that you've got, Mr Brown?'

'Everything. I've got Corinna, got my sugar, got you and Miss Effie to talk to sometimes, got this beautiful place to come to every day.'

Max Biedelman smiled a little smile. 'You're a fortunate man, Mr Brown, to want so little.'

'*No*, sir. It's not little at all.'

'Well, perhaps not.'

'Corinna, now, she's something different. She wants a way to get back at God, and that's a sad thing because there isn't a way to get back at God, never has been, never will be. Corinna, though, she won't believe that. She keeps turning her back on God and waiting for Him to notice she's missing from His flock. But the fact is, God doesn't notice people like me and Corinna in the first place, so how's He supposed to miss us? But Corinna, she just goes on taunting Him and being disappointed when He doesn't care.' Sam shook his head sadly.

'You have a harsh god, Mr Brown.'

Hearing Sam, Hannah had come over to slip her trunk into his fruit satchel, lifting out an apple. 'You having a nice

140

time out here, sugar?' he said. 'Yeah, I think so.' He watched her wander off a few feet. 'What about you, sir? What did you dream of when you were a little girl out there in Africa?'

The old woman regarded him for a long minute and then said softly, 'I dreamed of being a little boy, Mr Brown. Does that shock you? I dreamt about being a boy and growing up to be a man.'

'No, sir, that doesn't shock me. Makes me feel sad, though, like I do for Corinna. It's a hard thing to dream about what you can't have.'

'I don't believe that we have any choice about our dreams. I believe they simply come to us, like head colds and bad habits.'

'Maybe so,' Sam said. 'Maybe so. But it's a hard place you get to, isn't it? I had a brother Emmanuel who always wanted to be white, or at least light-skinned. Sad fact was, he was the darkest of all of us kids. He'd wear hats and long sleeves on the farm all summer long to keep from getting any darker, damn near killed himself with heatstroke more than once.'

Max Biedelman smiled. 'And did he stay on the farm?'

'Nah. He got killed in a bar in Yakima, trying to break up a fight between a couple of white men. Emmanuel thought white people were better than us, but those two white men didn't have enough decency between them to wash their hands after they went to the toilet. Crackers, trash, both of them. Turned out they weren't even fighting, at least not for real. They were just drunk and mouthy. Emmanuel got between them and they turned on him faster than a prayer reaches heaven. Shot him three times in the chest. Man didn't stand a chance.'

'That's a terrible story.'

Sam shrugged. 'Yes, sir, I guess it is. But Emmanuel would have probably found something else to get killed over, if those white men hadn't been there in that bar. Mama used to say, *That boy has a strange look about him, always has. We gonna lose him young.* And we did.'

'And yet, you're not bitter,' the old woman said. 'Why aren't you bitter, Mr Brown?'

'Bitter? No point in it. Emmanuel died because he was stupid and the Lord called him home out of pity for what else would happen to him if He let the boy stay any longer.'

Max Biedelman laughed.

'You bitter, sir?'

'No. I'm not bitter.' The old woman swayed to her feet, folding up her shooting stick. A small breeze had sprung up, and she pulled her coat collar up around her ears. 'I think our little experiment has been a success,' she said. 'Wouldn't you agree?'

'Yes, sir,' Sam said. 'But I guess it's time to go home, just the same.'

Now Sam sat in his chair in the living room, listening to Corinna washing up the dinner things. He had his recliner back and heaved his bad leg up beside the good one like a rotten old fish, burning from the inside out like he had fire for veins. Neuropathy, it was called; he'd read about it in the diabetes pamphlets Corinna had collected for him. Nerve death. There was going to come a day when he wouldn't have that foot to use anymore, wouldn't be able to stand beside Hannah and tell her everything was all right. And deep in his heart he knew that day was coming just as surely as nightfall.

142

Chapter 10

'**H**ey, baby,' Rayette greeted Sam at Dunkin' Donuts. 'This is the fifth morning in a row you been in here – you're going to ruin that elephant's appetite.'

'It'd take more than six donuts a day to do that,' Sam said.

'Yeah, for me, too,' Rayette said, patting her hips. 'I should've gone to work for a vegetable stand.'

'Now, you've got nothing to worry about, Rayette. You're a fine-looking woman.'

A customer pulled in behind Sam as Rayette handed him his coffee. 'There you go, baby. You be careful with that,' she said. 'I'll see you.'

'Yeah,' Sam said. 'I expect you will.'

He pulled out behind a big slat-sided truck full of garlic, headed to market from Spokane. It brought back memories. The summer he and his twin brother Jimmy were twelve years old, their daddy let them stay out in the fields on fine nights – just them and a few old blankets and the stars. There was no money for a tent, but Sam didn't care, wouldn't have stayed in one even if they'd had it, not when he could lie under the stars and see for himself what God would see if He was looking upside down.

Jimmy, though, had been a nervous camper, always going on about how coyotes were going to get them while they slept. They'd go way out into the farthest field, bed down in the hay, and Sam would just be rising up into the stars when Jimmy would punch his arm and say, *What's that? You hear that creepy kind of sneaky sound? That's coyotes. They know we're here, they're just waiting for us to drift off and then they'll come out and do their business. They're gonna teach the little ones to eat using us; a finger, maybe, or maybe your nose.*

Sam would laugh and Jimmy would yell at him, *You just shut up. We're lying down here in the grass, and that's the perfect height for a coyote snack.*

They'd never seen a single coyote, but right up until the end, all Sam had to do was look at Jimmy and give a little yip and that boy would shiver like God had stepped on his soul – and maybe He had. One day Jimmy didn't come home from a trip to town that he'd taken for no particular reason except he was twelve years old and he could. He'd wanted Sam to go with him, but Sam had promised to help hay one of the fields.

Jimmy didn't come home that night and still wasn't in his bed by morning. Sam's father went driving all through town, taking Sam into every store on Main Street and Fuller, pushing Sam ahead of him and saying, *You seen a boy lately looks just like him? We're looking for his twin, boy never came home last night. Sure appreciate hearing it if you know anything.*

144

No one did know anything, though. After a while there was nobody left to ask, so they headed back home. About a half-mile before they got there, Sam spotted a bunch of turkey vultures circling overhead, and he said what he always said when he saw turkey vultures rising: *Looks like something out there must have died.*

His daddy pulled off the road, and when he shut down the engine it was quieter than church, quieter even than Heaven, maybe; there was no sound whatsoever, not even when cars went by, not even trucks. Sam's father looked first and said, *Jesus God.*

Jimmy was on his back in the ditch, looking like he'd just gone in there for a nap except that his shirt was covered with blood, more blood than one skinny little kid was supposed to have, at least it looked that way to Sam. He and his father lifted Jimmy into the bed of their old pickup, and his skin was as cool as a snake's. But the way Sam really knew Jimmy was dead was, he had his eyes closed. Jimmy would have to have been dead to lie out there in a ditch all night with his eyes closed, because if he'd been anything short of dead he'd have had them wide open and swiveling in his head like searchlights, looking out for coyotes until morning.

Late that day the sheriff came out to the farm. He told them that a trucker long-hauling garlic from eastern Washington had pulled into a diner and told a state trooper he'd been rocketing through a small town outside Yakima when he felt a little something hit his front end, figured he'd clipped a deer or maybe an antelope, and kept right on going. It wasn't until he'd pulled off the road for coffee that he noticed a scrap of plaid flannel cloth stuck in the grille.

145

Boy wasn't nothing more than roadkill, Sam overheard his father tell his mother that night, spitting out words as hard as BBs. *Child was no more than a skunk by the side of the road.* Sam had heard his mother weep. His father just slammed out the porch door calling to the dogs to come on now, just *come on.*

He had never been the same after that, or Sam, either.

Now he and the garlic truck went their separate ways just outside the gates to the Biedelman Zoo, returning Sam to his senses. He'd been having visions of the past more and more lately. He wondered if it was something to do with the diabetes, but he didn't know how that could be, unless diabetes could make you crazy. Half the time he didn't know if he was coming or going anymore, what with dreaming the same damn dream almost every night. Every morning when he woke up, he felt like he'd climbed a mountain, or been worked over with a meat tenderizer like his mother used for tough old farm animals that had been butchered late in life.

Corinna was right: he was going to have to do something – talk to Neva Wilson, maybe, or get hypnotized like people did to quit smoking, so he could get some rest.

He parked out back of the barn, and saw that Hannah was already outside, taking in the thin November sun. When he got inside, he found that Neva had mucked out the barn, squeegeed and disinfected the floors, and was cutting up fruit.

'You must have gotten here hours before daylight,' he said. 'You trying to hurt yourself?'

Neva smiled and waved him off. 'It's okay. I couldn't sleep.'

146

'You got something on your mind? Harriet Saul, maybe?' Sam said wickedly.

Neva gave him a look.

'She's a nasty thing, isn't she?' Sam grinned, pulling on his zoo sweatshirt.

Neva tried to suppress a smile. 'So I didn't do too well with her yesterday, huh?'

'Nope. Seems like she especially doesn't like women, though, so it's not you, exactly. That's one tough old sheep who doesn't have much use for the rest of the flock. Even Truman Levy's been rubbing her the wrong way lately, and she's always been partial to him. Might be The Change coming on,' Sam said doubtfully. 'More likely, it's just her ornery nature.'

Neva just kept on chopping vegetables.

'Let me just give these to my girl, then I'll come in and give you a hand with that,' Sam said, holding up the Dunkin' Donuts bag. 'Be right back.'

'Take your time,' Neva said, waving him on. 'If I didn't have this to do, I'd have to think, and I don't want to think.'

Hannah heard the paper bag. Long before Sam was within range she'd headed for him with her trunk already reaching. He held the top of the bag open and let her choose for herself from a maple bar, an apple fritter, or a glazed donut filled with Bavarian cream. She started with the cream. 'I could sure use a donut myself,' Sam told her. 'I feel like I got sand for brains this morning. Neva, too. So you keep an eye on us, shug. Might be one day we'll need you to keep us out of trouble.'

When Truman woke Winslow, he found the boy running a low-grade fever all over again. Rather than leave him

147

home with Miles, Truman rounded up two boxes of apple juice, a fresh box of Kleenex, a couple of decongestants, and a few good books and brought him to work. Harriet was uncharacteristically tolerant when it came to bringing Winslow into the office, and this morning was no exception. When she saw the boy's school backpack sticking out of Truman's cubicle, she came right over. Winslow was crammed into a corner, drawing a picture of Hannah.

'Hey, sweetie, are you sick?' Harriet asked him.

Winslow shrugged. 'Kind of. I'm not throwing up or anything.'

To Truman Harriet said, 'There's not much going on today. Why don't you just take him home?'

'Thank you, Harriet—'

'Maxine.'

'—Maxine. I'll just finish payroll and then we'll go.'

'Paychecks aren't due until tomorrow.'

'Yes, I know, but this way if Winslow's worse tomorrow I won't have to come in. Half the kids in his class are out with whatever this thing is. Back into the germ pool after a long healthy summer. It's like this every year.'

'Well, don't stay longer than you have to.' Harriet gave her pith helmet a smart rap to seat it more firmly on her head and then she was gone.

Winslow waited a beat and then whispered, 'How come we're calling her Maxine?'

Truman shook his head and whispered back, 'She plays the role of Max Biedelman when she's here.'

'But I thought Max Biedelman was a man.'

'Yes, I know,' Truman said impatiently. 'But she wasn't.'

'Isn't she dead?'

148

Truman sighed. 'Yes, Winnie. Look, it's impossible for me to explain. You'll just have to go along with it.'

Winslow asked if he could go outside. It was a cool morning, but the sun was bright. Truman laid his cheek against Winslow's cheek, and they felt the same – the aspirin had kicked in. He let the boy go.

Winslow liked going to work with Truman, even if he was sick – a little sick, not sick-sick. It was a lot more fun than when his father had worked for Allstate Insurance, where the best thing about it was a coffee mug full of free Allstate pens that skipped when you wrote with them. Whenever Winslow cleaned his room another pen or two still appeared along with the lint balls, though he didn't know why that was – it was like they had legs and wandered freely through the halls and closets when no one was home. The zoo didn't have free pens, but Harriet Saul was nice to him even though she wore a helmet and pretended to be somebody dead.

They'd had Miles for a couple of weeks now. He was a nice pig, even if he liked Truman better than him. Winslow figured that was because Truman felt sorry for him and tried to make up for it. Truman had only begun to sleep in his own room again a couple of nights ago. As far as Winslow could tell, the pig didn't miss his mom much, though Winslow had worried about that when they first brought him home, because he was so small.

Winslow didn't miss his own mother exactly. It was more like he missed a woman who looked like his mother but didn't act like her. His real mom snapped at him a lot, mostly about his habits of folding his own laundry and getting his homework done ahead of time. His Other Mom smiled at him and said things like, *I love you more than anything else in the world, did you know that?* and *Why don't we just say to hell with it and go out for ice cream?* It helped a little that his real mom didn't seem to like Truman very much, either, although he did everything for her like washing the dishes and cooking. In fact, Winslow had noticed that the more Truman had tried to do for her, the less she seemed to like either one of them. When she'd moved out last spring her last words to him had been, *Well, god knows I don't have to ask you to behave, because you always do.* She'd said it like that was bad, and when she'd bent to kiss his forehead, she didn't quite touch him – all he'd felt was her departing breath. She hadn't even done that with Truman, just walked out with a backwards wave as she walked down the sidewalk to the car. To keep Winslow's spirits up, Truman had pretended it was okay, but a few days after his mom left for good, Winslow had seen his father staring at an old pair of moccasins she used to wear around the house and had apparently abandoned. He'd been crying. Winslow had gone to him and awkwardly patted his back, saying, *I'm pretty sure this will be better,* and it was, even in times like this, when he was sick. His mother had always acted like he got sick on purpose, just to mess up her schedule. Truman made him macaroni and cheese and felt his forehead a lot.

Winslow had gotten as far as the dik–dik exhibit when a boy about his own age fell into step with him.

'You work here?' he asked Winslow, seeing Truman's sweatshirt.

'Nah. I'm sick, so my dad brought me to work for a while.'

150

The boy looked him over. 'You don't look sick.'

'Well, that's because I'm not *sick*-sick. Just sick. How come you're here? Isn't it school?'

The boy shrugged. 'I faked a note saying I was supposed to go to the dentist.'

'Aren't you going to get in trouble?'

'Nah. I'll just hold my face when I get back to school, you know, like my tooth is hurting. I have a friend here I come see sometimes.' He puffed up a little. 'His name's Samson Brown. He's in charge of Hannah. She's the elephant here.'

'I know that.'

'Yeah? Well, me and Mr Brown, we take her for walks sometimes. You want to come?'

'Sure.' They headed off down the hill together toward the barn.

'What's your name?' Winslow asked.

'Reginald Poole. What's yours?'

'Winslow Levy.'

'Hey.' Reginald held out his hand and Winslow shook it. 'You're not going to throw up, are you? Because I don't want to be around if you start throwing up and stuff.'

'Nah, I'm okay,' Winslow said.

They trotted down to the elephant barn and found Sam in the yard with Neva, lashing a garden hose to a tree.

'Hey, mister!' Reginald called from outside the fence.

Sam turned around. 'Well, what are you doing here, boy?'

'I got excused from school this morning.'

'How come?'

151

Reginald shrugged. 'I'm ahead of everybody else, so my aunt, she wrote an excuse for me, said I didn't have to go until this afternoon.'

Sam frowned at him. 'I don't much like to be lied to. You know what I'm saying? Hannah doesn't lie, and Miss Wilson here doesn't lie, either. I can't respect somebody who lies, much as I'd like to.'

Reginald looked down at his feet.

'Who's your friend?' Sam said.

Reginald jerked his head toward Winslow. 'His name's Winfred, Winbad, Winberg, something like that.'

'Winslow,' said Winslow. 'My dad's Truman Levy.'

'I know who you are, son. So what's your excuse for being here? You too smart to be in school, too?'

'No, sir. I'm sick.'

'Don't look sick to me.'

Winslow groaned. 'Not *sick* sick. Just a *little* sick.'

'Hey, mister, what are you going to do with that hose?' Reginald asked Sam. 'You going to give Hannah a bath?'

'Did you hear something, maybe a little bug buzzing around my ear?' Sam asked Neva.

'I didn't hear a thing,' Neva said, poker-faced. 'Must have been the wind.'

'Aw, *you* ask him,' Reginald said, poking Winslow in the side.

'What's the hose for?' Winslow said.

'Watch.' Sam walked back to the barn and turned on the outside spigot. A perfect arc of water bloomed and fell fifteen feet away. Hannah had been watching the preparations with great interest. She lifted her head and trumpeted nervously.

'Go on, baby girl, you show that water who's boss.'

Sam encouraged her as Neva adjusted the hose to make the arc land farther away, closer to Hannah. 'You go, sugar, put your back under there now, you know you're going to love it,' he said.

Hannah watched him, watched Neva, watched the boys, watched the water.

'Why don't you get the brush,' Neva suggested.

Sam got a push broom, soaked it under the hose, and then brought it over to where Hannah was shifting her feet in an anxious little dance. Sam touched her side with the wet bristles until, little by little and with the added enticement of peppermints, Sam coaxed her toward the arcing water until she was finally standing directly under the stream.

'Baby's got it now!' Sam crowed, watching her turn every which way under the hose and then scoop up a big gob of mud with her trunk and toss it onto her back. 'Shug looks like a pig in heaven.'

'We have a pig,' Winslow said through the fence. 'Me and my dad.'

'That right?' Sam said.

'His name is Miles.'

'That's a fine name for a pig.'

'You going to walk Hannah today, mister?' Reginald asked.

'Not with you I'm not, *no* sir,' Sam said. 'No way some child too sneaky to be in school is going anywhere with me and Hannah. Now if it was just me, we might talk it over. But I can't have Hannah around someone who doesn't believe school's important. It might be a bad influence on her.'

'Aw, come on, mister.'

153

'Nope, I don't even want to see your face. You promised me you wouldn't cause your aunt grief, but I see you doing it anyway. You bring me some schoolwork with a good grade on it and then we'll talk.'

Reginald shuffled off and Winslow followed. Hannah was still flinging mud.

'He's pretty strict,' Winslow said.

'Yeah,' Reginald said with admiration.

They hiked up toward the zoo gates and administrative offices. 'You don't live with your folks?' Winslow asked.

'Nah.'

'We live with my dad, me and Miles, but my mom left.'

'Yeah?' Reginald said. 'My mom, she got into some kind of trouble, so I live with my aunt.'

'Where's your dad?'

'He doesn't live with us. It gets kind of complicated.'

'Yeah,' Winslow said, and stopped outside the Biedelman house. 'Well, I better go.'

'Okay, Windermere.'

'*Winslow*,' said Winslow. 'Maybe if you come to see Mr Brown this weekend, I could meet you here.'

'Yeah?'

'Yeah.'

'Okay. I'll see you Saturday,' said Reginald.

'Okay,' said Winslow.

Neva had come outside and was leaning against the barn door with her arms folded, smiling at Hannah and Sam. 'She sure is a good girl,' she said.

Sam beamed with pride. 'See that? You're already getting partial. I bet you talk to her, too, tell her stuff.'

154

'Yeah,' Neva said. 'She got an earful from me this morning.'

'Baby's always been good at listening to me, even after all these years.'

Neva looked at Sam closely. 'What do you think of Harriet Saul's pretending she's Max Biedelman?'

'I think it's a damn stupid idea. Disrespectful, too.'

'What do you think Max Biedelman would think?'

'She'd be cussing up a blue streak is what she'd be doing. Miss Biedelman sure could cuss, too, when she put her mind to it.'

Hannah bumped Sam with exquisite gentleness. 'Hannah doesn't think much of that Harriet Saul, either, do you, sugar?'

Hannah wrapped her trunk around Sam's head. 'You sure are in a lovey mood this morning,' Sam told her. 'If you're trying to get into my good graces, sugar, you're wasting your time. Donuts are all gone, and I'm saving the rest of the peppermints for later.'

'Listen, if she's in such a good mood, let's take a closer look at her foot,' Neva said.

'Yeah?' Sam turned to Hannah. 'Foot, shug.'

Hannah lifted her foot. Neva probed gently, and Hannah flinched. 'Can you see?' she asked Sam. 'Damn.'

'Yeah,' Sam said quietly. 'It's worse. You got any ideas?'

'I do, actually,' Neva said, handing Hannah two yams and a gourd as positive reinforcement for her cooperation. 'We're all done, Hannah.' She patted Hannah's knee and the elephant lowered her foot. To Sam she said, 'Let me run something by you. Last night I talked to a friend who works at the Pachyderm Sanctuary outside Redding. She's worked with elephants for twenty-seven years, and

155

she's seen more foot problems than anyone I know. I described Hannah's problem and she told me to soak the foot in apple cider vinegar for at least ten minutes twice a day, three times if we can get Hannah to put up with it.'

'Apple cider vinegar?'

'Bacteria doesn't like the acidity of vinegar. I know it sounds farfetched, but it certainly can't do her any harm. Hell, I'd try soaking her foot in fine whiskey if I thought it might turn things around.'

Sam nodded. 'What's that sanctuary you were talking about, miss?'

'The Pachyderm Sanctuary. You've never heard of it? It's a wonderful place, seven hundred fenced acres plus a barn that can house up to ten elephants. Alice McNeary started it with one old circus elephant about nine years ago – probably ten, now. Since then she's taken three other circus elephants and a couple more that were in bad situations.'

'What's it look like? The land and all.'

'I've only been there once, but it was beautiful. Mostly rolling fields and woods. Only about two acres have been developed for the barn and Alice's house. The elephants can go wherever they want. The idea is to give them a place where they can stop working and just be elephants.'

'I think I've been there, miss,' Sam whispered.

Neva looked at him. 'I don't understand.'

'What kind of bad situations were those other elephants in?'

Neva frowned, trying to remember. 'Well, one was at some tire dealership in Texas that was closing down, and no one wanted her because she was too old. The second

156

one had been by herself for twenty-eight years at some godforsaken zoo in Alabama.'

'Was that why the place took her – because she was alone?'

Neva frowned. 'How long has Hannah been alone here, again? It was forty years, wasn't it?'

'Forty-one, miss,' Sam said softly.

Neva's eyes locked onto Sam's. 'This might be a good time to start calling me Neva.'

Chapter 11

Sometime in the early morning – he would never be able to remember exactly when, or under what circumstances – Johnson Johnson got an idea. As soon as Home Depot opened he bought a length of plastic irrigation pipe, lined its bottom with carpet strips, and ran it from his kitchen window into the kitchen window of Neva's apartment. He made sure it was well sealed against the weather so Neva wouldn't catch cold. Then he went to the animal shelter. When Neva got home she found a white plastic umbilical cord connecting them across the backyard. She walked straight to the big house and knocked on the kitchen door.

'What's with that?' she asked when Johnson Johnson answered the door.

Johnson Johnson made his odd windmilling motion, urging Neva to come into the kitchen.

'Close your eyes,' he said.

'No – look, it's been a long day.'

'Here.' He scooped up a brown cat and thrust her into Neva's arms. The cat immediately started purring. Neva softened somewhat, running her hands down the cat's back and watching it ripple ecstatically. She stepped into the kitchen.

'Does she have a name?'

'Chocolate.' Johnson Johnson pointed to a black and white cat just walking into the kitchen. 'That's Chip. I got them so they could come visit you.'

'Come visit me? Through the tunnel?'

'Yes!' Johnson Johnson bounced up on the balls of his feet enthusiastically. 'It has carpet in it for traction. I'll wrap it with insulation so you won't get cold.'

'I love that! You've done a nice thing, you really have!'

Johnson Johnson beamed. 'I thought you'd, you know, like it. So, I could order a pizza.'

'Oh, I don't think so.' Neva set Chocolate down. 'I think two new cats and a tunnel punched through my kitchen window are more than enough festivity for today. But, listen.' He looked at her hopefully, his mouth slightly open. 'Thank you.'

'Welcome,' he said.

Neva wondered if she'd done Johnson Johnson a disservice by keeping him at a distance. Every time he saw her, he offered her pizza; every time he offered, she declined. And every time, like the phoenix, he rose again to make the same damned offer.

At some point soon, she'd probably have to let him order the pizza.

Just as she opened her apartment door, Chocolate

emerged from the tunnel, leapt over the kitchen sink, and minced along the countertop, high on her toes.

'So let's talk,' Neva said, scratching the cat's ears. 'I'd say you stand a good chance of convincing your new dad to buy you those incredibly expensive little cans of cat food with bits of seafood in aspic.'

The cat head-butted Neva companionably and walked on as Kitty, thuggish with one milky eye, slunk out of the tunnel and slouched off to explore. Neva had just started pulling odds and ends from her refrigerator for dinner – deli turkey, a bowl of grapes, a whole-wheat roll – when the phone rang. Piped through the answering machine was a nervous sigh and sounds of distressed throat-clearing.

'Neva? This is Truman Levy. Listen, I'm sorry to call you at home, but I need your advice. It's about Winslow's pig—'

Neva picked up the phone. 'Truman?'

'Oh, thank god.'

'Are you all right?'

'Yes, I'm all right, but there seems to be something wrong with Miles. He's congested, and he feels warm.'

'Have you taken his temperature?'

'God, no.'

'Do you have a rectal thermometer?'

'There's probably one somewhere from when Winslow was a baby. Do you think that's absolutely necessary?'

'Animal care is not for the faint of heart, Truman,' Neva said. 'Coat the thermometer well with Vaseline and insert it in his rectum for two minutes. If you don't have Vaseline, use butter.'

'Good Christ.'

161

'Do you want me to stay on the line?'

'Yes, yes. Please don't hang up,' Truman said, and she could hear him shudder. 'What's a pig's normal temperature?'

'I don't know, but I'll have found out by the time you've finished taking it. If I'm not here when you get back on the line, wait for me.'

'Okay.'

Neva set the receiver down and pulled one of her veterinary books out of a cardboard box. Kitty swaggered across the pages, his gut swinging. Neva picked up the receiver just as Truman was coming back on the line, breathing hard. 'His temperature's one hundred and four point two.'

'Well, it should be between a hundred and two and a hundred and three point six. Check his respiration – how many breaths is he taking per minute?'

Neva heard Truman counting under his breath. 'Twenty-five.'

'It should be between ten and twenty,' Neva read.

'He's snorting and gurgling. Listen. It's heartbreaking.' Neva heard loud congested snuffles being breathed directly into the receiver.

'Wasn't your son sick recently?'

'Winslow? Yes, all the kids were. There was some bug going around. It happens every fall.'

'Are you familiar with the term zoonosis?'

'My god, is it serious?'

Neva smiled. 'No, no, it means disease transmission between animals and humans. I think there's a good chance that Miles caught Winslow's cold.'

'His cold. Pigs can have colds?'

'Well, the porcine equivalent, anyway. We're not the only ones who can be under the weather sometimes. Anyway,

162

you might want to take him to see a vet tomorrow, if he isn't better. For tonight I'd keep him in a small room if you can – maybe a bathroom – so he isn't too active. Cover him with a blanket if he'll let you, or at least keep the room warm. Do you have a vaporizer? You could run that for him, if you make sure it isn't in a place where he can get at it and scald himself.'

The line fell silent.

'Truman?'

She could hear him sigh heavily. 'My parents are attorneys. I hold advanced degrees in business and English literature. I have never pictured myself as a swineherd.'

'Then it's a perfect personal growth opportunity.'

'Yes, well.' His voice trailed off. 'You might say a "Te Deum" for us.'

'A whole new future may await you in animal care,' Neva said cheerfully.

'I'd sooner eat flies.'

Truman stayed up most of the night, checking on the pig's breathing, topping off the vaporizer and tucking Miles's little blanket up around his shoulders, if pigs could be said to have shoulders. He tried and failed to remember the cut of pork that would roughly correspond. Eventually he concluded that he'd be better off just pulling up stakes and sleeping in a sleeping bag beside the damned pig on the bathroom floor. He and Rhonda had been less intimate in the last years of their marriage.

Either through nature's resiliency or the palliative effect of Truman's presence, Miles began breathing more easily at about three in the morning, and by five had fallen into a peaceful sleep, tucked into the hollow of

Truman's arm. By seven, the pig's fever peaked at one hundred and two and Truman had wracking pains through his entire body. He called Harriet's extension and left a message that he would be staying home, rallied just long enough to see Winslow off to school, and then crawled to the couch in the den. When the phone rang at nine o'clock Truman steeled himself for Harriet's voice, but instead it was Neva's.

'So?' she said.

'I kept him in the bathroom all night with the vaporizer – we slept on the floor.'

'We?'

'I no longer have normal feeling in my arms or legs,' Truman rasped.

'What's his temperature?'

'A hundred and two, same as mine.'

He could hear Neva snort into the receiver. 'Look, would you like me to check on you both at lunch? I can bring along some soup from the Oat Maiden.' The Oat Maiden was a café several blocks from the zoo and, from what Truman could deduce, it specialized in dishes made with obscure grains, husks, stems, hulls, rinds, and pith. He was too sick to care.

He gave her directions to his house and hung up, ruminating over the novelty of imagining that someone cared. His mother Lavinia had insisted that coddling bred weakness of character. Thus the list of sickroom comforts he had never received included chocolate ice cream, chicken soup, light reading materials, cinnamon toast, steaming mugs of tea, and a cool hand applied soothingly to the forehead. Lavinia had clapped an occasional chill palm to his brow with the air of a martyr. Perhaps

164

as a result, Truman was not a good patient, but given to whimpering and elaborate descriptions of the fresh hells of illness.

Now he let Miles outside, swallowed acetaminophen, and made a steaming mug of tea to breathe over. Creeping back to the couch, he wrapped himself tightly in an afghan and fell into an interminable fever dream in which, like Sisyphus, he was doomed to push his laden shopping cart through endless aisles at Safeway, only to arrive at the checkout lanes with a mysteriously empty basket. He didn't wake up again until he heard Neva letting herself into the house. She appeared in the doorway of his den, and in his fever-addled state her oversized zoo sweatshirt reminded him of the particular way men's shirts looked on slender women fresh from bed.

'Here you are – six-bean soup with veggie garlic sausage,' she said cheerfully, pulling a cardboard soup container from a brown paper bag.

'Why do they call it health food?' Truman said petulantly. 'It's not. No one healthy would eat this.'

'Go on, it'll be good for you. Have you taken anything? Because you look like you should be on major drugs.'

'I'm just preying on your sympathy.'

'Where's Miles?'

'In the backyard.'

In fact, Miles had his snout pressed pathetically against the sliding glass door.

'Can I let him in?' Neva said. 'Look, he's so *sweet*!'

'By all means. We wouldn't want him suffering out there all alone when we're having so much fun in here.'

'Do you always get ironic when you're sick?'

'Generally.'

Neva let Miles in, and when she crouched beside him he made brazenly seductive noises and fell like the dead at her feet. She listened to him breathe and ran her hand over his sparse coat. 'He feels cool, and his eyes are bright. I think he's probably over whatever it was he had. Is he eating well?'

'Oh, my god,' Truman said, stricken. 'I haven't fed him yet.' He told Neva where the pig kibble was, and how much to put in his dish. Miles set to like he hadn't been fed in days, and then, sated, circled twice and fell heavily into his basket beneath the piano.

'What a good pig,' Neva crooned.

'He's actually quite musical.'

'Really?'

'Yes. He especially likes Mozart. Winslow's working on several pieces right now, and Miles stays right there under the piano until he's done, no matter how long he practices.'

'Clearly a pig with discriminating tastes.' Neva bent down to pet Miles's head.

Truman watched as the pig snuffled with pleasure. 'Truthfully,' he said, 'I'd never envisioned pigs as being so—'

'Responsive?'

'Flatulent.'

Neva started laughing. 'Well, he's a pig. Pigs and gas go together.'

'I just wish someone had told me,' Truman said sadly, and pulled his afghan closer around his shoulders.

For the last nine days Harriet had driven an extra eight miles on her way to work so she could admire her new billboard with its prominent pictures of Hannah beside

166

herself as Maxine Biedelman. Since the billboard had gone up, zoo attendance had increased twenty percent – and in mid-November, to boot. Her one-woman performances were attracting larger audiences each day, and the question-and-answer periods sometimes lasted nearly as long as the talk itself. She was considering converting the house's capacious ballroom into an auditorium so her performances could continue in comfort through the winter.

Harriet loved her new persona. As Maxine, she was courageous and accomplished, a woman of sophistication equally at home in Cannes or on the Indian subcontinent. As Maxine she didn't walk, she strode; she did not merely see, but beheld. The very air she breathed was bracing. Here was a conqueror of worlds. There had been some awkward moments, of course, with disrespectful employees and forgetful managers who continued to address her as Harriet, but as Maxine she had discovered magnanimity: she merely smiled and reminded them of her policy. Sooner or later they would find that calling her Maxine had become second nature, just as they became accustomed to the new names of recent brides.

From the scribbled captions on the backs of Maxine's childhood photographs, she had sometimes been called Brave Boy, which Harriet thought was a wonderful name. Harriet's own childhood nickname had been Bucket, a reference to her appetite for fried chicken when she was small. Bestowed so many years ago by her father, the name had been only one among many unkindnesses. She had learned early that she was unlikable, but she didn't know why. Certainly it wasn't any child's intention to be disliked. Harriet understood very well that it was the least attractive children – the Dumbo-eared, the whiny-voiced, the clumsy, the loutish, the unpretty – who craved affection most of all.

When Harriet was seven, her father had died of pancreatic cancer. Five and a half months later, the school principal had come to Harriet's classroom and motioned to her that she should join him in the hall. She hadn't wanted to, but her teacher had nodded curtly in her direction: *Go*. In the hall, the principal had informed Harriet that her mother had been in a car accident and was being treated for serious head injuries in a regional hospital seventy-five miles away. Since Harriet had no other family nearby, someone from Social Services would come to pick her up and take care of her until other arrangements could be made.

Over the following six months she had stayed with a succession of foster families that had failed to like her. Sometimes she wet the bed; sometimes she woke the household with nightmares. At some homes, hands were too busy and hearts too closed; in others, hearts were open but already overcrowded. And at each home she left something behind: outgrown clothes, a stuffed dog, the memory of her mother's perfume, a pillow; her sense of belonging, of entitlement, of certainty. Already fat, she got fatter. Already homely, she slipped into shabbiness with bangs that went untrimmed and clothes that weren't always clean. She went to church or didn't, depending on the household, and if God was ever listening, He wasn't letting on.

During her mother's recovery, Harriet was brought to the hospital and then the rehabilitation center twice a month. But Thelma Saul no longer knew her. It became evident that in addition to impairments of memory and intellect, she had sustained a permanent blindness of the heart. *I'm sorry,* she would tell Harriet with increasing agitation, *but if you were my daughter, I would know you; I would love you.*

Month after month, Harriet would stand before her, imploring with every desperate beat of her heart, *See me. See me. See me.*

After five months, Thelma began to scream whenever Harriet was brought in, so the visits were stopped. Her mother was released from the rehabilitation center, and Harriet saw her from time to time on the street, but Thelma always fled from her. And then Harriet was taken to another town to live with Maude. Several years later, word reached her that her mother had remarried and had a little girl who was rumored to look very much like Harriet.

But all of that was in the past, and now she could hardly contain her exhilaration. It was a glorious thing, to be reborn. Harriet Saul – that clumsy, gauche, unliked, unlikable, unattractive woman – had dropped away, leaving her soul sleek and nimble. As Maxine she was the cherished daughter of a loving father; strong, successful, capable, and adored.

Bladenham News-Gazette reporter Martin Choi arrived ten minutes late for his appointment, perspiring heavily and clanking with gear. Harriet had been listening for him, and glided from her office with her hand extended to clasp his.

'Good to see you, Martin. You did a nice job on your article about the zoo. Is there something else you'd like to work on?'

Martin fussed with his little pad, dropped and recovered his pen. 'I'm thinking I might be able to put something together about' – he gestured at her safari gear – 'you know. This. You.'

'Do you mean Maxine Biedelman?'

'Yeah. The one who's dead and you pretend you're her.'

Harriet's smile became somewhat fixed. 'I take on her persona, yes. Living history is a very popular, proven educational technique. She was a remarkable woman. I give a lecture twice a day.'

'Yeah, well, how about we do an interview with you and then I'll take some pictures of you dressed, you know, in your safari outfit, and then after the lecture I can interview some zoo visitors.'

'That would be fine.'

She motioned him into her office and for the next half-hour laid out the marvel that was Maxine – her travels, her family, her experiences in Thailand and Burma, in Borneo and Sumatra. She offered photographs that illustrated her points, and waited patiently while Martin looked them over. She talked for exactly half an hour and then, at ten o'clock sharp, brought him outside with her. Several groups of schoolchildren and their adult chaperones waited at the foot of the porch, fidgeting in the late autumn chill. Harriet doffed her pith helmet and gave them all a hearty greeting. Martin Choi parked his camera bag at the foot of the stairs and began shooting pictures.

'Good morning to you all,' Harriet called. The gathering got quiet. 'I am Maxine Biedelmen. Welcome to my zoo!'

Her performance lasted forty-five minutes, followed by what was, today, a brief question-and-answer period, after which she bade her visitors farewell with a lifted hand. She was greatly moved by the end, the way she was every time. Martin Choi took picture after picture.

'Hey, what you just did, now that was really something,' he said admiringly when it was over. 'You were great – no kidding. You had those kids believing every word you said.'

She smiled broadly. 'Yes, I did. I always do.'

'So are there any other zoos in the country that do this kind of thing?'

'No. It takes a certain – calling. And of course, the institution has to have a colorful history to begin with.'

'Yeah? Well, you've got that. I have to admit I was pretty skeptical to begin with.'

'And now?'

'Yeah, well, it's like *theater*, isn't it, only at a zoo. Who's going to expect that?'

They had reached the door to the administrative suite. Harriet studied him closely for a minute or two and then said, 'I like you, Martin. You're a promising young journalist. Let me offer you something.'

'Yeah?'

'Depending on your article and how you portray me – me, Maxine Biedelman – I'll contact you first when things of interest happen here at the zoo.'

'Hey, sure, that'd be great. But I need to be up front here – I'm not promising to spin a story your way. I mean, I've got to report the truth, black and white, as I see it.'

'Of course,' Harriet said. 'You're obviously a man of

171

principle who's dedicated to your profession. I understood that about you the first time we met.'

Martin Choi puffed up. 'So, good.'

Harriet held out her hand. 'It's been a pleasure.'

'Sure. Okay.'

'We'll talk soon,' Harriet said, and saw him to the front door.

They would talk soon and frequently. It wasn't every day that you were handed a gift like Martin Choi. Finding him was a little bit like falling in love, and Harriet was shrewd enough to know it.

Chapter 12

Max Biedelman and Sam had fallen into a routine after their first excursion into the woods. The old woman would send word down to the elephant barn two or three times a week that she would enjoy their company, and Sam would bring Hannah right up to her porch so she wouldn't have to walk alone over uneven ground. Her hips were so bad some days that they only got as far as the edge of the woods, but on good days they'd go as far as a little clearing half a mile away, where there were logs to sit on and sunlight to enjoy. Miss Effie, more and more frail and flighty, rarely joined them.

'Is Miss Effie all right?' Sam ventured one early November afternoon when Max Biedelman was perched on her little stool in a puddle of sunshine, nose to the sky, eyes squeezed shut against the light, smiling the faintest smile. Hannah shuffled nearby, rummaging for windfall apples under the leaves.

'For the moment, but she's had a difficult autumn.

We're both failing, Mr Brown; our mortality is closer than we'd like. When I die, it will be with teeth and claws bared. Effie will go quietly, though, I think, like a mouse acquiescing to the cat. But then, Effie has never been strong. She was somewhat delicate even in her prime.'

'I sure would've liked to see her young.'

'And why is that, Mr Brown?'

'I bet she looked just like an angel, with that light curly hair of hers, and her being so fair to begin with.'

Max Biedelman smiled a faraway smile. 'She was visiting Crete with her parents when I first saw her. She had made her mother very angry by going out without a parasol, something a lady didn't do in 1897. Women wore white then, especially young women, and because of her lack of a parasol Effie's face was rosy and framed by lace and the fine summer straw of her hat. My father and I were in a café in a town square, lunching on goat cheese and olives and fresh bread and wine. All the time her mother was scolding her she was looking at me, and her eyes were simply brimming with mischief. Of course, I was in trousers and boots, brown as the devil and barely tame from spending six months in Africa. Effie's mother hurried her away from my father and me, sensing, no doubt, that she was about to lose control over her daughter altogether – which, in fact, she did.

'As it happened, Effie's family was booked on the same ship home as my father and I, and she wheedled the captain into including her family at our regular table in the dining room. She was a beautiful creature, twenty-one and all spun sugar and devilry.'

Sam watched Hannah stripping leaves from a small

aspen tree. 'First time I ever saw Corinna was in the grocery store on a plain old Saturday, nothing special about it except her and her sister Lula were in there buying a sack of yams. She was the most beautiful thing I ever saw. Big girl, round and brown with skin like milk chocolate or silk, maybe, with a smile that could light up the whole sky. I was lucky she didn't turn around and punch me right then for staring at her like that.

'Turned out she was visiting her aunt and uncle for the weekend. Her aunt and uncle were the only other black family for fifty miles. I figured God must have meant for me to meet her, to bring her to a place that was so far out of the way. There she was, right in my backyard almost, holding a sack of yams my daddy had grown on our farm and joking with Lula like they owned the place.' Sam shook his head, remembering. 'I knew right then that if I could marry that gal I wouldn't ask anything else from God or anyone.'

Hannah plodded out of the woods and approached them, coming to stand beside Sam. She wrapped her trunk around his head, even that long ago her special greeting for him. He patted her leg. 'It's okay, sugar, me and Miss Biedelman are talking. You can play a little bit longer.'

He looked at the old woman to confirm this. 'Yes, I believe a few more minutes would do us all good, Mr Brown. She may stay.'

'Go ahead, shug. We'll call when it's time to go.' The elephant padded off, swishing her tail. 'What did Miss Effie do when you were traveling, then?'

'Oh, it depended on where I was going,' Max Biedelman said, frowning. 'She was never one for safari

175

or for camping in the bush in Burma. She was afraid of the animals – afraid of the mahouts, too, for that matter. She was very much like my mother in that respect. No, Effie was made for fine hotels and continental cuisine, and on those trips she would happily accompany me. The rest of the time she lived with her parents in Seattle. Her father made her a generous allowance and eventually her mother resigned herself to the fact that Effie would never marry. As of course she did not, although there was a time when she longed for children.'

'How about you, sir? You ever want children of your own?'

'No. Oh, if I could have been the father of someone's children, I would have done that happily, but of course that wasn't the point. No, Mr Brown, I did not yearn for children.'

'Course, now you've got all these animals,' Sam said.

Max Biedelman cut her shrewd old eyes at him. 'Yes, I have my animals. And Effie, I suppose, has me.' She rose stiffly and folded up her little seat. 'I believe it's time to go home, Mr Brown. I would hate for Hannah to have to carry me back.'

'Yes, sir,' Sam said. Hearing them stir, Hannah was already hurrying back, clutching a small branch of alder. 'Time to go, sugar,' Sam said, patting her trunk. 'You got a souvenir? Why, you just take it along with you, then. It'll remind you of our travels until the next time.'

Max Biedelman chuckled and started the slow walk back. 'Our Hannah is also a traveler. One wonders, sometimes, what she saw in Burma. It's a beautiful country, you know. There are parts of it that are as close to Paradise as anywhere on earth.'

176

She fell into a ruminative silence for the rest of the walk, and Sam let her be. She had a lot to say goodbye to, before she died; a lot to dust off and look over one last time. Could take her years, like his grandmother, who was dying from the time she was seventy-two until she turned eighty; it took her that long to get the work done. He sensed that Miss Biedelman was doing the same thing, running her mind's hand one more time over what was beautiful and what had brought her peace. He had seen it come on, over the last few months. Seemed to him that sorting memories was just like carding wool: you combed and combed until you had all the fibers going in the same direction, the whole thing gleaming like a river.

'How're you doing, girl?' Corinna cried, holding open the door to the Beauty Spot for Neva Wilson. 'Come on in. Is it raining? When did that start?' She folded Neva into a quick one-armed hug against her substantial bosom.

'A couple of hours ago.'

'Really? My head must be in the clouds today.' Corinna hung Neva's jacket on a peg. It was a cheap, ugly thing. A pretty girl like her should have something better. Corinna settled her in her chair and gently fastened one of her salon drapes around the girl's shoulders. 'I hope you know you can come chew the fat over here anytime, without having to go and get your hair involved,' she said.

Neva shook her head, pulling her hair out from under the smock and letting it spill down her back. 'Come on. Who else am I going to trust with my finest asset?'

She was being flippant, but Corinna couldn't help

thinking she was also right; the girl had thick, glossy, dark red hair most African American girls would cut off their right arm for. Corinna was all for black people feeling good about what they had, but the truth was, the Lord shortchanged them in the hair department, and that was all there was to it. Corinna could relax, moisturize, condition, weave, braid, and style until the cows came home, but neither she nor any other beautician on earth, no matter how gifted, could come close to giving a black girl what Neva Wilson got for free, and that was all there was to it.

'So what are we doing, sugar?' she asked Neva.

'Just trim it, please – I've been doing it myself, and you can see what a bad idea that is.'

Corinna clucked and brushed. 'You sure you don't want a nice bob, maybe something a little different?'

'Cornrows would be nice,' Neva said. 'With lots of beads.'

'You got four hours? Because that's what it's going to take with all this hair you've got.'

Neva sighed. 'I guess I'll have to do that on a day off – I told Sam I'd be back in an hour.'

'Let's just clean you up for now. We can save the fancy stuff for next time.' Corinna got to work. 'So how's my Hannah today? Baby in a good mood?'

'She's in a great mood. We cut twenty-four honeydew melons in half, filled them with frozen raspberries, put them back together and hid them in the branches of trees all over the zoo. Sam took her for a walk an hour ago, and they still hadn't gotten back when I left to come here. I could see them way over by the house. Hannah had her trunk in the hedge.' Neva laughed. 'It was just like an Easter egg hunt, only in November.'

Corinna smiled broadly. 'Shug does like to get playful. You've done wonderful things for her, girl. She's got that old sparkle back in her eye, like we haven't seen for a long time. A mighty long time.' Corinna snipped, thoughtful. 'You think she ever waits for Miss Biedelman to come down those steps? Hannah and Sam, they used to go up to the house for Miss Biedelman when the weather was fine so she could come along on their walks. Course, it was her idea to take Hannah walking in the first place, but by then her poor hips were so bad – it was a damned shame.' She clucked gently. 'Sam used to worry about Miss Biedelman all the time. Said he'd had an old blue dog once that had hips like hers and they kept dislocating until they finally stiffened up and froze and they had to put that poor dog down. Man said he cried for a week.'

'He's told me about their walks in the woods,' Neva said, reaching up under the smock to scratch an itch. 'I wish the city hadn't put up that fence along the property line. We can't go there anymore.'

Corinna smiled, remembering. 'Baby would pad along next to Miss Biedelman just as easy as an old dog and every bit that affectionate. You know the way a dog will look at his owner, just head over heels in love.'

'She looks at Sam that way all the time,' Neva smiled. 'She thinks he hung the moon.'

'Yeah,' Corinna said. 'I've seen her.'

She worked quietly, wondering how forty years could have gone by, with her and Sam no older now than they'd been then, at least in their eyes. Sam was catching up, though; she'd seen it on him, these last few months.

'Sam ever tell you about Hannah's dream?' she said.

179

'What dream?'

'Guess not. There's this dream he has, been having it for years – close your eyes now,' Corinna said as she began trimming Neva's bangs. 'He dreams he's an elephant in a wide open place with other elephants. Go ahead and open again.' Corinna leaned down and blew hair clippings from Neva's forehead.

'Is there a pond?' Neva said.

'Why did you ask that?'

'He said something about a meadow and a pond.'

'Yeah. He used to have that dream maybe a couple of times a month, but lately he's dreaming it four, five nights a week. He says it's Hannah's dream, and he doesn't know what to do with it except to bring her more Dunkin' Donuts, and donuts don't make up for things beyond a point, though.'

The women's eyes met in the mirror. 'The funny thing is, when he described it to me, it sounded like a place just outside Redding, California,' Neva said. 'A real place, I mean. It's called the Pachyderm Sanctuary.'

Corinna stopped cutting. 'We've never been there, though – never even heard of it. What is it?'

'They take circus elephants that can't perform anymore, and zoo animals like Hannah, ones who've been alone or abused or are just too old for anyone to want them anymore. The sanctuary makes a commitment that the elephants that come to them will stay there and be taken care of for the rest of their lives. Their goal is simply to let elephants live within a community, a herd, with as little human interference as possible.'

Corinna's hands were pressing against her cheeks, her eyes welling. 'Oh, honey. You think they'd take shug?'

'I don't know. I honestly don't know – wait. *Wait.*'

Corinna had begun humming with excitement. 'Girl, I've been waiting for an apology from Jesus for years, for what He did to Sam and me with our baby and all,' she said. 'But if He can just make this happen, this *one thing*, I'll forgive Him for everything, I swear. I'll be singing hymns to the rafters, be praising His goodness so loud they're going to have to turn down the volume in Heaven. He can do what He wants with me, if only He'd let Hannah go there so Sam can retire.'

'Whoa – whoa! It's not that simple,' Neva said. 'The sanctuary won't take an animal before an endowment has been raised for its care – I think it's a minimum of a quarter of a million dollars, and that's *if* they agree to take Hannah at all, instead of some other elephant that's worse off. And you have to understand that there *are* animals that are worse off – animals that have been beaten, neglected, disabled.'

Corinna looked at Neva. 'I don't believe they'd turn my baby away if they got to know her.'

Neva sighed. Corinna drew a slow breath, a breath from the deep place where hope and intention begin. 'You just tell me who I've got to write to at that sanctuary and I'll write, and so will Sam. We've got some money put away, besides the social security. We'll send them everything we have. You just tell me who, and I'll send that check first thing in the morning.'

Neva turned in her chair to look Corinna in the eye. 'Look. I'll probably go straight to hell for even saying this, but I know the director down there. I've been thinking about approaching her. She's discreet, so there's nothing to lose by asking.'

Corinna took Neva's hands in hers and pressed so hard it hurt.

'You've got to promise to keep this a secret,' Neva said.

'Girl, you've got my word. You can count on Sam, too.'

Neva nodded.

'You do this thing and I'll take care of your hair for free for life. It's not much, but it's what I've got to offer.'

'Even cornrows?' Neva said.

'Amen, baby.' Corinna grinned. 'Even cornrows.'

Two hours later Bettina Jones came into the Beauty Spot singing 'Rock of Ages' and shaking out her plastic rain bonnet. 'Whew! I know what Noah must have felt like,' she said. 'It's raining out there like it's never going to stop.'

Corinna whisked Bettina into her chair and said, 'Wouldn't you just love to know what Noah told all those animals to make them hurry up and get on board? My daddy had chickens and goats, a cow or two, and those animals moved slower than grass grows.'

'You're sure in a good mood this morning,' Bettina said, examining Corinna's face in the salon mirror. 'Is that makeup you've got on? Your face looks different. Brighter or something.'

'I never wear makeup, you know that. The day you see me wearing makeup is the day you're going to be looking in my casket, because there is no other way I'd be smearing that stuff on my face. My mama used to say it was immoral and my daddy said anyhow we couldn't afford it, so I never got into the habit.'

182

'Is Sam feeling better?' Bettina said, fishing.

'No. The only thing that's going to help is for him to retire.'

'You finally set a date, then?'

'No, but I think it might be soon.'

'You sure are acting strange,' Bettina frowned.

'Nope, just the same old me. Come on, let's wet you down.'

Corinna held Bettina's smock like a train so she wouldn't trip on her way over to the sink. She noticed the woman was getting more and more little skin tabs all over her face, looked like raised black freckles. Some people were put off by things like that.

'Hon,' Corinna said, guiding Bettina's head back into the sink and turning on the water, 'you might want to see somebody about those little moles on your face. Get somebody to get rid of them for you before they take over.'

Bettina said stiffly, 'I don't want some doctor cutting on my face, Corinna. I am not ashamed of what the good Lord sees fit to send me. I'm beautiful in His eyes, and that's what counts.'

'They don't cut, honey, they freeze you. I do a girl who told me she had a wart frozen one time. She said they dip a Q-tip into a little ladle of steaming cold stuff, rub it on the wart, and wait a couple days till it falls off on its own. She said it didn't hurt a bit.'

'Thank you for telling me, Corinna,' Bettina said stiffly. 'But I can't afford a doctor like that, not on Social Security.'

Corinna wrapped Bettina's head in a towel and helped her sit up. 'Well, I tell you what. This appointment is on me, my treat.'

'Now, you can't do that!' Bettina cried. 'You've got to live, same as me.'

'Naw. It's my treat, so stop fussing.'

'Something's definitely up with you.'

Corinna waved her hand. 'Just in a good mood, hon. No particular reason. Just in a good mood.'

Johnson Johnson lay on his back in bed, in the dark, admiring the constellation of stars on his ceiling. It was a work in progress, applied a single star at a time with glow-in-the-dark paint and the finest brush he could find. He figured he'd painted something like ten thousand stars already, plus a bunch of planets, plotted out according to a celestial map he'd found in an issue of *National Geographic*. He'd broken the photograph into a grid, and lined off the ceiling to match. So far, the project had taken seven years. He figured he'd be done in another two if he kept up his current rate of three hours a week. He wondered whether, if he asked Neva nicely, she would come up sometime to see it. But he'd noticed she was edgy about things unless they involved cookies or animals. He was certain she'd been happy about Chocolate, Chip, Kitty, and the tunnel. He'd even considered running a second tunnel to her apartment, right through the wall and siding, but that could wait. Right now he had another project in mind.

He had come up with the idea of making Neva's elephant a musical instrument. He could buy several steel drums and hammer out their tops, maybe make them so they had different tonal ranges – a low drum, a high drum, like that. The elephant could play them using a rubber mallet. Or instead of steel drums, he could take

184

those big blue plastic bottles people used in water coolers and fill them up with different levels of water, so they sounded different from each other when you hit them – and if they broke, why, you could just get a drink. He'd go to Home Depot in the morning.

Johnson Johnson loved Home Depot. He'd gotten some of his best ideas there. Once, he'd been in Plumbing Fixtures and figured out that he could paint the inside of a toilet bowl bright colors and patterns, like a swirling design that would go in the same direction as the water when the toilet was flushed. Even better, he could put one of those toilet deodorizers in the tank that would turn the water blue, then use colors like yellow to turn the bowl green. He had brought home a white porcelain toilet and china paints and created tropical islands in an ocean at night, with the sky lit up by fireworks. Then he'd taken the painted toilet to a porcelain manufacturer and they'd let him fire it in their kiln. They'd wanted him to do some toilets for their customers, too, but he told them he didn't do something more than once. They'd made him promise to consider it, but that had been three years ago now, and he still didn't have the urge to paint another toilet – unless, of course, Neva were to ask him to. That wasn't likely, since she had never seen his toilet. Maybe she would sometime, though. You didn't know what good things were going to happen to you until you were right in the middle of them, so it was best to always be ready. He'd had good things happen to him before, so he knew. One night, a Ferris wheel had broken when he'd been on it, and he'd been able to sit up on top and look at the lights of Bladenham for half an hour for free. And another thing was, he'd found Kitty in a

185

ditch by the side of a road that he had never been on before and never went on again. Kitty had been bleeding from a cut on his head and one eye was swollen shut. Johnson Johnson had wrapped him in a blanket and brought him directly to a veterinarian, who'd asked Johnson Johnson if he really wanted the cat treated. *He's an old tom, son, probably sowed his wild oats a long time ago now,* the doctor had said. *You sure he's worth saving?* Johnson Johnson had been very sure then, and he was still just as sure now. Imagine Kitty dying unloved in some ditch instead of balled up all tight and cozy in the third hammock on the north wall in his living room. Johnson Johnson didn't like to think about it. And now he had Chocolate and Chip, and he wouldn't have wanted to miss them, either.

He pulled his covers up to his chin, basking in the faint light of the stars above his head and thinking with unfathomable wonder about how good the world was.

Chapter 13

N eva was outside hosing down the elephant when Truman and Winslow approached on the path to Hannah's barn. Neva smiled and saluted with the hose. Truman admired the way the sunlight set her hair on fire, like a Japanese maple in autumn.

'What brings you to my little corner of Paradise?' she called when they were within range. 'Especially on a Saturday?'

'Winslow. Have you seen a boy named Reginald around anywhere? He and Winslow cooked up a plan to meet here this afternoon.'

'He just got here. He's with Sam in the barn.' She opened the gate for them. Hannah stood in the yard, dripping with water, her eyes squeezed shut with pleasure, shuffling her feet in the mud. Neva turned on the water again, set the nozzle to the hardest stream possible, and pointed it straight into Hannah's open mouth. Hannah moved her tongue back and forth and let the spray hit

187

the back of her throat at full strength. 'She loves this,' Neva said. 'Go on in. I'm just finishing up.'

They found Sam and Reginald in the food preparation room, cutting apples. The boy lit up when he saw Winslow. 'Hey, you remembered!'

'Course,' Winslow said.

'Well, we're going to walk the elephant pretty soon,' Reginald said.

'Soon as she's done with her bath.' Sam handed a second knife to Winslow. 'If you're going to hang around here, you've got to work, though. Hannah doesn't like slackers.'

Truman said, 'You think it's okay for the boys to be here for an hour or so? It won't interfere?'

'Nah,' Sam said. 'Sugar likes the company, and we were going to take a walk anyway. You can come along, too, if you've got a mind to.'

Truman lifted his hand. 'Thank you, but I've got some things I need to take care of in the office. Have you seen Harriet?'

Sam frowned. 'No sir. I'm glad of it, too.'

Truman watched Winslow belly up to the counter beside Reginald and grab a couple of apples from a plastic wash tub. 'You knew Max Biedelman very well, didn't you?'

'We were friends. She was a fine lady, no mistake. It riles me to see that Harriet Saul strutting around here. You ask me, she's nothing but a cheap trick in a safari suit.'

Truman tried to suppress a smile and failed, shaking his head. 'She's a vision all right,' he said. 'Have you seen this morning's newspaper?'

'No, sir, I generally don't see the paper until I get home at night. Are you talking about the *News-Gazette*?'

'Yes. There's a full-page feature about Harriet and Maxine Biedelman on the front of the Lifestyle section.'

Sam glowered. 'Do they have any pictures of Hannah in there?'

'One or two,' Truman said, trying to remember. 'Most of them were of Harriet with zoo visitors.'

Reginald and Winslow appeared in the food prep doorway, holding the wash tub of apples between them. 'We're all done, mister,' said Reginald. 'We cut them real carefully, too. You sure she doesn't mind eating the stems and seeds? I'd mind.'

'Naw, she doesn't mind,' Sam said. 'It's good for her digestion. And she might just plant an apple tree along the way.'

Truman shook Sam's hand. 'I'll say goodbye, then. And thank you for letting the boys spend time with you. Next time we'll be sure to give you some notice before we show up.'

Sam clasped his hand. 'We don't need any notice. They're good kids, plus shug's always happy to have a new face to look at, especially a child's.'

'Winslow, stay out of the way, now, and do what Mr Brown tells you,' Truman said. 'I'll be back in an hour and a half.'

Neva was just stowing the hose when Truman left the barn. 'Beautiful day,' he said. 'It must be much harder to do what you do in the rain.'

Neva shrugged. 'You adapt. It's never good, but it's not so bad, either.'

'Well, I'd whine,' Truman said.

Neva smiled. 'So how's Miles?'

Truman hung his head. Just that morning the piglet

189

had chewed the bottom out of a plastic wastebasket in Winslow's bathroom, but why go into it?

'Listen, can I ask you a question?' Neva said, walking with him to the gate.

'Sure.'

'How much does it cost a year for Hannah's care and upkeep?'

Truman frowned. 'I'd have to look at the budget, but ballpark, it's around a hundred, hundred and twenty-five thousand dollars, if you include staff salaries and benefits. Maybe a little more. There's actually a separate trust Max Biedelman established so that Hannah would always be given the proper care. It includes the money for one salaried position, Sam's, and it's separate from the zoo's other operating expenses. It's something I didn't know about until recently. My father only unearthed it a couple of days ago. The money wasn't a surprise, but the fact that it was in a discretionary fund was. God knows how much of it has actually reached Hannah, all these years.'

Neva squinted in the sunlight. 'Hypothetically, if Hannah were to leave the zoo for any reason – not die, but be relocated, say – would the trust go with her?'

Truman looked at her, surprised. 'I have no idea, but it's probably addressed in the provisions of the trust. Why?'

Neva shrugged, but there was clearly more going on behind her eyes. 'No reason.'

'Ah.'

'Listen, would you have lunch with me some time?'

'I'd like that. Not at the Oat Maiden, though.' Truman shuddered. 'Anywhere but the Oat Maiden.'

Neva smiled. 'All right. You can choose the place. How about Monday, then?'

'That would be fine. Harriet is a bit odd about employee fraternization so it might be best if we make this our little secret.'

'Is that why her receptionist was fired?'

'No,' Truman said carefully. 'I believe Brenda failed to show the proper respect.'

'I wouldn't last five minutes up there.'

Truman sighed. 'Few do.'

From time to time, as they walked through the zoo, Hannah tucked her trunk under Sam's arm.

'How come she does that, mister?' Reginald said. 'Put her trunk in there like that?'

'Because she can't hold my hand.'

'What do you mean?'

'Watch her,' Sam said. 'She usually does it when something makes her feel nervous. Too many people around, especially on her blind side, or maybe she hears a noise she doesn't recognize.'

'She's *scared*?' Reginald laughed. 'She gets scared? Hell, she's bigger than anything I've ever seen.'

'Don't be disrespectful, boy,' Sam said sternly. 'If you're going to be disrespectful, you can just walk home right now.'

Reginald ducked his head. 'Sorry, mister. I didn't mean anything.'

'You say your sorries to Hannah, not to me. Do you have an apple in your pocket?'

'Yeah.' Reginald withdrew two apple quarters.

Sam nodded. 'Then you apologize and give her that apple.'

Reginald held out the apple pieces on the palm of his

hand. 'You can eat them if you want to,' he told Hannah. She picked the two pieces neatly off his hand and popped them into her mouth.

'Isn't that something, how she can be so dainty like that?' Sam said. 'I've never gotten over it, not even after all these years.'

Winslow spoke. 'Is she scared of us – of me and Reginald, I mean?'

'Nah, at least not right now. You're not doing anything but walking, and she's good about people walking on her seeing side, at least as long as they're people she knows. Guess she's seen you both enough to know you. Now, see that man right there, the one coming toward us who's walking real fast? Big man?'

The boys watched. The man passed close by her blind side and Hannah tucked her trunk into Sam's armpit. 'Baby doesn't like people coming at her fast like that when she can't see them,' he explained. 'She doesn't leave her trunk with me very long, because that's the business end of an elephant, but it makes her feel better.'

'What else is she afraid of?' Winslow asked.

Sam shrugged. 'I don't always know. It could be a small thing. You ever been afraid of a bee? Most bees won't do you any harm, but you jump anyway. Same for Hannah.'

The boys walked along thoughtfully.

'What are you afraid of?' Sam asked Reginald.

'Nothin'.'

'Now, that's not true. Everybody's afraid of something.'

'I'm afraid of trains,' Winslow volunteered.

'Trains?' Sam said.

'The noise when they go by, and that whoosh after they're gone, like they're going to suck you right up.'

192

Sam nodded. 'Well, I could see that.'

'I'm afraid of my aunt when she gets mad,' Reginald said. 'She starts talking and talking, and the spit just *flies*.'

'What does she talk about?' Winslow asked.

'How I'll end up in the gutter if I don't try extra hard, how it's in my blood. I don't think so, though.'

'She probably just wants you to make something of yourself,' Sam said. 'Woman is looking out for you, son. You remember that.'

'Yeah.'

Sam fished a small gourd out of his canvas pouch and handed it up to Hannah. 'Either of you suck your thumb when you were little?' he asked.

'I did,' Winslow admitted.

'Well, Hannah sucks her trunk sometimes, if she's feeling spooky, especially at night. Girl doesn't like the dark.'

The boys smiled at the thought.

'She ever cry, mister?' Reginald asked.

'I've never seen her cry, exactly, but she gets down-hearted from time to time. Could be she's thinking about her mama, who got killed on that plantation in Burma. Or maybe she's thinking about Miss Biedelman. We miss her, even after all these years.'

They walked in silence for a minute or two, watching people smile at Hannah as they walked past.

'She's got you, though,' Reginald said.

'Yeah,' Sam said after a minute. 'She's got me.'

Neva waited until she was at home that evening before making her call to Alice McNeary, the director of the Pachyderm Sanctuary, to talk about Hannah. Alice was a gravel-voiced, plainspoken, tough-as-leather old circus

193

trainer who'd been on the circuit for twenty-five years before giving it up to found the sanctuary. Neva gave her an overview of Hannah's circumstances, including the inadequacy of her yard and ending with the state of her feet.

'So when did you say she last lived with other elephants?' Alice asked.

'1954, I think. She lived with one old cow for about a year. She's been alone ever since.' Neva sat at the kitchen table, where Kitty was laid out, snoring loudly.

'How about keepers?'

'That's its own story: she's had the same man with her for forty-one years, a good man. But he's sixty-eight now, and his health is bad.'

'So how does he feel about Hannah's leaving? Would he support it?'

'If she were leaving to go there? Absolutely.'

'And the zoo? Which one is it again?'

'The Max L. Biedelman. In Bladenham, Washington.'

'What the hell are you doing in a place like that?' Alice said.

'It's a long story.'

'I didn't know they even had an elephant.'

'Give it another couple of weeks and everyone will know. The director's launching a big marketing campaign about Hannah and Maxine Biedelman.'

'I thought Max was a man,' Alice said.

'Max is short for Maxine.'

'Isn't she dead?'

Neva sighed. 'Yes. It's hard to explain. The zoo director is actually billing herself as Maxine Biedelman, walking around in period clothes, giving talks, stuff like that. I can send you an article that came out about her this morning.'

'Do that. How does she feel about the prospect of giving up the zoo's main attraction?'

'That's the thing – she doesn't know anything about it. She's a controlling harridan. We're going to have to get such overwhelming grassroots support that by the time she gets wind of it, there won't be any way out. And frankly, even if we can pull that off, which I doubt, it will probably get ugly by the end. You need to know that up front.'

Alice laughed. 'And when has that ever stopped me? You know I love a good fight. But we'll have to be very clear that I'm not raiding the zoo – the situation was brought to the sanctuary's attention, not the other way around. That's the only way my board would even consider her.'

'I know that.' Neva passed her hand over Kitty's flabby gut.

'Do you have other people working with you? You can't do this alone, you know; no one can do it alone. You're tough, honey, but you're not *that* tough.'

'No, it won't be me, alone. There are several of us, already. The trick will be to keep it away from the zoo until we're ready to go public.'

'Look, here's what we'll do. I'll brief my executive committee and go ahead and put her on a wait-list. There are four animals ahead of her, though, and I only have room for two. And my board's very tough on this. Any animal coming here has to bring two hundred fifty thousand dollars along as an endowment for their care. Those are the terms. No money, no dice.'

'Well, all right, then,' said Neva. 'I guess I'd better go out and find me some rich people.'

'Keep me informed,' said Alice. 'And I'll do a little

sniffing around, myself. I know a couple of people up in Seattle who might be willing to help.'

On Monday, Truman picked Neva up just outside the zoo gates and drove them to a place on the far side of town called Teriyaki Time, where he was relatively sure no one from the zoo would see them. The restaurant occupied a narrow slot at the center of an older strip mall – two tables wide, twenty-five tables deep, backed up by a stifling kitchen and one unisex restroom with wall fatigue. It was one of Winslow's favorites, a place they often resorted to after work when Truman lacked culinary inspiration. The owner greeted him enthusiastically.

'Hey, Truman! How's it going?' He shook Truman's hand and looked admiringly at Neva.

'Hello, Thomas. Neva, meet Thomas Kubota. This is his restaurant. Thomas, this is Geneva Wilson. She's an elephant keeper at the zoo.'

Thomas shook Neva's hand admiringly. 'No kidding?'

'No kidding.'

'I'll be damned. You're pretty small to be bossing a big animal around.'

'It's all in the wrist.'

Thomas handed Neva a menu. 'Take this with you. He won't need one.'

'Home away from home?' Neva asked Truman when they'd found a table at the very back of the restaurant.

'More often than I care to admit. Winslow puts up with my cooking, but there are times when neither one of us can summon the necessary forbearance.'

'So you come here.'

'So we come here. You don't see anyone from the zoo here, do you?'

'You'd probably know better than I would,' Neva said. 'But I don't recognize anyone.'

'Thank god. I've never been any good at cloak and dagger sorts of things. I hardly ever do anything illicit, and whenever I do, I get caught.'

'For example?'

'Sneaking things onto Harriet's desk to sign when I know she isn't in there. Leaving work ten minutes early.'

'You sneak?'

'From time to time. I'm not proud of it.'

'And that's the best you can come up with?'

Truman thought for a minute. 'Well, lately, anyway. I did steal a candy bar when I was six. It was a Payday. I slipped it into my pocket and the next thing I knew, my mother was hauling me up to the store manager's booth demanding that I make a full confession. My mother was the district attorney here for thirty years. I've never fully recovered.'

'So what did the manager do?'

'Winked. He winked at me. It was very confusing.'

While Neva examined the menu, Truman allowed himself to take her in. He had a nearly overwhelming desire to touch her. He imagined it would be like touching a lightly charged wire, that he would feel the hum and the heat. He was startled to realize that she was blushing. 'Was I staring?' he said.

'Yes.'

'I'm sorry. It's a novelty to be here with anyone older than eleven. Not to mention nice-looking.'

'Winslow's nice-looking.'

197

'Even so.'

A waiter arrived to take their order. Once he was gone, Neva appeared to marshal herself and said, 'Look, I'd like to talk to you about something.'

'Uh oh.'

'The thing is, it's got to be held in the strictest confidence. If you'd rather I not involve you, this would be a good time to say so.'

'It doesn't involve Paydays, by any chance?'

Neva looked startled. 'I can't promise that.'

'You're not planning a candy heist, are you?'

'What?'

'Candy? Payday bars,' Truman reminded her gently.

'Oh! I was thinking payday with a small "p", as in "to get paid". You're not the only one who doesn't lie or cheat very well.'

While their waiter slid plates of teriyaki chicken in front of them, Neva took a deep breath and said, 'Is there any chance at all that the zoo might get another Asian elephant to keep Hannah company?'

Truman looked startled. 'Not that I've ever heard of. We're certainly in no financial position to do that. Why?'

Neva picked at her teriyaki. 'There isn't any way at all?'

'I don't see how. The zoo's revenues haven't met operating expenses in years. Short of receiving a huge endowment, I can't see how we'd be able to support a second elephant. And, to be frank, if we *did* get a huge endowment, I'd recommend using it for physical plant maintenance and repairs, not acquiring another animal.'

Neva clasped her hands in front of her and said quietly, 'Okay, then here's the thing. I'm going to try to get

Hannah relocated to an elephant sanctuary in northern California. I can't believe I'm saying this to you.'

'What? Why?'

'Because she'll die if she has to stay here after Sam Brown retires.'

'*What?* Has something happened? Is he retiring?'

Neva poked at the ice cubes in her water glass with her fork. 'Look, I'm not very good at this. No, nothing's happened. Yet. But Sam's sixty-eight years old and he's got diabetes. It catches up with you fast, at his age. He doesn't want to talk about it, but I don't think he's going to be able to work that much longer. And once he's gone you might as well put a gun to Hannah's head, except it'll be worse than that because it'll be slower. Way slower.'

'I don't understand. You're very capable. Are you resigning?'

'No, no, that's not the thing. The thing is, elephants, especially female Asian elephants, are extremely social. They live in herds dominated by a single leader – usually a female, but in Hannah's case Sam is her herd. And her leader. Take that away and what she's left with is a yard that's way too small, a barn that's a hellhole, chronically infected feet, and advancing arthritis, especially when she has to stand on a concrete substrate all day, which she will once Sam's gone because she won't be going on walks around the zoo anymore. Sam keeps her calm, but without him I wouldn't trust her out there, she's too skittish. So her entire world will shrink to about three thousand square feet of concrete and up to fourteen hours a day chained to a wall.'

'Good god.'

'Look. I'm not anti-captivity and I don't have a bleeding

heart. I've been taking care of zoo animals for twenty years, and I believe deeply in what zoos do, what keepers do, and how we do it. But I also believe in doing what's right for the animals first. Hannah's a wonderful elephant and she's adapted amazingly well. She's not neurotic, and she's never hurt anybody. But that could change – it's almost guaranteed to change – once Sam isn't here. We need to get her out. And I'd like your help.'

Truman pushed his plate away. He didn't really know this woman, but he trusted her. He watched her knock rice around her plate with a fork.

'Yeah,' she said. 'Kaboom.'

That evening, Truman stood at the stove stirring a pan of spaghetti sauce while Miles and Winslow played nose hockey across the kitchen floor with a plastic puck. He didn't know who was more delighted, the pig or the boy. During a break in the cooking he got his camera and found two remarkably similar pairs of dark eyes dancing wickedly through the lens.

When it was ready, Truman set a plate of spaghetti on the round oak table for Winslow, and a second one for himself. On a placemat in the corner Miles received his own small dish of pasta, which he consumed in four gulps and a burp. Truman was discovering a certain charm in the little pig. His utter lack of guile, his naked and cheerful dedication to his appetites – food, warmth, and affection – were not so different from Winslow's or Truman's. By some obscure Darwinian chance eons ago, humans cared for pigs and not the other way around. But surely it could have gone differently another day. Admittedly Truman overcompensated. Miles ate cereal for his breakfast just as Winslow did, down to the brand name and the milk. At the end of each meal, his dishes were washed and stored in a cupboard. He had his own polar fleece throw in the den.

Truman remembered being similarly uneasy when he and Rhonda had first brought Winslow home. He could still remember the terror he'd felt when he looked down for the first time at the gently pulsing soft spot on the top of Winslow's skull. When he was anywhere near the baby he'd tiptoed, whispered, walked slowly. Rhonda, on the other hand, had seemed faintly disappointed with the entire experience, changing diapers indifferently, complaining about the unceasing demands Winslow made on her time and attention. It was Truman who had rocked, sung, burped, and borne the warm, damp weight of the baby as he slept. Even eleven years later there were moments when, in Winslow's presence, Truman felt stunned by love.

Miles slammed the plastic hockey puck into the side of Truman's foot, breaking his reverie. 'Winslow, I'd like your opinion about something.'

The boy looked up, strands of spaghetti arrested mid-suck. Truman smiled. 'Tell me about Hannah. What's she like?'

The boy shrugged. 'I don't know. Big. She's big.'

'Is she scary? Do you ever feel as though she might hurt you?'

'No, she's real gentle. *She* gets scared sometimes, though.'

'Does she? By what?'

'She doesn't like when people run. She's blind in her left eye.'

'I didn't know that.'

Winslow nodded solemnly. 'Sam says when he used to take her for walks in the woods she'd get upset if he got too far away. You can tell she likes Sam. She hugs his head with her trunk. He keeps a hand on her when we take her for walks. Me and Reginald do that sometimes, too.'

'I wouldn't think that would keep her from running away.'

'She'd never run away, Dad. Sam says he does it to keep her from getting spooked. Me and Reginald asked if we could take her for a walk by ourselves sometime, but he said she wouldn't go unless he was with her.'

'Ah.'

'She's real smart, though. Like, Sam says she can tell when he has a headache. I guess he gets these real bad headaches, and she'll just stand over him like she's guarding him until he feels better.'

'Does it help?'

'Yup.' Winslow twirled a huge forkful of spaghetti and continued talking through his food. 'Sometimes she'll give him stuff, too, like these little round rocks she likes to play with. She'll bring them to him. He says he doesn't know why. He says if it's a real bad day she'll even bring him her tire. You know, that car tire she sleeps with at night.'

'She sleeps with a tire?'

'It's not funny, Dad.'

'I didn't say it was funny.'

'Sam says she uses it to keep her company when she's chained up by herself all night.'

Truman wondered if he could bear to hear more. 'What do you think would happen to her if Sam couldn't take care of her anymore?'

'That'd never happen, Dad.'

'But if it did?'

'It won't.'

'Humor me.'

'She'd die.'

Truman stared. 'Why do you say that?'

Winslow shrugged matter-of-factly. 'Because she would.'

Truman let Winslow finish his meal and clear the table. Then he picked up the telephone and called Neva Wilson.

Chapter 14

A s the fall of 1957 deepened into winter, it was inex-
plicably spring in Miss Effie's heart. She unearthed
from her trunks delicate lace dresses with high collars
and mutton chop sleeves that had been the height of
fashion in 1905. She spent hours in front of her dressing
table mirror fixing her hair with combs and rhinestones,
a Gibson Girl once again. With Sam she was coy, asking
him to fetch the delicate accessories she had packed away
so lovingly a half-century before: ivory fans and silk-
tasseled parasols, silk shawls and kid gloves so fine you
could see the outline of each fingernail through the
leather. And then, one sad morning, she erupted into a
fit of temper at the inability of her servant to find a
button hook. There were no servants. Having journeyed
back to a better time, Miss Effie had mistaken Sam for
a household domestic.

'I believe Effie has left us,' Max Biedelman told Sam
when it seemed that Effie's departure this time would be

a lasting one. 'She's turned into a foolish old woman, and she would have hated that, had she known. She means no offense, Mr Brown, though of course her behavior is inexcusable.'

Sam brushed this aside. 'Miss Effie doesn't know any better. Where she's gone seems like a happy place, and that's something to be thankful for. I hope I keep my spirit half as good when I'm her age.'

To his astonishment, Max Biedelman turned from him with welling eyes. 'You are a good man, Mr Brown,' she said, clapping a hard hand on his forearm and then going to stand at the front room window to regain her composure. At last she said, 'Do you know, I've been in many frightening situations over the years, even times when I was in mortal danger, but I have never felt so powerless as I do now. It's humiliating to grow old, Mr Brown. One loses one's dignity.'

'That isn't true, sir. You're the most dignified lady I've ever met outside of my grandmother on my daddy's side. You stand right up and say what's on your mind. You're a shining example.'

Max Biedelman turned. 'I'd like to hear about your grandmother on your father's side. Please sit, Mr Brown. I've forgotten my manners.' She gestured to a fine, tapestry-covered chair across from her.

Sam sat down carefully. 'My grandmother, now, that's a story,' he said. 'The woman was as tough as an old boot, brought eleven children into this world and kept eight of them alive to over the age of fifteen, which was a rare trick in those days, at least where my folks were from originally, down in Arkansas. Corinna, her folks were real poor except for the land they farmed, but that land was theirs, homesteaded fair and square. My daddy's folks were townspeople, which was completely different. They didn't have so much as an extra "Howdy". My daddy's daddy worked the railroad, laying track eighty miles east of Jesus. The man was gone for months at a time. My grandma would get his pay, but it wasn't enough to feed all those children, so she worked as a washerwoman, did clothes for anyone who had a penny or two to spare. She did fine needlework, too, and taught all the girls in the family to do fancy work right along with her – nickel a hanky, dime for lace to trim a dress or a petticoat. Rumor was, she also hired herself out to keep a man company, but the family never believed that part, mainly because she was too tired most of the time to have anything left to hire out, if you know what I mean. Her name was Leeza, at least that's what everyone called her. Probably short for Elizabeth, now that I think about it. She had a proud head, always kept her nose up like she was smelling something sweet, didn't take guff off anybody. My daddy tells a story about her chasing a little bitty white man around the town with a hatchet for cheating her out of twenty-five cents he owed her for some washing. Dangerous thing for a black woman to do, but Leeza wasn't about to give up on that twenty-five cents. To hear my daddy tell it, half the town turned out for the showdown, which was her pulling him down into the mud on Main Street and sitting on his chest spouting scripture. Man not only paid her what he owed her, he promised to go to church the following Sunday.' Sam chuckled softly. 'The woman wasn't afraid of danger, *no* sir. No black person in their right mind stood up to white people back then, not even about money to feed their children. Old Leeza, though, she told the family she was too damned tired to put up with it anymore, fingers full of calluses and half-blind from the fancy work. I guess something just snapped. Funny thing was, she and her girls got plenty of work after that. People respected her. Feared her, too. Figured any black woman crazy enough to do what she did had to be someone to reckon with. The family was sure proud of her. By the time I knew her, she was just a scrawny little thing, old hen too tough to eat and too ornery to kill.'

Max Biedelman smiled. 'A splendid story, Mr Brown, and a remarkable woman.'

'Tell you the truth,' Sam said, shaking his head, 'the family steered pretty clear of old Leeza those last few years. You never knew when she might take offense at something and come after you with that crooked finger of hers jabbing at you like a steel spike. Woman might have been righteous in the eyes of the Lord, but she sure was touchy.'

Sam stood up, and Max Biedelman struggled to her feet, too. 'Do you know, Mr Brown, I believe you made that story up just to cheer me. And you have.'

'No, sir,' Sam protested. 'Every word of it's true.'

'Well then,' said Max Biedelman, a little bit of hell finally coming back into her eyes, 'I shall have to search my family archives for one that will top it.'

'That would be a tough thing to do,' Sam smiled. 'But I do love a good story, me and Hannah both. You just say the word, and we'll be here.'

Max Biedelman pressed his arm as she saw him to the door. 'I count on that, Mr Brown,' she said.

* * *

Harriet fussed over her finches, wondering if they knew how beautiful they were. They were no more substantial than a dandelion blown into the wind; their songs were heavier than their bones. So ponderous in motion herself, she had always wondered what it would be like to take wing, to no more than wish yourself airborne to *be* airborne. She'd built a large aviary in her home, devoting two whole rooms to her birds, so they could fly. In the last several weeks she had sat inside the aviary often, feeling the breath of their flight on her face as they passed. Now, late on a dark Thursday evening, she confronted squarely the fact that Truman Levy had abandoned her.

For months he had shared her deep devotion to the zoo. They had talked at length, familiarly; sometimes he even put his feet up on her second visitor's chair, crossing one neat ankle over the other, his brown leather loafers as spruce as he was. He often came in on weekends to take care of some detail or two, and he always stopped to chat with her before going home. Several times she had invited him out to lunch, and he had always accepted. He was only five or six years younger than she was; she had once or twice caught herself wondering if a more intimate relationship might be possible.

But that had all changed when Neva Wilson came to the zoo. Harriet was no fool – she could sense immediately that Truman was different toward her. He was a courtly man, but his slight distaste for Harriet bled through his exquisite manners. It was true that she'd been featured in a number of newspaper articles as well as the new advertising campaign, but it was all for the good of the zoo, not for Harriet's personal aggrandizement. She had expected his enthusiastic support and congratulations, but instead she detected a certain impatience, even a degree of discomfort. Whatever the exact reason, their shared commitment to the zoo − which was to say, to each other − was clearly eroding.

Harriet was never sure at what age she had recognized that she would probably never marry. She had been young; younger than thirty-five, certainly. Younger than thirty? Impossibly young, if she'd been younger than thirty, and yet her final descent into the hell of the department store makeover had been the end of a journey, not the beginning. It marked the death of her last fading hope that she might yet rise above her plain heritage, conquer her big bones and overstated features, her mannish hands and dull hair. By the time she was in her late twenties, the list of social opportunities that she had never experienced was already long: make-out parties, high school proms, homecoming dances, festival courts, double dates, drive-in movies, sorority pledges, fraternity weekends. Instead there had been an endless string of weddings, weekend after weekend during which she was politely added to the guest lists of cousins, colleagues, neighbors. She had worn permanent creases in her one good suit from all of them; had spent money she didn't have on silver plate and cheap crystal for the gifts. And she was greeted the same way at each one: *Why, Harriet! How good to see you! How long has it been − yes? Well, really. That long?* As though it was her fault, as though she had been deliberately withholding herself from their loving if absent-minded arms, rather than left to fend for herself for yet another Christmas, another Easter or Thanksgiving. *Harriet, dear! How grown-up you look!* they'd say, when what they meant was matronly, dowdy, plain.

She was not deluded. Nor, however, did she believe in self-pity. She was a woman of strength who believed that productivity was, if not a substitute for beauty, at least a damned good second. For every lover she'd failed to attract, she'd achieved a new promotion, a new title, a raise. She began to decline the endless string of baby showers that had replaced the wedding invitations, using the saved gift money to buy finches instead, and then to build an aviary in the first small house she had bought for herself on her thirtieth birthday.

In all those years, there'd never even been a serious boyfriend. Not that she was a virgin; there had been men from time to time, more or less interchangeably. As marriage prospects, however, they had lacked luster and freshness. At first they phoned several times a week, proposing movie dates or dinner at inexpensive ethnic restaurants. Credit cards being too ambiguous for the cheapskate, cash was often laid on the table so Harriet could see for herself that she was expected to come up with the balance of the bill. Then the calls would come less and less frequently until finally they failed to come at all. Harriet rarely noticed until weeks had gone by.

But she'd thought that Truman was different. He had the smooth cheeks and clear, light eyes of a younger man, coupled with hands so beautiful they might have belonged to Michelangelo, hands capable of pulling a soul out of stone. But clearly she'd been wrong. As her birds muttered and trilled peacefully all around her in the aviary's artificial sunlight, she picked up the telephone and called the zoo to listen one more time to Truman's recorded voice regret that he was not available.

★　★　★

211

Across town in her apartment, Neva was in a less philosophical frame of mind. Another gale had blown in off Puget Sound, the third in a week, with wind and rain keeping inside anyone who had a choice – including Hannah. Neva and Sam had treated her to a long indoor bath with warm water, and later Neva taught her to blow bubbles using a child's bubble hoop and Dawn dishwashing liquid. But despite their best efforts they were losing ground. From what Sam had said about the weather, it would rain more or less continuously until spring, making it nearly impossible to keep Hannah's feet dry. Even now, and in spite of the apple cider vinegar footbaths, the abscess under her toenail was worse, and so was Sam, judging by his rapidly diminishing energy and noticeable limp. Time was becoming an increasingly pressing issue all over.

Now Neva sat in her Goodwill armchair in her one-room apartment, scratching Chip's ears as he dozed in her lap. Someone must be missing him tonight. He was a gentlemanly soul, sturdy and calm, an ankle-winder, a lap-sitter, a champion sleeper with a deep, resonant purr and excellent Manchu whiskers. He usually appeared in the tunnel from Johnson Johnson's house as soon as he heard Neva open her front door.

The windows rattled as sudden hail clattered against the glass like BBs. Sam had told her he and Corinna spent evenings like these in the barn because storms made Hannah anxious, and there were a lot of storms in this part of the Northwest. Neva sometimes found their devotion unnerving, as though Hannah's Hannah-ness were more important to Sam than her elephant-ness – as could certainly be the case, given that Sam had never worked

212

with or visited another elephant, or even another zoo. He and Corinna were also childless; if she remembered right, there had been something about a baby many years ago, some tragedy. She resettled Chip on her lap and contemplated the nature of loss. Six months ago, she had been sitting in the waiting room of a dental office in Yonkers, New York, when across the room a boy reading a book went off in her mind like a bomb. He had a long, slender face and hair that blazed like autumn, the exact shade of red that children hated the most because it was all people saw. He might have been her, twenty-five years earlier.

Or he might have been her son.

She'd left the office with a pounding heart. In putting her baby up for adoption she had agreed that she would never try to find the child, or assign or retain anyone else to do so. But she had asked if the dental office could slip her appointment back by an hour, went to a nearby Barnes & Noble, and bought a book about dragons that the clerk assured her would suit an eleven-year-old boy. Then she returned to the dental office.

'I just noticed this book in my backpack,' she said, lying to the receptionist. 'I must have picked it up by accident – it belongs to the boy who was here this morning, and I'd like to return it to him. Can you tell me his name, or maybe an address where I can drop it off?'

'You can just leave it with me and I can call for you,' the girl had said brightly, tapping her teeth with blood-red fingernails. 'His mom was in for a cleaning. Valerie Nightingale. Pretty name.'

Neva had slid the book into an envelope, put a card

213

inside that simply said, 'I've heard this is a great book,' and sealed it up. No signature, no phone number. No harm. The boy was as good as dead, for her; she might as well have seen a ghost in that waiting room.

Truman sat at the kitchen table with his father. Matthew Levy had the build of a boy and the large, agile brain of a man perfectly suited to receiving and processing information. He had just explained to Truman that he'd unearthed no unexpected bounty for the Biedelman Zoo in either the city's or the law firm's archives.

'I hope you weren't counting on my finding a pot of gold,' he told Truman. 'It's very rare to find a windfall, you know, except in the movies.'

'No, it was just a wild hope,' Truman said. 'Did you by any chance review the provisions of Hannah's trust while you were there?'

'The trust?' Matthew hesitated, as though he was trying to remember. Truman recognized this as a trick of humility he'd learned years before as a prosecutor. Undisguised, his prodigious memory had given him a certain machine-like quality in the courtroom. "Yes, I did," he said now. 'Its provisions were very straightforward. Max established it to provide for Hannah's food, upkeep, and veterinary care. Unfortunately, it doesn't generate a great deal of money anymore.'

'That's an understatement. It probably seemed like a fortune when she set it up, though.'

'Yes, well, money isn't what it used to be,' Matthew smiled dryly. 'But then, it never was.'

Truman cleared his throat. 'Dad, if Hannah ever left the zoo, would the trust go with her?'

'Is she leaving?'

'No, but one of the keepers asked me that question, and I didn't have an answer.'

'I'd have to read the provisions again to be sure, but I don't recall anything stipulating that Hannah has to live in Bladenham as a condition of the trust. An error of omission, no doubt. I'm sure Max never even considered the possibility of Hannah's leaving – though, oddly, she didn't leave the trust with the Zoo in perpetuity. When Hannah dies, the money is to be disbursed by the trustee to an individual elephant or an elephant welfare organization of his choice. I'm sure your new director will fight that, when it happens.' A small glint appeared in the old man's eye. He had met Harriet Saul.

'Then who's the trustee?' Truman asked. 'I always assumed it was the zoo director.'

Matthew consulted a slim, leather-bound folder. 'No, no. I wrote down the name because I wasn't familiar with it. Here: Samson Brown. Is that someone you know?'

Truman leaned forward. 'He's her keeper. He's been with her since Max Biedelman was alive.'

'Yes, well, she named him as sole trustee, with no provisions for how his replacement should be selected if he predeceases the elephant. That struck me as odd – she was exceptionally thorough in arranging all the other details of her estate. Perhaps she and this man had some understanding between them. In any case, he'll be responsible for choosing the trust beneficiary after Hannah's death. If he doesn't predecease her, of course.'

'And if he does?'

Matthew frowned. 'Well, it would certainly be best if he names a successor beforehand. If he doesn't, the

215

position would most naturally fall to someone at the zoo – Ms Saul, in all likelihood, based on her position as chief administrator.'

Truman thought for a minute. 'So does this mean that Sam is Hannah's owner?'

'No, no. Technically the zoo – the institution – is her owner, since she's part of the property Max left to the city. But Samson Brown is, essentially, her appointed guardian. All decisions concerning her care and well-being must be made or approved by him.'

'You're kidding.'

'I take it this is a surprise.'

'To me, anyway.'

Matthew looked at Truman mildly. 'By the way, after her death Hannah's remains are to be interred on the Havenside grounds, beside Max's own grave. The city apparently granted her that variance.'

'She arranged for Hannah's burial?'

'As I said, she was thorough,' Matthew said. 'I suppose it's also possible she wasn't entirely in command of her faculties when she had the papers drawn up. Or maybe her attorney wasn't in command of *his* faculties, which strikes me as more likely.'

'What are you saying?' Truman said. 'Wasn't Tim Roscoe her attorney? He was with your firm.'

'And old as the dickens by then, too. I had no idea you were so interested in all this – I don't believe you've mentioned it before. I'll look into it a little more thoroughly if you'd like me to.'

'It would be information that might come in handy,' Truman said. Matthew raised an eyebrow but said nothing.

Winslow shuffled into the kitchen in his baggy socks. 'Why are you guys talking about Hannah? Is she okay?'

'She's fine,' Truman said. 'I was just asking your grandfather some hypothetical questions.'

Hearing a change in the tenor of the conversation, Miles rose from his bed beneath the piano in the den and thrust a slobbery rubber dog bone through the baby gate. When none of them responded he maneuvered a shred of towel onto his head. Matthew considered him doubtfully. 'Does he know what we're saying? He certainly seems to be very . . . involved.'

'He doesn't sleep,' Winslow said. 'Ever.'

'Of course he sleeps, Winnie,' Truman said. 'Just not at night.'

'*Ever*,' Winslow insisted.

'He's exaggerating,' Truman told Matthew.

Matthew finally turned in his chair to regard the pig head-on. Miles, encouraged, put on his most ingratiating pig-smile and perked up his ears. 'You know,' Matthew said, 'you might have just gotten a dog.'

After Matthew left, Truman stayed at the kitchen table listening to Winslow do warm-up scales on the piano and pondering the fact that by siding with Neva he was participating in a deception, not to mention one involving Harriet. He was uncomfortable with that, and he'd said as much to Neva when he'd called her last night with his decision.

'Look, I'm not comfortable with it, either,' she'd told him. 'I don't do things behind people's backs and I never have. If I thought there was any other way to get Hannah out, I'd jump at it. But I don't think there is. Do you? I'd love to hear another plan.'

217

Truman didn't have one.

'Then let's move on to something else. How's Miles?' she'd said.

In fact, the pig was being particularly solicitous these days, snuffling underfoot as Truman made dinner or packed lunch for Winslow. He had taken to bringing Truman love tokens – a stub of carrot, a savory kibble, a Wiffle ball; once, one of Truman's own slippers, slick with slobber. These the pig presented with a strangely Old World flourish, shifting from foot to foot until Truman looked down and feigned delight at such a gift.

'He hasn't rooted up the kitchen floor,' Truman had told Neva, 'or eaten anything that isn't generally acknowledged as food, so I'm cautiously optimistic. On the other hand, I worry about his happiness. Maybe he longs for other pigs. Do pigs need other pigs, to be fulfilled?'

He'd heard Neva laugh softly on the other end of the line. 'Truman, Truman.'

'What?'

'He's not us, you know. He's not human. Don't make things more complicated than they are.'

Truman wished he could ask her what she was wearing. He also wished he could ask her why there were fewer freckles on her hands than her forearms, when it should have been the other way around. Did she wear gloves a lot? If so, why? He also wished he could kiss her. A nice, slow, easy kiss, the kind that happened between two people who were completely at ease. He wished he could be at ease. Wanting the other person to be at ease made him uneasy. Intimacy was a complicated business.

In any event, Neva had gone someplace else. 'Look,' she'd said. 'Would it help you to know that Hannah is the most tractable elephant I've ever worked with? I can't believe I'm going to say this, but I also believe she's capable of deep feeling. I don't normally believe in attributing human emotions to animals, but I've seen her hover around Sam all afternoon when he isn't feeling well. If he goes into the barn and she can't follow, she'll wait by the door, sometimes for hours, until he comes back. Her behavior on his days off is totally different than it is when he's working. She's less sharp, less observant. She'll stay all day in one part of her yard, rocking or sucking her trunk. It takes a lot to engage her, and when you do, it doesn't last. Is this making sense to you? On Sam's days off, he and Corinna always come in after-hours to watch a movie or two with her, and Hannah knows that, so she'll start perking up, finally, at closing time.' Neva had sighed. 'It's hard to know what's right, but she can't stay here if she's going to have any quality of life after Sam's gone. I've gone over it and over it, and I still keep coming up with the same answer. Let's just start quietly and see where it takes us. Raising the money is going to be the hardest thing to do, never mind being discreet about it. You wouldn't happen to have half a million dollars lying around that you've just been waiting for the right moment to tell me about, would you?'

'If I did, I'd hand it over to you right now.'

Harriet had been sitting in her aviary for several hours with a bottle of wine, and now she poured out the last glass. Somewhere around the middle of the bottle she had gone to her bedroom briefly to change into her Maxine Biedelman clothes. She couldn't say why; no one was going to see her tonight. But she felt better in them,

219

much better. Maxine Biedelman would never call up Truman Levy or anyone else just to hear his voicemail message. Maxine Biedelman went her own way, shining the dual beams of her strength and independence far ahead into the darkness. No one would have dared to call her Bucket. Maxine was a force to be reckoned with.

Harriet took a yellow legal tablet from a little Indonesian teak table she'd bought recently and fished a pen out of her breast pocket. She had had reading lenses made for a pince-nez she'd found among Maxine's things in the attic, and now she clipped these on her nose as she consulted her notes.

She was developing a budget for renovating Havenside. The house had once been a place of glory, well-documented in the sheaves of photographs Harriet had winnowed from the files upstairs several nights before. In the styles of the great houses in Newport, Rhode Island, there had been painted skies on the ceilings, with birds and scudding clouds; ornate moldings and gothic arched windows and claw-foot bathtubs with taps in the shape of griffon heads. Though Maxine herself had been largely indifferent to these charms, she had evidently maintained the house's original architectural integrity for her father's sake.

According to the notes on Harriet's legal pad, it would cost between seven hundred and fifty thousand and one million dollars to return the house to its original splendor. She had already found a tent and awning vendor who would recreate Maxine's original campaign tent from photographs for twenty-three thousand. Restoring and maintaining Havenside's paths and gardens would cost another twelve thousand dollars.

One million thirty-five thousand dollars. It wasn't that much. Harriet estimated that she could raise the money through an aggressive capital campaign in less than two years. She would have Martin Choi run periodic articles keeping the citizens of Bladenham informed, fueling their civic pride. She would have the ad agency convince Seattle and Tacoma newspapers to write features, too, and see that the stories were picked up by the Associated Press, Reuters, and the other wire services, maybe even *USA Today* and CNN.

As Maxine, Harriet was also ripe for television coverage, including regional and even national morning programs and evening news magazines like *60 Minutes*. National Public Radio was another must-have, not so much for the audience it reached as for its prestige among the country's intelligentsia.

Harriet made a note to investigate the cost of commissioning original theme music – a signature piece, something robust and memorable that could be used in future zoo ads, but which, in the meantime, TV and radio producers could pick up and include in their coverage. Maybe the ad agency had green talent who would write the music for free in exchange for exposure.

And then, while sipping the last of the wine and paging idly through a stack of old photographs she had brought home from the zoo, Harriet Saul experienced an epiphany. Skipping over animal images, she studied for a long time a picture of Maxine Biedelman at the turn of the century on the Serengeti Plain in Africa. No girl now, but a woman standing tanned and clear-eyed, Maxine regarded the camera with a straight back and a faint smile, solidly grounded in her heavy brown boots. An energy beat from

221

the paper like a drum, not civilized but primal, elemental, a throbbing in the gut, in the belly like an oath. *I am, I am, I am.*

For the first time in her life, Harriet understood what her spirit had known for some time: she was in love.

Chapter 15

S am sat on a hassock in his living room, gently rubbing Corinna's poor flat feet and swollen ankles. 'You're getting too old to stand up all day, Mama,' he said.

Corinna dismissed his remark with a wave of the hand. 'That apple cider vinegar footbath helping the baby at all?'

'Not much.'

'A little?'

'I'm hoping,' Sam said.

'Yeah.'

Sam gently massaged Corinna's toes, lovingly running over each one the fingers of a healer who knows his limitations.

'You think it's really going to happen?' Corinna asked.

'What?'

'Moving the baby.'

'Don't know, Mama, but Neva's a tough little thing – determined, too. She doesn't like that Harriet Saul, either, so we've got a little bit of spite on our side, that and knowing it's the right thing to do, taking shug to that place.'

'I never thought of her living just with elephants.'

'You mean I've been dreaming it all these years and you never saw it?'

'No,' Corinna said.

'Why?'

'I don't know, exactly. The baby's people. I never thought of other elephants as people, not like shug.'

'They are, though,' Sam said, frowning. 'At least, they're *her* people. It doesn't matter if they're not ours, as long as they watch out for her.'

'Think she'll know what to say to them?' Corinna asked.

'If she doesn't, she'll learn. She must have known how to do it over there in Burma.'

'That was a long time ago.'

'I know that, Mama,' Sam said quietly. 'But she's going to be all right. I can feel it, like I felt she'd be all right as long as she was with us, all these years.'

'Yeah,' Corinna said, unconvinced. 'Do we have to get our money ready soon?'

Sam worked her flat arches with his thumbs. 'Not yet. Neva says Truman Levy's working on something.'

'Does she know we mean it when I said we'd give the money if it's going to make the difference in getting the baby to that place?'

'She knows, Mama.'

Sam stopped rubbing, holding Corinna's feet quietly in the palms of his hands.

'What are you thinking about?' she asked.

'Don't know who I'll be, without the girl.'

'I've thought that, too,' Corinna said softly.

'I guess we'll find out, when the time comes,' Sam said. He lowered Corinna's feet into her slippers, arranged her skirt over her ample lap, and kissed her hand.

'You think they'll let us visit her at that sanctuary?' Corinna asked.

'Neva promised, Mama. She gave her word.'

'Well.' Corinna heaved herself out of her chair and patted his cheek. 'I think I'd better see about supper.'

'Something I can do?'

'Nah, you just put your legs up.'

Sam stood until she was gone, then lowered himself into his own chair with gratitude. His legs were on fire from the knees down, and the ulcer was moving down onto the sole of his foot. He didn't know how much longer he could hold on, though he'd never tell that to Corinna. She worried too much as it was.

He parked his eyes on the far wall and found himself thinking about the baby they'd lost. At first Corinna had gone so far away in her mind, Sam had thought he might lose her, too. He didn't think he could bear that, thought that if it happened, he'd stop being himself altogether and change into a mean and bitter man who didn't give a single goddamn. But Corinna hadn't died, not outside or in, and except for her everlasting feud with God, she'd healed. Maybe not completely, maybe not perfectly, but mostly you couldn't see the scar, not even when you knew where to look.

But since Neva Wilson had started talking about moving Hannah to the sanctuary, Corinna had been suffering; Sam, too. They were too set in their ways to move to California, and neither of them had much experience with travel. They'd pretend they were planning to visit that place, but they'd never do it. They'd grieve. Hannah would go and they would not, and that was just the way it had to be.

Miss Effie died quietly at Havenside on Thanksgiving Day, 1957, attended only by Max Biedelman. In the weeks before her death, a series of strokes had reduced her to an angelic presence no longer capable of speech but lit from within by a gentle light.

Even in her grief Max Biedelman preferred privacy, handling all the arrangements herself. In any case there were very few to make. Neither she nor Effie had living family anymore, and the women had been too isolated in their last years even for friendships. When Effie's ashes had been returned from the crematorium, Max Biedelman had reached Sam at the elephant barn and asked him to accompany her on a walk.

He and Hannah went up to the house as quickly as they could and found the old woman on the porch waiting for them, dressed in black trousers and an exquisitely cut black coat. 'They used to call them widow's weeds, Mr Brown,' she said with a certain irony. 'I had my tailor prepare them some months ago.' She had a canvas satchel over her shoulder, heavy enough for her to bow slightly beneath its weight.

'You want me to carry that for you, sir?'

'I'm fine, Mr Brown. Thank you.'

They proceeded in silence, Max Biedelman leading them with quick steps. Sam wondered if the doctor had given her some kind of pain-killing medicine to ease her grief, but even if he had, Sam doubted she'd have taken it.

226

No, he guessed her vigor was shock, like people who walked ten miles out of the wilderness on broken feet. Sam and Hannah fell in behind her, not slowing down until they had reached the little clearing where she and Miss Effie had liked to come with books and a picnic lunch. As soon as they stopped, Hannah lifted the old woman's arm gently in her trunk and tucked it between her own leg and the wall of her chest.

Max gave her a firm pat with her free hand. 'I'm all right, Hannah,' she said, offering her a peppermint she pulled from her pocket. 'That's very nice of you, but I'm perfectly all right. Go along, now.'

Hannah stood for a minute, considering, and then freed Max Biedelman's arm.

Sam said, 'You go ahead, sugar. We'll call you if we need you.' Hannah padded off, but only as far as the edge of the clearing, where she stood with her back to the woods she loved, keeping Sam and Max Biedelman in her line of sight.

The old woman lowered her satchel to the ground in the watery sunshine and took out a fancy enamel urn Sam had never seen before. 'The ashes,' she explained. 'I would be honored, Mr Brown, if you would help me scatter them.'

They took turns releasing ashes around the clearing, into the breeze. They didn't speak, and when they were done the old woman simply unfolded her shooting stick and sat on the little stool with her back to Sam. He hunched on a stump nearby, bits of dry leaves falling through his fingers like tears. He and Corinna hadn't cremated the baby, but dressed her in a white lace christening gown Corinna had made when she'd still been

227

on good terms with the Lord, and buried her in a small pink casket with a white satin lining like God's angels must wear.

Finally Max Biedelman turned back to him, pulling her composure around her like a tattered coat. 'Well, Sam,' she said.

'You want me to take you home now, sir?' he said softly.

'Not yet. But you may stay with me a little longer. I would like that.'

'I'm right here.'

Max Biedelman sat quietly, her hands in her lap. Then she raised her worn eyes and said, 'I didn't intend to grow old, Mr Brown, but apparently it's happened anyway.'

'Yes, sir.'

'I shall miss her terribly.'

'You're mighty strong, sir. You're going to get through this all right.'

Max Biedelman regarded her hands holding each other in her lap. 'I don't know that I want to get through it. I don't know what the point of getting through it might be.'

'You've got your animals. You've got this place.'

'Yes.' The old woman rose wearily, calling to Hannah. 'You've reminded me that there are things to do.'

Sam stood, too. It had taken his grandmother seven years to die. He could see that Miss Biedelman meant to get it done quicker.

Johnson Johnson paced in his kitchen, waiting. He knew that Neva had gotten home because all three cats had disappeared down the tunnel. Finally there was a knock on his door.

'What surprise?' Neva said, holding the note he'd taped to her front door. He breathed in the smell of animal dung and musk and fruit and hay that wafted around her like a fine perfume. He smelled her sometimes at night, when he ran through his favorite memories at the end of the day.

'I made something,' he said. 'Come on.' He was out of the room and headed upstairs before Neva had even closed the outside door. He could feel her following warily. She'd be pleased, though, once she saw what he'd done.

'Here,' he said. Three steel drums sat on the wide landing outside his bathroom, where he'd been working on them under his yellow light bulb. He used the yellow light when he needed to hear as well as see something he was making. He didn't know why it worked that way, just that he'd always been able to hear better when it was turned on.

Neva inhaled sharply, running her hands over the drums. Johnson Johnson had cut them at different heights, and hammered their tops into different shapes. Around the outsides he'd painted friezes of elephants. From a rivet on the side of each drum he'd hung a rubber mallet with foam tape wrapped around the wooden handle as a grip.

'I thought, you know. For your elephant,' he explained.

'My god, they're *beautiful*,' Neva breathed. 'Can you play them?'

'You can.'

Neva gonged one of the drums tentatively. It returned a perfect C major. 'You've calibrated the entire drum to play true tones?'

229

Johnson Johnson blinked anxiously. 'Well, it's supposed to be for music.'

'You're amazing.'

'You think maybe she'll like them?'

'How could she not like them?'

'Well, I mean, she's an elephant,' he pointed out.

'Listen.'

'Huh?'

'Let's take them down to the zoo together,' Neva said.

'Me?'

'Sure. Don't you want to see her play them?'

'Okay.' Johnson Johnson hadn't ever been to the zoo. As far as that went, he hadn't ever seen an elephant, either, at least not in person. He went into his room and pulled on a sweatshirt. When he came back out, he found Neva reading his bathroom sink, which was painted in a swirling pattern and was accompanied by sayings like, THEN IT ALL WENT DOWN THE DRAIN and WE'RE REALLY GOING TO CLEAN UP, AREN'T WE?

'So you did this, too?'

'Uh huh,' Johnson Johnson nodded. He hadn't ever had anyone up here before. He wondered if the real reason he'd made the drums was because he'd have to make them under the yellow light bulb, which meant he'd have to show them to Neva up here, which meant she'd see his bathroom. He wasn't sure.

'Come see this,' he said, pulling her into his bedroom by the arm. She looked alarmed, and tried to pull away. He quickly closed the door behind them to make the room dark.

'No, let me—'

'Look up,' he said, letting go of her arm.

230

'What?'

He pointed to the stars. Neva looked up and did a double-take. 'You did this, too?'

'It's not done yet, though.' They both stood still, heads back, mouths slightly open, watching the evening stars. Then he opened the door and switched on the light again in case she was afraid of the dark. The walls of this room, too, were fully outfitted with a funhouse of ramps, stairs, launching platforms, hammocks, and perches for the cats. Chocolate popped up like a gopher through a hole in the floor.

Neva looked at Johnson Johnson, paused momentarily for effect, and said, 'What would you think about getting a pizza?'

'Pizza?' Johnson Johnson breathed, unsure of what else to say in the face of such an unexpected gift.

'Pizza,' Neva confirmed. 'I'll order it. There's something I want to ask you first, though, and it's got to be a secret for now.'

'Yeah, okay.'

'You know Hannah's the elephant I take care of.'

'Course.'

'Well, here's the thing. The zoo's not a good place for her anymore, and it won't ever be again. She needs to be moved to a big elephant park in California, but it's really expensive.'

Johnson Johnson nodded, wondering if he was supposed to say something yet. Neva kept going, though. 'I mean *really* expensive.'

'Okay,' he said. He could see Neva inhale. He thought she should really breathe more.

'So here's the question. Would you be willing to make

more drums like these, or maybe something like your sink or toilet, and let us sell them to raise money for Hannah? We'd buy the materials for you, so you wouldn't be out any money, just time.'

Johnson shrugged. 'Yeah. Okay.'

'Really?' Neva rocked up on the balls of her feet like he did himself when he was excited about something. 'You can think about it. I mean, are you sure?'

'Uh huh.'

She brought her hands to her mouth and said, 'You just don't know.'

He looked down at his feet. No, probably not. He usually didn't.

She grabbed his wrists and squeezed. 'No, no, what I mean is, you have no idea how much this means. There's someone I'd like you to meet, and I'd like to do it here, if you don't mind, so he can see your work.'

'Okay.'

'Can I ask him to come over now? Would that be okay?'

'Okay. He can have pizza.'

Neva went down to the kitchen and called Truman, who promised to be there as soon as he and Winslow had eaten dinner. She told him not to bother; they'd have food waiting for them. Then she called another number from a magnet on Johnson Johnson's refrigerator and ordered an extra-large pizza with everything. When she looked up she saw him standing in the doorway, nearly shivering with pleasure.

Half an hour later – five minutes behind the pizza delivery guy – Truman and Winslow knocked on Johnson

Johnson's door. Neva introduced them all around, passing out paper plates she'd fetched from her apartment. Johnson Johnson extended the pizza box to them with the utmost dignity.

Neva tore through her own slice. 'I can't wait to show you these drums Johnson's made for Hannah. And his sink.' She caught the look Truman gave her. 'I know. Just wait until you see them. Let's show you now. It won't take long, and then we can finish eating.' She turned to Johnson Johnson. 'Is that okay with you?'

'Okay,' he said. They'd already sampled perfection; eating the rest could wait.

Neva led the way upstairs. Johnson Johnson trailed behind. When they reached the landing, Neva put her hands over Truman's eyes until he was in position, then pulled her hands away. 'Ta-dah!'

Truman looked, tapped, gonged. 'These are extraordinary. Really – they're *beautiful*.'

Johnson Johnson flushed with pleasure.

Truman turned to Neva. 'You know, folk art has really come into its own in the last decade or so.'

'Any idea what they might sell for?'

Truman frowned. 'Well, if people knew they were to benefit Hannah – or, say, an anonymous but needy elephant – I'd bet a set like this could sell for two thousand, twenty-five-hundred dollars. Maybe more. I have friends who own an art gallery in Seattle. They could give us a better idea.' He turned to Johnson Johnson and said, 'Would you be willing to make some of these for us to sell?'

'He's already said yes,' Neva cut in.

'We couldn't pay you at all,' Truman continued. 'You understand that.'

Johnson Johnson pulled himself up to his full height and said, 'Course.'

'Look,' Neva said. 'Why don't we get dinner over with and bring the drums to Hannah? I want Johnson to see what she does with them. Harriet won't be there this late, will she?'

Truman consulted his watch. 'Probably not,' he said. 'Though with her, you can never be sure.'

'Can I use your phone?' Neva asked Johnson Johnson.

'Okay.' He watched her, liking the way she went around his kitchen absently touching everything. Blind people did that. Johnson Johnson did that, too.

Neva called Sam and Corinna's house. She let the phone ring eight times, but no one answered. Then she dialed the elephant barn. After four rings, Sam picked up.

'Sam? Is Corinna there, too?'

'Uh huh. We're watching Laurel and Hardy. Shug likes them, though I'll be damned if I know why.'

'Well, stay even if the movie ends. We're bringing something for Hannah.'

'We?'

'Just wait for us.'

'Now you've got me wondering.'

'You'll never guess,' Neva said, and hung up.

Johnson Johnson followed her down to the elephant yard. Neva carried one drum and Johnson Johnson carried two. Truman and Winslow had headed off to the mansion to make sure Harriet Saul wasn't there.

'You're sure Hannah won't ruin them if she hits them too hard?' Neva asked as they set the drums down while she unlocked the gate.

'Well, if she re-tunes them it'd probably be so she can

play her own songs better. Maybe elephant music doesn't sound like people music.'

'Huh,' Neva said, amazed anew by the cottage industry that was Johnson Johnson's mind. Sam met them at the barn door and helped them bring the three drums inside. Once they were safely through, Neva introduced him and Corinna to Johnson Johnson.

'Well, it's a pleasure to meet you,' Sam said, shaking hands and then turning to inspect the drums. 'Just look at these,' he said. 'Shug, come over here and see what this man's made for you. Music!'

Hannah shambled over from the television, cradling a small rock in the crook of her trunk. Neva patted her. 'Johnson, meet Hannah. Hannah, this is Johnson Johnson.'

Johnson Johnson held out his hand to shake, Hannah put down her rock to stretch her trunk, and they met someplace in the middle. Then Hannah walked her trunk up Johnson Johnson's arm, sniffing.

'Cats,' Neva explained.

'She's big,' he said.

'Well, she's an elephant.'

'Uh huh.'

Truman and Winslow slipped in the door. 'We're all clear,' Truman said. 'How'd she like them?'

'She hasn't actually noticed them yet,' Neva said. 'We're still making introductions.'

Done assessing Johnson Johnson, Hannah stretched her trunk toward Sam, nosing around his pocket. 'No treats left in there, shug,' he said. 'Here's your treat, right here. You sure you're okay with her giving them a test drive?' he asked Johnson Johnson.

Johnson Johnson just colored and hugged himself a little

235

tighter. Sam gave Hannah one of the mallets, and she wrapped her trunk around it and swung aimlessly.

'Baby girl, you've got to try banging it on Mr Johnson's drum like this.' Sam brought the second mallet down on one of the drums, producing a ringing G major. Hannah opened her eyes wide and lifted her trunk in great excitement. Sam slapped her shoulder supportively. 'You can do it, too, shug. Go on, now.'

Hannah hit the drum once, and then again, and soon there was a halting chain of notes, all perfectly pitched. Johnson Johnson rose up on his toes and bounced. Sam turned to him and grinned. 'You've done something awful nice, Mr Johnson. Sugar's never made music before.'

'Well, you know.' Johnson Johnson tucked his chin in embarrassment and pride. Sam clapped him on the back reassuringly.

Truman leaned toward Winslow and said, 'What do you think Miles would make of this?'

'He'd probably wish he had a trunk.'

Sam said, 'Is Miles your pig?'

'Yeah.'

Sam chuckled. 'Most pigs think they're God's gift. You put one of those drums on the ground, I bet he'd just pick up that mallet in his mouth and whale away.'

Neva watched Hannah play a riff between the two drums. It might have been music. Even if it wasn't, the notes were pleasing.

'I think we might want to talk about something,' Neva said.

All eyes turned.

'I think we need to talk about money.'

'The bad word,' Sam said.

'I know, but I think it's going to be up to us to get started. Even if we got the okay to move her out tomorrow, we'd need two hundred and fifty thousand dollars for the sanctuary to take her. Plus whatever it'll cost to transport her.'

'That's a whole lot of money,' Corinna said. 'We're ready to give what we've got, but it won't look like much against that kind of need.'

Truman cleared his throat. 'Let's wait before we have this conversation. It's getting late, and I've asked my father to do a little snooping. I don't want to say anything more at this point, because it's too soon to get our hopes up.'

Hannah had wandered off to find her tire, and everyone else began yawning and searching for jackets and car keys. Sam shackled Hannah to the wall for the night, whispering reassuring words Neva couldn't make out.

As Neva let the door swing shut behind her she looked back at Hannah, alone and chained to the wall in the gloom. The elephant was already rocking slowly from side to side, silently and relentlessly. By morning, Neva knew, her ankle would be bleeding beneath the shackle, as someone might cut bright, secret wounds with a razor blade.

Chapter 16

Martin Choi had a plan, and that plan did not include covering a beat for the *Bladenham News-Gazette* for the rest of his life. He was going places, and to do that he needed page-one bylines, unexpected story angles, scoops. He felt that his newfound access to the inner workings of the Max L. Biedelman Zoo might help him get there. Harriet Saul had made it clear that he would be on the inside of breaking news. That didn't mean he was going to sell out and become her boy, though. He would use his investigative skills, look around, develop inside sources. He was twenty-four years old. He wanted to be working for the *Seattle Post-Intelligencer* by his twenty-sixth birthday. He had sixteen months to get there.

'So where'd Brenda go?' he asked the new girl behind the zoo's reception desk.

'Dunno. She was canned.' The girl cracked a piece of gum. Her fingernails were two inches long – wicked, curved things that Martin regarded with a certain amount of horror. She was pretty, though, at least prettier than Brenda, who'd had a surgically repaired harelip. This one might have an incipient weight problem, though. He couldn't tell for sure.

'You like working for the zoo?'

She shrugged. 'It's okay. It's a job.'

'Yeah.' Martin shifted on the uncomfortable plastic chair in the zoo's waiting room. Harriet's door was still closed, and he could still hear her on the phone. 'So, hey,' he tried. 'You read the *News-Gazette* much?'

'Nah.'

'I had a page-one story a couple of days ago.'

'Huh.'

'It was about the landfill, and how people are throwing away more and more stuff instead of donating it to charity. Kind of a different angle, you know?' He'd worked hard on that story, even going so far as to rummage around for a couple of hours to document a sample of what was there: two working black-and-white television sets, a perfectly good exercycle, four coffee tables, and a clock.

He'd kept the clock.

'So you think she'll be done pretty soon?' he said, jerking his chin over his shoulder toward the closed office. 'I mean, I've been here for half an hour.'

'I don't know,' the girl said. 'She can talk, I'll tell you that.'

Martin subsided, promising himself he'd wait just fifteen more minutes. He had his limits.

The phone rang and the receptionist picked it up, nodded at it, and put it down. 'Mrs Biedelman will see you now.'

'I didn't think Maxine Biedelman ever married.'

'Yeah? Well, anyway, Herself is in.'

Martin lifted and stood in stages: first his camera bag and accessories, then his cameras and several lenses, finally his bandoleer of film canisters. It took a while. The office door opened and Harriet appeared looking impatient.

'Hey, yeah, great to see you again,' Martin said, freeing a hand and extending it. 'I appreciate your taking the time, you know, on so little notice.'

'It's fine.' She led him into the surprisingly grimy inner sanctum of her office, showed him to a chair, and sat down herself like royalty behind her desk. 'What story are you working on?'

'Tell me about the drums,' he said.

'Drums?'

'Yeah. The elephant was playing a couple of steel drums, real fancy. Drew a big crowd and everything.'

'When?'

'Now. This morning.'

Harriet's left eye twitched. 'Why don't we just go down there and see?' she said ominously. Martin wouldn't want to work for the woman; wouldn't want to work for either of them, Maxine Biedelman or Harriet Saul.

Clanking like Marley's ghost, he set off after Harriet, who was steaming ahead so fast Martin lost her in the crowd when they got to the elephant exhibit. By the time he found her, she was talking through the fence to a woman employee inside the exhibit – hissing, really. 'And when did you think you'd let me know about this?'

'Look, it was strictly spur-of-the-moment,' the woman said. 'No one planned it. The man who made them is my landlord. I didn't even know he was working on them until he gave them to me last night.'

241

'Did anyone else know about this?'

'No.'

'I'll bet. I'm going to have Truman put a letter in your personnel file, documenting that you're now on probation.'

'You're kidding.'

Harriet turned her back and walked away.

'You've got to be kidding!' the woman called after her.

'So do you care to make any comments?' Martin said, trotting up beside Harriet.

'What?'

'Comments about the drums.'

Harriet gave him a withering look. 'I think you can see for yourself that Hannah's received a set of drums, which she's using. It's all part of our environmental enrichment program, to improve the quality of Hannah's life.'

'Has there been something wrong with her quality of life?'

'Don't get smart with me, Martin.'

Martin subsided. 'Sorry.'

'You have enough for a story,' Harriet said. 'Stay as long as you want to, but don't interview my employees. If you need any more comments, come to me, not to them.'

'Hey, sure, okay,' Martin said, and watched as Harriet's sizable khaki haunches receded from the exhibit and up the hill to her office. Then he looked around and took stock. A crowd of visitors was still watching Hannah bang on the drums. Two boys stood on the periphery of the crowd, kicking dust at each other.

'Hey! You guys have a minute or two to talk to a reporter?'

The boys exchanged looks, then shrugged. The African-American one said, 'Yeah, sure. You gonna take our picture, too?'

242

'I might. So tell me what's going on here.'

'Hannah – she's the elephant – she's playing these cool new drums someone made for her.'

'Johnson somebody,' said the other boy, a pale kid with a few extra pounds on him.

'That his first name or his last name?' Martin asked him, taking notes.

'Both,' the pale kid said.

Hannah seemed to be playing a slow-motion riff on the drums, banging one, then the other. Martin watched, scribbled some more. 'So what does she think of them?'

The boys rolled their eyes at each other, and the black kid said, 'You better ask Hannah that.' Smartass.

'Oh, yeah, right,' Martin fake-laughed. 'Hey, you're quick, kid.'

'Uh huh,' he said.

'Yeah, Speedy Gonzales,' the pale boy said, elbowing the first one in the ribs.

'Cut it out!' The boys started sparring but subsided as the crowd of visitors around them applauded for Hannah, who had walked away from the drums, dropping the drumstick in the dust so she could pick up her tire.

'What now?' Martin asked.

'Hell, you're the reporter,' said the smartass.

'Yeah, well, thanks, kids.' Martin started moving away toward the heart of the crowd when he heard the pain-in-the-ass kid holler after him.

'Hey, mister! You going to get our names so you can put us in the paper?'

Martin turned back. 'Okay, shoot. Why aren't you guys in school, anyway?'

'It's Thanksgiving break,' the smartass said. 'Man, aren't you supposed to know that kind of thing? You write the damn newspaper—'

'Yeah, well, it must have slipped my mind, okay? You bust my chops, kid, and I'm leaving without names,' Martin said.

'Sorry, mister. He's Winslow Levy, funny name, his dad works here,' the other boy said, jerking his thumb in Winslow's direction.

'Your father works here? Really?' Martin asked Winslow, perking up. The kid might have potential as a source.

'Uh huh,' said Winslow. 'And he's Reginald Poole. It has an "E" on the end. The Poole part, not the Reginald.'

'Yeah,' Reginald said. 'I help out here sometimes.'

'Oh, yeah? So what do you do exactly?' Martin asked. This could be rich.

'I help when Sam takes Hannah for walks.'

'She goes for walks? You mean like a dog? Must be a pretty big leash, huh, kid?' Martin cracked himself up. 'Jeez, I'd sure hate to see the bone.'

Both boys looked at him with disgust. 'She's an *herb*i-vore,' Winslow said.

'Okay, okay, hey, sorry. Jesus, doesn't anyone have a sense of humor around this place?' Martin said.

'So how come they're not called florivores, anyways?' Reginald said to Winslow.

'Florivores?'

'Flora, fauna, like that. Florivore.'

Winslow considered this. 'Well, they don't call carni-vores faunivores, either.'

'Hey – Boy Wonder!' Martin broke in. 'How about standing over there by the elephant and the drums so

244

I can take your picture? How do you call her over, anyway?' Martin made kissing noises, the way you'd summon a household pet.

'That won't work, mister,' Reginald said.

'Yeah? Well, show me something that will.'

Reginald turned around and waited to catch Hannah's eye. When he did, he said as softly and precisely as Sam, 'Hey, sugar.'

The elephant walked toward them, getting as close to Reginald as she could from the other side of the fence. The drums were in the background, but it was good enough. Reginald and Winslow posed for him. Martin snapped three, four, five pictures.

'Are we going to be on the front page?' Winslow said.

'Probably not, sport, but you might be in tomorrow's edition someplace.'

'Hey, Reginald,' Winslow said. 'We'll be in the paper. Did you hear?'

But Reginald was paying attention only to Hannah, who was shifting her feet and making low noises to him. 'She knows me,' Reginald said. 'Did you see her come over? She knows me.'

Truman sat at his desk, looking at a memo Harriet had tossed there with instructions that it was to be placed in Neva's personnel file immediately. She obviously meant for him to read it; otherwise she would have put it in the files herself. It was an ugly thing, closing with, *I, Harriet Saul, recommend immediate termination if or when this employee acts without prior authorization in the future.*

Christ.

Truman slipped the memo into the file, locked the drawer, and called the elephant barn. Neva answered.

'Hey,' Truman said.

Neva said, 'Hi. How's life up there in the gulag?'

'Scary. Would you have dinner with me tonight?'

Neva sighed. 'I don't think I'd be very good company.'

'Please say yes.'

'All right, as long as I don't have to be perky. I'm definitely not up for being perky.'

'I'm not feeling all that perky myself. How about meeting me at Teriyaki Time at six-fifteen?'

'Okay.'

Truman hung up the phone and pressed the heels of his hands hard against his eyes. It was only 10:05 and he could feel a pounding headache coming on. He decided to martyr himself and attend Harriet's morning lecture – she might find his attentions soothing.

He came out the front door just as Harriet prepared to make her salutations from the porch. Not to be up-staged, she nodded to him regally and gave him a moment to pass, descend the stairs, and find a place among the visitors.

There were probably a hundred people gathered around the porch. Even in November the zoo was comfortably full. Yesterday they had received a phone call from a tour bus operator, asking about group rates.

'Good morning!' Harriet boomed, slapping her riding crop smartly against her puttees and doffing her rough-rider hat. 'My name is Maxine Biedelman. Welcome to my zoo!'

Applause broke out, and several women shushed their children. The group pushed forward as one to hear better.

'The thing is, she's weird as hell, but you've got to hand it to her, this whole Maxine Biedelman thing works,' a young man laden with camera gear whispered to Truman as they stood together on the outskirts. Truman hadn't even noticed him there. Now he recalled having seen him at the zoo once or twice.

'You've seen her do this before?'

'Sure, a couple of times.' The young man extended his hand. 'Martin Choi, *Bladenham News-Gazette*.'

'Truman Levy.'

'Hey, then I just talked to your kid down at the elephant barn.'

'He's a big fan of Hannah's.'

'Yeah, well, he and a buddy of his were telling me they help with her sometimes.'

'Not officially,' Truman said, alarmed. He could only imagine what Harriet would say if she saw Winslow quoted in the paper.

'Gentlemen,' Maxine boomed, sending death rays out to Truman with her eyes. 'If you aren't fans of mine, kindly move along so others can hear.'

The crowd laughed and Truman apologized, calling, 'Yes, Maxine, I was only discussing your new lemurs with this fellow. He wants to know if they should be met at the station with a cage or a net.'

'Ah,' Harriet said, accepting her cue. 'It seems that the people of Bladenham don't always know what to make of me. Why, when I brought my first zebra home, there was nearly pandemonium. That was only one of many times we've found ourselves on the front page of the *Bladenham News-Gazette*. Isn't that right, Martin?'

Martin Choi grinned and acknowledged the crowd.

247

Truman slipped away under the cover of laughter. This wasn't the first time he'd seen someone transformed by a theatrical role, but it was certainly the most startling. Harriet's performance was electric, though god knew if she was actually basing her role on the real Max Biedelman. Rhonda had had a theatrical bent, too. Her whole life was a play, with herself occupying center stage. There had been moments during their marriage when Truman could almost hear her practicing her lines. He'd pointed that out to her several years ago, and she'd said, *Oh, really, Truman, grow up. Nothing is truly spontaneous, it's all been rehearsed before. The only difference is, most people aren't honest enough to admit it.*

The thought had depressed him then, and it depressed him now.

Just as he reached his desk he heard muffled applause from the lawn – Harriet taking her bows, no doubt. A half-hour later, she appeared at his cubicle, flushed with success.

'You're really very good,' Truman told her, because she was.

'Yes, I am,' Harriet agreed. 'I think it's time we talked about renovating the ballroom.'

Sam removed his zoo ball cap and said to the receptionist, 'Miss Saul wanted to see me.'

'Who?'

Harriet called out through her open office door, 'Come in, Sam.'

Sam walked in slowly and stood in front of her desk, cap in hand. 'Yes, ma'am.'

'Were you here last night when Neva Wilson brought in the drums?'

'Yes, ma'am.'

'She lied, then. She said no one else knew about it.'

'I didn't know, ma'am – I was already here.'

'Why?'

Sam ducked his head. 'Me and Mrs Brown come in the evenings sometimes to keep Hannah company.'

Harriet frowned. 'Do you? I wasn't aware of that. How often?'

'Not often, ma'am,' Sam said, alarmed. 'Maybe once a week, sometimes twice.'

'And how long do you stay?'

'Maybe an hour or two. It does Hannah good to—'

Harriet was shaking her head. 'I can't have that, Sam.'

Stunned, Sam said, 'Why?'

'You're an hourly employee. I can't have you here working hours I'm unprepared to pay you for. There are liability issues.'

'I don't do it to get paid, ma'am. I'm just giving Hannah a little extra company. She gets lonely chained to that—'

'I'm sorry.' Harriet's attention was already moving on. She began sifting through a pile of papers. 'Please let Geneva know, also. You may not be on the premises except during your regular hours.'

Sam scrambled. 'We could change our shifts around, so one of us is here early and the other is late.'

Harriet paused, frowning. 'No, I don't think so. I need you both here during regular zoo hours, to keep up the exhibit.'

'But, ma'am,' Sam protested with growing alarm. 'Hannah's already alone in that barn for twelve, fourteen hours a day sometimes.'

'That's all, Sam. Thank you.'

'Miss Saul, you're doing the wrong thing, the *wrong* damn thing for that elephant,' Sam said bitterly.

'I don't appreciate being sworn at, Sam. And I really must insist that you call me Maxine.' Harriet began to write notes in the margins of a document on her desk. 'Maxine Biedelman.'

Teriyaki Time was packed when Truman got there, but Thomas had saved a table for them. Truman stood until Neva had slipped into the booth, a gesture of respect his parents had drilled into him early. *Women are stronger and smarter than we are, Truman, as your mother will tell you,* Matthew had often said ruefully. *If the world is ever in the throes of Armageddon, it's the women who'll be left standing.* Nothing in Truman's experience had ever successfully challenged this.

Now, as he slid into the booth, he thought Neva looked strained and tired. Even her hair seemed at odds, pulled into a messy bun from which strands kept escaping. He'd never seen anyone less able to disguise what she was feeling. Whatever toughness she had achieved must have come at a high price. Was there a man? Had there ever been a man? Or had her life been invested in a succession of needy animals? He envisioned her standing on the deck of an ark, Noah-like, surrounded by pairs of animals stretching all the way to the horizon.

'What?' Neva said, blushing. She attempted a smile, but it failed before it even reached the corners of her mouth.

'Nothing. You look tired. Tired and discouraged.'

Neva opened a packet of sugar, shook some onto the

table, and absently pushed it around with her finger. 'How do you do it?' she said.

'Do what?'

'I've known rhinos with better dispositions. And I hate rhinos.'

Truman conceded the point.

'So where's Winslow?'

'Ah. He's with his mother. She got into town last night. He'll be with her through Thanksgiving.'

'Is that okay?'

Truman shrugged. 'Rhonda's always believed in spontaneity. It plays hell with planning, but I think Winslow was glad to see her.'

'How long have you been divorced?'

'Just about a year.'

'Why?'

'Why did we divorce?' Truman blew out a ruminative breath. 'I guess you could say we had trouble synchronizing. You know that carnival ride where two cages swing in opposite directions, going higher and higher until they go over the top? That was us. We passed each other all the time, but we never actually stopped in the same place until it was time to get off the ride.'

'So that doesn't sound good,' Neva said.

'No.'

'How is Winslow dealing with it?'

'Mostly okay — frankly, I think he's relieved that she's not around very much. She tends to take up a lot of space.'

Neva looked at him for a long moment, weighing something. Then she said, 'I have a son Winslow's age.'

Truman put down his fork.

'Surprising, I know. I don't seem like the motherly type. I *wasn't* the motherly type. I gave the baby up for adoption. I was twenty-five.'

Truman leaned toward her across the table. She leaned back, shrugging. 'It's not glamorous. My birth control pills failed.'

'But you went through with it.'

Neva nodded.

'Did you ever think about keeping him?'

'No. I only saw him for a minute, and then he was gone.'

'Why?'

'Why didn't I keep him? My work doesn't mix with child-rearing. I didn't think it would be fair. He deserved not only to live, but to live with someone more suitable than me. If it were to happen again today, I'd probably make a different choice, but then I still had too much to do, to prove.'

'Do you know where he is?'

'No. I thought I saw him once in New York, but that's not likely. I lived in San Diego when he was born.'

Truman stirred his rice.

'It's okay,' Neva said. 'It was a long time ago. I can't believe I even told you.'

'Have you ever been married?'

'Not then. A couple of years later.'

Truman raised his eyebrows encouragingly. Neva pushed some rice around on her plate. 'His name was Howard. His dream was to become a securities analyst. My dream was to *shovel shit*, as he liked to put it. Shit and securities don't mix. Luckily, it only took us two years to discover that.'

'So you got out,' Truman said.

'So I got out. It was all very amicable – we did much better as friends than spouses. We still talk from time to time. When he remarried a few years ago, he invited me to the wedding and neither of us thought it was strange. I would have gone, too, but I thought it would make the bride's family uncomfortable. She was a good choice for him. I think they're happy.'

'So it's not a sad story,' Truman said.

'No.'

'Good.'

Truman suddenly stood and beckoned with one raised hand to Sam and Corinna, who had just arrived.

'Now I know why you had Thomas put us at a big table,' Neva said. 'How nice!'

Truman helped Corinna into a seat. 'Thanks, baby,' she said, and then to Neva, 'How are you, honey? Sam said it was a bad, bad day.'

'Yeah, it was,' Neva said.

'Well, I have some news that might help,' Truman said. Three faces turned to him as one. 'Though we're not quite sure what it means yet.'

'Spill it, honey,' Corinna said. 'I think we could all use something good.'

Truman crossed his hands on the tabletop. 'My father's a retired judge. You probably know that the zoo's financial situation isn't the best, so a few weeks ago I asked him to go through some old city records to see if there might be a long-forgotten fund or an endowment that could help make up the zoo's shortfall. He found something interesting. Sam, when Max Biedelman passed away, did anyone say anything to you about Hannah?'

'No, sir.'

'Not anything?'

'Not that I remember. Except that I got to keep my job.'

'Well, they should have. Before she died, Max Biedelman set up a trust that would be used for Hannah's upkeep. It isn't enough to cover all her costs anymore, but it helps.'

'She told me she was going to do that,' Sam said. 'She said she didn't want me or Hannah to worry about things after she was gone.'

'But she didn't say anything else?'

Sam shook his head.

'Well, there was another piece to it. I wonder why she didn't tell you. The trust was to be overseen by a trustee whose job was – is – to make sure Hannah's being well cared for. The trustee is empowered to make decisions about anything that involves her welfare.'

'I never heard anything about that,' Sam said.

'You should have,' Truman said. 'Because it's you.'

'What?'

'You're the trustee!' Truman grinned. 'How d'ya like *them* apples?'

'Yes!' said Neva, and pumped her fist in the air.

'But what does it mean, honey?' Corinna asked Neva.

'I'm not sure yet, but I know it's good,' Neva said.

'It means that Sam is Hannah's legal guardian,' Truman said. 'Technically, it means if he feels Hannah's at risk in any way, or that her care doesn't meet her needs, he can ask the zoo to make whatever changes he feels are necessary. And if the zoo refuses, he can withhold or withdraw the trust's funds. In other words, what Sam says, goes – the zoo has to comply, or it loses roughly

254

seventy-five thousand dollars a year. Which, let me tell you, it cannot afford to do.'

'Are you saying that the trust owns her?' Neva said.

'No. On the surface of it, the zoo owns her, because she was gifted to the city along with Max Biedelman's other property when she died.'

'Rats.'

'*But* — and here's where it gets fun — what if Sam deems that the *zoo itself* does not and cannot meet Hannah's needs? Does he have the legal right to move her to a facility that can?'

'Like the Pachyderm Sanctuary,' Neva said.

'Like the Pachyderm Sanctuary. My father needs a little more time to look into this before he gives us his final opinion. And no matter what, we'll probably wind up in court. But the bottom line is, things are going to get better for Hannah. Sam has the power to make that happen.'

'Someone going to tell that to Harriet Saul?' Sam asked.

'My father's offered to talk with her and the city as soon as he's had a chance to find a precedent or two and feels like we're on absolutely solid ground. You know lawyers — they move like molasses. But he'll get back to us as soon as he can.'

Truman and Neva sat in Truman's car watching the rain outside Teriyaki Time long after Sam and Corinna had driven away. 'I don't understand why no one ever told Sam he was the trustee,' Neva said. 'That makes no sense. And it had to be on purpose, because who would forget to do something like that?'

Truman smiled and said, 'I'd never have guessed it — you're naïve!'

'Me? Naïve?'

'Think about it. Sam is a black man. He was a black man in 1958 when Max Biedelman died.'

'So you're saying it was racial?'

'I'm saying it's a lot of money, and it seemed like even more money back then. I'm saying some small town leaders probably weren't going to put an uneducated black Korean War veteran in charge of seventy-five thousand dollars a year.'

'Seventy-five thousand, is that how much the zoo gets? That's less than a third of what we'd need for the sanctuary to take her.'

'No, no. That's just the annual earnings — that's how much goes into the zoo's operating budget,' Truman said. 'The trust itself is worth more than half a million.'

'God, I *love* you,' she crowed, and then she folded herself over the emergency brake and the gear-shift column and kissed him in a way he hadn't been kissed in years or maybe longer; maybe ever.

In bed on their backs, side by side in the dark, Sam took Corinna's hand and placed it flat on his chest, over his heart. It was a gesture that went way back to when they were young and Corinna liked to tell him that with each beat his heart was saying, *I'm yours, I'm yours, I'm yours.* Who was Sam to disagree?

'She told me this afternoon we couldn't go and sit with shug at night anymore,' he said after a while.

'Who said that?'

'That Harriet Saul,' Sam said bitterly.

'Big old mean-spirited cow. Why'd she say something like that?'

'She asked me if I knew about the Neva drums, and I said yes, which was my first mistake – I know, Mama, you were about to say it – but I didn't want to get the girl in trouble so I said we only knew because we were there at the barn when she brought them in. So of course she wanted to know why we were there, and when I said we came in sometimes to keep shug company in the evenings, that's when she said we couldn't anymore. Said it was because she couldn't pay me for the time – like I care about that. I told her, too, but she said it didn't matter. She couldn't pay me, plus something about liability, so we can't be there. But maybe now this news, this other, means we don't have to do what she says.'

'Maybe I'll just put a little something nasty in her hair color next time,' Corinna said. 'Grind up a little Hannah-doo, maybe.'

'Woman, you're *bad*.' Sam started laughing and then Corinna started laughing, too; and both of them laughed so hard they thought they'd never stop, and if they didn't, it might not be such a bad thing, after all they'd been through. When they finally returned to their senses, Sam took Corinna's hand in his and said, 'Looks like the Lord might have performed a little miracle for us today.'

'Do you know,' Corinna said, 'He might just have.'

Chapter 17

Miles was dancing with excitement when Truman came home from work – it had been another long day alone for the pig. Truman squatted beside him, Miles did his Fall of the Dead trick, and Truman scratched him all over, armpits included. Then he scooped some pig kibble into a dish and tuned the radio to a classical station that was likely to play Mozart for Miles in Winslow's absence.

It was odd, being at home without the boy. They had developed a way of life together and there was a sort of companionable, bachelor comfort to it. He couldn't imagine losing a child, the way Sam and Corinna had, or giving one up, the way Neva had. But then, Neva Wilson was a different flavor of fish. She was going to lose her job before this mess was over, and she must know it, yet she'd said nothing at dinner about the likely effect their rescue mission would have on her person- ally. For that matter, Truman would probably lose his job, too, once his role in the intrigue became clear. In Harriet's eyes, you were either loyal, traitorous, or an idiot; her childlike worldview lacked nuance. She sulked; she pouted and stewed and wheedled and undermined; she was as maddening as a nine-year-old. And yet her portrayal of Maxine Biedelman had been powerful and entertaining and fully developed. Was it possible to be better at being someone else than you were at being yourself?

Truman opened a bottle of beer and took it with him to the telephone, speed-dialing his parents' number. He filled Matthew in about the disastrous day, and then spent the next hour with the telephone receiver pinned between his ear and shoulder, listening. Before they hung up, they agreed to meet with Sam and Neva before work the next morning.

At seven a.m., Truman, Sam, and Neva sat at a table farthest from the door of the Oat Maiden, nervously fidgeting with thick, mismatched mugs of coffee. It was the first time either Truman or Sam had been inside – and most likely would be the last, at least as far as Truman was concerned. The café's walls were painted navy blue and all the tables and chairs apparently came from moth-balled public high school classrooms. Cheerful little notes were taped to the walls everywhere, written in a childish hand and proclaiming, TRY THE ORGANIC HAND-PRESSED CIDER! and WE CHEERFULLY SUBSTITUTE SOY MILK. Only Neva seemed at ease.

Matthew and Lavinia arrived with heavy briefcases and broad smiles. They each shook Neva's hand, and then Sam's. 'It's a pleasure to meet you, Mr Brown,' Matthew said. 'I've heard a lot about you.'

'Don't know what there'd be to say about me, sir.

But me and Hannah and my wife are real grateful to you for helping like this. You can call me Sam.'

'All right then, Sam,' Matthew said pleasantly.

Truman tapped the third envelope of sugar-in-the-raw into his mug of coffee in a vain attempt to render it drinkable. No doubt it was some variety harvested exclusively by the last virgins of an indigenous people living high on some obscure mountaintop in South America. After vigorous stirring, the coffee still tasted like roasted dirt.

Matthew spread documents across the tabletop and described to Sam and Neva what each one established, and what he felt was the best plan for opening up a discussion with Harriet Saul.

'Will you be there?' Sam asked after he was finished.

'Yes, if it's all right with you, Sam. I think that might be best.'

Sam slumped in relief. 'Yes, sir, that would be just fine. I'm not much good at talking about things sometimes. I lose my way, if you know what I mean.'

'Well, this is complicated stuff.' Matthew smiled disarmingly, and Truman felt a rush of affection for this man who had taught him to value integrity and humanity above everything. Matthew continued, 'Lavinia and I thought it might be best for me to open up the meeting with an overview of the changed situation in which we suddenly find ourselves. Let me take the fallout from Ms Saul. Mostly we need to establish that you, as Hannah's legal guardian, have the privilege, right, and responsibility to ensure that Hannah's care and surroundings are of the highest quality. Is this all right with you so far?'

'Yes, sir,' Sam said gravely.

'After that, you may say whatever you feel needs to be said – for instance, that you and your wife will continue to provide company for Hannah in the evenings as often as you see fit.'

'She doesn't do well being alone, sir,' Sam said. 'I hate to be stirring things up, but shug just doesn't do well when she's alone too much.'

'You don't need to justify yourself to me, Sam. Truman has described the situation, and I believe you are every bit within your moral as well as your legal rights to act as you have done and no doubt will continue to do.' Matthew pressed Sam's forearm reassuringly.

'Any reason why we've got to tell her today, instead of waiting until after Thanksgiving?' Sam asked. Thanksgiving was only two days away. 'Seeing as how it's going to spoil her holiday and all.'

Lavinia touched the cameo at the throat of her cashmere twin set and smiled. 'It's very thoughtful of you to worry about the holiday,' she said, 'but we're going to need a governmental permit in order to legally move Hannah, and that will require the zoo's cooperation. The process will take weeks, at best. We'll follow your lead, of course, Sam, but we'd recommend that in this case we get our first hand of cards out on the table right away.'

Sam looked alarmed. 'You going to tell her about us taking the girl to the sanctuary?'

Lavinia said, 'For now we think it would be best not to talk about moving Hannah. We have a little more legal work to do before we're comfortable scaling that wall.'

'Yes, ma'am,' Sam said, visibly relieved.

'This is new and somewhat confusing ground for us all, Sam,' Lavinia said gently. 'I hope you'll ask us questions

262

any time you have them. We're pretty good at finding answers.'

'Yes, ma'am.'

Truman drove back to the zoo alone, while Sam, Lavinia, and Matthew stayed behind to go over their talking points before they met with Harriet at nine o'clock.

When he arrived at the zoo Sam checked in at the elephant barn, but then turned right around again to leave. Neva looked at her watch. 'You've still got almost half an hour,' she said.

'I'll only upset sugar if I stay here, nervous as I am,' Sam said. 'Naw, there's something else I've got to do. I believe it's time to meet this Maxine Biedelman.'

He reached the front porch of Havenside just in time to hear Harriet Saul calling, 'Welcome to my home!'

Sam's father had had an old tom peacock that had mooched around the farm dragging its raggedy tail feathers in the dust. That bird was as ugly an animal as Sam ever saw, but you would have thought he was king of the world, for all the preening and strutting he did. Sam hadn't thought about that old peacock for forty years or more, but Harriet Saul brought back the memory like it was yesterday, she was so desperate for everyone to look, to pay attention, to say nice things. If Miss Biedelman could see the woman she'd laugh out loud. The small crowd around him was clapping, so the talk must be over. Sam saw by his watch that it was time to go to his meeting, and his heart hopped right up into his throat and stayed there.

Matthew and Lavinia were already in the reception area when Sam arrived. They shook hands all around, and then Lavinia told Sam, 'I forgot earlier that I have something for you, Sam. In going through the city's files, I stumbled across this. Apparently Ms Biedelman had left it for you.' She handed Sam a yellowed envelope of rich, heavy paper stock. 'I don't know why you never received it. I'm sorry.'

Sam recognized Max Biedelman's personal stationery. He put it in his pocket for later. The receptionist got a call, listened, then hung up.

'She'd like you to meet in the conference room. It's across the hall.'

'All right,' said Matthew, with the faintest twinkle in his eye. 'Come, then, my dear.' He put his hand under Lavinia's elbow and nodded to Sam once, firmly, to strengthen his resolve.

'You don't expect me to take your word for any of this, do you?' Harriet Saul said after Matthew and Lavinia had finished their presentation. Sam hunched in his seat at the conference table.

'Of course not,' Matthew soothed. 'You'd be wise to talk with the City's legal counsel. In the meantime, however, I trust we've been clear that Mr Brown will be on the premises whenever he feels it's necessary, day or night, but that he does not intend to request compensation beyond his usual and customary wages. And if you consult the zoo's insurance carrier, I'm sure the liability issues will be easy to resolve.'

Harriet stared at him hostilely. Matthew continued, 'Let me remind you that Mr Brown's wages are not paid by the zoo itself, but by the trust, which is held and administered by the City of Bladenham. Technically, Mr Brown wouldn't require your authorization for overtime compensation. But never mind – we're acting in good faith, and we're confident that you'll proceed in the same spirit.'

Harriet turned and stalked out of the room without a word, slamming the door behind her.

'Well,' Lavinia said brightly. 'I think that went well, don't you?'

Sam caught just the hint of mischief way deep down in her eyes.

'What happens now, ma'am?'

'A rebuttal from the zoo, I would imagine. Challenging the validity of the trust, challenging your appointment as trustee. Don't you think so, dear?'

'Yes indeed.' Matthew winked at Sam. 'My wife's an excellent predictor of these things. Now, Sam, we'll be off, but you know how to get hold of us. I want you to call if you have any concerns or questions, or if Ms Saul takes any action that you're uncomfortable with.'

'Like what?' Sam said.

'Oh, there are a number of things she can do to make things difficult for you,' Matthew said. 'Taking away your keys to the facility, or changing the locks on the gates or doors. Firing Ms Wilson. Attempting to fire you. Denying you access to the zoo property. Harassing you in any way, such as directing the security staff to maintain a watch over you and Hannah around the clock. Demanding that you sign in and out, so there's a record of your presence at the zoo. I'm sure you get the idea.'

Alarmed, Sam said, 'You think she's going to do any of those things?'

'Ah – that I don't know,' Matthew said. 'But I'd say she's certainly capable of it. Wouldn't you say so, dear?'

'Oh, certainly,' Lavinia said serenely, standing and straightening her pearls. 'Absolutely.'

As Sam walked out he noticed that although the room

was badly overheated, neither Lavinia nor Matthew had so much as broken a sweat.

On the way back to the elephant barn, Sam opened the thick, creamy envelope Lavinia had given him. It looked like it had been opened before – a wax seal he had seen Max Biedelman use on other correspondence was broken. Nevertheless, he handled the envelope with great care, wanting it to remain, as nearly as possible, the way it had left Max Biedelman's hand so many years ago. Unfolding the paper, he read:

April 15, 1958

Dear Sam,

I am entrusting Hannah to your care, dear friend. She needs you as much as you need her. I suppose she is the legacy of my last foolish act, for how selfish it was to bring her here to Havenside knowing she would outlive me. I trust that the attorneys will fully explain Hannah's circumstances to you, as well as your powers as her guardian, but please accept this note, however inadequate, as my thanks for your friendship and for the love you have shown Hannah, Effie, and me. It has been my great privilege to know you. May you and Hannah prosper.

– *Max L. Biedelman*

The note was dated just two weeks before her death. Miss Effie had died five months before, and Max's decline had been precipitous. She still accompanied Sam on walks from time to time, but she had had her gardener remove the campaign tent that, except for its periodic replacement, had stood on the grounds for fifty-eight years. Increasingly unsteady on her feet, she often held Sam's arm when they walked.

'I promised you a story of my family, Mr Brown,' she said one warm afternoon as they moved slowly across the lawn with Hannah ahead of them. 'And I always make good on my word. I shall tell you about my mother's cousin. His name was Ernest, though he himself was not. In fact, Ernest was a shyster, a born con artist. But my mother was fond of him, and supported him off and on for years.

'Once, Ernest claimed that he had come up with a patent medication that cured pustular tonsillitis. Of course there was no such treatment available back then, but he placed advertisements in all the major newspapers in the country, all the way east to New York and Boston. Well, the advertisements proved to be persuasive, and soon Ernest was flooded with orders he couldn't fill, not having put by an ample supply of bottles. He became quite frantic, as you can imagine, and solicited my mother's help. She showed him a little bottle of medicinal opium my father had obtained for her in Morocco, beautifully made out of cobalt glass, and told him that my father knew of a Turk here in the United States who might produce similar glass bottles for Ernest's tonic. They could be filled with anything – tincture of violet or laudanum. It could hardly matter, since the product was a sham to begin with. Ernest, however, had forgotten that, and insisted on filling the bottles with some foul-smelling,

267

execrable concoction he made himself, the secret of which he swore he would never reveal to anyone.

'Soon the little bottles were speeding across the country, to households large and small. Do you know, Mr Brown, that women began to write to him that whatever was in those little blue bottles *cured* them and their children? This came as quite a surprise, as you can imagine. It turns out that Ernest, whose only goal in life was to make easy money off the misfortunes of others, had accidentally brewed up a natural antibiotic, using tincture of Echinacea in addition to toadstools and swamp water, or whatever other god-awful ingredients he'd chosen. He died a wealthy man.'

Max Biedelman laughed heartily. 'So you see, Mr Brown, it is possible that even the most despicable people can sometimes do good.'

Chapter 18

After work that day – the day before Thanksgiving – Truman found a message from Winslow on the answering machine. Winslow said that he and Rhonda were going to have Thanksgiving dinner at the Ramada Inn, and asked if he could come home right afterwards. The boy had been whispering, as though he hadn't wanted his mother to hear him. The original plan had been for Winslow to stay with Rhonda until sometime Friday afternoon. Truman called her cell phone with a sinking heart.

'He says he wants homemade pies,' Rhonda said grimly when Truman reached her. 'I can't imagine what he's thinking. I am not Betty Crocker.'

'He knows you're not Betty Crocker.'

'Have I ever baked a pie – have I ever even *once* expressed an interest in baking a pie?'

'I bake. He's probably just forgetting.'

'That child has never forgotten a thing in his life.

He's unnatural. We were in a Walgreen's and he remembered the brand of moisturizing cream I use. It's not normal for a child, a *boy* child, to commit his mother's toiletries to memory.'

'Is he there? Can he hear you?'

'No. He's in the tub,' Rhonda said ominously. 'He's bathing.'

'Bathing is okay.'

'It's the second bath he's taken.'

'Well, he's been with you for a couple of days,' Truman pointed out. 'You've showered, haven't you?'

'That's different. I'm forty-five. I'm supposed to care about being clean. He's eleven. He's supposed to like dirty socks and his hair sticking up.'

'Well, he never has before, so I can't think why he'd start now.'

Rhonda blew out a breath, and said, 'Let it be on your head.'

'What?'

'His emasculation. Let it be on your head.'

'Yes, all right. Would you ask him to call me when he's out of the tub? He left me a message saying he'd like me to pick him up tomorrow after your Thanksgiving dinner. That's fine with me, if it's all right with you.'

Rhonda's tone was frosty. 'He gets more like you every day.'

'Like me?'

'Stuck. Rooted. He has no sense of adventure or spontaneity. I can't image what he'll be like at twenty-five. Planning his retirement, no doubt.'

'I don't think that's true. I'll see you tomorrow, then. Please ask him to call me when he's out of the tub.'

270

Almost as soon as he hung up, the phone rang again. It was Neva, calling to say that she, Sam, and Corinna would be at the elephant barn for Thanksgiving dinner, and they'd like him to come, too. 'I guess they spend every Thanksgiving and Christmas there,' Neva told him. 'Hannah gets two of her own pumpkin pies, plus one banana cream. Anyway, they've asked us and your mom and dad to join them. Bring mashed potatoes, if you can. They're bringing the turkey, stuffing, and green beans.'

'God,' Truman said. 'I wouldn't miss it. What did my folks say?'

'Exactly the same thing.'

Corinna had dressed for the occasion with a Thanksgiving holiday apron and Indian corn fingernail decals. Sam wore a sweater, khaki wash pants, and suspenders. Matthew, predictably, had dressed down in a sport coat and tie; Lavinia, elegant as ever, wore her pearls, a cashmere twin set, and a Pendleton wool skirt. Neva had on jeans because she always wore jeans, plus a thick, soft chenille sweater the color of tangerines; she wore her hair down, falling softly around her face. Truman's heart ached when he looked at her. Truman himself had chosen a tie with embroidered turkeys all over it that Winslow had given him as a gift the year before. Winslow, fresh from Rhonda's loving arms, had chosen to dress in his sweater vest, oxford cloth button-down shirt, and sharp-creased slacks. Truman could only imagine – and with a wicked little smile – the wrath his clothes had probably incurred at Rhonda's. All in all, they were a festive group, perched around the inside of the barn on lawn chairs, sharing TV tables. Hannah stood in their midst, rolling

271

several round pebbles in the crook of her trunk while she watched Corinna take foil off the tops of several pies.

'Baby sure loves these,' Corinna said. 'The first year we tried mincemeat, too, but she didn't take to that one so much. Whipped cream, though, that's a whole other thing.' She turned to Sam. 'Remember, baby, when we gave her that plate full of nothing but a quart of heavy whipped cream? Hannah blew half of it across the barn before she figured out what it was. We were wiping old whipped cream off those walls for days, but ever since, she's been a whipped cream kind of girl – whipped cream and banana cream pie.'

Lavinia stretched out her hand toward Hannah, but hesitated. 'May I touch her, Sam? Will I startle her?'

'Naw, she likes being touched, as long as she isn't afraid of you. She's real physical that way. Just give her a good, firm pat – or you can just leave your hand on her, let her know you're friendly. She likes that, too.'

Lavinia reached up and thumped Hannah smartly on her side. Hannah stretched her trunk toward the older woman, zeroing in on her pearls and twin set en route to her face and neck. Lavinia held very still as the questing trunk made its way around her.

'She's telling you she likes you, putting her trunk by your ear like that,' Sam said. 'Baby always was one for bath powder and perfume. If you've got either of those on, she'll be stuck to you like glue.'

Matthew smiled, watching. Truman thought that much of his life had been spent just this way, watching Matthew watch Lavinia, or watching Lavinia watch Matthew. Theirs seemed to be the perfect union, two people who not only respected but delighted in one another, and always had.

272

Matthew was saying, 'Your elephant has good taste, then, Sam. Lavinia wears nothing but Chanel Number Five.'

Sam went over to Hannah's probing trunk and headed her away. 'It isn't good manners to smell a lady for too long, shug, even when you're doing it out of admiration.' Corinna passed him a large baked yam with marshmallow melted inside. Sam brought the yam to Matthew and placed it in his hand. 'Hold it out flat, just like that.'

Hannah rolled her eyes and stretched her trunk in Matthew's direction, scooping up the yam in one fluid movement of her trunk and popping it in her mouth like a bonbon. Matthew laughed. 'She reminds me of a goat my father used to have, Sam. Gloria Lee, that was her name. That goat couldn't get enough biscuits with honey, just loved 'em. My mother used to make a double batch on Sundays just for her.'

Truman suspected the story was apocryphal; he'd seen his father spin more incredible yarns to put a man at his ease.

'My father had a farm,' Sam said. 'Just outside Yakima. Poor kind of hardscrabble place, took every bit of will he had to pull a living out of that dirt, but he was proud of it just the same.'

'Yes? Then you must remember farm animals from over the years, too. I'm embarrassed to admit this, but to this day I find myself matching our animals up with people. My son, for instance, reminds me of a cocker spaniel my mother had, a good, gentle dog called Fanny, always very sensitive to the moods of her family. If she thought you were upset or sad, she would lie beside you day or night, until you'd convinced her that the worst had passed.'

'How about Harriet Saul, Dad?' Truman said, coloring. 'Who does she remind you of?'

'Well, now that's a hard one. Most animals don't have that kind of temper.' Matthew frowned, thinking. 'I'd have to say Caesar. You remember him? No? Caesar was a very large Black Angus bull with a legendary temper. He tended to charge first, look later. Nobody went into the pasture with Caesar, neither man nor cow.'

Sam laughed hardest. 'You got her just right,' he said. '*Just* right. Now, Neva here, she reminds me of an old lop-eared rabbit I had once, a girl by the name of Shirley. That rabbit had the busiest nose you ever saw, working working working all the time. Pretty thing, too.'

Neva gave Sam a one-armed hug and returned to her chair with a second piece of pumpkin pie. Corinna made the rounds with what was left. 'Come on, now, we've got food to spare,' she cried amidst groans and cries of overindulgence. 'Hannah doesn't like to see food wasted.'

There was a knock at the barn door. Everyone else looked concerned, but Neva said, 'It's okay,' and jumped up as though she'd expected it. 'I'm glad you're here,' she said, pushing the door open. 'Come on in.' Behind her Johnson Johnson dipped his head self-consciously and worked the hem of his coat between a thumb and forefinger. His hair was plastered down with something, and he wore a strange, nubbly brown sports coat over a brilliant tie-dyed T-shirt.

'Matthew, Lavinia, this is Johnson Johnson,' Neva said. 'He's my landlord, Hannah's patron, and folk artist extraordinaire. Johnson, I think you know everyone else here.'

'He's the one who made those drums for the girl? I've never seen anything so beautiful. You just come on in, sugar,'

Corinna said, taking Johnson Johnson's arm and leading him to a chair beside her own. 'We got pumpkin and banana cream. Which one do you want to start with?'

Johnson Johnson looked up at her. 'Pumpkin,' he said and then, flushing, 'Pumpkin, *please*.'

Matthew stood and held up his paper cup of cider. 'A toast,' he said, and everyone turned to him. 'To Hannah, to her trustee, and, most of all, to safe journeys.'

No one made a sound; no one even breathed.

Matthew grinned and raised his cup high. 'The trust is fully transferable.'

Across the zoo property, Harriet Saul sat in her office in the dark, sipping her fourth plastic cup of wine. It was a cheap bottle of Merlot from an unknown Argentinean vineyard, something she had found in the grocery store close-out bin. Outside her office, in the now-deserted reception area, an electric Christmas wreath blinked red, green, red, endlessly like a conflicted heart. *Stop! Go! Stop!*

Harriet had seen lights on at the elephant barn when she came in, heard faint laughter as she crossed the parking lot to her office. They had betrayed her, all of them, and she couldn't understand it, knew she'd never understand it, except to realize that once again she had misplaced her trust. In the end, the mistake had been hers.

She stared into the darkness of her office and allowed her mind to drift to other Thanksgivings. Maude had never cared for the holiday, celebrating with an indifferent succession of dry turkeys and packaged gravy. Harriet had eventually taken over the holiday cooking, but even so it had been a cheerless affair. She recalled a

Thanksgiving table, and her mother and father arguing until her father slammed a wine glass down on the table so hard it had shattered. That had been the end of the holiday. He'd needed nine stitches, and within two months he was gone.

Harriet tapped out the last drop of wine, hid the bottle among others in her office closet, and re-enabled the security system. As she pulled the outside door to, a fresh volley of laughter rang out from the elephant barn, mocking her; mocking everything she was and ever would be.

After they came home from the elephant barn, Winslow practiced at the piano and the pig lay insensible beneath it, eyes tiny slits, mouth lifted in a stuporous porcine smile. He had just polished off the half a pumpkin pie that Winslow had brought back for him, as well as four yams and a drumstick.

'He missed you,' Truman said, sitting on the sofa in the den, when Winslow was finished. 'I missed you.'

'Nah, he only missed my music,' Winslow said. 'Why do you think he likes it so much?'

'Perhaps he *is* Mozart,' Truman said. 'Reborn as a pig.'

Winslow looked at his father to see if he was serious. 'Do you think he could be?'

'Anything's possible.'

'I like that,' Winslow said.

Truman made room for him on the sofa. 'So tell me about your visit with your mother.'

Winslow shrugged. 'She kept saying things made her mad, like how I probably kept my crayons in order from dark to light.'

276

'Well, you do.'

'I know, but what's wrong with that?'

Truman shook his head. 'There's no accounting for a mother's ways, Winslow. Yours has a low threshold for tidiness.'

'Did she yell at you for being neat, too?'

'Sometimes.'

'Well, the inside of her car was full of old half-empty water bottles and potato chip bags and old napkins and stuff with her lipstick all over it.' Winslow shuddered faintly. 'Plus she had an air freshener hanging up. How come she'd need an air freshener in her car? I think she might' – he lowered his voice – 'smoke.'

'Really?'

'Well, I could definitely smell something.'

'Ah.' Rhonda had smoked pot when they'd first met. Artists, she believed, did. She had quit only in deference to Winslow's allergies; perhaps she'd started again, now that Winslow was away from her. Truman didn't think the boy needed to know that, though. 'I think it's safe to say your mother has always done things a little differently than most people. She's a strong-willed woman, and she's always had a lot on her mind. More than most people do.'

'Like what?'

'Well, Art, with a capital "A". Beauty, with a capital "B". Creativity, with – '

'A capital "C".'

'You get the point, I think.'

'Design, with a "D", Excellence, with an "E",' Winslow said.

'So you see, your mother is full up a lot of the time

277

dealing with all these things, especially when they're important enough to be capitalized.'

'Fantasy, Greatness – '

'Yes, Winnie, I think we've beaten this particular horse.'

'Happiness,' Winslow said, subsiding. 'Don't forget
happiness.'

'Oh, no,' Truman said. 'I would never forget happiness.'

For Martin Choi, Friday morning came late and brought
with it one hell of a hangover. That's what he got for
spending Thanksgiving at No Place Special, the *Bladenham
News-Gazette*'s bar of choice. He had won nearly fifty
dollars at darts, but after that things got fuzzy. He woke
up in his clothes, lying on top of his bed with one
shoe on.

The phone on his desk rang. Closing his eyes so that
the assault would be limited to just one of his senses, he
lifted the receiver and mumbled something that was
meant to resemble his name.

'Yes, good morning,' a well-modulated male voice said.
'Are you the reporter who has written several features
about the Biedelman Zoo recently? If you are, I believe
I have a story for you.'

Martin straightened up: Hell yes, he was that reporter.
He cleared his throat several times, desperately re-assembling
himself into a soon-to-be-award-winning *Seattle Post-
Intelligencer* reporter.

The caller identified himself as Matthew Levy. Martin
knew the name – Matthew Levy was something of a
legend around Bladenham, one of the youngest judges
ever appointed. Martin straightened his shirt collar.

'You may be interested to know that a forty-one-year-old document has surfaced at the City of Bladenham archives that establishes that Hannah – of course you are familiar with Hannah, the elephant – has a trustee, a guardian, if you will; and that he, not the zoo, has the responsibility of overseeing her care and monitoring her health. Would this story be of interest to you?'

'Hell, yes!'

On his way to the judge's house Martin dry-shaved and picked up and bolted a desperately needed double shot of espresso from the Java Hut. It was a good thing he did, too, because the Levy sun porch was glaringly, even agonizingly, white, with white walls, floral chintz, and white wicker. Martin ran his palms down his own wrinkled rugby shirt, which since its last laundering might or might not have been worn.

'Please sit down, Martin,' Matthew said, gesturing to a chair. 'You've already met my wife Lavinia, of course.' Indeed he had: Lavinia had met him at the door, scaring the shit out of him by calling him Mr Choi and showing him to the sun porch through airy rooms filled with antiques and art. 'Lavinia will join us if that's all right with you. She's also an attorney. She's been assisting me in looking into this matter.'

'Sure, yeah, okay.' Unfortunately, Martin's journalistic acuity was masked somewhat by a coughing fit that sent Lavinia into the kitchen for a crystal pitcher of ice water and a glass.

'Whew, whoa,' Martin said when he was able to speak again. 'Hey, sorry. Big night last night, you know, Thanksgiving and all.'

'Yes, of course,' Lavinia said. Could she possibly be

279

wearing as much solid gold as it looked like? If so – and he had no reason to think otherwise – her net worth, just sitting there beside him, was probably twice the value of Martin's car. He struggled to focus on Matthew.

'—could require that her facilities be altered or upgraded, if he felt the current conditions warranted it,' Matthew was saying.

That got his attention. 'What? Could what?'

Matthew smiled and nodded to Lavinia, who poured a cup of coffee from a carafe and handed it to Martin.

Matthew started over. 'Have you met Samson Brown? Good. Well, as it turns out – and this knowledge is brand-new, Martin, fresh news – that Mr Brown is Hannah's legal guardian, and has been since 1958, though no one informed him of that until now. I was simply explaining that with the power Max Biedelman vested in him, Mr Brown could – indeed, is obligated to – require that the Biedelman Zoo make modifications to Hannah's accommodations.'

'That right?' Martin said, squinting at his notepad.

'Yes, that's right.' The old man handed off to Lavinia, who lifted a thin china cup to her lips. Then she talked about some trust fund that the old woman had set up before she died; and about how some money flowed into the zoo's operating budget each year, and what formula determined the exact amount. And how, now that there was a trustee involved – that would be Samson Brown, Martin was pretty sure – the zoo would spend the trust money at the trustee's behest – possibly even reallocating it, 'if he finds that the zoo's facilities are inadequate. Theoretically, of course,' Lavinia set her teacup neatly in its saucer. '*If* he deems that there are inadequacies. Isn't that right, my dear?'

'Yes,' said Matthew. 'That's right.'

Martin squinted. 'So *are* there inadequacies?'

'I'm afraid I'm not qualified to make that judgment.' Lavinia took a sip of tea. 'Her yard is a bit small, I would think.'

'Small, huh? Okay, so what else? Food okay? Is she treated right? I mean, she always looks kind of depressed when you go down there, now that I think about it. She's usually just standing around with this crummy old tire. Except when she's painting or something. Playing the drums.'

'All of those are excellent questions,' Lavinia said. 'Perhaps that's where you should begin your investigation.'

He didn't remember having said anything about an investigation. But now that she mentioned it, this could be just the launching pad that would propel him through the doors of the *Seattle Post-Intelligencer*. Yeah, boy.

Matthew helped him gather up his things and walked him to the door, saying, 'Stay with this story, Martin. I believe this is just the beginning.'

'Oh yeah?' So what did he know that Martin didn't? 'Such as like what, exactly?'

But Matthew just smiled enigmatically and clapped him on the shoulder, saying only, 'I envy you, young man. You have a great story to tell – now go and tell it!'

'Well, sure,' Martin said. 'Okay.'

In his side-view mirror as he pulled away, Martin could see Matthew watching with his hand raised in heroic farewell.

And suddenly he felt like a million bucks in spite of the wracking headache. This was what investigative reporting was all about – finding that story, pulling off

281

that scoop. He had a tiger by the tail, now. He could handle that. He drove straight to the zoo, striding into the reception area only to find yet another new receptionist. The place sure had a high turnover rate, worse than the *News-Gazette*, and that was saying something.

'Yes, Martin,' Harriet Saul said from the door to her office before he'd even finished introducing himself to the girl. It was creepy how she always seemed to know when he was there.

'Hey, how are you? Have a great Thanksgiving? Look, I just heard about Hannah's trustee thing. Can you fill me in?'

'No,' Harriet said flatly.

Martin blinked. 'No?'

'No.'

And then, to Martin Choi's lasting astonishment, the woman stepped into her office, turned her back, and closed the door.

The next morning, Matthew left the house at seven o'clock to buy the newspapers. Truman and Winslow arrived just as Lavinia brought coffee, orange juice, and English muffins to the sun porch table. Beside her place lay a pair of white cotton gloves, her customary protection against the drying effects of newsprint. She had long, white, beautiful hands, even at seventy-two.

Matthew handed around three copies of the *Bladenham News-Gazette*. A front-page, above-the-fold headline in forty-point type proclaimed, TROUBLE AT THE ZOO? FAVORITE ELEPHANT HAS NEW BOSS. It was bylined, of course, Martin Choi.

The three of them fell to, while Winslow read the comics.

282

'Well,' Lavinia said brightly when she was done. 'One can only wonder what he would have written had he been sober.'

Matthew looked at his grandson, who had finished the comics and was playing a piece of music on the arm of the sofa. He beckoned the boy over to stand beside him, put his arm around him, and began to smile puckishly. 'Winslow, have you learned to play chess yet?'

'No.'

'A pity,' Matthew said. 'It has so many useful analogies.'

'Such as,' said Truman.

'The one that first comes to mind is "check", because that is what we have done so far.'

'And?'

'And then, of course, there's "checkmate", which is, of course, the endgame.'

Winslow stood still within the half-moon of Matthew's arm.

'Now then,' Matthew said, 'I have a story to tell you. Just a story, you understand, but it's an instructive one that you might choose to pass along to your friend – is it Reginald? yes? – when you see him at the zoo today. Shall I tell you?'

'Okay.' Winslow loved Matthew's stories. He waited, slipping Lavinia's discarded white cotton gloves on and off.

'I believe you know that Hannah is a social animal, a big-hearted girl with a very small family. And who might that family consist of?'

'Sam Brown?' Winslow guessed.

'Exactly. And who else?'

283

'Neva Wilson?'

'Well, she certainly helps Mr Brown take care of Hannah, but they aren't very well acquainted yet, not enough to be considered family. Who else?'

'Harriet Saul?' Winslow said doubtfully.

'Ah! Now there's a good guess. But Ms Saul is a busy woman, an excellent administrator who is responsible for running a very complicated business, namely the zoo. So who does that leave Hannah with?'

Winslow frowned. 'I don't know anyone else. Just Sam.'

'Exactly! Mr Brown to you, Winslow, but yes, she has nobody except Mr Brown – and Mrs Brown, of course. But here's a problem: Mr Brown is ready to retire. He's worked hard for a very long time, but he's not in good health anymore, and he's earned the right to rest. Who does that leave for Hannah then?'

Winslow looked alarmed. 'Nobody.'

'Precisely! That means – hypothetically, you understand – that Hannah must either find a new family or be alone for the next twenty years, since I gather that elephants can live into their sixties. And who would make a better new family than other elephants? They have no plans to retire, they don't have to go home at night, they don't want to take a summer vacation, and they don't have any interest in getting a different job. Ms Saul knows all this, because she's a woman with a big heart. But she's also an excellent administrator, so she knows it's too expensive to bring another elephant to Havenside. So there's really only one alternative. What would that be, Winslow?'

The boy looked at Matthew. 'What?'

'Sending Hannah to other elephants!' Matthew crowed.

'Is she going to do that?' Winslow said. '*Really?* Because, oh boy, I bet Hannah would rather play with other elephants any day than hang out with an old guy.'

'Let's not cast aspersions on old men,' Matthew said.

'Sorry, Grandpa.'

'Now, Ms Saul is a good woman, and any good woman who cares more about an elephant's quality of life than about a zoo's financial well-being would send Hannah away, wouldn't she, if there were a place where she'd be better off?'

'Is there?' Winslow asked.

'As a matter of fact, there is. It's a place called the Pachyderm Sanctuary near Sacramento, California.'

'Do you think they'd take Hannah?' Winslow said, leaning close to Matthew.

'I believe Harriet Saul is working on that right now.'

'That was masterful,' Truman told Matthew as he saw them to the car.

Matthew shrugged disparagingly. 'It's what we old dogs call "seizing the higher ground". School him a little on the ride home.' Matthew waved a disingenuous, grand-fatherly goodbye to Winslow through the back window. 'Especially about Harriet Saul's goodness.'

Chapter 19

With a freshly minted, bylined, front-page, above-the-fold story to his credit, Martin Choi was a man on the move. God, it was good to be him. And it wasn't over yet! Matthew Levy had as good as promised that. So for the second day in a row, he made tracks to the Biedelman Zoo despite the fact that, technically, it was his day off. But he was a professional newspaperman. It wasn't always just about the paycheck.

To his disappointment, the zoo's administrative offices were locked. He pounded on the front door several times, but if Harriet Saul was there – and when *wasn't* she there? – she wasn't showing herself. He headed down to the elephant yard and found Samson Brown outside, scooping slippery green muck out of Hannah's tiny mud wallow. Martin could smell it clear across the yard and outside the fence, where he was standing. The stuff was ripe enough to fell trees.

'Hey! Do you remember me?' he called.

'Don't think so,' Sam said, squinting. 'Am I supposed to?'

Martin stood a little straighter. 'I'm a reporter with the *Bladenham News-Gazette* – actually, I'm the one who broke the front page story in today's paper. Have you seen a copy of it yet?'

'Yeah, I've seen it. Someone had it out at the Dunkin' Donuts when I stopped.'

'What did you think of it?'

'Didn't think anything. I didn't read it.'

'But you're Hannah's guardian. Aren't you interested in the way the story's being covered?'

'Naw. Seems like something that should stay between me and Hannah – me, Hannah, and Harriet Saul,' Sam said, pitchforking Hannah droppings into his wheelbarrow.

'Yeah, what about Harriet Saul, huh?'

'Couldn't say,' Sam said. 'Ask her.'

'I tried, but yesterday she wouldn't talk to me, and today I can't find her. You have any idea why?'

'Nope.' Sam moved the wheelbarrow to the next manure pile.

Martin deflated a little. 'Well, look, I don't want to stop you from working.'

'Does it look like I'm stopping?' Sam said. 'God Himself couldn't stop me some days, so there's no need for you to worry.'

'You know anyone else I could interview?'

'No.'

'All right, well, hey, let me give you my card in case you think of something you want me to know about. This is a multifaceted story, you know what I mean?'

'Don't know anything about facets,' Sam said. 'I just

know about me and shug, and none of that needs to go in the paper.'

Martin held out his business card. 'So you won't take this?'

'Nope. Save it for someone who might use it.'

'Okay, well, the name's Martin Choi. Martin Choi. If you think of something you want to talk to me about, just call the *News-Gazette*.'

Sam lifted his hand in a vague farewell and disappeared into the elephant barn.

Nuts.

Two boys – Reginald and Winslow, Martin remembered – rounded the barn with a pitchfork and wheelbarrow, scuffling and shoving each other. Martin called, 'Hey! You want to be in the newspaper?'

'Sure, if you promise to put our pictures in,' Reginald shouted back. He and Winslow walked over to the fence.

'I might be able to arrange that. Can I come inside there with you?'

'No,' Reginald and Winslow said in unison.

'How come?'

'Because,' Reginald said.

'Because why?'

'*Because*,' Reginald said. To Winslow he said, 'Jeez.'

'Watch your mouth,' Martin said, turning to a fresh page in his reporter's tablet. 'I might just forget your name.'

'R-E-G-I-N-A-L-D P-O-O-L-E.'

'Yeah, yeah. So tell me what you think about this whole Hannah thing,' Martin said. 'What kind of stuff are you overhearing?'

Winslow frowned at Reginald. Reginald held up his empty palms: nothing.

289

'You boys are going to make me work, aren't you?'

'What kind of stuff do you want to know, mister?' Winslow said.

'I want to know whether the trust is going to do anything, you know, radical. Like, say, changing the way Hannah lives. Or *where* she lives.'

Winslow looked startled. 'How did you know that?'

Martin was just as startled. He'd just been talking; he hadn't even been paying attention. 'What — she's going somewhere?'

The boy regarded Martin Choi for a long moment and then nodded.

'*Yes?* No shit! Hey, excuse me, kid. Where's she going? When's she leaving? Oh, man, this is it — this is *it*!'

'I don't know. Someplace in California,' Winslow said. 'Someplace where there are other elephants. They found out yesterday for sure.'

'So who's working on this? Jesus, kid, this is big stuff!'

Winslow started to get nervous. 'You should probably ask my grandfather. He'd know. His name is Matthew—'

'Yeah, yeah, I know him, kid. What's your name again? Winfred. Odd name. Got it, kid. Look, hey, I owe you. You ever want a paper route, you just let me know.'

Less than half an hour later, Martin Choi was once again seated in Matthew and Lavinia's sun porch.

'Hey, thanks for talking to me. I've heard the most amazing story from your grandson at the zoo. I wanted to run it by you, see if there's anything to it.' Martin reviewed his facts while Matthew sat quietly, fingertips joined, listening.

'Yes, yes, all those things are true. There is also something else, but I can't share it with you without an absolute guarantee of anonymity,' Matthew said.

'Yeah, hey, no problem,' Martin agreed. Sometimes people wouldn't say the really ugly stuff except anonymously. Martin was okay with that.

'Then I would like to tell you something about Harriet Saul that she would never tell you herself – might even deny if you confronted her with it.' Matthew took a deep breath, lowered his voice, leaned forward, and said, 'Harriet Saul is personally spearheading the effort to move Hannah to the Pachyderm Sanctuary. *Personally*, Martin. She's committing an act of keen integrity, I might even say courage. I'm sure you understand fully how much more difficult her job as the zoo's managerial and financial overseer will become without Hannah.'

Martin looked up from his tablet, squinting suspiciously. 'So if she's such a hero, how come she won't talk? Because she still won't. She's *pissed*.'

'Come on, Martin. Think. Harriet Saul's not doing this to draw attention to herself; she isn't doing this for self-aggrandizement or even basic recognition. She's doing it for Hannah, *because it's right*. Because it's right. Pure and simple.'

'Well, sure,' Martin said, squinting. 'Sure! That's why – Jesus, picture being the head of an operation like the Biedelman Zoo, and knowing that the one animal you need most to put you on the map is the one who needs *you* to let it go? How are you going to explain that? You're not! You're not going to explain that! You're just going to do it, because it's right. Let the chips fall where they may!'

'So you understand,' Matthew said gravely.

291

'Damn right.'

'Martin.'

'Huh?'

'Report it, son. Report it.'

Harriet crackled with fury as she huddled with Mayor Howard Bolton and City of Bladenham counsel Bob Medford at City Hall. 'I'm not going to accept this – you can't possibly expect me to accept this. It's ridiculous, Howard, and you know it. You might as well shut down the zoo. Just go ahead and lock the gates right now and hang up a sign saying CLOSED FOR LACK OF INTEREST. Without that elephant, the zoo's nothing but a collection of hoofed stock, barnyard animals, and a couple of ratty primates.'

'Now, that's not true,' the mayor said. 'The people of Bladenham love their zoo. They're not—'

'Oh, shut up, Howard,' Harriet said.

Howard turned to his legal counsel. 'Bob, in your experience, how much of a loophole might this thing have? If we contest it, would we win?'

'Probably not. The documents establishing the trust and setting its provisions are very straightforward.'

'Oh, we'll contest it,' Harriet said in a low, dangerous voice.

'Now, Harriet,' Howard said. 'We don't want to get into any expensive, drawn-out legal battle. Especially one we're likely to lose.'

'I assume the candidate who ran against you was a moron,' Harriet said bitterly. 'Because why else they elected you I can't imagine.'

★ ★ ★

Sam was the first one at work on Saturday morning, bearing a sack of pumpkin crème donuts and a custard one Rayette had slipped in for free. Juggling the bag, a leftover turkey sandwich, and cranberry sauce in a mayonnaise jar, he fumbled for his keys and tried the gate. The key wouldn't work. He looked at his key, looked at the gate, reinserted the key. Nothing. While he was trying to figure out what was going on, a relief zookeeper Sam had only seen once or twice before came out of the barn. They saw each other in the same instant. The zookeeper, a pasty-faced man in his twenties, looked uncomfortable.

'My key won't work,' Sam said. 'You break this lock?'

'Nah. She had them changed.'

Sam could hear shug in there rocking. The shackle rang against the wall like a tolling bell. 'What?'

'She had security change the locks this morning.'

'Why'd she do that?' Sam said.

'Look, dude, all I know is she told me to come in and feed the elephant, so that's what I'm doing.'

Sam tried to stay calm. 'You unchain the girl yet?'

'I'm supposed to leave her chained up for now. I gave her some hay, though.'

'Let me in,' Sam said.

'No can do, bud. I'm really sorry.'

Sam was struggling to stay reasonable. 'Just unchain the girl. You can do that. Just let her outside. Won't hurt you to at least do that.'

The zookeeper headed around the barn. 'Sorry, man, but I don't want to piss off the boss.'

Sam called as loud as he could, 'You hold on, shug! Papa's going to be right back, and then we'll get you out of that place. Just hold on, sugar.'

He tore up the hill and straight into the house. Before he even came into the office suite he could hear loud voices: Truman and that Harriet.

'For god's sake, Harriet,' Truman was saying. 'You can't lock them out.'

'Oh? And why not?'

'He has twenty-four-hour access. Legally.'

Sam stood outside the door.

'And I'm not contesting that,' Harriet said. 'But the zoo is my domain. I can deny access to anyone I feel might be a destructive presence.'

'Oh, come on, Harriet,' Truman said. 'What are you going to gain? You have no legal basis for keeping Sam from her. Or Neva.'

Sam could tell Harriet was smiling, one of those mean, pinched little smiles. 'I do, as a matter of fact. Neva Wilson no longer works here.'

Sam couldn't stand by for that. He pushed through into the office suite. Truman was standing in the door to Harriet's office, his back to Sam. 'You're kidding,' he was saying.

'I knew I shouldn't have hired her. She's been trouble since the first day she got here. I blame myself.'

Sam could see muscles tighten in Truman's back. 'Harriet, as the director of this zoo your first obligation is to the animals. You can't keep that elephant chained up.'

Harriet's voice got tight and shrill. 'Oh, so you're an animal expert now? Don't you *dare* get sanctimonious with me, Truman. You've taken her side ever since she got here, and I won't have it.'

Truman turned around and saw Sam standing by the reception desk. Truman beckoned for him to follow.

294

'Truman!' Harriet yelled. 'Don't you walk away from me!'

'Go back to the barn and wait for me there,' Truman told Sam in a low voice. 'I'll call my father and see what we can do. We'll get you in.'

'Shug's going to hurt herself if she's left in there. She doesn't understand.'

'I know,' Truman said. 'We'll fix this.'

Neva was waiting at the elephant yard fence when Sam got back. Truman must have called and warned her. She trotted to meet him.

'She said you don't work here anymore,' Sam said.

Neva waved that off. 'Look, this is crap. I'm going to call down to the sanctuary and ask Alice to get emergency clearance from her board so we can bring Hannah down as soon as we can get the permit through the USDA.'

'How long's that going to take?'

'I don't know. A week. Maybe a little longer.'

'Shug ain't got a week.'

Truman pulled into the parking lot by the barn and he and Winslow hopped out of his car.

'Shug's going to hurt herself if she's left in there,' Sam said to him again. 'You hear that noise, sounds like a hammer on an anvil? That's shug tearing up her leg. She doesn't understand.'

Truman bowed his head. 'I know, Sam. My folks are working on it. They'll get you in as soon as they can. They're sure it'll be by this afternoon, and hopefully sooner.'

Sam looked at Neva in despair.

'It's going to be okay,' Neva said with as much confidence as she could muster, though the only card in her hand was the certainty with which she wished it. She walked away to her car and pulled out her cell phone.

Sam, Truman, and Winslow settled down behind a hedge outside the fence line to formulate a plan and keep an eye on the relief zookeeper. As soon as he left, locking the gate after him, Sam gave Winslow a nudge and the boy dashed to the twelve-foot-high chain link fence, climbed over the top, and dropped into the elephant yard. He came back to open the gate from the inside. Sam rushed into the barn and to Hannah's side. Blood was running down her ankle and had made a sticky pool beneath her feet. Sam unfastened the shackle, retrieved the girl's tire, and started petting and talking as reassuringly as he could manage with his own heart nearly broken.

'It's okay now, sugar, Papa's here. You're going to be just fine. It's over now, sweet thing, we're going to get you out of this nasty place. Come on, sugar, let's get you out of here into some daylight.'

Sam threw open the barn doors, picked up Hannah's tire, and started walking with it. Hannah came out of her trance and trudged after him.

Winslow came over. 'Is she okay? She's sure bleeding a lot.' He pointed to her ankle.

'She'll be better once we get her out of here,' Sam said.

It was two fifty-eight — two minutes before Harriet's afternoon performance.

Truman backed his car up to the gate to the elephant

yard and Neva pulled up behind him. She hopped out of her car and disappeared inside; a minute later the hayloft door opened and she pushed out four bales of hay. Truman loaded two in his trunk, then two in Neva's car. While he was doing that, Neva reappeared with two huge plastic totes full of uncut produce. Truman loaded these in the back seat of his car.

'Go,' Neva told Sam. 'Go! We'll see you there.'

'Let's go now, shug,' Sam said quietly. 'We're going on a little adventure.'

Reginald Poole appeared at the top of the hill. 'Hey, wait up, you guys!' he shouted.

Sam put his finger to his lips. Reginald ran down as fast as he could.

'You going on a walk?'

'Yeah, we are, but it's going to be a longer walk than she's used to. You got your aunt's permission to be here?'

'She says I can stay until five.'

'Fall in, then. We got to make some tracks today, though. No dawdling. And no sassing, either. I'm not in the mood for any sassing.'

'How come?'

'No reason you need to know. You got on a pair of comfortable shoes?'

Reginald looked down at his Nikes. 'Yeah, they're comfortable.'

'Okay, because between the girl and me, we got enough bad feet already to last us 'til Judgment Day.'

Sam brought Hannah out of the gate, but he headed in a different direction than Winslow was used to.

'Where are we going?' he said.

'You just give the girl a yam now and then and be

patient,' Sam said. 'You'll see.' And that was all he would say.

Harriet put on her pith helmet with grim determination. Her zoo was hemorrhaging like a leaking dike, spewing money, personnel, control. It couldn't go on. But first she had a performance to give. She gave her clothes a grim little tug and walked onto the front porch with her portable amplification system, riding crop, and large-format camera. Several hundred visitors were gathered at the foot of the stairs.

She raised the microphone. 'Good morning, friends!' she called. 'I am Maxine Biedelman. Welcome to my zoo!'

Light applause broke out. Martin Choi, clanking with his usual excessive gear, pushed forward through the crowd, which parted to let him up onto the stairs with Harriet. He seized the microphone. 'Ladies and gentlemen, let me introduce you to Harriet Saul, the director of this terrific zoo of ours.'

Harriet hissed, 'Martin, for God's sake.'

He kept right on going. 'Let me tell you about this woman,' he said into the mike.

'*What?*' Harriet said. She tried to grab the microphone away, but Martin lifted it high over his head and spun away, out of her reach.

'This is a wonderful woman, ladies and gentlemen. A *brave* woman. Do you all know Hannah, our elephant?'

Sounds of concurrence rose from the crowd.

'Well, this woman is going to save Hannah's life. That's right. Hannah lives alone and in lousy conditions – nobody's fault, just the truth, and Harriet Saul knows it. So here it is: she's working to relocate Hannah to someplace better, someplace where she can get healthy and live with other elephants.'

A general gasp rose from the crowd. Martin went on. 'Friends, you are looking at a woman who's putting it all on the line to make sure Hannah can go to an elephant sanctuary. It's where Hannah should be, not here, and this woman' – and here he actually *grasped Harriet's hand* – 'is big enough to see it. That's integrity! That's courage! Folks, you are looking at a hero. A hero.'

Harriet struggled to free her hand, but Martin kept it in an iron grasp. He was rolling, now. 'I've had the privilege of interviewing Ms Saul a number of times recently for the *News-Gazette* – which you can buy at all major area supermarkets and street corner vending machines – and I can attest to her bravery, her dedication. She's a woman who's doing something not because it is easy, not because it's popular, but because it is *right*. Right, ladies and gentlemen! And I, for one, am proud to stand here beside her!'

And to her astonishment, he lifted her sweating hand high overhead in a victory salute.

Sam walked beside Winslow, with Hannah on his other side; and beyond that, Reginald. Hannah carried her tire and she moved fast – faster than she had in a long time. The Lord only knew where she thought she was going. She hadn't come this way, up the far side of the zoo property, in thirty years or more.

Sam asked Winslow, 'You got the fruit like I asked you to bring?'

Winslow held up a gallon-sized zip-lock bag of yams and carrots. Sam knew the boy had it; he was just talking to calm his nerves.

'You bring some for me, too?' Reginald called. 'I didn't have time to cut anything, what with you all being so damn secretive.'

'When we get there,' Winslow said.

'Get *where*? What's the big damn secret?'

'You watch your mouth, boy,' Sam warned, and Reginald subsided. Sam looked over at Winslow beside him, and thought the boy looked a little peaked. 'You okay?' Sam asked him. 'Did you have a good time with your mama?'

Winslow shrugged.

'Nah?'

Winslow hunched his shoulders. 'We didn't have that good a time, but now I miss her anyway.'

'When are you going to see her next?'

'Dunno. She doesn't usually say. She travels a lot now so, you know.'

'Sounds exciting.'

'She's going to Ecuador next week. She's doing sculptures based on countries in Latin America. She says it'll be a miracle if she doesn't get dysentery.'

'You ask her to bring you back a souvenir?'

'No. She'll bring me back something, though.'

'Yeah,' Reginald called. 'A tapeworm, maybe.'

Sam chuckled. Bright kids. Winslow didn't have as much to prove as Reginald, though. Nice boy, too. He'd been real well-behaved at Thanksgiving, listening to the grownups, not wisecracking. Neva had kept watching him like she knew him real well, maybe, or like she was trying to figure him out. Too bad that girl had such a shell around her. Inside she was nothing but sweetness and butter, but she made people punch through the crust

300

to get at it, and he guessed a lot of them didn't have the strength.

'You think someone's going to come after us?' Winslow asked Sam.

'Nah. They probably won't even notice we're gone for a little while yet.' He hoped he sounded more convinced than he felt. All they could do was keep walking straight and as fast as the girl would go. 'So tell me something about your mama,' he said to Winslow, to keep his mind off worrying. 'What's she like? Besides being a famous artist.'

'She's not famous.'

'Tell me what she's like anyway.'

'I don't know. Tall. She's tall.'

'What would she say if we walked by her right now?'

'"You don't *always* have to tuck your shirt in."'

'Odd thing to say.'

Winslow sighed. 'Yeah.'

They'd arrived at a chain link fence. Sam brought wire cutters out of his jacket pocket and, working fast, cut the links until he'd freed a section of fence wide enough for Hannah to fit through. They walked on, into the woods now, farther than either Winslow and Reginald had ever been.

'Is this okay?' Reginald called from Hannah's far side.

'Is what okay?'

'Our being here. I didn't think we were supposed to come here.'

'Today is different,' Sam said. 'Today it's okay.' Hannah padded ahead of them now, following the same route she'd often walked so many years before.

'Do you like living with your daddy?' Sam asked Winslow.

'Yeah. Miles does, too.'

'The pig.'

'Yup.'

'Wouldn't normally picture your daddy with a pig,' Sam said.

'Miles likes him, though.'

'Pigs have a good sense of people. Old Hilda, she's the sow here, she doesn't like kids, but that's because she can't see too good and she's afraid they'll sneak up and throw something at her.'

'Why would she think that?'

'Someone tossed a firecracker in with her once, just one of those little poppers, but it scared her so bad she didn't come out of her shed for a week.'

'That was mean,' Winslow said.

'People are, sometimes.'

'My grandpa told me Hannah's not going to live at the zoo anymore,' Winslow said.

'Yup. Shug's going to go to a retirement home for elephants.'

'Do you think she'll be okay down there?'

'Yeah, I do. Course, she's going to miss us at first, like we're going to miss her. But it'll be good for her, all the same. She'll get her feet nice and healed up, get to roam around where there's grass and trees and a pond. And other elephants, of course. She's going to be better than okay. I expect she's going to think she landed in the Garden of Eden.'

Reginald came around. 'It's lonely over there,' he said. 'What are you guys talking about?'

'Heaven,' Sam said. 'You boys want to switch sides? Winslow, take shug's blind side for a little while and let

302

Reginald come over here. Remember to keep your hand on her, so she knows you're there.'

Winslow crossed over and Reginald took his place.

'So tell me something about yourself I don't already know,' Sam said.

'Like what?'

'I don't know. Tell me about your daddy.'

Reginald's shoulders hunched up a little bit. 'I haven't seen him for a while.'

'You talk to him, though?'

'Nah. My aunt says the less I have to do with him, the better.'

'That right?'

Reginald seemed to reach a decision. 'He's in prison. He broke into a liquor store in Bothell. Said he didn't mean to hurt anything, just needed a little something to take the edge off a bad headache. Why would you break into a liquor store for that? He should have broken into a drug store. He probably wouldn't have been caught, there. No one cares about drug stores. They probably figure if someone's desperate enough to steal aspirin or something, they must really need it.'

'Sometimes people do wrong things, son. Bet he'd take it back if he could. He's probably real sorry he isn't around to watch you grow up.'

'Yeah,' Reginald said without conviction.

'People can do all manner of stupid things. Doesn't mean they're bad people, necessarily.'

'My aunt says my dad's a worthless piece of junk.'

'Women can be hard sometimes,' Sam acknowledged. 'I can't imagine what Corinna's thought about me over the years. Probably be right, too. We're just people. We get

303

up some days and do something we shouldn't, and we can't even explain why. That's human nature. Maybe that's the way it was with your daddy.'

They walked along quietly, listening to the sound of Hannah snapping twigs underfoot. Sam said, 'You know, sometimes the folks we're given at the beginning don't end up being the ones who raise us. Someone loves you, why, then they're raising you. You got your aunt. Hannah, she found Miss Biedelman, and then she found me and Corinna. She's been lucky that way. And now she's got you, too.'

That perked Reginald up. 'You think she knows me? Because I can call her, and she'll come right over.'

'Of course she knows you, son. She might have a buggered-up eye, but she's not blind, and even if she was, she's plenty smart enough to recognize the people who've been good to her. You're the man with the treats. Plus she trusts you. There's something about you she just likes.'

'Yeah?'

'Sure.'

'How about Winslow?' Reginald asked.

'Not so much,' Sam said in a voice too low for Winslow to hear. 'At least, not yet. But he's got Miles, so there's that – Hannah doesn't necessarily like to share.'

'So she chose me.'

'Yep.'

The boy spread his chest, walked a little higher on his toes.

Sam elbowed him lightly in the side, grinning. 'She also likes handsome. You think you're handsome?'

Reginald grinned back. 'I *know* I'm handsome.'

'Couple of more years and you're going to be hard to be around,' Sam laughed.

'Hey, you guys!' Winslow called. 'It's getting creepy in here.' Dusk was well underway. 'Can I come over there with you?'

'Yeah, just tell shug where you're going and keep your hand on her when you cross behind her, so she doesn't startle,' Sam said.

Winslow circled around and joined them. 'Either of you ever have nightmares?' Sam asked.

'I do,' Winslow said. 'I dream my mom's mad at me.'

'Why's she mad?'

Winslow shrugged. 'I don't know. She was always mad about something. It was more at my dad than me, though.'

'How about you?' Sam asked Reginald.

'Nah.'

'Hannah, she dreams,' Sam told them.

Reginald rolled his eyes at Winslow. Sam just smiled. 'Everything dreams, son.'

'Aw, you don't know that.'

'Sure I do,' Sam said. 'If you look in her eyes you can see it there as plain as day. Shug dreams about grass. Grass and elephants.'

Chapter 20

Harriet closed herself in her office with a pounding headache. The Trojan Horse had wrought less havoc than Martin Choi's declaration on Havenside's front stairs. Within an hour of completing her show she had declined interviews with the Associated Press, the *Tacoma News-Tribune*, Northwest Cable News, the *Seattle Post-Intelligencer*, the *Seattle Times*, and Reuters. She had had the receptionist tell them all she would return their calls after four p.m. She figured by then she'd either be dead from a stroke or her blood pressure and pulse would have returned to a sustainable range.

She checked the wine bottles at the back of the closet in vain.

She ate an old, stale half-order of nachos and coagulated cheese.

She paced the perimeter of her office, hitting her shin repeatedly with Maxine's riding crop. *Thwack. Thwack. Thwack.* For the first time in her adult life, she didn't know what to do. Her experience centered almost entirely on rejection, not courtship. She'd been sabotaged by praise.

Her security radio crackled and then one of the security guards said, 'Security to Ms Biedelman-Saul. Ma'am, there's no elephant down here. Over.'

'What do you mean? How can there not be an elephant?'

'I don't know, ma'am. Over.'

'Well, are you saying she escaped?'

'No ma'am, I wouldn't say escaped, because there aren't any gates open or anything. Nobody in the barn, either, for that matter. Over.'

'Well, was the lock broken open?'

'No, ma'am, I don't see any sign of that. Over.'

'Oh, for God's sake.'

'Yes, ma'am. Over and out.'

Just when Sam's flashlight batteries began to die, they broke from the woods into a meadow. 'Hey!' Winslow said. 'Now I know where we are! This is my grandpa's farm. How come we're—' Then he saw the barn, golden light flooding through two small windows. 'We're going to keep Hannah here, aren't we?'

'Smart boy!' Sam said, clapping Winslow on the back. 'Shug's going to stay the night, give us a chance to sort some things out.'

Matthew came out the back door of the house as they neared the barn. Winslow ran to meet him.

'Look who we've got!' he called.

Matthew gave the boy a hug and walked with him toward the barn, where Sam, Reginald, and Hannah were

308

standing. 'Well, now!' Matthew said, shaking Sam's hand warmly. 'Did you run into any problems?'

'No, sir,' Sam said. 'Least, not once we got out the gate.'

'Good, good.'

Matthew slid open the barn door. The barn was a clean, dry, open place neatly holding the tools of a gentleman farmer – a ride-on tractor, hay mower, wheelbarrow, hay rake, and a few tools. The rest was a hayloft, several horse stalls with hay strewn over their dirt floors, and a lot of air. Matthew hung several Coleman lanterns to boost the golden light of the overhead bulbs. Hot white lantern light threw shadows into the corners.

'Think this'll do, Sam?'

'Yes, sir. I think this should be about perfect.'

A car crunched up the gravel drive and stopped in front of the barn.

'Ah!' Matthew said. 'Here's my son.'

Truman joined them in the barn, closely followed by Miles. Miles snuffled his way in while Hannah watched him with rolling eyes, reached toward him tentatively with her trunk. The little pig twitched his tail and gamely turned in a circle so Hannah could sniff all of him. Truman took the wheelbarrow to the car and came back with his two bales of hay.

Reginald poked Winslow hard in the ribs. 'That your pig?'

'Yeah. He farts a lot.'

Reginald snorted appreciatively, looking around. 'This is real nice. You get to come over here often?'

'Yeah,' Winslow said. 'Sometimes I get to drive the tractor.'

309

'Yeah? I visit my grandpa sometimes, too. He lets me do whatever I want. One time I ate twenty-two Eskimo Pies in a row.'

'Yeah?' said Winslow.

'Yeah. I'm going to see him again soon, and we're going to stay up all night and play paintball.'

'You're lying,' Winslow said.

'Nuh uh,' said Reginald.

'So where does he live?'

'Here.'

'Where's here?'

'Bladenham.'

'Yeah, but what street?'

'I don't know. I never paid attention.'

'I bet you don't even have a grandpa.'

Reginald kicked Winslow hard on the shin, and then they were scuffling in the hay.

'Boys!' Truman called. 'Knock it off.'

'He's telling all these lies,' Winslow said.

'Then he probably has a good reason,' Truman said. 'Find something else to talk about.'

Sam was telling Matthew, 'Shug must think she's died and gone to heaven with all this nice hay and pretty barn. It's been a long time since she got to go anyplace new.'

'Did she get through the day without too much harm?' Truman asked. He looked down at Hannah's bloody ankle and winced.

'She got a little upset earlier, but she'll be okay,' Sam said. 'Nothing a nice little meal of hay and fruit won't make right again.'

Truman's gaze went from Hannah's leg to Sam's.

'Sam – good god!' The cuff of Sam's khaki pants was wet with blood. 'What happened?'

'Just a nasty sore I've got. Bleeds sometimes, but the doctor's got me on a new medicine that should fix it right up – that and getting off my feet for a while once shug's settled.'

'I hope so,' Truman said, and then car tires crunched over the gravel again. Neva pulled up and jumped out. 'Did she make the trip okay?'

Sam said, 'She did just fine. I'm proud of the girl. She hasn't been that far into the woods in a long time, but she just went right along.'

'Thank god.' Neva approached Hannah, who had come to stand quietly beside Sam with her trunk tucked under his arm. 'You're a brave girl,' Neva told her, 'and it's just going to get better and better.'

Sam, Truman, Winslow, Reginald, and Matthew all turned.

She broke into a grin. 'I just heard from Alice. They'll take her as soon as we can have her ready!'

A whoop rang out, followed by a general clamoring for information.

'Tell us about it, for god's sake,' Truman said. 'Details – we want details!'

Neva said, 'Well, evidently this lockout was the final straw. Alice said she was pretty sure the board would have voted to accept Hannah anyway, but they weren't planning on dealing with it until their next regular meeting in February. When she told the board chairman we'd been locked out, he called the executive committee together, and I guess they just about set the room on fire. Apparently they drew up a motion to accept Hannah on the spot, and the full board passed it by a phone vote

311

without a single dissension.' She turned and said quietly, 'Congratulations, Sam.'

Sam shook his head. 'Don't know what to say.' Hannah bumped him with her trunk. 'Baby always knows when something's up.' The elephant wrapped her trunk around his head, explored his ear. He reached up and patted her. 'It's all right, baby doll. It's all right now. You're going to see the world.'

Off to the side, Matthew was saying to Winslow, 'Come with me, my boy.' The two of them trotted off.

'What on earth?' Neva asked Truman, but he just shook his head.

'Could I borrow your phone?' Sam asked him. 'I'd like to call Mama and tell her the news. She's going to be on the moon.' Truman extended his cell phone and Sam walked deeper into the barn.

Truman turned to Neva, whose eyes were bright. She said, 'If I know Alice, she incited a riot. The woman's a Valkyrie when she's pissed off.' She laughed. 'God, I'd have loved to be in the room.'

Matthew came back into the barn with Lavinia and Winslow. Winslow carried two cream sodas; Matthew had a bottle of wine and a bouquet of glasses.

'You know we're going to have to tell Harriet,' Truman said to Neva.

'I thought I would do that myself in a little while. Unless you'd rather do it, of course,' Matthew said to Sam, who'd come back with Truman's phone.

'No, sir,' said Sam, returning Truman's cell phone.

'Is Corinna all right?'

'Woman's beside herself. I never heard her stuck for words before.'

312

'Then I believe a toast is in order.' Matthew uncorked the wine and had Winslow pass around the filled wine glasses, and cream sodas for the boys.

'To Hannah!' Matthew called.

'To Hannah!' they all echoed.

Sam pulled Reginald aside and pointed to his watch: five-fifteen. 'I forgot all about the time. When was your aunt picking you up?'

'Five. It's okay, though.'

'No it isn't.'

'She won't care.'

'Course she'll care. She's probably worried sick or mad, one or the other, and I wouldn't want someone to feel either way about me. You ask Mister Levy over there if you can use his cell phone, and then you tell her I'll drive you home myself.'

'Aw, man,' Reginald said, and shuffled over to Matthew.

'He seems like a nice boy,' Matthew said to Sam, watching Reginald shuffle away, punching a number into Matthew's cell phone.

'Yeah, he just needs some attention.'

'What kind of attention?'

'The man kind, mostly.'

'I gather his father's in jail,' Matthew said.

'Yeah,' Sam said. 'It about killed him to tell me that.'

Reginald headed back looking dejected as they both watched. 'She's real mad,' he said when he reached them.

'She should be, you promising her something and then breaking your word. Your word is the only thing a man's got, so don't you go wasting it. You tell her I'm going to bring you home?'

313

'Yeah. She said good.'

'I bet she did. All right, son, let's go. Say goodbye to everyone.'

'Bye, everyone!' Reginald yelled to the barn in general. 'Bye, Windermere!'

Goodbyes rang out from all over. Sam put his hand on the boy's back and steered him to the car.

'I think we got some things to talk about, you and me,' Sam told him as they drove away.

'Yeah? Like what?'

'Like what you want more, a future or a past.'

'What's that supposed to mean?' Reginald said.

'Looks like I'm going to have a little time on my hands pretty soon, so you stick with me and I'll show you.'

Neva hauled an air mattress, sleeping bag, pillow, and toilet kit out of her car and into the barn. She told Matthew, 'I'm taking first watch, if that's okay with you.'

Matthew nodded. 'You know best. Just come into the house anytime you need to. Walk right in. I'll set some towels out for you, and Lavinia's preparing supper.'

Sam, back from driving Reginald home, said to her, 'You sure you don't want me to be the one to stay over? Mama could bring me a sweater and some blankets and I'd be fine.'

'Nope. Your turn will come,' Neva assured him.

'Uh oh,' said Winslow, pointing across the lawn.

Approaching from across the lawn were Lavinia and Harriet Saul. Matthew stepped forward to greet her. 'Hello, Harriet. What a pleasure.'

Harriet nodded at him curtly, and then at the others. 'Sam. Neva. Truman.'

314

'Ma'am,' Sam said, stepping between Harriet and Hannah.

'Martin Choi has publicly declared me Saint Francis of Assisi. If I'm going to be beatified, I'd better at least understand why.'

Neva said to Sam, 'Let me talk. She's already fired me.'

'That might have been a bit hasty,' Harriet said.

'Oh, probably not.'

'Look, I need to know. Is it absolutely necessary for Hannah to leave?' Harriet asked. 'You know what it'll do to the zoo.'

'She'll die if we don't move her,' Neva said.

'And you agree?' Harriet asked Sam.

'Yes ma'am.'

'I assume you have someplace lined up to take her.'

'The Pachyderm Sanctuary has agreed to take her as soon as she can be moved,' Neva said. 'It's an excellent facility near Sacramento.'

'No doubt,' Harriet said dryly. 'And what will you do, Sam? I'm sure you understand that you can't stay at the zoo.'

'No ma'am. I'll be retiring,' Sam said. 'I've got some medical things I need to take care of.'

'Medical things?' Harriet said.

'Diabetes, ma'am. I've got diabetes.'

'You never said anything about this.'

'No, ma'am.'

'Believe it or not, I do care about these things.'

'Yes, ma'am,' Sam said. 'I didn't know.'

'Yes, well, people rarely give me the benefit of the doubt,' Harriet said. 'I don't know why that is.'

'Yes, ma'am.'

315

Harriet nodded at Sam and Neva. 'And I assume you have a plan for moving her.'

'Yes, ma'am, we do,' Sam said.

'All right, then,' she said. 'I'm listening.'

Matthew brought a glass of wine and a folding chair for her, and the others dragged over boxes and a bench. Harriet pulled her barn coat around her more tightly and they began.

At ten o'clock that night, Truman and Neva were sitting on wooden crates at an upturned industrial spool they were using as a table. The remnants of a late spaghetti dinner had been loaded into black trash bags nearby, and in one of the stalls Miles blinked in porcine contentment, bedded down in fresh straw. Winslow lay on a straw bed one stall over, cozy in his down sleeping bag; Hannah stood near Neva and Truman, dozing over her tire.

'I admire your dedication,' Truman was saying.

'It's just selfishness – I love what I do. I can't imagine doing anything else.'

'You're lucky. Most of us don't feel that way. Lives of quiet desperation and all that.'

'Are you desperate?'

'Me? No. There have been moments, but no – I have choices. Actually I've been thinking about going to law school.' He smiled ruefully. 'Three lawyers in two generations. People will run when they see us coming. Imagine being a student again at thirty-six.'

From his stall, Miles heaved a mighty sigh. Truman smiled at Neva, who smiled back. 'Actually, it's a relief to have him here,' Truman said. 'He's begun rearranging the furniture in the den at night.'

'Well, he is a pig,' Neva pointed out. 'They're smart. Smart and busy.'

'I only wish I'd known,' Truman said. 'I'm going to tell Winslow goodnight. I'll be right back. Are you all right – do you need anything, while I'm up?'

'Are you coming back, after?'

'I was thinking I would.'

'Then no, there's nothing I need.'

Truman stretched out beside Winslow, smelling the magical essence of sweet hay and animals. The boy lay on his back, looking at the barn ceiling, deep in thought.

'Isn't it late to be thinking so hard?' Truman said.

'How come you put Mom's shoes away?'

'Shoes?'

'Her moccasins. The ones that always used to be by the front door.'

Truman thought about this. 'I don't know. I was just ready, I guess. I used to love the way your mother sounded when she walked around the house in those shoes. They were way too big for her – they'd been mine, to begin with – and when she walked around the house in them you could hear them patting on the wood floors. It was the most peaceful sound, knowing we were all at home and safe together.'

Winslow rolled onto his side, ready for sleep.

'But now we've got Miles, so that's all right, too,' Truman said.

Winslow smiled drowsily. 'We should have gotten a dog.'

Truman adjusted Winslow's sleeping bag, kissed his forehead, and stood up stiffly. Hannah dozed nearby, shifting her weight and flapping her ears. Who would have ever

317

thought he'd be here minding an elephant in a barn on a late fall evening, side by side with a woman with whom he believed he was falling in love. It had been a long time since he had felt anything even approximating joy, but here it was – deep contentment; contentment and hope. With Rhonda, disaster had always been imminent, inspiring the exhilaration he imagined you might feel when handling explosives or diving out of a moving plane, but there had been no contentment. And then there hadn't even been the threat of disaster by the end, because it had already happened.

Neva broke up a piece of straw. Truman watched her until her ears turned rosy.

'What,' she said.

'You remind me of the kind of person who spends her summers alone with grizzly bears, or who can splint her own leg with a sleeve and a stick and hike five miles to civilization.'

Neva laughed. 'Am I really that fierce?'

'You're pretty fierce.'

'I never really learned to do the girl thing.'

'I think you're very girl – just a very *fierce* girl.'

'Sounds bad.'

'It's not bad.' Truman held his hands close to the Coleman lantern on the table in front of them. 'What will you do, once Hannah's gone?' Harriet had reinstated her to the ranks of a zoo employee, but only until Hannah was moved.

'Oh, there are lots of places I can go,' Neva said. 'I've been in the business a long time, and I have a good reputation. It's a small pond out there where man and elephant meet, and I'm a pretty good-sized fish. I've had some offers.'

Truman drew a fortifying breath. 'Well, here's an idea Winslow and I have come up with. We think what Bladenham needs is a top-drawer miniature pig breeder and trainer. No, now, wait, hear me out. Pigs are cute when they're young. I know this from experience. And by the time they grow up, they're someone else's problem.'

Neva laughed. 'Me, a pig breeder?'

'*And* trainer. Winslow and I will teach you everything we know.'

'That wouldn't take long.'

'It might,' Truman said. 'It depends on how quickly we reveal our secrets.'

'Do you have secrets?'

'Not many, but we could string them out. Think about staying. Please.'

'We'll see,' said Neva. 'But in the meantime, listen: if you climb into my sleeping bag tonight, I won't kick you out.'

'Ah,' said Truman. 'I should warn you that Miles may try to get in with me.'

'And that,' said Neva, 'is where I set my limits.'

The next afternoon at the Beauty Spot, Corinna was coloring Bettina Jones's hair at last. Some of the little moles on her face were gone, too. Something was up.

'You don't have to tell me everything, but give me a little hint,' Corinna said, lowering Bettina's head backwards into the sink. 'Did you find a pile of money in your backyard, maybe? Did Mr Solomon propose?'

Mr Solomon had been courting Bettina for nearly fifteen years without making a single commitment. Corinna didn't think much of him; he was a skinny man

319

with a stingy attitude. He was more than happy to let Bettina cook him dinner every Thursday night, but when it came time to give back again, he was sorely lacking. So far his greatest extravagance had been to take Bettina to a cafeteria for her sixtieth birthday; the entire meal had cost him twelve ninety-nine, and that included a seventy-five-cent tip for the busboy.

Bettina sat up a little straighter. 'As a matter of fact, there's a new man in my life.'

'No.'

'Yes, and I want to look my best for him.'

Corinna took her hands out of Bettina's newly black hair. 'Well, go ahead. Or do I have to guess?'

'I can't tell you much,' Bettina said, ''cause he's married.'

'*No.*'

Bettina nodded coyly. 'Yeah.'

'Well, you've shocked me. Is he someone I know?'

Bettina nodded.

'Do I like him?'

'Not much, but I believe that'll change.'

Corinna put the back of Bettina's chair upright so she could look her in the eye. 'Who?'

'You know Darla Kinney?'

'Didn't she die last year?'

'Thirteen months ago this March.'

'Billy Kinney? But honey, that's not married, that's widowed.'

'Yeah, only he says he still feels like he's married. Says he needs another couple months to sort it all out and then we're going to tell the world. He told me last week he loves me.'

'Aw, honey,' Corinna said, pressing Bettina's shoulder

320

through the cape. 'Why'd you say I don't like him? I like him.'

'I never thought you did.'

The women moved over to the chair in front of the mirror as one, Corinna holding the back of Bettina's cape like a train so she wouldn't stumble. Bettina adjusted her skinny hips in the chair, and Corinna started setting her hair with rollers. She said, 'He's just kind of a strong flavor, is all. But I never didn't like him. You tell Mr Solomon yet?'

'Cheap old thing,' Bettina picked a piece of fuzz off her tongue.

'You tell him?'

'Yeah, I told him. You know what he said?'

'What?'

'He said, *Honey, if you got someone falling over in love with you, why, you take that road, 'cause the one to my house don't go all the way through.*'

'He said that?' Corinna stabbed a pick through a roller.

'Yeah, he said that.'

'All those years of your feeding him pork chops and lamb stew, and he says a thing like that.'

Bettina sighed. 'Don't I know it.'

'Funny the way things work out. You and Billy Kinney. Now I think about it, it makes a lot of sense. You and him and Darla have always been good church friends, and you never could get Mr Solomon to church except on Christmas and Easter.'

'He never felt strongly about Jesus,' Bettina said primly.

'You and Him, you on pretty good terms?'

'Yeah, we are,' Bettina said. 'I work real hard at it every day. Me and the Lord, we talk.'

'Is that right? About what?'

321

'Mostly what you'd tell a husband, I guess. How I'm feeling, what worries I've got – nothing special. An old woman like me, I've got nothing to say that will exactly raise somebody's blood pressure, but He listens just the same.'

'Well, you know me and the Lord, we've had our differences over the years,' Corinna said, separating out a section of Bettina's hair with the end of a rat-tail comb. 'I never made a secret of that.'

'Uh huh.'

'But with Hannah going to the sanctuary and all, I believe I've got some answering to do to Him for a change, instead of the other way around.'

'When's she going?'

'Soon, maybe a week or two. Sam's all jittery about it. Me, too. We worry about the girl.'

'Well, tell that to the Lord, honey. He's up there right now listening for you.'

Corinna pinned the last roller in place. 'To tell you the truth, I'm working on getting up the courage. It's been an awful long time since I've been in touch.'

'That's no more than a blink of an eye to Him.'

'Yeah, well, I've got to figure out an apology, that's the first thing. It doesn't feel natural, though, after all these years of being mad.'

'Well, tell Him that. Tell Him you're ready to put your hand in His and walk down that path of righteousness and joy.'

'Yeah,' Corinna said doubtfully.

'Come on now, you got to have faith. He's taking care of Sam, isn't He?'

Corinna set the last roller in place. 'I didn't see it before, but I guess He is.'

322

'Then you got no reason to doubt His goodness. You talk to Him, honey, and you'll feel your cares just lift away like magic.'

'Well, I sure could use that.'

'Yeah, you could.'

As Bettina drove away, Corinna saw Sam just pulling into the driveway. As they often did, the two of them closed up the shop together, Sam sweeping up Bettina's hair clippings while Corinna emptied bowls of old disinfectant and poured in new. Sam seemed like he was in a pensive mood. He'd been changeable ever since they'd gotten word that the sanctuary had made a place for Hannah. As though he could hear her thinking, he said, 'Now that shug's going, I don't know what I'm going to do with myself, Mama.'

'We'll figure it out,' Corinna said. 'Like we always do.'

'Don't know that I want to figure it out.'

'Sure you do, honey. I guess we've got some mourning to do first, but once that's over we'll still be right here, together.'

Sam stowed his broom in the closet and came over to put his arms around her. 'We're a fine pair,' he said softly.

Corinna looked up at him, her eyes brimming. 'Yeah, we are.' She raised her hand to his face, his cheek as familiar to her as her own. 'Aw, sugar man,' she whispered, 'now we get to be old.'

Harriet wondered why the expression stopped at a glass half empty. It could be a lot emptier than that, and she was in a position to know. She'd been in her aviary power-drinking a bottle of Merlot that was definitely more than half empty – the only thing left was its tears, not even enough to fill a teaspoon.

She wandered out of the aviary with the grieving wine bottle in one hand and her empty glass in the other, moving from room to room to visit the framed photographs she had hung everywhere – photographs of Maxine and the pretty little woman who had accompanied her to France, to New York, to Italy; photographs of Brave Boy and Arthur, of Maxine in the company of mahouts in the jungles of Burma. Here was a successful woman, a woman who had loved passionately and inspired love in return, and who was now mocking her: *You can look, but you may not have.* Harriet had been betrayed by her employees, by her circumstances, by family, by genetic inheritance, by love in general and men in particular – and now, unkindest of all, she was being betrayed by the dead. A bolt had appeared from on high, and it had come from the distant hand of Maxine Biedelman herself, Harriet's angel and savior, her beloved. The elephant would not be staying.

From her night table Harriet pulled a thick stack of unframed pictures and fingered them like rosary beads. She left on top a close-up of the face of a young elephant, its left eye mangled and swollen shut, the eyelid pulpy and weeping blood. Under the picture was written in faint pencil, OUR DEAR GIRL. The photograph was of Hannah, freshly orphaned: Hannah, Maxine's crowning achievement, the object of her final passion. A big, awkward, wounded creature who was lucky enough to be loved by a woman who saw beauty where there wasn't any. Along the bottom of the photograph was written, THE FINAL RED TAPE IS DONE, AND WE SHALL HAVE HER!

324

Harriet turned the photograph on its face and regarded the next one, a picture of Maxine in safari-wear, striding up the path of her property, neatly thatched huts on one side – a balloon-animal kiosk stood there now – and, on the other, an open yard with two gentle-eyed dik-diks and a zebra.

And just like that, from the ashes heaped around her, Harriet found her salvation. She was not, never had been, and never would be Maxine – Max – Biedelman. But she could be her agent, could keep the flame of Max's legacy alive by devoting herself to restoring Havenside, all of it, to its old and original glory – the whimsical gazebos and pavilions, the lush grounds, the grand home, the campaign tent, the lifetime of photographs; and yes, gradually, the animals. She would tell Max's story to anyone who would hear her, visitors, guests, donors, and historians, and with the money she raised she would rebuild the zoo. All of it.

And maybe one day there could be elephants again.

Chapter 21

People lined the streets of Bladenham two and three deep despite the drizzle. From inside the closed cab of the transport truck, Sam watched them cheering and holding up homemade signs and balloons to say goodbye to Hannah. His shug had been loved.

He hated that she was riding in an open cage like she was, even with the wooden windbreak on three sides. It was cold out, and it nearly broke his heart, seeing her chained to the transport cage by one front foot and one back foot so she couldn't turn around. It kept her safe but he hated it anyway, his sugar being driven out of town like a criminal, like something wild and dangerous. What was she thinking, all by herself in those chains, with no idea where she was going, or that it would be someplace good? Sam wasn't allowed to ride back there with her, in case she shifted suddenly and crushed him, but he'd have chanced it, if it had been left up to him – ridden in his old chair from the elephant barn, feeding her a donut from time to time and telling stories, making up some foolishness to pass the time. He was glad Corinna had stayed home. Seeing her shug in chains like that would have broken her heart.

Satellite trucks were broadcasting Hannah's departure live throughout the Pacific Northwest and feeding news services around the world. Harriet Saul had been giving interviews continuously since *Good Morning America* powered up at three a.m. It was now nine. Sam had been at the zoo all that time, too, getting Hannah watered, keeping her calm while the transport truck was backed up to the barn. Hannah had gone into the cage easily, despite Neva's worrying, and they were getting on the road earlier than they'd expected. Neva was ahead of them someplace, driving her run-down little car. She'd meet the transport truck at designated rest stops on I–5 heading south – two in Oregon, three or four in California. It would probably take them twelve hours in all to reach the sanctuary.

The truck driver didn't have a lot to say, and that was all right with Sam. His heart was too sore for company, all his feelings riding high and tight in his throat. If Max Biedelman was watching, he hoped she'd be proud – proud of Hannah, and proud of him, too. It reminded him of a conversation he had had with her several months before Miss Effie's death, when it had become clear that she needed to prepare herself for it. She'd been stumping along beside him with her walking stick, wearing a jaunty Irish cap against the fall drizzle.

'Do you know, Mr Brown, when my father died, I wasn't sure I would go on. He passed away on safari about seventy miles from Nairobi. It was some sort of hemorrhagic fever, and came on so swiftly that by the next morning he was too sick to move, and by the following evening he was gone. We buried him there. It was what he'd have wanted, though my mother never forgave me. We'll stop here, I think.'

She'd unfolded her little campstool. Hannah had explored the nearby trees and Sam had crouched in the damp, running his fingers through the dew and the clover while she talked.

'My father was a fine man and an ideal traveling companion, Mr Brown, curious about everything. He taught me astronomy, botany, zoology, anthropology, biology – he was a great admirer of Charles Darwin. Before he retired each night he read poetry. I never could stand the stuff, but he claimed it sang to his soul.' She'd smiled fondly. 'I never found another traveling companion who suited me as well, though I've traveled with other men over the years.'

'Ladies, too?'

'Very few. My mother despised travel. She was a vain, silly woman to whom a length of Italian lace was more important than either my father or me – or anyway it seemed that way to me. I could never understand why he'd married her. He claimed she had been more daring when she was young, and perhaps she was, but it would have been quite out of character. Effie, of course, was nearly as bad, though Effie is not and never was a silly woman. No, women were not my traveling companions of choice, Mr Brown. Wonderful when they are in civilization, but best left there.'

She stood, folded up her campstool, and they'd set off again, Hannah lumbering along beside them.

Sam said, 'My father got old early, busted up by Jimmy and Emmanuel dying like they did; no sense to it, no sense at all. I tried to be real careful with myself after that, so I wouldn't multiply his misery. My mother died younger than she should have, from grief. Woman was only fifty-three, and *strong*, but I guess that was just on the outside. She loved us children. First there was Jimmy, of course, and then eight years later there was Emmanuel. When a couple of old boys from the bar brought the body home, she started to scream so loud my daddy had to send her upstairs just so he could hear the story straight. Not that it was much of a story. No story at all, really; no point to it, none whatsoever. Her heart broke, right up there in their bedroom with the bureau and wash-stand her father had made as wedding presents, and the bed my father built. There was nothing else in that room, not so much as a rocking chair. Her heart was like that, too – all the basics but nothing extra, no padding to soak up all the sorrow when it spilled over. Drowned her soul.'

'Tell me, Mr Brown, do you ever hear their voices?'

'No. Wish I did.'

'Nor do I.' The old woman kept her eyes on the ground ahead. 'I've asked God for that, but He has not seen fit to answer.'

'To tell you the truth, where God is concerned, me and Him are only distantly connected,' Sam said. 'The way I figure it, we're aware of each other, we're respectful, too, but we don't exactly sit down for a meal at the same table.'

Max Biedelman smiled. 'Nor do I, Mr Brown. Nor do I.'

★　　★　　★

330

The truck driver pulled into the first prearranged rest stop, ready, as he'd put it to Sam, for a crap and a cuppa joe. Sam was out of the cab the minute the truck stopped, headed around back to check on Hannah.

She was quiet behind the bars, and calm. Sam dug into his first box of Dunkin' Donuts and handed in a custard-filled imperial.

'How you doing, sugar?' he said softly. 'You keeping warm enough? If we would have known how cold it was going to be, Mama could have knitted you a sweater, maybe, or a blanket. Sure would like to see you riding down the road in a purple-striped coat – wouldn't you just look fine.' Sam smiled in spite of himself, the first real smile in hours. It did him good, seeing Hannah so calm and composed – the truth was, she was doing better than he was, and he wasn't even the one out in the cold. He was so proud of her, he could have just spit.

He handed her a Bismark.

'How is she?' Neva, who had been waiting for them, hopped out of her car with the engine still running. A small crowd was growing around the truck and the cage.

'Good – she's doing good.'

Sam offered a raspberry jelly donut and stooped to look at Hannah's ankles. They'd wrapped the steel shackles with soft leather strips to keep them from rubbing so much. He didn't see any abrasions yet. That was good.

Neva hauled over a hose. 'Do you want a drink?' she asked Hannah. 'Yes?' She sprayed the hose into Hannah's open mouth for a good long drink. Sam gave her two Bavarian cream-filleds and a cruller, which she popped into her mouth one by one.

'Ain't she a dainty thing, though?' Sam said, smiling.

331

Neva smiled, too, and looked him over. 'How are you holding up? Are you tired yet?'

'Nah,' Sam said. 'I figure I've got the rest of my life to be tired. I'll be tired when sugar's out in that meadow making friends. How about you – you okay?'

Neva had been up all night, getting Hannah's food and gear ready. She shook her head. 'I'm okay. It's pure adrenaline, but I'll grab a cup of coffee before I head out. It was a nice sendoff back there, wasn't it?'

'Yeah. Baby sure had friends.'

Neva smiled and squeezed Sam's arm.

When they got back on the highway again heading south, Sam thought about Corinna, about the day he'd brought her home from the hospital after the baby died. Sam had taken the trash out to the alley, and when he came back he'd heard her upstairs keening, a fury and a wildness to it. By comparison, his own grief had been a puny thing, a narrow dark place like a well sunk deep in his soul. After that, there had always been this thing between them, this inequality of grief, this unfinished mourning.

People had asked him sometimes what they'd said to each other, as though there *had* been something to say to each other. There hadn't been. There had only been Corinna's eyes, awful things, and the milk stains on the front of her dresses.

Last night, when Corinna had said her goodbyes to Hannah, she had been composed, at least mostly. Sam had stood back while she'd let Hannah's trunk explore her hands one last time. Hannah had moved close and rumbled deep down in her throat, as though she knew.

'Honey girl,' Corinna had said, 'you've been the best

thing that's ever happened to Papa and me, and I think you know that. We love you, and that won't ever change, no matter how far away you are.'

With her trunk, Hannah nudged Corinna gently to one side and wrapped her ear around the woman, holding her close. Sam had never seen the girl do something like that before. 'Lord, but I'm going to miss you,' Corinna broke down. 'It's all right, baby – they're tears of joy. You're finally going to have the life the good Lord intended all along. And if that's not a joyful thing, I don't know what is.'

Now, the driver called Sam back so they could get on the road again. Sam gave Hannah one more donut, patted her with what he hoped was reassurance, and climbed back up into the cab.

'You been driving elephants for long?' Sam asked the driver, mostly to keep himself from entertaining sad thoughts. The driver was a big man – big belly, big face, stubbly cheeks. He had nasty, wet-sounding lungs, a cough full of junk.

'A few years,' the driver said, resting a meaty forearm on the wheel. 'Not just elephants, though. I done 'em all – elephants, tigers, lions, giraffes. Walrus, one time; a killer whale one time, too. Big box of water sure made a mess when you stopped, slopping all over the place.'

'You worry about them, when you're driving?'

'Nah,' the driver said. 'I figure that's someone else's job. Yours, today. I just keep us on the road and steer. He doing okay back there?'

'She. Yeah, she's doing okay. I'll sure be glad when it's over, though.'

'Yeah. One time we had an elephant go down, a circus

333

elephant. They're not supposed to have room to lie down, but this one must have fallen. Hoo boy.'

Sam looked over. 'She get back up?'

'Not without a winch. Busted up her leg real good. Don't think that elephant ever went back into any circuses, if you know what I mean. Elephant's not worth much with one leg that's no good.'

Sam crossed his arms tightly across his chest and prayed.

Forty-one years ago, Max Biedelman had taught Sam how to ask Hannah for things: lie down, lift a foot, rise.

'When you ask her to do something, Mr Brown, you must ask her nicely, and in a normal speaking tone,' the old woman had said. 'She is every bit as civilized as we are; indeed, more than some people I've known.' She'd smiled to herself when she said that. 'Hannah will understand you perfectly, so there is no need to shout, or to speak to her as you would to an idiot. Never underestimate her intelligence, or her desire to please you, once you've earned her trust. It's all about trust, Mr Brown. That's the glue that will bind her to you. Trust and respect.'

Sam had never stood beside something so big before, or so soulful. The old woman had stood back, arms crossed, watching him, watching Hannah.

'Come, Hannah,' he'd said.

The elephant had just stood there.

'Try again, Mr Brown.'

'Come, Hannah.'

The elephant had stood there.

Max Biedelman's eyes twinkled. 'You're unsure, Mr Brown. If you're unsure, she will be, too, and it's in an elephant's nature to want to be sure of things before doing them.'

Sam took a deep breath. In a low, quiet voice he said, 'Come on now, sugar. You and me got places to go.'

And from that moment on, they had.

'How long you been with this one?' The truck driver jerked his thumb over his shoulder.

'Forty-one years.'

'Jesus.'

They'd had to bind Corinna's breasts to make her milk stop. She had done the binding herself, wrapping her breasts so tightly she'd had trouble breathing. When he'd asked her about it, she said she'd have had trouble breathing anyway, so it didn't matter. She had worn those bindings like a hair shirt every day for a year, eleven whole months beyond what she'd needed to, but Sam had left it alone after that first time asking. If the bindings made her remember the baby, why, that was her business, no one else's, not even Sam's. They'd learned privacy, that year. They'd also learned that not everything broken could be fixed, and that not everything ruined could be thrown away. Sometimes the damaged things were all you had to work with. Sam had built Corinna the Beauty Spot because he couldn't build a road to God.

By Yreka, California, Hannah's legs were raw from the constant friction of the shackles. Neva stood beside Sam, handing him strips of foam tape to wrap the leather in. Not that it would help much.

'Sam,' she said softly, closing her hand around his wrist, and that's how he knew he was crying.

The day after she and Sam scattered Miss Effie's ashes, Max Biedelman closeted herself with a team of lawyers. Over the next week she called Sam to the house several times to help her move boxes. 'What does one do with all the detritus of one's life?' she asked one afternoon as he was pulling a trunk from a closet for her. 'In the end it means so little to anyone.'

Sam moved the trunk to a place in the room where she could get to it easily.

'I've lived a long time, Mr Brown, longer than most. I should be grateful – indeed, I am grateful. And yet, I would give everything, *everything*, to do it all again.'

'You're lucky to have had the life you did, sir – done so many things, been so many places.'

Max Biedelman stood silhouetted in the parlor window, silent. Finally she said, 'Do you know what I've been thinking lately? I've been thinking that we're animals, like any others – we senesce, we sink into decrepitude just as they do. But I've wondered if it isn't our special hell that we are able to register the swift passage of time, the lightning speed of it all, and the absoluteness with which it is gone. I feel my age, Mr Brown, I feel every bit of it, and yet I can recall so very clearly what it was like to be young. It torments me. I should like, just one more time, to feel the winds of Africa, to hear and feel the din and the heat of the Indonesian jungle. The mahouts used to sing as they prepared their supper. They were a joyful people who believed in a joyful world. And indeed, the world is a fine place when one sees it from the back of an elephant.' Her voice sank to a whisper. 'You cannot know how hard it is, saying goodbye to it all. There are moments when it is unendurable.'

'You're alive,' Sam said. 'You still got life all around you, so God isn't ready to bring you home yet. When He's ready, you'll be ready, too. Like Miss Effie was.'

Max Biedelman wiped at her face with her shirt cuff and looked at him. 'I hope so, Sam. I do hope so.'

'Yes, ma'am,' Sam said softly.

Maxine Leona Biedelman died one week later, alone by intention in her room. Sam thought she would have wanted it that way. On the next fine day he mingled her ashes with Miss Effie's in the clearing, just as she'd asked him to do.

And that night, for the very first time, he dreamed Hannah's dream.

'Looks like this is the place,' the truck driver said, startling Sam, who must have dozed off. His eyelids felt like sandpaper. When they drove past a wooden sign saying PACHYDERM SANCTUARY, his heart began to pound.

Out the window he watched as the gravel road led them through woods and clearings, then into a huge meadow that disappeared over the top of rolling hills.

He had already seen it, right down to the rocks and hillocks.

They pulled up to a big white barn, newer than the newest building back at the zoo. A tall, long-legged, weathered woman came outside and signaled the driver where to park the truck. Neva shot by in her car and stopped alongside the barn, hopping out to embrace the woman. When the driver stopped the truck, Sam got out of the

337

cab slowly, all of a sudden reluctant to be here, not sure he could bring himself to do what he'd need to do.

Neva brought the tall woman over. 'Sam, this is Alice McNeary.'

'Nice to meet you, Sam. Neva's told me a lot about you.'

Sam shook her hand. 'Ma'am.'

And then he'd turned and walked away.

Alice put her arm around Neva's shoulders and hugged her reassuringly. 'It's always tough,' she said quietly. 'And they're always fine.'

'The keepers or the elephant?'

'Both.'

'God,' Neva said, wiping her nose.

'You sure you won't stay with us?'

'I'm sure. I promised someone I'd come back, at least for a little while.'

Alice raised her eyebrows. 'Oh?'

'Yeah.'

'Well!' Alice gave her a quick one-armed hug and then strode to the truck, where Sam was fumbling with the cage's locking mechanism.

'Neva's told me Hannah is a good animal, Sam. One of the best.'

'Yes, ma'am, she is.'

'It's going to take some time to get the cage open and for us to get ready for her. Why don't you go into the barn and bring down a flake of hay for her? You'll find a wheelbarrow inside the door, and a pitchfork in the loft. It's good timothy hay. We grow it ourselves.'

Sam drew a deep breath. 'Shug sure does love her hay.'

'Has she had much to eat?'

'No, ma'am. Just some Dunkin' Donuts.'

338

Alice cracked a smile. Sam smiled back.

'So she's spoiled, is she?'

'Yes, ma'am, she is.'

'Well, she won't have to lower her standards on our account. We talk a good story, Sam, but deep down everyone here is a pushover.'

Sam's smile faded. 'Yes, ma'am. I'll go and get the hay.'

In the barn he breathed in the good rich smells of elephant. He found the hayloft and the wheelbarrow and the pitchfork and brought the flake to the truck. Alice McNeary and Neva had put the ramp in place against the side of the cage and slid back the gate. All that was keeping Hannah inside were the chains and shackles.

'All right, Sam, I think we're about ready for her,' Alice called. 'Can you put the hay at the bottom of the ramp? Maybe a little on the ramp, too. That should give her some incentive to leave the truck.'

Sam put down the hay. 'Hey, sugar,' he said softly, climbing into the open gate of the cage. Hannah turned her head and reached for him with her trunk. 'How's my baby girl? You tired of standing in this mean thing? How about we get you out of here and let you see some things. You're in your new home, now.'

Alice had been standing to one side, watching. Now she handed him a wrench. 'We've found that it's better for everyone if we let the elephants come out under their own steam. Whenever you feel she's ready, Sam, you can do the honors.'

Sam looked at her, not understanding.

'You can take off the shackles.'

'Yes, ma'am,' he said. 'Me and shug have a couple things to talk over first, though, if that's all right with you.'

'Of course. Take all the time you need. She's here now. There's no hurry.'

Neva started toward him, but Alice caught her by the arm and shook her head.

Sam reached into his pocket and pulled out the last donut, wrapped in a napkin. He held it out to Hannah on the palm of his hand. 'I suppose that's the last Dunkin' Donut you're going to get for a while, baby girl. I bet they've got other treats for you, but I didn't see a Dunkin' Donuts on the way through town.'

Hannah nudged his hip anxiously with her trunk. He leaned into her and said, 'Let me get through this, sugar. You're going to be with elephants now. You won't need me and Mama anymore.' Sam turned the wrench over and over in his hand. 'But no matter what, you can count on me thinking about you up there at home, so if you feel a little breeze or smell a donut smell sometimes, why, you know it's just my thoughts passing through. I won't leave you, is what I'm saying. Not in my mind. You just keep that in your thoughts, sugar, like a great big bull's eye.'

Hannah wrapped her trunk around Sam's head gently, whistled in his ear. 'That's all, shug. That's what I got to say.' He took a deep breath.

'Foot, baby girl.'

Hannah lifted her front foot. Sam unwrapped enough of the shackle to get at the fitting, and then the steel clattered onto the bed of the truck. He walked around behind her and she lifted her foot before he'd even asked. The second shackle came undone like a well-oiled lock. Sam caught it before it could fall, staring at it in his hand.

Then, still holding the shackle tightly, he turned and walked down the ramp. Hannah followed him the way she'd followed him so many times before, over so many years.

At the bottom of the ramp, he stopped and looked around. He could see Neva and Alice McNeary starting toward him. From the other direction, cresting the hill Sam knew better than his own backyard, he saw four elephants. How many times had he seen them in his sleep – six hundred? A thousand? How many miles had he walked in his dreams, trying to catch up?

He felt Hannah see them, too. She pulled up short like she'd been touched with something electric. One of the elephants trumpeted, and then the others trumpeted, too.

Sam could feel what she was feeling: that it had been so long.

He pushed her gently, willing her to leave him. His had been a long and solitary vigil, but it was over.

'We're going to be all right now, shug,' he said. 'This is how we begin.'

The Aspinall Foundation

The Aspinall Foundation is an international charity leading the way in conservation across three continents and managing two wild animal parks in Kent. Founded in 1957 when John Aspinall bought Howletts Wild Animal Park to house his famous animal collection, the Foundation expanded in 1973 when Port Lympne Wild Animal Park was bought to accommodate the growing collection. Today, the parks are home to over 1,000 animals and 120 different species.

Howletts Wild Animal Park has the largest herd of African elephants in Britain, and has had more African elephant births than all other British zoos combined. The elephants are cared for by highly qualified and devoted keepers and are able to roam freely through nine acres of lush paddock.

THE
ASPINALL
FOUNDATION
REGISTERED CHARITY NO. 326567

2 for 1 entry

See The Aspinall Foundation's herd of African elephants for yourself at Howletts Wild Animal Park in Kent with this amazing offer.

Simply detach this coupon and produce it at the visitor box office.

Terms & Conditions: Two for One offer expires 28th Februar⬛
Offer valid on full price adult tickets only, higher priced ticket mu⬛
Offer valid at Howletts & Port Lympne Wild Animal Park⬛

Visit **www.totallywild.net** for information and directions.